The Lost Sisters

Lindsey Hutchinson

W F HOWES LTD

This large print edition published in 2017 by
W F Howes Ltd
Unit 5, St George's House, Rearsby Business Park,
Gaddesby Lane, Rearsby, Leicester LE7 4YH

1 3 5 7 9 10 8 6 4 2

First published in the United Kingdom in 2017
by Aria

A CIP catalogue record for this book is available
from the British Library

ISBN 978 1 51008 495 7

Typeset by Palimpsest Book Production Limited,
Falkirk, Stirlingshire

Printed and bound by
T J International in the UK
Printforce Nederland b.v. in the Netherlands
Ligare in Australia

For my children Matthew and Esther
who make me so very proud in
everything they do.

CHAPTER 1

The sound of the slap echoed around the quiet parlour. Orpha Buchanan's head rocked on her shoulders from the impact.

'You are a spiteful, vindictive woman! Why ever did you have me in the first place?' Orpha shouted then listened with horror to the answer her mother gave.

'It was your father's fault, I never wanted you! I would have left you to die but for your father finding a wet nurse and nanny! If I had had my way, you wouldn't be here now!'

Hortense Buchanan smirked as she watched her daughter's face. The girl's bravado suddenly crumbled.

'What is it that makes you hate me so much?' Orpha sobbed as she slumped into a chair.

'You were born! With your dark hair and green eyes like your father's; your sweet nature . . . you make me sick!

Finding her courage once more, Orpha shouted, 'I didn't ask to be born! That was your mistake, if you hadn't wanted a child . . .'

Another sharp slap halted the girl's words.

1

'How dare you speak to me in such a manner!' Hortense's fury reached boiling point as she landed blow after blow on her daughter. In a frenzy of anger, she slapped the young girl who tried desperately to fend off the attack. Hortense screamed abuse as she rained down the blows with her open hand until finally she fell into a chair exhausted.

'Get out of my sight girl!' Hortense said in hardly more than a menacing whisper.

Orpha shot from the parlour to the safe haven of her bedroom. Sitting on her bed, she allowed the tears to fall at last. Her face was stinging from the slaps, and the hurt to her body told of yet more bruises to come.

Slowly and carefully she took off her blouse and allowed her long skirt to fall to the floor. Bathing the sore areas around her face and shoulders with cold water from the bowl on the dresser, Orpha stared into the mirror.

Why was it that she and her mother could not get on? Why did they have to argue over the most trivial of things? She was at a loss as she searched for answers to these questions. From as early as she could remember, Orpha's mother had shown only her dislike of her daughter. Hortense was jealous, that much Orpha had worked out, jealous of the fact that she and her father had the same features and character as well as sharing a good relationship. Even Orpha could see there was nothing of her mother in her, and she, at least, was grateful for that.

As she stared at herself in the mirror she wished she had been born in another century. Would the future be any different? Would she have been better placed to fight her own corner in a time yet to come? Tears flowed freely as she feared that time may never come.

Looking again at the marks that covered her body, Orpha turned away. Drying her tears, she carefully began to get dressed once more. Finally managing to lie on her bed, her thoughts swirled. Why did she put up with the constant physical and mental abuse from her mother? She didn't really have a choice. At fourteen years old, what could she do? She could tell her father, but then Hortense would make her life unbearable. She contemplated what might happen if her father knew about what was going on. Would he divorce her mother? If he did, would he hold her, Orpha, responsible for the break-up of the family? She could not risk her father's displeasure, she loved him too much for that. She could run away, but where would she go? She had no working skills, no trade to fall back on. She would starve or end up in the workhouse. No, even taking the beatings was better than that! She realised at that moment there was no way out for her . . . at least not yet.

As she lay on her bed, Orpha heard the singing and joviality from the people in the streets around her home in Wednesbury. She had hoped to be allowed to join in, but instead she had received yet another hiding. The day had been declared a bank holiday in celebration of Queen Victoria's Diamond Jubilee – 20th June 1897, and street parties were in full swing everywhere. Orpha had asked her mother's permission to go out and enjoy the day with the other people of St James' Street, but Hortense had refused.

Orpha slowly stood and walked to the window, looking out longingly at the revellers. She heard the music and laughter of the road's residents as they enjoyed their day off from the daily grind of work.

She pursed her lips as she thought about those fortunate enough to have a job. This celebration day off was welcome indeed for them. If she had a job herself it would give her freedom and independence from her mother, but finding work would be nigh on impossible in the poverty stricken town.

As she watched the festivities she thought about the people who were singing and dancing in the street. She thought about where she, and they, lived.

Wednesbury was a small town in the heart of the industrial 'Black Country', so named due to the pall of smoke constantly hanging over the place, belched out daily from chimneys both domestic and industrial. The coal dust from the three collieries combined with the dark smoke from factories and furnaces coated every building with a layer of grime. Housewives spent many hours cleaning their closely packed terraced houses money was the opinion of Hortense. At least Abel could only spend his money on one daughter now.

The tea having gone cold in the cup, Hortense didn't notice as she remembered Abel's other daughter. Hortense had given birth eighteen years ago to a girl they had named Eugenie. With a mop of dark hair, the baby blue eyes had soon turned emerald green . . . just like Abel's. Hortense hated the child on sight, as she had with Orpha, and quickly made up her mind the baby had to go . . . one way or another.

The pictures formed in her mind of how she had instructed the stable lad to ready the horse and trap; to leave it outside the front door before going back to his business in the stables. When she had been sure the boy was nowhere to be seen, Hortense had laid Eugenie in a large basket covered by a blanket. Placing the basket next to her on the seat of the trap, she had flicked the reins for the horse to walk on.

She saw again the child sleeping peacefully as the trap rumbled over the cobblestones of Holyhead Road. Through the smoke-blackened streets of Wednesbury and out across the Monway Colliery, keeping to the well-worn tracks and avoiding the disused coal pits, Hortense had guided the horse for hours. Tracking her way over the Old Moorcroft Colliery, she had eventually come to what appeared, at first, to be a deserted cottage. Halting the horse and seeing no signs of life in or around the cottage, she had lifted the basket down, putting her arm through the handle. Walking across to the cottage, she noticed the building was run-down but the garden was full of vegetables. Someone lived there, that much was evident, but were they inside the cottage? Hortense walked up the tiny path where she knocked on the front door. There was no answer, so she walked round the side of the house to the back. Laying the basket on the doorstep, she peeped round to the front, and seeing no one, she walked swiftly back to the trap. Climbing aboard and turning the horse around, she set off for home.

As she had driven the trap homeward through the streets of Wednesbury once more, she'd glanced around at the dirty buildings and houses. Coal dust from the mines and soot from the chimneys hung over the town. The factories and furnaces working night and day added to the pall of smoke and Hortense was not surprised people were dying of diseases of the lungs.

Without realising, she shook her head as her thoughts roamed. No wonder it was called the Black Country, for everything was covered in a layer of dirt. Children who were dressed in rags, barefoot and dirty ran around the streets. The amount of poverty was appalling but Hortense had ignored it. She had plenty, thank you very much, so why should she care whether the kids of the town had enough to eat.

Her mind slipped back to the day she had met Abel. She had spotted him across the crowded room of the Mayor's inaugural ball. She had ignored the businessman who had invited her along for most of the evening. The man who she had set her sights on was tall, with raven black hair. His skin was the colour of mahogany from spending many months in the sun. As she had wandered closer, she saw he had the most unusual eyes – emerald green.

She had been introduced to him and during their conversation had learned about his adventures in Colombia and working the emerald mine.

Hortense had lived in Wednesbury all of her life, and had hated it from the moment she was old enough to understand the poverty of the smoke blackened drab little town. This handsome man, Abel Buchanan, would be her ticket to a better life, and she had actively pursued him with a view to marriage.

As time wore on and they eventually *did* marry, she had tried her best to entice Abel to take her to live in a more salubrious area, even suggesting they move abroad. However Abel would have none of it, he loved the 'Black Country' and was busy building up his consultancy business.

Then had come Eugenie. She continued her previous train of thought.

On reaching home, Hortense had left the trap by the front door and rushed into the house. Calling for the maid and getting no answer, Hortense had quickly put the perambulator in the garden in the last of the weak sunshine. Going back into the kitchen, she made herself some tea as she thought about what she had done and how she could tell Abel about his missing daughter when he got home from the Gentlemen's Club.

She smiled as she watched the moving pictures in her mind's eye.

'Abel, Abel! Thank God you're home . . . Eugenie's gone!' Hortense had cried as her husband had walked into the parlour.

'What? What do you mean she's gone?' he'd asked.

She saw again the concern that had etched his face.

'She's gone! As in, she's not here! She's disappeared!' Hortense had made a show of being the distraught mother – a standing-ovation performance in fact.

'Calm down, woman, and tell me what's happened.' Abel had guided his wife to a chair.

'I put her in the baby carriage in the garden for some fresh air and when I went to fetch her back in . . . she wasn't there! The gypsies must have taken her!'

'Right,' Abel said as he strode out of the room, leaving Hortense with a sly smirk on her face. Abel had mounted his horse and ridden to the newly built police station in Holyhead Road. The police had been given all the details and Abel had returned home saying the search for his daughter had begun. The police were out in force, asking questions everywhere and of anyone in an effort to glean any information that would lead to the missing child.

stopped looking for her. Every available opportunity he had gone in search of her; to no avail. She had simply disappeared leaving him in torment. Now Orpha, who had been like a blessing when she arrived, had gone missing too and Abel felt his heart would surely break. Choking back the sobs threatening to erupt, he rode onward, looking desperately for the easily recognisable raven black hair of his daughter who had filled his world.

Abel searched up one street of Wednesbury and down another until the darkness drove everyone indoors. Riding to the police station on the Holyhead Road where he had gone eighteen years earlier in a horrifically similar situation, he tearfully reported his daughter having gone missing to the officer in charge. Then he made his way slowly through the cobbled streets back to his home in St James' Street. He cried openly and allowed his tears to flow freely down his cheeks and drip onto the saddle.

Sitting before the fire, Abel spoke quietly to his wife, 'I couldn't find her, Hortense . . . I couldn't find our daughter!' Tears formed and lined his lashes as he wondered where a girl of fourteen years could possibly be, out alone in the town late at night.

'She'll come back when she's hungry!' Hortense said nonchalantly.

Looking up, Abel caught the quick smile before it left her lips. He knew his wife had a sharp tongue when it suited her, but this seemed different. That one action caused him to suspect his wife knew more than she was letting on about the whole affair. For the first time, Abel saw a slyness in her he didn't much care for. 'Hortense,' he said, his voice thick with tears, 'what have you done with Orpha?'

'You what!' Abel's wife stood up and walked to stand in front of him. 'I haven't done anything with your precious daughter! How dare you accuse me, how dare you lay the blame at my feet!' Turning from him, she marched from the room, her indignation evident.

For days, Abel trawled the streets looking for Orpha. All the searching brought him no information as to the whereabouts of his daughter. No one had seen her. No one had any idea where she might be. The police were searching too, but their enquiries around the town brought no word of the missing girl.

Abel now sat in his study as exhaustion and distress washed over him. Two daughters lost to him . . . and he had the overwhelming feeling this was no coincidence.

Looking at the velvet bag lying on his desk, Abel touched a finger to its softness. The box it had lain in beneath the floorboards was open next to it. Opening the bag, he tipped the contents onto the desktop. A little part of his treasure lay before him. Running his fingers over the contents, Abel felt his tears again begin to fall.

Crystal tears fell from emerald eyes onto emerald gems which lay scattered on a mahogany desk.

Staring at the emeralds spread out before him, Abel recalled the adventure he had undertaken to acquire them. As a young man he had secured a working passage on a ship sailing to a foreign land. He had felt the urge to see the world as well as get himself far away from the monotonous grind and filth of industry in his home town. He needed fresh air in his lungs rather than the dense smoke-filled air of Wednesbury. Months of sailing had taught him the ways of the ship and the sailing of her. Eventually the ship had docked . . . at Colombia.

Taking himself off the ship without telling its captain he would not be sailing home with them, Abel had managed to secure a job on a team who were mining for emeralds. The work was deep underground, which was dusty and dirty and took strength and determination to strike the hard granite with a pickaxe to loosen the gems. When the emeralds fell from the rock, they were jagged and dull but he soon learned they could be cut by an experienced jeweller to make them sparkle as brilliantly as any diamond. The company Abel worked for were naturally insistent on filling their quota of emeralds mined . . . and they were extremely harsh on anyone digging out the gems from their mine for themselves. A man could go missing in the dense jungle and no one would be any the wiser. This threat kept the workers in line;

no one wanted to die out there. Abel, however, was wily, and knowing he would never become wealthy from the wages paid for his hard work, he had struck a private deal with the foreman in charge of the workers. They had agreed for a percentage of what Abel earned from the gems he collected to be given over to the foreman, he could sneak back to the area and then find himself a spot away from the company mine to dig where he wouldn't be seen by anyone. Night after night he dug for the tiny emerald chips, muffling his chisel with rags in order that his banging with a hammer would scarcely be heard in the quiet of the night. He'd also squirrelled away the tiny jewels that the other workers left behind, deeming them not big enough to be worth their efforts of collecting them; within a year he had gathered enough of these rare gems to make him a very rich man indeed. Staying true to his word regarding paying the foreman, Abel swiftly booked a first-class passage on the next package boat to England, and returned home in search of a wife to share his good fortune.

Dropping the emeralds back into the bag and then into the box, Abel replaced them in their place of safety beneath the floorboards. On his return from Colombia, Abel had sought out a gem expert in London to broker deals on his behalf for the sale of a few emeralds now and then when the price rose to its highest. The remaining jewels were kept in the bank for safety as well as easy access should he decide to retrieve them in order to sell them on. His broker kept him abreast of the fluctuating market in precious gems and at the moment the price was extremely high. However, the sale of these emeralds would have to wait a while; his first priority was to find his daughter.

Pouring a brandy, he sat again at his desk. Abel had his health and wealth but not his daughters. Eighteen years ago Eugenie had disappeared and now Orpha was missing. On a sob, he thought, '*I would give up all of this wealth to have my daughters back with me once more.*' His gut tightened as he wondered again if Hortense had anything to do with it.

Sipping his brandy, savouring the burn of it in his throat, Abel suspected his wife knew far more than she was saying, and he made up his mind to discover exactly what that was.

Earlier in the day, Hortense had enjoyed her ride on the heath, especially as she'd picked some mushrooms for Abel's evening meal. It was the maid's day off and Hortense had not found a suitable cook as yet, so finding an old pan she had cooked the mushrooms over a gentle heat; they would go very nicely with a piece of lamb . . . Abel's favourite.

Singing softly, she peeled potatoes, scraped carrots and putting them in a pot with the lamb, she pushed the pot into the oven. She had heard Abel come in earlier, after another day searching for Orpha, and retreat straight to his study where he would sit until it was time to eat.

Going to the fire, she poked it with the fire dog, making sure there were no traces left of the gloves she had burned there moments before.

Making tea, Hortense sat in the parlour and looked around her. It wouldn't be long now before this house belonged to her. Leaning back in her chair, she smiled; in a few weeks Hortense Buchanan would be a merry widow and a very wealthy one at that!

Hortense served Abel his meal without a word said between them. Sitting opposite him, she watched him push his lamb stew and mushrooms around the plate with his fork without having taken a bite.

'Not hungry, Abel?' she asked.

Abel just shook his head, continuing to push the food around.

'But it's your favourite . . .!' She tried again feeling the irritability build inside her.

Nodding, he muttered, 'I ain't got no appetite,' and dropped the fork on the plate with a clatter.

'Abel, you have to eat something!' Her voice was sharp as she slammed her own cutlery onto the table.

Abel shot back, 'No, I don't have to eat anything! I said I'm not hungry!' With that he picked up the plate and threw it against the wall, shattering it and scattering food and broken crockery all over the floor.

Hortense stared at the mushrooms. Such a waste of her time preparing them!

Standing, she strode into the kitchen, returning with the hand brush and dustpan. Brushing the mess together onto the dustpan, she returned the whole to the kitchen thoroughly annoyed at having to do this cleaning up which should be the servant's domain, but then it was the maid's day off after all. As she stuffed the food, broken plate and dustpan and brush into the fire in the range she was fuming.

What a waste of perfectly good poison mushrooms!

Hortense had watched her husband slam the door behind him as he left the house. The time had come to confront the man she called husband. He was hiding something and she determined to discover exactly what it was. Her instinct was sharp, and she knew it was somewhere in the study where he spent so much time.

Standing at the doorway of Abel's study, Hortense wondered what she might find if she searched. Entering the study, she moved to the desk and lit the oil lamp standing on the shiny surface. In the pool of dim light, Hortense pulled out a drawer and lifting out the papers she held them closer to the lamp to scan them. Business papers. Replacing them, she searched the other drawers in the desk, which threw up nothing of interest to her.

Hortense felt her anger build as she looked around the room . . . nothing. She was not sure what she hoped to find, but she searched the whole room nevertheless, to no avail. Dousing the lamp, she strode from the room and banged the door behind her in sheer frustration suffused with disappointment.

CHAPTER 2

Orpha Buchanan had walked for hours not knowing where she was or where she was going. Her legs ached and her heart was heavy with sadness.

Darkness was descending and fear began to take hold. She knew she would have to spend the night out on the heath and as she looked around for some form of shelter, it all became too much for her. Orpha burst into tears. She was cold, hungry, and alone, besides being on scrubland in the middle of God knew where. Trying to pull herself together, she glanced around again. A little way ahead was a small hedge. Walking towards it, she sat down, leaning her back against it. This would have to be her bed for tonight, and as it grew darker, her fear heightened.

Orpha awoke the following morning unaware she'd even fallen asleep. After a moment, every-thing came flooding back to her in a rush – she was out on the heath because her mother had thrown her out and warned her never to return.

Getting to her feet, she stretched out her aching muscles and answered a much needed call of nature.

Not sure of the direction in which she'd come, her mind retraced her steps of the previous day and making her decision she strode forward. Again, she walked for hours and saw nothing and no-one. She was all alone and it felt like she was the only person left in the world. Before she realised, darkness began to surround her once more. It was time to stop for the night, again. Seeing the crumbling wall of what she considered might have once been a cottage, she walked towards it. Sitting on the scrubland she felt her despair envelop her and tears begin to form. On a huge sigh she lay down. She had spent one night out on this God forsaken heath; she could do it again. Eventually she would come to an inhabited area and then she could maybe look for work of some sort to earn enough to feed herself. The thoughts cheered her a little and feeling thoroughly exhausted she fell asleep.

Orpha woke in the early hours just as dawn was breaking. She had slept well considering she had been lying on the bare earth. Rising, she rubbed her aching back before setting out once more. As she began to walk across the heath, she heard the rumble of cart wheels coming towards her. Standing aside for the cart to pass on the track, she was filled with fear as it stopped close by her.

'Hello wench,' shouted a man sat on the driving seat.

'Good morning,' Orpha replied warily.

'Where you off to?' the man asked as he jumped from the cart and stood facing her.

'Wednesbury,' Orpha gave the timid reply. An uneasy feeling crept over her as the man stared into her eyes. She knew the man was going in the direction she was coming from; the place she was fleeing, so thinking quickly she had blatantly lied to him hoping he would go away and leave her alone.

'Wednesbury eh? Well you're going in the wrong direction.' Rubbing a hand over his whiskers, the man added, 'I can give you a ride if yer want.'

Orpha watched the stare turn into a lascivious grin. 'No . . . thank you, I prefer to walk' she said as firmly as she could muster whilst taking a step backwards. This was what she had feared might happen which had given rise to her telling the lie in the first place.

'Now then, girlie, don't be like that,' the man said, stepping towards her. 'A girl with such pretty green eyes as yours shouldn't be so offhand.'

Her senses screamed at her to walk away, so Orpha began to stride out without acknowledging his words.

'Oi . . .' She heard the word and then footsteps behind her before she felt the grab of her arm, then she was swung round to face the man from the cart.

Snatching her arm away, Orpha rounded on him, 'You let me go this instant!'

'You don't yell at me, young lady!' the man said, grabbing for her once again.

Terror gripped her as she tried to snatch her

arm back for the second time, but he had a firm hold on her.

Shaking her, he yelled into her face, 'Stop yer wriggling, girlie, I only want to talk to you.'

'Get away from me!' Orpha yelled back, still struggling to free her arm.

Grabbing the front of her dress, he pulled her hard towards him and Orpha heard the material tear and saw his eyes feast on her. Wrapping his arms around her, she felt herself leave the ground as he lifted her. In a split second, Orpha landed on her back on the heath all breath pushed from her lungs. Before she could get to her feet he was on her, pulling again at the cloth of her dress.

As his weight pressed her body into the ground, Orpha pushed on his shoulders, but he was too heavy for her; she could not escape from beneath him. The man laughed as she grabbed the back of his jacket, trying now to pull him off her. She kicked out and screamed into his ear, 'You get off me . . . leave me alone!'

'I don't think so, girlie,' the man laughed in her face before clamping his lips on hers.

Shaking her face free, Orpha screamed again, 'Get off me!'

The man's chuckle turned into a gurgle as he was lifted into the air and thrown aside like a puppet.

'Best do as the lady says,' a sonorous voice said.

Scrambling to her feet, Orpha tried with fumbling fingers to pull her dress together at the front where the man had tried to rip it from her. Looking up now, Orpha saw who had come to her aid. A young man with blonde hair and bulging muscles stood with legs astride in a protective stance in front of her.

'She's a whore!' the carter spat.

'She's a lady!' the young man shouted as he rounded with a hard punch to the other man's jaw, sending him sprawling on the hard ground. 'Now get yerself off and don't let me see you again, or else . . .'

Seeing the bunched fists and the stance of a bare-knuckle fighter, the man scrambled to his feet and after rubbing his jaw he climbed back onto his cart. Spitting on the ground, he said through clenched teeth, 'I'll be seeing you again, lad.' Flicking the reins, he urged the horse away.

'Not if I see you first!' the young man shouted after him, then turning to Orpha he asked, 'Are you all right, miss?'

'Yes . . . yes, I think so. Thank you, Mr . . .?' Orpha again was trying to close her torn dress.

'Lucas, Ezekiel Lucas . . . most people call me Ezzie.'

'Thank you, Mr Lucas, I'm most grateful,' Orpha said, fumbling with her clothes. She felt the blush rise to her cheeks as she saw him stare at her. Looking up, she noticed his blue eyes twinkle as they gazed into her green ones.

'Erm . . . if yer sure yer all right . . .?' Ezzie began to step back.

Suddenly his kindness overwhelmed her and,

unable to control herself any longer, Orpha fell to her knees on the heath and burst into tears. The feeling of loss and distress enveloped her and her shoulders shook with the force of her crying.

Then Ezzie was on his knees before her, taking her hand in his gently. 'Look, you'd better come along with me . . .' Seeing the fear in her eyes, he clarified his statement with, 'I live with my mother on a boat on the "cut". We're moored up in the Basin near Bradley Lock. It's not far, and my mother will take care of you. Please don't be frightened of me, I promise I won't hurt you.'

He helped her to her feet, before letting go of her hand. Her other hand still held her clothes together tightly as Orpha watched him turn and walk away. In a quandary as to what she should do now, she looked around her. She could either go her own way and risk being accosted again, or she could follow Ezzie and pray what he said about his mother was true. Swallowing her fear, Orpha followed Ezzie.

Orpha's mind whirled as she walked slowly behind the man who had saved her from the clutches of another. What was she doing following this man? He could be leading her anywhere! But then what choice did she have? She had nowhere to go and no-one to turn to.

On they walked, Ezzie not looking behind but knowing she was following him by the sound of her tread on the heath.

Eventually reaching the canal and seeing all the

boats lined up, Orpha's fear began to dissipate a little. Watching as Ezzie climbed up onto a boat named 'The Sunshine', she saw his hand extend out to her.

Biting her lip, Orpha held back then heard a woman shout, 'Is that you, our Ezzie?'

'Yes, Mother,' he called back, his arm still stretched out towards Orpha. 'I could do with a bit of help here, Mum.'

A woman's head popped out of the hatchway followed by an ample body as she looked at Orpha standing on the towpath holding onto a torn dress. Casting a stern look at her son, he shook his head saying, 'She was being attacked on the heath, and I thought it best to bring her here to you.'

'You did right, lad, c'mon wench don't hang about there, get yer arse on the boat so we can get going.'

Still hesitant, Orpha looked from mother to son and back again, then the woman shuffled to the side of the boat and very nimbly jumped down.

'It's all right wench, I can see you're afraid, my name is Edna and we're making for Birmingham if you want a ride. You'll be safe enough with us.'

Orpha burst into tears, her heart-rending sobs shaking her young body.

'Now, now . . .' Edna said as she took Orpha's arm and helped the girl aboard 'The Sunshine'. With Ezzie at the steering, Edna pulled the girl down through the hatchway and, giving her an old dress, said, 'It ain't much but it's better than the one you got on. I'll be up top when you're ready.'

Orpha calmed somewhat as she looked around her. Never having been on a boat before she was amazed how cramped it seemed, and yet there was a place for everything and everything in its place. She shuddered as she thought of the saying her mother was so fond of using. Her situation was dire, and yet the mother and son who were now busy navigating the canal had come to her rescue. She'd heard the stories about the 'cut-rats' being looked down on for choosing to live on the canals rather than in houses, but these people seemed very nice, at least what she'd seen of them so far. Orpha smiled to herself as she imagined what she must look like in the dress Edna had given her, but she was grateful for the woman's kindness. Climbing up through the hatch she smiled and nodded her thanks to Edna who was talking with her son. Orpha's eyes roamed the deck of the boat and its cargo which seemed to stretch out a long way forward. She wondered how Ezzie managed to control the craft from the back just by moving a piece of wood from side to side. Edna made tea and brought cake up from the tiny galley and again Orpha felt indebted to this woman and her son.

As the boat chugged along, Orpha thought about what she would do once they reached their destination. She could try to find her father, but she guessed he might not be in Birmingham, where he sometimes had work. It was a chance in a million she would see him there. Orpha wanted so much to tell her father about the abuse she had suffered at her mother's hand, but she could not return home; she was too afraid. These thoughts left her none the wiser as to what to do when they eventually docked.

After a couple of hours, they moored up once more. The three of them sat around a tiny table in the belly of the boat.

'Now then, what's yer name, wench?' Edna said, sipping tea from a tin mug.

Glancing at the stew and dumplings and a massive chunk of home-made bread set before her, Orpha muttered, 'Orpha Buchanan. Thank you, Mrs Lucas, this looks delicious . . . but I have no money to pay you.' Shyness descended on her as she eyed the food hungrily.

'I don't want no bloody payment, Orpha!' Edna said sharply, then seeing the girl's tears fall silently she softened, 'Eat yer dinner, girl, it's good for you.' Cuffing her son round the ear playfully, Edna said to him, 'This wench has good manners, you could learn a lot from her.'

'Thank you, Mother, this is scrumptious,' Ezzie said sarcastically then blew her a kiss.

Despite her misery, Orpha managed a smile along with mother and son before they all began to devour their food.

Over tea later, Orpha related how her mother had thrown her out after years of physical and verbal abuse; of trying to find her father without having to go home where her mother was and then getting lost; she finished her tale with the assailant on the heath.

'Blimey wench!' Edna gasped. 'All that and you're only what . . . fourteen?'

Orpha nodded shyly, although of late she had felt much older.

'Well, as I told you, we are on our way to Birmingham, maybe you'll see yer father there, and don't worry . . . Ezzie can sleep up on top of the boat, so you can have his bed.'

'Thank you, Mrs Lucas, but I couldn't impose on you and your son further, you've already been so kind,' Orpha said, lowering her eyes. Secretly she wished she could stay with these lovely people, but propriety had forced her hand.

'Edna, my name's Edna, wench, and it ain't no imposition. Now, Ezzie, get yer stuff and get up on top.'

Smiling, the young man grabbed a blanket and climbed through the hatch, closing it quietly behind him.

Lying in Ezzie's bed, Orpha heard him settle himself for the night on the deck of the boat. A shudder ran through her as she remembered the attack on the heath, to be replaced by the warm feeling of seeing Ezzie throw the man away from her.

Orpha slept soundly for the first time in years that night not being at all disturbed by Edna's snores.

CHAPTER 3

In another town far from where Orpha was fleeing for her life, Peg Meriwether looked out of the window of her tiny cottage. The sky was blue but she could see grey clouds beginning to gather. She needed to visit the market in the town to sell the vegetables she had grown in her large garden which sprawled at the side and behind her cottage.

Peg's two-bedroomed cottage stood in St George's Ward of Wolverhampton, which was very close to the small heath which separated her from All Saints Road. If she crossed over the road, it would take her into Raby Street which ended at Cleveland Road. This was where the cattle market stood and just behind it the makeshift street market had been set up by a group of people who had elected a market inspector. It was he who dealt with the powers that be to allow the market to stand each week. The Great Western Railway sliced the town into two halves and wharfs and basins for the mooring of barges were dotted everywhere. Wolverhampton & Staffordshire General Hospital was situated on Cleveland Road and the Wolverhampton Union Workhouse lay further down the same road.

Grabbing her shawl, Peg began to carry the baskets of vegetables out to her two-wheeled handcart kept at the back of the cottage. Closing the back door, she grabbed the handles of the cart and, dragging it behind her, she walked in the direction of the town. It wasn't too far across the heath and before long she was nodding to the other stallholders of the market as she steered the cart to her pitch. As the H-shaped legs flipped down from near the handles, Peg took the boulder from the cart and wedged it behind one wheel. Satisfied the cart would not move, she began to arrange the baskets of vegetables, laying them out for all to see.

She watched as the market filled up with women who rushed from one stall to the next in an effort to beat the oncoming bad weather, to be home before the threatened downpour started. A crack of thunder caused all eyes to turn to the sky. Grey clouds rolled together and a chilly wind blew around the market stalls. Peg pulled her shawl tighter around her shoulders and keeping one eye on the sky she prayed the rain would hold off until she got home.

At last, having sold all her produce, Peg replaced the boulder wedge on her cart; flipped up the legs and secured them under the cart. Then waving her goodbyes to the other stallholders she set off for home.

Halfway across the heath, she cursed when one of the cart wheels slipped into a deep rut and stuck fast. Peg pulled then pushed the cart trying to free the wheel, but it wouldn't budge. Standing back, she looked at the wheel and muttered, 'Bloody hell!' Again she tried to extricate her cart, energy spent, to no avail. Lightning flashed around her and a rumble of thunder sounded, then the first few drops of rain began to fall. Peg looked up at the darkening clouds and under her breath said, 'That's just what I needed . . .'

Another flash of lightning and a crack of thunder immediately followed; the storm was overhead now. The rain fell quickly and in no time at all it was lashing her face as she worked furiously at the trapped cartwheel. The ground was beginning to turn muddy and Peg's side button boots slipped as she pushed and pulled the cart. Out of sheer frustration, Peg gave the wheel a good kick, yelling, 'Oh bugger it!' Kicking viciously again at the wheel, she saw it move slightly in the rain-soaked ground. Holding the handles of the cart, she pushed and at the same time kicked the wheel. Again it moved. 'Right you bugger,' she said as she gave another good hard kick. The wheel sprang free and as Peg yanked on the handles, she muttered, 'Thank the Lord for that!'

She'd had no intention of leaving her cart on the heath overnight, she relied on it for transporting her vegetables to market, which was her only form of income. Besides, some thieving bugger would have pinched it by the time she went back to reclaim it.

When she finally reached home, Peg was soaked to the skin and shivering with cold. Pushing the cart to the back of the cottage, she dashed in through the back door. Taking off her shawl, she shook it in the tiny kitchen, then she took off her muddy boots. The living room was warm and she was glad she'd banked the fire up before leaving for the market. She'd piled 'slack' – tiny coal chippings mixed with water – onto the embers in the grate. This helped to keep the fire in, and as the water evaporated, the coal chippings fused together to burn slowly. It was a practice used at night in the winter and by morning a good fire would be burning in the hearth.

Draping her wet shawl over the back of a wooden chair, Peg removed the fireguard and stood the chair in front of the fire. Before long, steam began to rise as her shawl started to dry out. Swinging the bracket holding the kettle over the fire, Peg dashed upstairs and slipped off her wet clothes. Dragging a thick cotton nightdress over her shivering body with another warm shawl about her shoulders, Peg took her wet clothes to dry out by the fire next to her shawl.

Another bracket on the opposite side of the fireplace held her dinner. In the pot were vegetables from her garden which had cooked gently while she'd been at the market. Slicing some cooked lamb from the tiny pantry, she dropped it into the pot and replaced the lid. Making a cup of tea Peg salivated at the aroma of lamb stew with home-made bread for her dinner.

Her meal eaten, Peg glanced around the small living room, leading her to recall the story of being found on the step of the back door to the cottage by the woman who had lived there, Rufina Meriwether, many years before. Peg remembered the woman fondly as she sat toasting her toes by the fire. Rufina had told Peg the story many times and as she gazed at the flames dancing in the hearth, she heard it again in her mind.

Rufina, on returning from the market one day, had found the child in a basket on the doorstep. Rufina had never married and although she would have loved to have had children of her own, she did not want the burden of a husband. Consequently she had carved out a life for herself in her small cottage giving up all hope of ever having a child. She had determined whoever had left the child on her doorstep obviously couldn't care for her, so she had taken her in. If the mother wanted the baby back, she would know where to find her. And if not, the baby was better off without her. Rufina had vowed to be the best mother she could be and named the baby Peg, added to which was her own surname of Meriwether. They had lived together for those last eighteen years – for no one had ever returned to claim the child – until Rufina had died of pneumonia the previous winter.

Peg felt again the sadness at the loss of her foster

mother, the woman who had been all things to her; mother, teacher and friend. Rufina had taught her how to grow the vegetables she now sold in the market; what to plant in which season; how to harvest and what to sell or keep. Peg had an affinity with the land and she was well rewarded for her efforts. Rufina had taught Peg to read and write; how to do her numbers and how to calculate money. She had also left her this cottage and the means to support herself which was more than many women in the area could hope for. Rufina had been the only mother Peg had ever had and she had loved her with all her heart.

With a sigh, Peg climbed the stairs to bed, and pulling the bedclothes over her head, she shut out the noise of the storm raging outside. Comfortable, warm and with a full stomach, she was soon sound asleep.

Peg rose early the following morning seeing the sun pouring in through her bedroom window. As she ate her breakfast, she suspected the ruts on the heath would be like a quagmire despite the morning sunshine, so she decided to stay home and rescue any vegetables in her plot that the storm had not ravaged.

Sitting in the sun, she strung onions to be hung in the pantry, boxed shallots for the market and collected and washed the green beans the wind had ripped from the plants that grew around their wigwams of canes. By midday the sun was hot in its zenith and Peg decided to chance a trip over the heath to the market. Loading her cart and filling a bottle with water, she set off.

Dragging the cart in the heat of the afternoon was hard work and Peg stopped to take a drink from her bottle of water. As she quenched her thirst, her peripheral vision caught sight of a rider coming from the direction of the market. Reining his horse close to her cart, he jumped down.

'Hello wench,' he said.

Warily nodding her greeting, Peg eyed him suspiciously.

'You off to the market then?' he asked, casting a glance at the produce on her cart.

Peg rolled her eyes as she said sarcastically, 'No, I'm walking my dog!'

'Hey, there ain't no need for that,' the man said as he stepped towards her.

Peg placed her bottle of water on the cart near the boulder which she used as a wedge and rested her hand there.

'Cat got your tongue?' the man laughed as he stepped closer to her. Peg ignored the question but kept her eyes on him. She knew where her boulder was without having to look down. 'You know what . . .' the man began, 'you are ignorant! You should answer when someone speaks to you.'

Shrugging her shoulders, Peg moved one hand to the cart handle, the other she left near the boulder. She didn't like how this was going and she felt her stomach clench at the uneasy feeling.

Shaking his head and with a smile lifting only the corners of his mouth, the man walked forward and grabbed Peg's arm, yanking her hand from the cart handle.

In one movement, Peg picked up the boulder and snatched her arm from his grip as she took a step back. Holding the rock high so he could see it, she snarled, 'You touch me again and I'll stove your head in!'

Throwing back his head, he laughed, 'I don't think you will, pretty wench . . .' His eyes roamed her body with a lecherous grin.

Seeing his intent, Peg raised the rock higher and took another step backwards away from the man, in an effort to widen the distance between them. 'What is it you want?' she asked through clenched teeth.

Closing the gap with another step forward, the man said, 'I love a girl with spirit, how about you and me have a little fun before I go home to the wife?'

As he rubbed his hands together, Peg's anger rose and she shouted, 'You think you can accost me on the heath, have your way with me then ride off home to your wife? I think not!'

Looking around him and seeing no one, he spread his arms and said, 'And who, may I ask, is going to stop me?' The grin creased his face again.

Chancing a quick look at the ground around her Peg saw loose rocks and boulders lying within easy reach. Her eyes quickly snapped back to the man standing in front of her. 'I will,' Peg said, showing a bravado she didn't feel.

'I doubt that,' the man said. 'Now then, let's you and me have that fun I spoke about.' Stepping towards the girl with the pretty green eyes, he faltered as the rock glanced off his forehead above his right eye. 'You bitch!' he shouted as his hands covered the injured spot.

Peg used that moment wisely to gather more rocks and stones and began to hurl them at the man. Each finding its mark, the man covered his head with his arms before he fell to his knees cursing. Peg aimed a rock at the man's horse standing grazing nearby and caught it a sharp blow to its flank. With a whinny the horse bolted away in the direction of its home.

Turning his head to see his horse galloping off, the man scrambled to his feet glaring at Peg.

'Want some more?' she said, a rock held firmly in each hand.

'You bitch!' he said again. 'You'd better hope we don't meet again!' Turning away from her, he began to run after his horse.

Collecting her boulder then grabbing the handles of her cart, Peg pulled hard and ran in the direction of the market, her strength fuelled by the adrenaline coursing through her body.

'Bloody hell, wench, what's got your knickers in a twist?' Lottie Spence, a friend and fellow stall holder asked as she helped Peg pull the cart next to her own stall.

'I've just been accosted on the heath!' Peg puffed.

'Christ! Are you hurt?' the older woman asked, her concern evident.

'No, but he scared me, Lottie.' Peg felt the adrenaline drain from her body leaving behind an ache in her arms and legs.

'Hey wenches,' Lottie called across the market, 'Peg's been accosted on the heath, be careful on your way home.'

Stallholders gathered to discuss the incident, deciding to return home in pairs or groups as far as was possible.

Turning back to Peg, Lottie said, 'You need to tell the police about this, see what they can do about it.'

'I can't walk all the way to Walsall Street to the police station, it's miles away, besides there's not enough time now . . . I'll go tomorrow,' Peg answered as she shakily set up her cart.

Staying Peg's hands, Lottie said sternly, 'Then run down to the ironworks over the back of the timber yard and tell the men what's happened and ask for an iron bar for protection. They'll give you one for nothing when they know what it's for. Go on, I'll watch your cart.'

Thanking the woman, Peg ran hell for leather to the iron works in All Saints Road. Lottie had been right, Peg got her small iron bar free of charge once the workers heard her story.

Dragging the empty cart home that afternoon with her iron bar on the top, Peg's heart sank as she trudged the heath and saw a rider coming towards her. She wished some of the other women lived out her way then she wouldn't have to make this journey alone. Stopping and grabbing the bar, she hid it behind her long skirt. This could just be someone riding home. But then on the other hand . . .

The horse's hooves rucked up the heath as the rider yanked hard on the reins, bringing them to a stop near Peg's cart.

Seeing the man jump down, Peg thought, *God help me . . . it's the same man!*

Standing in front of the girl, legs astride, his hands on his hips, he said nastily, 'I thought you'd be coming back this way.'

'Well you thought right,' Peg said. Despite the fear and panic she felt, she noted he had, once again, not bothered to tether his horse, Peg thought, *Some people never learn.*

Balancing her weight evenly on both feet Peg waited, her heart beating like a drum and her breath coming in gasps.

The man glanced at Peg's hand still on the cart handle and realised her other one was behind her skirt. He was sure the hidden hand held a boulder.

'I've got a lump the size of an egg on my head,' he said, pointing to his forehead where the rock had hit him earlier in the day.

'So it would seem,' Peg answered.

'It's your fault!' he shouted.

'I can't argue with that,' Peg stood her ground.

'Good, because you're gonna pay for it now,' the man said, striding towards her.

Leaning slightly forward at the waist gave Peg a solid stance and she brought her arm round, revealing her iron bar which was far easier to manipulate than the boulder had been.

The man stopped abruptly as he saw the bar in her hand. 'What do you think you're gonna do with that? I'm a man and it stands to reason I'm the stronger!'

'You may be stronger . . . but I've got the weapon!' Peg said as she waved the bar in front of her. 'You want to chance your arm . . . see who comes off best?'

Anger blazed in him as he strode towards her, his arms stretching forward in order to grab her, and he yelled, 'I'm gonna teach you a lesson you'll never forget!'

Peg shouted, 'Forget this!' and she swung the bar up before bringing it smartly down on his left arm. She heard the bone break a split second before the man screamed out his agony.

Grabbing his injured arm with his right hand, he said through jaws clamped together, 'You bitch! You broke my bloody arm!'

'Yes, and I'll break the other bugger an' all if you don't leave me alone!' Peg's voice rose in anger even as she moved away from him. Watching him weighing up his options she thought, *This bugger's not going to stop!*

As if he'd read her mind, Peg watched as fury

bubbled up in him and he began stepping forward and kicking out at her. As he neared her again, Peg held the bar with both hands. She stepped back as he strode on one leg and kicked out at her with the other. To an onlooker it must have looked like a bizarre dance out there on the heath, the man stepping and kicking as he approached the girl. Peg chose her timing well and as he lifted his left leg to kick her again, she swung the bar in a sideways swipe and caught him hard at the side of his knee. Again she heard the bone crack just before a scream left his throat.

Dropping like a stone onto his right side, the man yelled, 'You're bloody mad!'

'Yes I am!' Peg said as she carefully moved towards him, the bar held above her head, 'Mad as hell that you thought to accost me for the second time today!' Knowing, due to the injuries he sustained, she had the upper hand, Peg went on. 'So you thought to teach me a lesson I'd never forget, did you? Well, now, it seems to me, you'll be the one never to forget. I suggest you listen very carefully to my next words. Don't you ever try this with another woman, and should you see me in the future . . . you turn and go another way. Do you understand me?'

The man lay with closed eyes moaning in pain and said nothing.

'DO . . . YOU . . . UNDERSTAND . . . ME?' Peg yelled down at him. The man opened his eyes to look at her and nodded. 'Then we have reached an agreement,' Peg said as she lowered the bar. Walking to her cart, she placed the bar on the top, grabbed the handles and dragged it to where the man lay writhing in agony.

Spotting the horse nearby, she stopped to pick up a stone. Tossing it slightly in the air and catching it again Peg shook her head at the man. He groaned as he saw her intention. Peg swung her arm and the stone flew from her fingers, hitting the horse on the rump. The man groaned again as he watched his horse gallop away once more.

'How the bloody hell am I to get home now?' he rasped through the pain of his broken bones.

'That's your lookout, you should have thought of that before,' Peg said before adding, 'and, while you wait to be rescued by a kind passer-by, think about this . . . how will you explain to your wife how you got to be in this state?'

Peg smiled as the man closed his eyes again and let out a sob.

Grasping the cart handles, Peg Meriwether walked home without even a backward glance.

CHAPTER 4

Hortense Buchanan drove the trap to Birmingham herself in order to be fitted for some new gowns and dresses; it was high time she and Abel resumed an acquaintance with the socialites of the town. Having failed at trying to poison Abel with the mushrooms in order to inherit his wealth, she had decided to make the best of living with him for now. At least she would still have money and the niceties of life. She had already inspected her wardrobe; she had decided new gowns were definitely the order of the day. Abel's depression at losing his daughter was dragging her down too, so she thought to lift her own spirits with her favourite pastime . . . shopping.

Stopping the horse outside Lawsons Dressmakers shop in the high street, Hortense berated herself; Birmingham city was becoming far too busy to bring the trap, she should have travelled on the railway. Carters, horses, traps, people walking and milling about, it was extremely uncomfortable to even walk down the street. The smells of unwashed men and the sight of dirty children rampaging around began to thoroughly annoy her.

With a huge sigh, Hortense stepped down from the trap and instantly collided with a young man walking past her. Losing her grip on her bag, it fell to the ground and the young man bent quickly to retrieve it.

'Madam, please forgive me, I was entirely at fault,' he said.

Moving her eyes from the bag being passed to her, Hortense allowed them to roam over the boy in front of her. He wore a fine-fitting tailored outfit and his brown leather riding boots shone in the sunlight. Her gaze swept upwards and Hortense gasped as shock rattled her to her core. A wide smile showed even white teeth and a mop of unruly raven black hair fell over sparkling emerald green eyes!

'I hope you are not hurt,' the young man said as Hortense tried to regain her composure.

'No . . . no, I'm fine thank you,' Hortense stammered.

'I'm glad to hear it,' the boy said, 'in that case I'll be on my way. Good afternoon.' With that the boy marched down the high street, leaving a bewildered Hortense standing with her mouth open.

Sitting in Harrison's Tea Shop a few moments later, Hortense tried desperately to gather her wits. The boy's smile, his hair, his eyes . . . It could not possibly be a coincidence. The likeness between the boy and her husband had taken her breath away.

The waitress came over and stood by Hortense's table and waited, saying nothing.

'Tea!' Hortense snapped.

'Would *madam* like anything else?' the waitress asked sarcastically.

'Had I wanted something more I would have asked for it!' Hortense snapped again.

The waitress said nothing as she turned on her heel and strode away, bristling with indignation, her white cap bobbing on her head. Moments later she returned with a tray of crockery and slammed it on the table in front of the woman who had been so rude to her. *Let her pour her own tea!* she thought as she walked away, her long black skirt and white apron swishing around her side button boots.

Hortense did pour her own tea as thoughts of the young man whirled in her brain. She guessed him to be around sixteen years old. She knew Abel had no siblings, so if he and the boy *were* related this could mean only one thing – Abel had a son!

Her heart tightened in her chest as she considered the ramifications of the situation. Her husband had, or had had, a mistress! Moreover, she had given him a son!

Throwing coins on the table, much to the disgust of the disgruntled waitress, she dashed outside in the hope the young man would still be in sight. Hortense realised her hopes were in vain as she looked up and down the street . . . the boy was gone.

Finally sitting in her kitchen again, tea in hand, Hortense worked through the scenario in her head.

After Eugenie had 'disappeared', she and Abel had struggled in their relationship; he had blamed her for the loss of his daughter. Yes, she was to blame, but he'd never know that for sure. Abel had been distant with his wife for a very long time and now she thought of it, he had stayed at the so-called business meetings in the Gentlemen's Club longer than at any time before, even staying overnight on occasions. So, she suspected he had lied to her . . . he had not been at the Club at all . . . he'd been with another woman! Why had she not seen it before? Feeling stomach acid burning her insides, Hortense poured milk into a cup and drank it down.

Returning to her thoughts, she recalled how, quite suddenly, Abel had seemed happier, not appearing to dwell so much on the loss of Eugenie. Was that when the boy had been born? His spending more and more time away from home made perfect sense to her now. When he was not here with her, he was away with his mistress and their son!

Snapping her mind back to the present, Hortense realised she had to be rid of Abel's boy too – she didn't want an heir out there when Abel died. She had resigned herself to continue to live with Abel and his money, but this discovery of him having a son had spurred her desire to be rid of him once more. But what of the boy's mother? Who was she? Where was she? Maybe Hortense could dispose of them all at the same time . . . If they lived as a family – then they could die as a family! *It would serve them right!* She thought spitefully.

Hortense watched Abel scan the daily newspaper over the breakfast table the next morning and her thoughts turned back to the young man on the street in Birmingham. Seeing again in her mind his sparkling green eyes and mop of raven black hair, the anger swelled in her. Abel was taking her for a fool and she would not stand for it!

Grabbing her shawl, Hortense strode out to the stables and was delighted the trap stood ready for her. Nodding to Jago, the stable boy, she climbed aboard and set off on yet another jaunt to Birmingham. She had decided against taking the train as she hated being cooped up in the carriage with other people, especially those with unruly children. She also didn't like the noise of the engine and the smell of the steam constantly surrounding it. At least the air was a little fresher outdoors, provided one didn't breathe too deeply, otherwise the lungs would clog with the filthy waste from the collieries. Hortense needed to see that boy again. She needed to discover the truth about him and whether or not he was, in fact, Abel's son.

The noise of the people assaulted her ears and the smell of the town made her nose screw up as she guided the trap through the streets. She could smell the engine at the station, which was still belching out steam; it was a quick way to travel but the odour of that awful steam clung to everything. Searching the crowds as she walked the horse through the throngs of people, she looked for sight of the boy.

Coming again to the dressmaker's in the high street, Hortense scanned the street before she made her way into the shop. Ordering more gowns, although her heart was not in the choosing of the material, she left the dressmaker who was gushing her thanks. The time spent in the shop had allowed her to contemplate the boy, his mother and where and how they lived. Moreover, she contemplated how she could dispose of them in one fell swoop. Looking up and down the street once more, Hortense's eyes scanned for sight of the boy. She hitched up her skirt and wandered along pretending to look into shop windows, but she looked only at the reflections of the people passing by. Finally reaching the conclusion she would probably not see the lad again she strode off back towards the trap in a foul temper.

Hortense felt disappointment sting at not seeing the young man again. She needed to find out who he was and, most importantly, if he had any ties to Abel. She needed proof of identity before she could construct a plan that would see her free of the green-eyed family.

A thought sent a barb to her heart as Hortense only now realised that if the boy *was* Abel's son, there may be more of his children in that household. She had only seen the boy . . . but there could be others . . . Abel could still be producing for all she knew. She *had* to find that boy, she *had* to discover all there was to know about him and his family – but how?

A couple of days later, Hortense halted the buggy outside Harrison's Tea Shop and she climbed down. She had decided that if she sat by the bullion-paned window with tea, she could see people passing by. She had made up her mind to do this every day if needs be.

Struggling to get the nosebag over the horse's head, a voice floated over her shoulder.

'Can I help you with that, madam?'

As she let go of the nosebag into the strong hands that lifted it over the head of the horse, Hortense turned and found herself looking into green eyes once more. *What a stroke of luck!*

'Thank you, young man,' she said, smoothing her skirts with her hands in order to get her surprise under control.

'I see you are quite well despite our collision the other day,' he went on with a smile.

'Indeed,' Hortense managed as she searched his face for anything that could possibly give her a clue to his identity.

The boy smiled, holding out his hand, 'My name is Zachariah Buchanan,' he said politely.

Hortense felt the colour drain from her face as she stared at the boy with her husband's surname smiling at her. Rapidly trying to regain her composure, she shook his extended hand, saying, 'Hortense . . . Eldon.' Thinking quickly, she had used her maiden name.

'I'm pleased to meet you, Mrs Eldon,' Zachariah said, smiling again. 'Are you feeling unwell, madam?'

'No, Mr Buchanan, I am just a little tired,' Hortense felt only the corners of her mouth tilt up in a tight smile.

'Then if you will excuse me, Mrs Eldon, I am late for an appointment at Beaty Bros., my tailor.' Extending his hand once more, they shook before he went on his way.

Rummaging in her bag on the pretext of looking for her purse, Hortense watched the boy out of the corner of her eye. She saw him step into a shop with the name Beaty Bros., above the door. Beaty Bros., was an expensive shop . . . how could he afford the clothes from there? Did he work? Could it be Abel's money the boy was spending?

Going into the tea shop, she sat by the window, keeping a keen eye out for Zachariah Buchanan leaving the tailor's. Hortense knew meeting the boy again was a chance in a million and she was determined she would not waste the opportunity to learn more about him. She hardly dared blink in case she missed him coming out of the shop and her eyes watered as she stared hard through the window.

The waitress ambled over to the woman sat in the bow window and cursed under her breath

58

when she recognised her as the customer who had been so rude to her a few days before.

Hortense kept her eyes on the street as she said, 'Tea . . . please.'

Wonders will never cease! the waitress thought as she shuffled away. Returning with the tea tray, the girl poured the tea before being dismissed with a wave of Hortense's hand. *Maybe they will,* the waitress added to her previous thought.

Suddenly Hortense's view was blocked by two women who stopped to chat with each other outside of the tea shop. Damn! She could lose sight of the boy if he came out of the tailor's now! Throwing coins on the table, she rushed out through the tea shop door just as Zachariah Buchanan strode out onto the street. Dragging the nosebag from her disgruntled horse, she climbed up into the trap and very slowly urged the horse forward to follow where the boy would lead. Seeing him pay a lad who held his horse's reins, Zachariah swung into the saddle and trotted away along the cobbled high street.

Flicking the reins, Hortense felt the trap pick up speed as she kept the rider in full view. Feeling excitement flow through her, she kept the horse to a pace that allowed her to watch where Zachariah rode, but that would not allow him to realise she was following him.

The trap rolled and bumped over the cobbles, shaking her to the bone. Hortense began to wish she had left the trap at home and rode the horse instead. She prided herself on being an excellent horsewoman and the thought of a saddle was preferable to the hard seat of the trap.

Passing riders and carriages on their way to Wednesbury, Hortense continued her journey in the opposite direction. She fervently prayed she would not lose sight of Zachariah now. Her heart was beating fast as she followed the boy on the horse. If he should glance backwards, he would see her, he would know she was following him. She swallowed hard and, listening to her better judgement, she slowed the trap.

Trailing him along Corporation Street, then between the rows of houses either side of Aston Street, she saw him quite suddenly turn into a driveway on the left of the row of houses and she slowed her horse. Glancing into the driveway as she passed, she nodded with a smile as she watched the young man jump down from his saddle. Assuming she had just discovered where Zachariah Buchanan and therefore her husband's illegitimate family lived, she encouraged the horse forward and turned the trap for home revelling in her good luck.

CHAPTER 5

The narrowboat made its way along the canal system and Orpha delighted in waving to other 'cut-rats', canal people, as they passed by. She heard the news shouted from boat to boat as they chugged along the waterways in the sunshine. Unable to contribute to the coffers, Orpha made herself useful making tea and helping with the meals as the boat pulled into the stopping places along the way. She washed the dishes and put everything back in its place before joining Edna and Ezzie on deck to chat away the evening hours. She felt guilty at Ezzie giving up his bunk for her and being relegated to sleeping on deck, but he didn't appear to mind one little bit. Orpha found herself slipping easily into the ways of the canal people and thought how hard they worked for such little reward.

Having eventually reached Birmingham, Orpha gave her thanks to Edna and Ezzie Lucas as she jumped down onto the towpath of the Basin at Old Wharf. She was sad to be leaving them but headed off with the woman's words ringing in her ears . . . *If you don't find your father, come back here to us, we'll be here a while to unload the boat.*

Orpha walked down Bridge Street not really knowing where she was going, or if she would see her father. Knowing he conducted business there at times, she felt it a safer bet than returning home to face the wrath of her mother. All around her were factories and houses, and as she walked on she began to realise just how big Birmingham city was.

The fear she had felt on leaving the boat and heading for the town was swamped by awe as she took in the sights, sounds and smells. People pushed past her as she slowly walked along looking all around her. She wrinkled her nose as the smell of boiling meat reached her nostrils. She heard children laughing as they ran down the cobbled road. She didn't notice women staring at her attire. The dress she'd been given hung from her small frame and was held up by an old belt to prevent her tripping on the hem. Having visited the large town regularly with her father, Orpha was now traversing the streets alone in an area not familiar to her.

Passing Queen's College and the General Post Office, Orpha was amazed at the network of streets spread out around her; she stopped quite suddenly as she turned into the high street.

Catching her breath, Orpha's eyes settled on a horse and trap stood outside a shop. That was her mother's trap she was certain of it! Squinting in the sunlight in order to see better, she saw a woman step through the shop doorway onto the street. It was not her mother! Orpha's heart skipped a beat as she watched a woman glance anxiously around her.

Leaning against the wall, she took a deep breath; she'd had a nasty scare. Looking again around the corner, she released her held breath. Orpha shook her head; her fear of her mother had her imagining things.

As the afternoon sun began to set, Orpha made her way back to the basin where the barges moored up. The search for her father had been fruitless and although at one point she saw a young boy who looked like him, but of course it was not him. Not knowing now what she should do, her mood was disconsolate as she trudged back to the basin. At least Edna said she could stay with them overnight on their boat. Checking the names on the boats as she walked along the towpath, her heart weighed heavily as she realised 'The Sunshine' was not in its mooring place on the canal. It was gone . . . she was too late!

Turning back towards the town, Orpha wondered where she could spend the night now. She had no money and as darkness began to creep over the buildings like a shroud she again wandered the streets watching as the shops closed down for the night.

Feeling the fear grip her of being alone at night,

in a strange town, she once more found herself near the canal towpath. Why did she keep coming back here? What was it that kept pulling her back to this place? Was she hoping to see 'The Sunshine' return to its mooring place? In her heart she knew the boat would now be well on its way to some other destination. Sadness weighed heavy as she thought she might never see Edna and Ezzie again.

Orpha sat beneath one of the few trees that lined the towpath, leaning her back on the trunk – at least she felt safer here than in the town. Closing her eyes, Orpha knew sleep would evade her; thoughts tumbling over themselves about the predicament she found herself in. She could trudge the streets forever and never find her father. Sitting with her eyes closed, listening to the sounds of the canal people settling for the night, Orpha made her decision. Tomorrow she would head for Wednesbury and her home regardless of the consequences.

Sitting alone beneath the tree, Orpha heard some revellers coming back to their boats after a good night in one of the many public houses in the town. Drawing her knees up, she tried to push herself into the tree's trunk in order not to be seen.

She need not have feared; the men laughed out loud when a woman on one of the boats shouted, 'Shut yer bloody row, you lot, folk here are trying to sleep!'

With that they clambered aboard their own boats and quiet settled once more over the canal. The few lights showing from the candle jars on the boats cast an eerie glow on the towpath and fear crept over the young girl once more.

Wrapping her arms around her drawn-up knees, she dropped her head onto them and sobbed quietly into the night. How had she come to this? Loneliness and despair crawled over her as she wept her unhappiness into the darkness.

The morning sunshine woke Orpha and she instantly felt panic not knowing, at first, where she was. Then she realised she had slept beneath the tree at the basin at Old Wharf. Getting to her feet, she stretched out her aching muscles. Looking around her, she heard the people on the boats begin to stir, and she knew she had to get moving.

Walking the same streets she had trudged the previous day, Orpha made her way into the town. She was hungry and thirsty, not having eaten since the day before, and as she walked, she thought about how to go about getting a day's work so she could feed herself before going home. Knowing work was hard to come by in Wednesbury, she wondered if it would be as difficult to find here. What could she do? What jobs were available for women? Waitress, barmaid, or going into service . . . she could knock on a few doors to see if a parlourmaid was needed for the day. Not holding out much hope, she strode on with determination filling her mind.

Walking down Carr's Lane, Orpha continued on, her new-found determination fuelled by the growl of her empty stomach. Coming at last to the market, she wandered between the closely packed stalls, the sight of the fruit making her hunger all the more acute. The marketplace seemed to stretch out for miles as Orpha wound her way up and down the narrow gaps between the stalls. People pushed and jostled in search of a bargain and Orpha felt giddy with excitement.

The noise of the stallholders shouting out their prices across the market assaulted her ears, but Orpha hardly noticed it, being so deep in the wonder of it all. The aroma of freshly cooked pies drifted on the air and Orpha breathed it in greedily. Once more, her stomach growled its protest of being deprived of food.

Pushing on through the stalls, Orpha found herself at the end of the market and faced with yet another tangle of streets. Walking down Moat Street, she turned into Moat Row, and passing the slaughterhouse Orpha gagged. Rushing forward away from the dreadful smell emanating from the building, she passed a carriage works and walked down into Cheapside. Orpha continued her journey until she found herself in Martineau Street, which ran parallel with Union Street and then into Lower Priory. She had walked three sides of a square and ended up not far from where she had started!

Walking through the market once more she asked at the pitches if anyone could help regarding her search for work. Heads shook as she moved from stall to stall, asking the same question.

All day and into the evening she walked the city asking for work, but it looked like she would have to spend another night without a comfortable bed to lie in. As evening drew in, Orpha migrated back to the tree by the canal and chastised herself for not trying to get home to her father. She desperately wanted to see him, but fear of her mother had kept her away.

Orpha wrapped her arms around her knees and lay her head down. Her tears soaked into the ends of her shawl as she cried for her father and what she wished could have been a good relationship between her mother and herself. For all the woman had done to her, she missed her in a strange way.

As her tears subsided she knew she would have to make up her mind about what to do. She wanted to go to her father but she *needed* to stay away from her mother. Whatever her final decision she had to eat in the meantime and that meant finding some work.

After another miserable night, Orpha took to the streets again the next morning.

Exhaustion, despair and hunger settled on her as she leaned against a shop wall. Her feet and legs ached and looking down at her boots she wondered how long they would last her. She did not hear the man who approached her until he spoke.

'Out for business?' the burly man asked.

Looking up, Orpha said, 'Pardon?'

'I said, am you out for business?' the man

repeated. Not understanding what he meant, Orpha frowned and shook her head. 'Shame,' the man muttered as he walked away.

Orpha frowned again as she watched him go, wondering what his question meant. Quite suddenly the shop door opened, startling her.

'What you doing here?' a plump woman yelled, standing with her hands on her hips. 'You get away from here and ply your trade somewhere else!'

'I don't understand . . .' Orpha began. 'I am looking for work.'

'I can bloody well see that for myself!' the woman snapped. 'I ain't having you trying to attract custom outside my shop, so bugger off!'

A sudden intake of breath showed Orpha's understanding at last . . . the woman thought she was a whore! 'You misunderstand . . .' Orpha tried again.

'Oh no I don't!' the woman interrupted. 'I saw you talking to that bloke. What happened, couldn't he afford what you were asking?'

Orpha gasped before her body folded onto the street and she sobbed like her heart would break.

Completely taken aback by this turn of events, the woman blustered, 'Now then, wench, don't take on so,' looking around her as she spoke. 'Come on, get up and move along.'

'I . . . I have nowhere to go.' Orpha sobbed into the corner of her shawl.

'Well you can't stay there,' the woman answered. As Orpha got to her feet, a dizziness whirled in her head and all sound muffled her ears. She felt the colour drain from her face as her legs gave way beneath her. She felt nothing more as blackness engulfed her.

Opening her eyes, Orpha glanced around her. She was lying on a couch in a small living room and the woman who had yelled at her was sitting close by.

'Back with us, I see,' the woman said, holding out a cup of tea.

Orpha took the cup gratefully and sipped the hot sweet liquid which gave her some sustenance and helped her feel a little better.

'I'm very sorry to have put you to this trouble, it was not my intention,' Orpha said before sipping her tea once more.

The woman eyed her from her chair next to the couch. *This girl ain't no whore,* she thought, *she's too refined for that.* Instead she said, 'Drink yer tea, girl, then we can have a little chat.'

Orpha did as she was bid while the woman brought her a piece of cheese and a chunk of home-made bread. 'Thank you,' Orpha said, 'but I'm afraid I'm without funds and cannot pay you for your kind hospitality.' She was desperate to eat the food offered but didn't want to take advantage, the woman had done enough by bringing her here.

Waving a hand, the woman pushed the food into Orpha's hand. 'Now then, firstly what's yer name?'

'Orpha Buchanan,' she said.

'Well Orpha,' the woman went on, 'I am Henrietta Toye and I run this shop with my husband Henry.' Seeing the girl smile, she went on, 'That's why everybody calls me Hetty, saves any confusion.'

'I'm very pleased to meet you, Hetty, and I'm so sorry to have put you to this trouble . . . I don't know what happened out there on the street.' Orpha looked in the direction of the door as she spoke, eyeing up the food.

'You fainted, that's what happened. When did you last have something to eat?'

Shaking her head trying to remember, Orpha replied, 'I can't remember.'

'Christ, wench!' Hetty's exclamation was loud in the small room, as she set the kettle to boil again. 'Get yer chops around that food girl, then I think you should tell me all about it, but first I have to apologise for mistaking you for a whore. Mouth open and in with both feet, that's me. I am sorry, Orpha.'

'Please, Hetty, think nothing of it, I can see how you drew your conclusion,' Orpha smiled as she tried to eat with some decorum despite being famished and Hetty smiled back.

Over another cup of tea, the green-eyed girl related her tale of being thrown out by her mother; of having been accosted on the heath and given a lift to the Old Wharf basin on a boat by Edna and Ezzie Lucas; of having slept beneath a tree, then walking almost in a circle before finding herself leaning on the shop wall to rest a while.

'Christ A'mighty!' Hetty gasped as Orpha finished speaking. 'So what are you planning to do now?'

Tears coursing down her face, Orpha shook her head. 'I don't know, Hetty. I have to find some work in order to feed myself. Maybe then I can return home to my father.'

'What about if yer mother is there?' Hetty asked, her concern etching her face.

'I'll have to cross that bridge when I come to it,' Orpha replied, 'but for now, finding work is my first priority.'

'Right!' Hetty slammed her hand on a nearby table. 'You can stay up in my spare room until you decide what to do.' Lifting her hand to stay Orpha's protest, Hetty went on, 'You can help out here in exchange for board and lodging. Now, how does that sound to you?'

Jumping up from the couch, Orpha flung her arms around the woman's neck, saying, 'Oh thank you, Hetty, it sounds wonderful to me!' Standing back a step, she then asked, 'But what about Mr Toye, how will he feel about having a stranger in his house?'

'Oh don't you worry about Henry, you leave him to me!' Hetty grinned. Never being blessed with children of her own, Hetty relished the idea of the young girl staying with them. 'Now then, how about you have a little taste of what we make and sell?'

Orpha's eyes widened as she saw the plate of sweets and chocolates placed before her.

Hetty smiled as she saw Orpha bite a chocolate

in half and close her eyes as it melted in her mouth. Her smile turned into a grin as Orpha pushed the rest of the confection into her mouth without opening her eyes.

'Hmmmm . . .' Orpha groaned, 'Hetty, that was the best thing I've ever tasted!'

'Ar well, we used to work for Mr Cadbury in the factory down in Bourneville and when this little shop came on the market, we were fortunate enough to be able to buy it. We'd already learned the trade of chocolate making so decided to try and make a living by going it alone.'

'Well obviously it worked,' Orpha said, licking her fingers.

'Ar, we do all right here, we can't compete with George Cadbury o'course, but we manage to earn a nice living,' Hetty said with a contented sigh.

Cursing and banging announced the arrival of Henry Toye on his return from the sugar refinery, loaded down with sacks of sugar, and he was introduced to his new 'assistant'. Hetty brought him up to date regarding how the girl had come to be at their shop.

Henry tutted and shook his head and Hetty said, 'I already apologised to the girl for my mistake, so don't you say a thing Henry Toye!'

To Orpha he said, 'You can take over the tasting from Hetty an' all . . .' giving the girl a sly wink, 'she's fat enough as it is.'

Orpha gasped at the insult but Hetty roared with laughter.

'You got room to talk, that shirt is bursting under the strain of that belly!'

Henry's laugh boomed out. 'Take no notice of us, girl, insults abound in this house. We don't mean anything by it; besides, the world would be a sad place if you can't insult your best friend.' Orpha noticed the warm smile pass between the two and thought she'd never seen her mother and father smile at each other like that.

'Right, you come along with me, wench and I'll show you where you'll be sleeping.' Hetty grabbed Orpha's hand and led her upstairs. 'It's only a box room but . . .'

'Oh Hetty, it's lovely!' Orpha said, looking around. It was smaller than her room at home but much more homely.

'Ar well . . . tomorrow we'll begin your tuition.' The woman smiled.

'Tuition?' Orpha asked.

'Yes lovey, we'll show you how to make chocolate!'

Hetty closed the door quietly as she left Orpha to settle into her new bedroom.

Looking around the tiny room, Orpha couldn't believe her luck. She had been down on her uppers and the Fates had stepped in. Sitting on the edge of the bed, she thought how there were still good people in this world of misery and greed. She determined to work hard to repay Hetty Toye for her kindness in taking her in off the street. Orpha smiled as she realised she had board and lodging;

she would be fed good food and would be taught a trade. She had come so far in such a short time and began to feel being thrown out by her mother could be a blessing in disguise. She would put her all into her work for Hetty, then when she went home to her father she could show her mother she was someone to be proud of.

CHAPTER 6

Zachariah Buchanan rode home from the tavern where he'd spent a few hours drinking with his friends and strode into the house, hearing his father's sonorous voice emanate from the parlour.

'Father,' he said, excitedly shaking his hand, 'it seems like forever since we last saw you.'

'I know, lad, I've been really busy with business meetings, I ain't had time to spit!' his father laughed.

Zachariah watched his parents sitting close together holding hands, they looked for all the world like a courting couple with him as their chaperone.

Abel and Mahula Buchanan, a match made in heaven. It was just a pity he and his mother saw so little of his father. He was always away at some meeting or other; he always looked so tired of late too, the boy noted. As he watched them, he wondered if there was anything he could do to enable his father to rest more.

Suddenly a thought struck him and Zachariah said, 'Father, isn't it time you found me some work at one of your friend's factories or maybe you could teach me the ways of advising in business?'

The explosion of his father's reply shook him to his core. 'No, lad!' Registering his shock, his father went on more gently, 'There's nothing for you, lad. Besides, you're a young buck . . . you should be out sowing your wild oats.'

Zachariah watched his mother tap his father's arm and berate him gently for the statement.

'Don't you go encouraging our son into sinful ways!' his mother said playfully.

For the first time in his life, his father had raised his voice to him, and as Zachariah sat watching, he tried to work out why that had been.

Abel Buchanan had left early the next morning as he had so often in Zachariah's sixteen years, and after breakfast Zachariah sat with his mother in the parlour. Watching her knitting needles clack together, Zachariah thought again of his father shouting at him the previous night.

'Mother,' he said quietly, 'why do you think father yelled at me last night?'

'Oh Zachariah, he hardly yelled,' his mother answered, looking at him, her needles continuing their fast clicking, 'you just took him by surprise that's all.'

'I suppose,' Zachariah muttered.

'Besides, your father is exhausted . . .' Mahula continued.

Cutting across her sentence, he shot, 'I know!

That's why I thought I might be able to help . . . If I worked, father could rest more.'

'I understand that, son, but you have to understand something too. Your father works hard to provide for us, and you know yourself we want for nothing,' Mahula said as she watched him over her knitting.

'Except his time!' Even to his own ears he sounded like a petulant child. Zachariah stood and began to pace the floor.

'Don't be a baby!' His mother's words were sharp. 'Now go and find something to do.'

Striding from the room, Zachariah heard his mother sigh as he closed the door quietly behind him.

Sauntering into the garden feeling bored, Zachariah caught sight of Seth Walker, the boy mucking out the stables.

To hell with it! he thought, *I'm going to see Father at the Club no matter what Mother says!*

The ride from Birmingham to Wednesbury was invigorating. At last, Zachariah had made a decision for himself and acted on it. Laughing loudly he spurred his horse on. His father would be so surprised to see him; he felt sure he would be welcomed with open arms.

Trotting down Brunswick Terrace, Zachariah turned his horse into Squires Walk and arrived at the Gentlemen's Club, where he knew his father would be at this time of day. He nodded his thanks to the man who took his horse but who had merely stood staring at him. Striding through the doors of the place he had never visited before, Zachariah asked a man close by where he could find Abel Buchanan. The man stared; he said nothing, he just pointed his finger. Thanking him, Zachariah marched into the quiet club room. It was as he guessed; older men sitting snoozing with newspapers over their faces. Others in quiet conversation turned to look at him as he stood looking around.

Abel was sat at a table talking with a man Zachariah presumed to be a businessman. Catching sight of his son, Abel gasped his surprise. He held up a hand to the approaching boy in a warning to hold his tongue, then apologised to the businessman who left the room with an open mouth at the likeness between the man and the boy standing next to him.

'What the bloody hell are you doing here?' Abel snapped, his tone sharp.

'I came to see you, Father,' Zachariah said slightly taken aback at Abel's words.

'I can bloody well see that! Sit down before someone sees you!'

Zachariah watched a bead of sweat roll down Abel's face as he took a chair and said, 'Oh, I have already been seen, Father . . . I came in through the front door.'

'Oh Christ!' muttered Abel, covering his face with his hands.

'Father, what's wrong?' Zachariah asked, thinking his father was feeling unwell.

'Nothing, lad . . . why on earth have you come here?'

'I want you to give me some work . . . I want to do something . . . anything . . . with you!' the boy announced, feeling pleased with himself.

'You what!' Abel was now beside himself with worry. 'You can't work with me, lad!'

'Why not, Father?' Zachariah asked in all innocence.

'Because . . . because . . . you can't! Now let that be an end to it. You get yourself back home right now . . . and go out by the side door!' Abel stood and pointed in the direction of the door.

Zachariah felt hurt and confused to say the least and quietly left the club room . . . by the side door.

Abel Buchanan slumped back in his chair, a feeling of abject terror claiming his mind. The men in the Club had seen the boy and there was no mistaking they were related. Everyone knew he had two girls and had lost them both, they also knew Hortense and he had no other children.

He could not even say Zachariah was a brother to him, the lad was far too young for God's sake! His thoughts jockeyed for first place in his mind . . . gossip would be rife on every factory floor by now. What could he say? How could he explain this? Christ! Hortense would hear of this in no time!

Abel felt sick to his stomach as he thought about what he should do. Why had Zachariah come to the Club? Seeking work, the lad had said. It was only natural the boy would want work at his age; he was most likely bored and that would probably see him getting into some trouble or other eventually. Why couldn't Zachariah have waited until Abel had gone home to him and his mother? He chastised himself for his infrequent visits there. Had he gone home more often, Abel may have averted what he now saw as a catastrophe.

It was too late to worry about that now!

Abel ran his hands through his hair as he faced his dilemma . . . go home to his wife, Hortense, in Wednesbury or . . . go home to his mistress, Mahula, in Birmingham?

The choice swung like a pendulum in his brain until his head ached with the strain of it. If there were two ways of doing something, Abel Buchanan could always find a third. Grabbing his jacket, Abel strode from the Club amid the silent stares of its members. The third way in this case seemed the safest, and so he set out for Wednesbury and . . . The Green Dragon Hotel!

'Where on earth have you been?' Mahula asked as Zachariah entered the parlour.

'I went to see Father,' he answered, dropping into a chair still feeling the disappointment of the day.

'Why? I told you he would be busy!'

'I know, Mother, and he was. He didn't seem at all pleased to see me,' the boy said.

'Oh?' Mahula could not hide the surprise in her voice. 'Even though you went against my words, I would have thought he would have been pleased to see you for all he was busy.'

'Well he wasn't!' Zachariah sulked, knowing petulance was again showing on his face. 'He even made me leave by the side door!'

Mahula kept quiet as she poured tea for them both.

'Father was worried . . . worried I might be seen by the other members of the Gentlemen's Club. Why would that be, Mother? What is he afraid of?' Zachariah looked up at her and saw the hurt in her eyes.

'I don't know, son, but we'll ask him when he comes home,' Mahula tried to soothe the hurt she knew her son was feeling.

Unable to settle and the clacking needles driving Zachariah to distraction, he suddenly rose from his seat and said he was going out for a ride.

Once his horse was saddled, Zachariah climbed into the saddle and trotted down the driveway, and out onto the streets. He didn't know what was going on but Zachariah intended to find out. Steering his horse gently with his knees, he started in the direction of Wednesbury where he hoped to find his father and some answers.

Guessing his father would have left the club by now, Zachariah's intention was to visit as many of his father's 'watering holes' as time would allow and arriving in Dale Street he investigated The Woodman Inn. With no sign of his father, Zachariah continued his search in The King's Arms on the High Bullen. Cutting across Union Street, he tried the Joiner's Arms in Camp Street; the Museum Tavern in Walsall Street; the Golden Cross Inn in the Market Place and finished his search in The Market Tavern in Russell Street.

The men in the taverns had stared openly at the young man as he looked around each one. What were they staring at? Perhaps it was because he wasn't in working clothes as they were. Ignoring the muttering, he left to continue his search.

Zachariah had not found his father in any of the drinking establishments, but out of seventeen in Wednesbury he had only visited six. The day was wearing on and he wanted to be home before nightfall, so he turned his horse and set off back to Birmingham. After a fruitless search, Zachariah's mood was disconsolate, and knowing he had yet to face his mother, his mood turned downright sour.

Mahula's mood was no better than her son's as he strode into the house. Asking where he'd been, she received a sulky answer of 'Out riding!' Mahula asked no more questions and they ate their evening meal in silence.

Sitting with a tankard of beer on the table before him, Abel reflected. All this nonsense was telling on his health; it was easier when he was young and full of energy, but now the travelling from town to town and the worry of being found out was making him feel ill. Abel had to grab his courage with both hands and leave Hortense. He wanted a simple life and he wanted it with Mahula and Zachariah in Birmingham. He also wanted desperately to find his daughters . . .

Closing his eyes, Abel leaned back in his chair and followed his mind into memory. He remembered how, searching for Eugenie, he did not see the woman walking towards him until it was too late. Deftly, she had stepped to the side and they had bumped into each other. Grabbing her arms to prevent her falling, he had given his apologies. He had received a scolding that set his ears alight. In that moment, Abel realised he had found the love of his life. With Mahula, he had been so very happy and when Zachariah came along he felt he could burst with the joy of it. However, the doctor had told Mahula she could have no more children, complications with Zachariah's birth having put paid to that. Abel had lost his daughter Eugenie and he felt Zachariah's coming was a blessing to him.

An overwhelming guilt swept over him as he opened his eyes. Why had he been so stupid? Trying to keep two women on the go at his age was more than ridiculous. He felt guilty also about the hurt they would feel if they found out about each other. It had never been his intention to cause hurt to either woman; he had only wished to do his best by both of them.

If Abel left Hortense would she cause a scene in Wednesbury? Very definitely . . . it would be all over the newspapers and then Mahula would hear of it. He could just imagine the gossip – *fancy that Abel Buchanan keeping two women!* The headline in the local papers would read, *Wealthy Business Consultant commits bigamy!* For all that would be untrue – as Mahula was not, in fact, his wife – it would matter little to the tabloids. It would, however, have a drastic effect on his business dealings and his good reputation would be ruined. Abel knew he was in a precarious position whichever path he took. He had chosen the life he was living and now he was stuck with it. Abel felt he was living on borrowed time. He had no way out.

Downing his beer, he called for another. What should he do now? Abel had made up his mind, he was going home to Hortense to tell her he was divorcing her. But first he needed to get drunk!

CHAPTER 7

Waking with a hangover Abel was sure had been supplied by the devil, he wondered how he had negotiated the stairs to his room above the bar in the Green Dragon Hotel the night before.

Rising slowly, he splashed water on his face from the bowl on the dresser. Looking at himself in the mirror, Abel decided a hair of the dog was definitely needed and made his way carefully downstairs to the bar.

Sitting with a tankard of beer, he tried to think about what he should do next. In no fit state to be out in the town or at the Club, he elected to stay where he was . . . for a few hours more at least.

Feeling slightly better at last, Abel decided it was time to take a gentle ride into Birmingham. He had to face his son some time, so why not now?

Walking to the stables at the back of the Hotel, he waited while his horse was saddled by the stable boy. Riding out, Abel slowed the horse from a canter to a walk as his head still pounded from too much to drink the previous night. Abel tried to formulate a plan but thinking made his head ache even more. Zachariah would surely want an explanation as to why Abel didn't want him working alongside him. What could he tell his son? How could he explain his aberrant behaviour? Mahula would want answers too. Abel couldn't tell her he didn't want his son working in Wednesbury because of his wife Hortense finding out!

His head threatening to explode, Abel walked the horse along the cobbled streets to his house in Aston Street. Reaching the building, the stable boy took the reins as Abel climbed wearily from the saddle. With a nod to the lad, he walked up the steps and into the house, mentally preparing himself for the verbal onslaught he knew would come.

Stepping into the parlour, he saw Mahula and Zachariah sitting by the fire.

'Hello Father,' Zachariah said with a smile.

'Hello son,' Abel answered, trying to paste a smile on his face. Leaning down to give Mahula a kiss, she turned her face away from him.

So I'm definitely in the dog house, he thought as he took a seat next to her.

'Right,' Mahula snapped before his trousers met the chair, 'are you going to tell me what all this is about?' Lifting her eyes from her knitting, she tilted her head towards their son.

'What all what is about?' Abel asked, feeling distinctly uncomfortable and playing for time.

'Abel, don't you play games with me!' Mahula

shot the words in his direction. 'The lad came to see you at the Club and you all but threw him out!'

'No . . .' Abel began.

'Yes!' Mahula snapped before he could finish his sentence.

Abel winced and said, 'Look, I haven't any work for him with me.' Then to Zachariah, 'You'd be better off looking for work closer to home, lad.'

Seeing him nod, Abel felt relieved at least his son could see the logic of his words. He also felt ashamed for hiding the truth of his situation.

Mahula, however, was not going to let the subject rest. 'Why were you afraid he'd be seen, Abel? What do you have to hide? Are you ashamed of us?'

Abel saw the hurt in her eyes and his heart went out to her. 'No, of course I'm not ashamed of you . . . either of you . . .' Abel looked at each in turn.

'Then why?' Mahula's voice cracked as she spoke.

'I . . . I can't tell you . . . I have something to do before I can explain everything to you both.' Abel hung his head, feeling shame engulf him once more.

Standing up smartly, Mahula threw her knitting on her chair, then turning, she jabbed a finger at him and said, 'Fine! But I want you to leave this house . . . and don't come back until you have done whatever it is that needs doing!'

Getting to his feet, Abel nodded his acceptance and walked quietly from the room, leaving his son with his mouth hanging open.

Riding back to Wednesbury, Abel thought to himself, *Well that didn't go so well!* What should he do now? Should he go back to the Club? No, he couldn't face the questioning stares from the members, his friends. Should he go home to Hortense? Certainly not! He definitely couldn't face that option!

Ah well, he thought, spurring his horse to a canter, *back to the Green Dragon it is then!*

After drinking himself stupid in the Hotel once more, Abel finally gathered his courage and set off for Buchanan House in Wednesbury to see his wife, Hortense.

'Mrs Buchanan went to Birmingham in the trap, sir,' Jago, the stable lad, said as Abel jumped from his horse in front of the huge house he rarely spent any time in especially now as Orpha, his beloved daughter, had disappeared too. As often as he was able he continued to search for his missing daughters.

'You know what for, lad?' Abel enquired.

Shaking his head, a wry grin on his face, the boy said, 'The missis don't tell me nuthin' sir.'

Nodding, Abel said, 'Ar, her don't tell me much more either. Leave this one saddled up, lad, I may be off out again in a minute or two.'

Dashing into the house, Abel strode into his study and locked the door behind him. He needed to check that the emeralds were still in their hiding place beneath the floorboards. Satisfied all was well with his treasure, Abel marched from the house to the stables.

'I'm off to the Club,' he told the stable boy, 'you can tell the missis I'll be home for dinner.'

The boy doffed his cap in reply and watched the master of the house – sitting skewiff in the saddle – gallop down the long driveway.

CHAPTER 8

Meanwhile, Hortense Buchanan steered the trap into the driveway at the house in Aston Street, Birmingham, the house she had followed Zachariah Buchanan to a few days before.

Stepping down, she looked at the large building before mounting the three steps to rap on the door. Taking a pace back, she looked over the house once more as she waited, a sneer plastered on her face. Knocking the door again, Hortense continued her wait . . . no one was at home it seemed.

As she turned to walk away, the sound of the door opening caused her to turn back.

'Can I help you?' the woman in the doorway asked.

Hortense stared at the dark-skinned beauty stood before her. Dark hair, dark eyes, olive complexion, Hortense wondered if she had foreign blood somewhere in her lineage. Was she the maid? No. She wore no uniform – in fact her clothing was of the best quality. *So this is the other woman!*

'I hope so,' Hortense answered, 'is this the home of Zachariah Buchanan?'

'Yes,' the woman answered, 'it is.'

Extending her hand, Hortense said, 'I am Hortense Eldon and I came by to give my thanks to the young man for the help he gave me recently.'

The woman shook hands, saying, 'Thank you, Mrs Eldon, won't you come in?'

Stepping into the house, Hortense felt her breath catch in her throat as she cast a glance around at the opulence; it was even more impressive than her own home. Being led into the sitting room, Hortense sat on an overstuffed chair and sank into its comfort.

Hmmm, she thought, *I shall order one of these on my way home!* Instead she said, 'Beautiful home you have,' looking at the shining furniture and paintings on the walls.

'Thank you, Mrs Eldon, Oh where are my manners . . . I'm Mahula Buchanan.'

Hortense felt her colour drain as the implications of the situation hit her like a lightning strike. There was no denying it now – Abel had deceived her!

'Pleased to meet you,' Hortense said haughtily but thought, *You have no idea how pleased!*

'And I, you. Would you care for tea?' Mahula asked.

Hortense nodded once and Mahula left the room.

Thoughts swam in her head as she waited for her tea. Mahula could be Abel's sister of course, but he'd never talked of having any siblings. But then the boy's name was Buchanan too . . . why would that be? If it was that Mahula was Abel's sister, maybe she'd had a child out of wedlock and Abel, in his infinite kindness, had given the boy his name in order to save his sister from cruel gossip and ridicule. The fly in that ointment, however, was that Mahula had dark eyes – not green like Abel's! If she was sister to Abel, wouldn't they have the same features?

The sitting room door had been left open and Mahula returned placing the tea tray on the table between them. Hortense noticed the china laid out on the tray and her smile turned to a grimace. *Better china than mine!* she thought. However, she would remedy that on her way home too.

'So, Mrs Eldon, you said Zachariah gave you some assistance recently?' Mahula said as she poured tea for them both.

'Indeed, Mrs Buchanan,' Hortense watched the woman sat opposite her. Mahula had not corrected her on the use of her married status. 'The lad kindly helped me with the nosebag for my horse.'

'Ah,' Mahula said as she leaned back in her chair, 'he's a good boy, Mrs Eldon, I'm proud of him.'

'And so you should be,' Hortense took up, 'is he in work, might I ask?'

'No,' Mahula's look turned sour, a look Hortense did not miss. 'His father has nothing for him as yet.'

'I see,' Hortense said with a deprecating smile before sipping her tea.

Mahula went on, 'I'm sure Abel will find something for him soon though.'

There it was! Zachariah *was* Abel's son! As told from the lips of his mother. Hortense's emotions ran wild. She was angry at Abel for deceiving her in the first place, then producing a son who would be party to inheriting the estate. Her jealousy of Mahula and her surroundings, which were far grander than her own, swelled in her.

For a short while the women chatted, then Hortense rose to leave. 'Please pass my thanks to your son,' she said.

'I surely will, thank you for calling, Mrs Eldon,' Mahula smiled.

'No, thank you Mrs Buchanan, this really has been most enlightening.' Hortense said with a straight face.

Guiding the trap back through the busy streets, Hortense mulled over the conversation in her mind. Mahula was Zachariah's mother; Zachariah was Abel's son and there were no other children in the family; all information gleaned from her visit to the house in Birmingham.

Mahula Buchanan, she mused though, had not introduced herself using the married title. Was she actually married to Abel or was she 'living in sin' with him and using 'Mrs' Buchanan in order to save face? Was Zachariah born to married parents, or was he born a bastard?

The questions rolled through her mind making the whole scenario more complicated the more she tried to understand it. The one thing she was sure of was . . . Abel would pay dearly for this – very dearly indeed!

Anger rising, Hortense flicked the reins, setting the horse to a trot as she reached the heath.

'Damn you to hell, Abel Buchanan!' she said aloud as the horse picked up speed.

By the time Hortense reached home, the horse was exhausted and foaming at the mouth and she was in a red-hot temper. The questioning look the stable boy gave her as he took the reins was answered with eyes that he felt sure could shoot fire and burn him to a crisp. He quickly led the horse away to see to its welfare, wisely keeping his mouth shut.

Hortense watched him go, satisfied her withering look had kept the boy firmly in his place. On her way home she had tried to make a mental inventory of what furniture should be replaced, then she made her decision . . . it would all go! So she had ordered the new furniture, new china and had visited the Servants' Registry, saying she was in need of a cook and butler. Abel would baulk at this, she knew, but she could threaten to reveal his secret to all and sundry if he caused her too much trouble.

Hortense's anger slowly melted as she began to realise that Abel's secret might benefit her in countless ways and for as long as she wished it to. Then, when she had all that she wanted from him . . . she would hang him out to dry before the people of Wednesbury.

As Hortense made her way inside, she looked at the door to Abel's study. There *must* be something in there that could shed light on his marriage to Mahula, if indeed a marriage had taken place.

Striding across the tiled floor of the hall, Hortense flung open the door to the study. Standing in the doorway, she made up her mind – if there was something hidden, she was going to find it!

Going to the desk, she pulled out drawer after drawer. Taking out the papers, she scanned them quickly before piling them onto a chair. With the drawers now empty, she pushed them back into place before getting to her knees and feeling the underside of the desk. Maybe there was a secret drawer. Maybe the catch to it was beneath the desktop. Feeling all the way round the desk revealed nothing and Hortense felt the frustration rise as she looked around the room. Going next to the bookshelf, she removed each book in turn, shaking it out before returning it to its original place. Nothing. She slumped into Abel's chair by his desk.

As her eyes roamed around the room, she noticed the corner of the rug was bent back on itself. Curiosity consumed her and she grabbed the rug and threw it into the corner of the room. Looking at the floor where the rug had lain, she saw a small hole in one of the wooden floorboards. Kneeling down she stuck a finger into the hole and pulled. The board came up! Looking down into the hole the floorboard had covered, she saw a box. Lifting the box from its resting place, she took it to the desk and sat down. Putting the box on the desktop, Hortense stared at it. What was inside? Why was it hidden beneath the floor? What was it Abel did not want her to know about? Could it be the certificate of his marriage to Mahula? Could it be the certificate of his son's birth?

She had made her decision not to waste another moment in discovering what was inside. Hortense threw caution to the wind and flipped up the lid.

Peering into the box she saw the little velvet bag and taking it out she tipped its contents onto her hand. Sunshine cascading through the window shone over the glittering green stones in her palm and Hortense released the breath she was holding. Screwing up her hand holding the small emeralds tight, Hortense lifted the hand to her lips then threw back her head and laughed out loud across the silence of the study.

Opening her hand again, Hortense counted the gems lying there – twelve. If she took one, Abel probably wouldn't notice and then she could pilfer the rest at a more opportune moment. Replacing everything back into place, she left the study the emerald clutched tightly in her hand. Placing it in an envelope in her drawstring bag she hid the bag at the bottom of her underwear drawer in her bedroom.

Abel had returned earlier in the evening going straight to his study as usual. Now he sat by the fire reading his newspaper. He had said nothing to her regarding the missing gem, therefore she concluded he had not discovered its loss. Hortense watched him, her eyes occasionally slipping back to the book she had little interest in reading. Inwardly she was rubbing her hands together in glee at getting one over on her husband. Finally he was beginning to get what he deserved.

The tiny emerald she had stolen, she intended to sell in the Jewellery Quarter in Birmingham at the first available opportunity.

The following day there was a loud banging on the front door. Her new furniture had arrived. Instructing the delivery men to take out the old before bringing in the new, Hortense watched a new chapter of her life begin to take shape.

Simmons the Butler and Mrs Jukes the new cook would be arriving the following day, the Servants' Registry office had informed her, so some of the old furniture was to be used in their rooms.

'Anything of no use to me you can take away,' she informed the men now working in her house, 'you can have whatever you want from that which is left over.'

The men doffed their caps in thanks.

Abel returned from his meeting to a house full of new fixtures and fittings. Shaking his head wearily, he retired to his study for a little peace and quiet. Seeing his business papers piled on the top of a new desk and his old comfortable chair replaced by one that looked distinctly uncomfortable, Abel's anger surged.

Striding from the study, he yelled, 'Hortense! What the bloody hell have you done with my desk and chair?'

Hortense called back from the parlour, 'they're in the butler's room, dear; I thought you could do with some new things.'

'Butler?' Abel shouted, looking around the parlour at the strange couches and chairs, 'What bloody butler?'

'Simmons . . . he starts tomorrow as well as our cook Mrs Jukes. She's a widow and—'

'I don't give a bugger what she is!' Abel snapped. 'You have *my* old desk and chair put back in *my* study first thing tomorrow or else!'

'What about the new ones?' Hortense asked in all innocence.

'Give them to the bloody butler!' On the last, Abel turned and strode from the room.

Hortense heard the bang of the front door as Abel yelled, 'I'm off to the Club!'

Abel had been so distraught about his old desk and chair, he hadn't thought to check his treasure beneath the study floorboards.

Hortense ignored Abel's request to replace his study furniture and the following morning busied herself showing Simmons and Mrs Jukes to their rooms as well as the butler's pantry and kitchen.

'You're a little young to be a butler, aren't you?' Hortense asked as she took in the dark hair, brown eyes and rigid posture of the tall man.

'Nature has been kind to me, ma'am, I'm older than I look,' Simmons replied.

Hortense harrumphed then explained haughtily, 'I hope to be entertaining the higher echelon of society in the near future.' Satisfied that both understood her intentions and instructions, she left them to unpack and settle in.

Sitting in her luxurious surroundings in the parlour, Hortense congratulated herself on a job well done. However, her work was far from finished; she had an emerald to sell for the highest price she could get. She wondered whether to visit Mahula in Birmingham again. Perhaps it was time to put a cat amongst those particular pigeons . . . but how could she do that? What, other than personal satisfaction, could she gain from her action? She could confront Abel about his other family, but that could prove disastrous for her. Once he was aware she knew about his mistress and son, he might choose to divorce her and move in with them permanently. Then she'd find herself with no money and no way of acquiring any. With her husband and money gone, her prestige would soon follow. With a scowl, she decided to think on the matter a while longer. She would upset the family in Birmingham only when it served her purpose.

In the meantime, Abel strode into the Gentlemen's Club in Squire's Walk, giving the doorman a nod in passing. Sitting in his usual chair, he gave his thanks to the waiter who brought a glass of whisky to the table.

Bloody woman! He brooded. *Changing my study around. She's a bloody menace!* Something had to be done about her and the sooner the better. How could he be rid of her? Did he know of anyone who could help him dispose of her?

Realising where his thoughts were taking him, Abel rubbed his hands over his eyes in an effort to push the thoughts away. Tipping the wink to the waiter for another drink, Abel settled himself in for the evening . . . maybe he would stay over. When the waiter delivered his second whisky, Abel placed a key on the tray. Nodding his understanding, the waiter moved off to instruct a maid to ready Abel's bedroom, one of a select few above the Club's bar room kept strictly for their members to spend the night rather than travel home in the dark. Yes, Abel would be staying the night at the Club.

CHAPTER 9

Orpha Buchanan had settled in nicely with the Toyes and worked hard learning the art of making chocolate. She often helped out in the shop and became a favourite of the customers, who warmed quickly to her good nature.

It was at night when loneliness crept in; when Orpha missed her father. She wanted him to know that, on the whole, she was happy. She desperately wanted to see him, but she knew she would have to save some money for the journey back to Wednesbury. However, in order to save, she had to find a paying job. The Toyes were good to her, she pondered one night as she stared at the moon through her window. They fed her and taught her a trade and she liked them both immensely, but she needed to earn her own money.

Watching the clouds pass across the moon, she wondered how to tell them she would have to look elsewhere for paid work.

Orpha sighed into the quiet of the room as the moon emerged from its cloud cover. Would the Toyes be hurt by her moving on? Would they think her ungrateful for all their help? She didn't think they were in a stable enough financial position to pay her a wage, and she wouldn't dream of asking anyway.

Long into the night, she considered her predicament. She simply could not bear to leave the people who had saved her from a life spent in the workhouse.

Both Henry and his wife Hetty had come to look on Orpha as they would their own daughter; she brought light into their lives.

Henry Toye asked one morning, 'You want to come along with me to the sugar refinery, wench?'

'Yes please!' Orpha answered full of excitement. 'As long as Hetty doesn't mind.'

'I managed afore you came, girl, I can manage one day without you,' the woman's smile said no slight was meant by her words.

Trudging through the streets, Orpha asked, 'Henry, why don't you have your sugar delivered?'

'They charge for delivery, my wench, and I don't order enough to warrant that charge.'

'What if you ordered more?' Orpha went on.

'Not sure we could use more . . . what do you think? Could we make more? Enough to request delivery? Could we sell it if we made more?' Henry asked.

'Goodness yes!' Orpha exclaimed. She wondered if she could help them build up the business which would then provide an opportunity to earn a wage, and even if not, at least she could leave having repaid their hospitality in some way. So she determined to stay a while longer and see how things panned out.

'Right then, I'll tell you what, you conduct the deal today and see how it goes.' Henry smiled.

'Really?' Orpha was aghast.

'Really.' Henry laughed.

'What's this, Henry Toye, you having a young wench doing your dealings now?' the manager of the refinery joked.

'I am Mr Toye's assistant and will be dealing with you in the future,' Orpha said with far more confidence than she felt.

'Now then Toye . . .' The manager ignored Orpha as though she wasn't even there.

Orpha felt the little confidence she'd been feeling evaporate and she looked at Henry with pleading in her eyes. This was going to be a lot harder than she thought.

'Give the girl a chance, hear her out,' Henry said protectively.

The manager clamped his mouth shut, leaning his elbows on the arms of his chair. His eyes met Orpha's, giving her leave to continue.

'Well, Mr Toye intends to double his order as of today and would appreciate that order being delivered to his shop,' she said as she watched the manager for his reaction.

'Well now, we only deliver bulk orders . . . and we charge for the privilege,' the manager began as he looked Orpha directly in the eye.

Again, she looked to Henry for help. He provided it by saying, 'How's about you waive the delivery charge as I'm increasing the order?'

The manager blew through pursed lips. 'Not sure I can do that, Henry; if others found out, they'd all want the same courtesy.'

'No one else need know. Besides, I'm sure the recommendations of your good business acumen will see more people seeking to order from your good self,' Orpha pushed. Leaning back in her chair, Orpha folded her hands in her lap, trying to stem their shaking, and also in an effort to ignore the grin creeping across Henry Toye's face.

The manager's mouth opened and closed like a fish out of water before he nodded once.

'Thank you,' Orpha said as she stood to leave.

Henry and Orpha howled with laughter once outside the gates of the refinery. 'Now for the dairy!' he said.

By the time they reached home, the dairy and flour mill also had agreed to deliver without charge to the shop, and Orpha had promised to sing their praises to all in exchange.

Hetty listened as they related the tale over their evening meal. 'Now we have to make more and sell more,' she said quietly, 'is it possible?'

'Only one way to find out!' Orpha said as she cleared the table of crockery.

CHAPTER 10

Having discussed the menu for the evening meal with Mrs Jukes, Hortense made her way to the train station. Boarding the train to Birmingham, the stolen emerald safe in her bag, she settled down for the journey.

Leaving the train at New Street Station in Birmingham, she walked through Stephenson's Passage onto Corporation Street. Checking her whereabouts, she saw Martineau Street to her right and a little further up was Lower Priory. Striding out along Corporation Street, Hortense came to the place she was looking for: Abyssinian Gold Jewellery Company.

Immediately Hortense walked into the luxurious building, a salesman came to her. 'Welcome to Abyssinian Gold Jewellery Company, madam. Please, take a seat and tell me how I may help you.'

Hortense sank into a deeply upholstered chair and took the envelope from her bag, handing it to the man sat opposite her. Tipping the content onto his palm, the man's eyes lit up with admiration. Nudging the emerald gently with his little finger, he saw darts of light shoot over the gem's emerald cut.

'Ahhh,' he said almost sensually as he reached into his pocket for his small magnifying glass. Looking at the gem from every angle, he asked, 'Colombian?'

Hortense nodded out of ignorance but giving the impression she was knowledgeable about gems, as she watched him inspect the jewel before he spoke again.

'Yes, I thought so. Only the very best emeralds are mined in Colombia. This stone has been cut into what is known as the emerald cut . . . rectangular with the corners trimmed off, then further into a step cut . . . the rectangular facets are each cut one on top of the other, and expertly too, if I may say. It is fairly clear, with few inclusions, and being of the darkest green, I suspect it will be worth rather a lot, madam,' Looking at the stone once more, he said on a sigh, 'This gem is perfect!'

Hortense nodded once more before saying, 'I wish to sell it.'

The man's eyes shot to hers, his magnifying glass still over one eye making it look twice the size of the other. 'I see,' he said, looking back to the gem sitting on his palm. 'Well, firstly I have to weigh it and then I can give you my price.'

Hortense followed the man to the counter where he took a weighing scale and placed the emerald on the top. Using tiny specially made weights, he said with surprise, '1.08 Carats!' Lifting a book from beside the scales, he ran his finger down a column of figures. He eyed the woman as he lay the book back on the counter. 'Madam, this emerald is worth £500!'

Nodding again, Hortense kept her elation well hidden.

'Are you sure you wish to sell it?' the man asked.

'Yes,' Hortense said, 'I am.'

Disappearing into the back room, the man was gone only a few moments before returning and placing a banker's draft on the counter, he was sporting a huge grin.

Hortense placed the paper in her bag.

The man picked up the new-fangled telephone and rang the bank, informing them that Mrs Buchanan would be arriving to cash the banker's draft.

'Thank you,' she said.

Shaking her hand, the man said, 'No madam, thank *you*!'

Leaving the building, Hortense visited the bank to cash the order before she strode back towards Birmingham New Street Station, feeling immensely pleased with herself, the £500 tucked safely in her bag.

Mrs Jukes was a widow of ten years, her husband having passed from pneumonia during a severe winter. She had applied at the Servants' Registry Office in Scotland Passage, and the owner Sarah Benton had recommended the position with

Hortense Buchanan. Simmons, the Butler, had come from the same office it seemed.

As the two now sat in the kitchen of Buchanan House, they chatted about people they knew, of places they had previously worked at, and their present employers.

'Well, it's a nice house and my bedroom is pleasant albeit small,' Mrs Jukes said.

'Hmmm,' the butler eyed the cook over his teacup.

'Now then, Simmons, don't you go looking down your nose at me! We have to work together after all.'

'Quite so, Mrs Jukes, you have my apologies.'

Nodding her acceptance, she glanced around the kitchen. 'This place could do with a good clean,' she said haughtily and they both smirked.

'What do you make of the mistress?' Simmons asked.

'Mistress!' Mrs Jukes harrumphed. 'Married into money did that one! I tell you now, Simmons, I'll be watching my back with her and I suggest you do the same!'

'I agree with you, Mrs Jukes,' the butler said thoughtfully.

'Call me Beulah, it ain't as though we'll be strangers for long, living in the same house an' all.'

'Very good . . . Beulah,' Simmons said quietly.

'Did you hear the tale of the Buchanan girls?' Beulah asked.

'No, I missed that one,' Simmons said with a grin, knowing how household staff loved to gossip.

'Well . . .' Beulah drew the word out as she settled her ample weight more comfortably on the kitchen chair. 'It would seem that about eighteen years ago their baby girl was took off by the gypsies, although none were in the area.' Simmons raised his eyebrows before the cook went on. 'Ar, and then just a few months ago, their fourteen-year-old daughter went missing!'

Simmons shook his head in disbelief. 'Have either of them been found?' He asked.

'Would appear not,' Beulah said before drawing her chin into her neck, her mouth forming a tight line.

'How very sad,' the Butler mumbled, putting his cup and saucer on the table.

'Ar, the master almost went mad with grief, so I heard.'

'And the mistress?' Simmons asked.

'Oh the mistress, she went out and bought new frocks!' They both collapsed in a fit of laughter before the cook screwed up her mouth as she watched Simmons nod his head. It would seem they were both of the same opinion, their new mistress was a bit of a tyrant. In addition to watching their own backs, they agreed to watch each other's.

In the meantime, the maid, a young girl by the name of Alice Danby, had arrived back and had introduced herself to the other staff. It had been Alice's day off when the new staff arrived, and she had dared to stay overnight with her family in

George Street, not far from the marketplace. Fortunately, Mrs Buchanan was out when she arrived and had left early so wouldn't have realised Alice was not yet in the house. Alice had joined the family a few years earlier, her predecessor having stormed out in a fit of temper which Alice could well understand, her own relationship with the mistress could never be construed as a good one.

'Blimey!' Alice said. 'The missis has been busy . . . all the furniture has been shifted and changed.'

'Ar well,' Beulah Jukes responded, 'it ain't nothing to do with you what the *mistress* does, so you mind your business.'

'I know my place,' Alice said in answer.

'You mind you keep it an' all!' Beulah retorted.

'I'm a parlourmaid!' Alice said with her nose in the air.

'You're a kitchen maid an' all!' Beulah said sharply. 'So get the kettle on and let's have no more lip from you.'

Simmons shook his head; this setting of the pecking order of staff was probably going on in houses all over the district. It was necessary so everyone knew their place in the household.

Right on cue, the little bell in the kitchen tinkled, and looking at Alice, Simmons said, 'That'll be the mistress wanting her afternoon tea.'

Alice sighed as she set the tea tray ready to go upstairs to the 'Dragon Lady'.

⋆ ⋆ ⋆

Hortense was in an excellent mood, and why not? She had a cook, maid and butler, as well as new furniture throughout the house. She was not hampered by children and . . . she was £500 better off!

After breakfast in bed, Hortense set off to put the money from the sale of Abel's emerald into her own account in the bank in Wednesbury. As she walked she revelled in the luxury of being the mistress of the staff in her employ.

Lost in her thoughts, Hortense walked from the Holyhead Road into Dudley Street. As she passed the Shakespeare Inn, the door opened and she heard, 'Ah, Mrs Eldon, so nice to see you again.' Looking at the young man who spoke to her, Hortense sucked in a breath. It was Zachariah Buchanan. The boy was here in Wednesbury!

'Oh Mr Buchanan! You gave me quite a start. I didn't think to see you here in my home town.'

'Ah yes,' the boy went on, 'I'm searching all the alehouses . . . I'm looking for my father.'

'Lost him have you?' Hortense gave a deprecating smile.

With a little laugh, Zachariah nodded before adding conspiratorially, 'Mother and father had somewhat of a disagreement and I'm afraid we haven't seen him since.'

'Oh dear,' Hortense saw her chance. 'Could you describe him? Then maybe if I should see him I could tell him you were looking for him.'

'Mrs Eldon, that is so kind, although you would

know him in an instant. He is very like me, except a little older of course,' Zachariah grinned cheekily. 'He has the same black hair and green eyes. Unmistakable really.'

'Indeed.' Hortense felt her tension rise, 'Should I see him I will inform him. Now if you will excuse me . . . good day, Mr Buchanan.'

Saying his goodbye, the boy walked up the street as Hortense walked down it.

Well now, it seemed Mahula and Abel had fallen out.

Damn shame! Hortense thought sarcastically.

CHAPTER 11

The wind had a cold bite as the beauty of autumn finally spread her colourful cloak over the landscape.

Orpha Buchanan stood in the kitchen of 'Toye's Chocolate Shop' mixing cocoa powder with butter into a smooth paste. Adding water and milk, she stirred the mixture over the range until it was hot. Adding flour and sugar, she mixed it thoroughly until the creamy chocolate slid from the back of the spoon smoothly. Spooning it into the small moulds, she sat the whole on the cold slab in the pantry to set.

As she worked, Orpha considered how fortunate she was living with Mr and Mrs Toye, and how she had learned the process of chocolate making and now she was being paid a small wage too. Her mind drifted to her father, as it often did, and she felt a pang of regret. Orpha had not continued her quest to go home and find him. It was fear of her mother which had prevented her doing so. Hortense had threatened to kill her if she did, and after years of abuse and hurt, Orpha didn't feel strong enough to face any more. Maybe one day soon she would seek out her father and be able to confide in him about her misery and anguish regarding her mother – but not yet. Knowing she should have, she felt the guilt colour her cheeks as Hetty Toye ambled into the kitchen.

'To celebrate the New Year, Henry and I can afford to up your wages a little.'

'Oh Hetty! That's wonderful, but are you sure?' Orpha asked, 'You know I'd do this for nothing.' She couldn't believe how well she'd settled in here and meant what she said about working for nothing.

'Ar well, you did when you first come to us, I seem to remember, but we felt so bad we had to pay you something. Now business is better we can afford to give you a rise.'

Orpha mumbled her thanks as she gave the woman a hug; the woman who had taken her in off the streets.

'Leave that a minute,' Hetty said, watching Orpha clear the table, 'Sit down because I want to ask you something.' As Orpha sat down, Hetty continued, 'Now then, we've been doing really well in the shop since you came. We've made and sold more chocolate with your help.' The woman watched Orpha nod in confirmation that Hetty was speaking the truth. 'Right then, what I want to know is . . . have you any ideas as to how we can sell even more than we do now?'

'You are asking me? I haven't been here that long Hetty, and I wouldn't presume to tell you about the chocolate-making business!' Orpha was amazed the woman had asked for her opinion.

'Ar, I know you ain't been here long, but two heads are better than one, so if you have any ideas, I'd like to hear them.' Hetty began to bustle about the kitchen, making tea.

'Well,' Orpha said, drawing out the word in her hesitation, 'if we could get hold of a few walnuts and some condensed milk we could make some fudge. I've eaten it before whilst at home and I think it might sell quite well.'

Hetty banged a cup on the table with, 'Bloody hell, wench, that's a damn good idea!'

'I had wanted to suggest this before, Hetty, but didn't feel it was my place.'

'Good ideas are always welcome, gel, don't be afraid to speak out.' Hetty smiled to reassure the girl.

With their tea drunk, Orpha once again set to making more chocolate as Hetty stood the counter in the shop. Henry was dispatched to the town for the new ingredients.

Later, when the shop closed for the evening, husband and wife sat in the kitchen, watching Orpha crushing walnuts finely and mixing them into the other ingredients to a smooth mixture. She poured the whole into a shallow baking tray and set it to cool on the cold slab before clearing the table and washing up her utensils.

'You think it will work?' Henry asked sheepishly.

'We'll know by the morning,' Orpha said with a smile.

All three were up early the next day, dying to try the new confection. Orpha tipped the fudge out onto the scrubbed table and, taking a sharp knife, she cut it into small cubes. Unable to contain herself, Hetty snatched up a square of fudge and dropped it into her mouth. She closed her eyes as she began to chew before finally saying, 'Henry, get down to the town and set a regular order for them ingredients. Orpha . . . we're onto a winner with this!'

After tasting the sweet mixture, they agreed with Hetty, and Henry set off for the town yet again, thanking his lucky stars for Orpha as he went.

Orpha's fudge was selling well and she and the Toyes worked long hours to keep up with demand. The small wage she was paid was saved each week and before long she had quite a little pile of money kept safe in her room. She knew this would come in handy when she felt it was time to go home to her father. She contemplated whether that time was now.

In her room, Orpha counted her savings. She had more than enough money for a third-class ticket on the train to Wednesbury. She could go home and see what sort of reception she would get. Sitting on her bed, Orpha considered the idea. Yes, she wanted to see her father, although seeing her mother would be something else again. It would mean leaving Hetty and Henry who had been so kind to her over the last weeks, but she felt they would understand her need to go home. Orpha thought out her options, and taking her courage in both hands, she swept down the stairs to inform the Toyes she would be leaving them at the end of the week. Orpha Buchanan was going home.

Orpha sat in the kitchen quietly, her previous confidence having fled. She didn't know how to broach the subject of her decision to leave the couple who looked after her and taught her a trade. She felt torn: on the one hand she wanted to stay, she was happy here; on the other, she wanted to go home to her father, but then she would have to face her mother again too. She shuddered at the thought.

'Penny for your thoughts?' Hetty asked as she sat at the table with Orpha.

'I was thinking about my father,' Orpha said quietly.

Hetty nodded knowingly. 'Well why don't you go and visit him? It's probably time you did, I daresay he's been worried sick about you.'

Hetty didn't want the girl to leave but she could see the unhappiness in Orpha's eyes as she spoke of her father.

'I want to Hetty but – I'm scared!' Her tears stung the back of her eyes.

'Scared of what? Is it your mother you're afraid of?' Hetty asked gently.

Orpha nodded and her tears began to fall.

Hetty was up and round the table in an instant, wrapping the girl in her arms tightly. 'Oh my poor wench. Come on, you cry it out, it does no good hanging on to it.'

Just then Henry entered the kitchen and seeing the scene before him he raised his eyebrows in question.

'Her's missing her dad,' Hetty said by way of explanation.

Orpha's tears subsided and Henry patted her arm as he sat at the table.

'Look gel, we don't want to see you go, but we will understand if you feel the need. Just remember, if you go home and it don't work out, you can always come back here to us, can't she, Hetty?' He looked at his wife and saw her sobbing into her apron. 'Oh blimey, now I've got two of you at it,' he smiled as Orpha burst into tears once more, having seen she'd upset Hetty.

'Thank you,' Orpha eventually sniffed.

Henry placed an arm around her shoulder and the other around his wife. 'Right, now that's settled have you enough money for the train fare?' Henry asked.

Orpha nodded.

'Good. Now go and get your things and we'll take you to the station,' he added.

'I'd rather go alone, it will be hard enough saying goodbye here, I couldn't bear it at the station,' Orpha said.

Glancing at Hetty still sobbing in Henry's arms, Orpha ran upstairs to collect her few belongings, her own tears beginning to form again. She hugged the Toyes in turn on her return to the kitchen. She was leaving the two people who she had come to love, but she was determined that, whatever happened, she would see them again.

Waving a sad goodbye, Orpha left the shop and walked briskly to the train at New Street Station full of trepidation. As she stood at the ticket kiosk she debated whether to go straight to Wednesbury or go to see a little of another town before returning home. On impulse, she bought a ticket for Wolverhampton.

Climbing aboard the steaming giant of a train, Orpha sat on the wooden bench in the train compartment, she deliberated the decision she had made. She was excited at the prospect of seeing another large town and she couldn't wait to get there. However, she was fully aware of her prevarication. She'd been so set on going home and now she had changed her mind – again. She knew what was preventing her returning to Wednesbury – it was her mother. The more she thought of the abuse she'd suffered at the woman's hands, the more afraid she became.

Orpha sighed as she stared out of the train window but she missed the delight of the sights passing by. Her mind was fixed on her mother's cruelty over the years, and she knew without a scintilla of doubt this was why she could not go home yet.

Alighting the train at Monmore Green Station, Orpha followed the throng of people out onto the street. Standing a moment, she looked around. Wolverhampton, she noticed, was much like any other town. A maze of streets were filled both sides with houses and businesses. Buildings crammed so tightly together she wondered if the sun ever reached between them.

Having lived in the city of Birmingham for the last weeks, the prospect of walking through a big town held no fear for her now.

The cold wind raced along the cobbled street and whipped around her long skirt. She was glad of her boots, knowing the weather would deteriorate soon enough.

As she walked, she considered her options. Never having been here before she tried to decide which way to go. Her first priority was to find a bed for an overnight stay. She knew she was prevaricating about going home, but the thought of facing her mother continued to fill her with dread.

Striding forward, she noted the street sign: Wesley Street. She looked at the buildings as she passed; all were covered in a layer of grime. She heard the shouts of cabbies as they drove towards the station in the hope of a fare. People dressed in clothes which had seen better days bustled alongside her, pushing and shoving their way through the mass of bodies on the street.

Moving into Collier Street, she heard laughing and banter as she came upon the wharf. Chillington Wharf was alive with folk loading and unloading cargo from boats and barges. Orpha stopped to watch, enjoying the sight before her. Then she strolled along Chillington Street which lined the wharf. With a smile she waved to a woman on a narrowboat who called down to her, 'How do gel?'

Orpha's stomach rumbled as she passed a boat loaded with fresh vegetables, their aroma reminding her she should eat.

Crossing over the bridge, she made her way into the town proper. She felt a shiver down her spine as she glanced at a huge building. The sign for the Wolverhampton Union Workhouse stood proudly over the huge iron gates. Increasing her pace, she moved on, until she reached a fork in the road and she stopped. To the left she could see the General Hospital and the Tramway Depot. To the right were houses and shops; a better bet for finding a room for the night. Making her choice, she walked up into Bath Street. Every building was joined to its neighbour to form a long line of brickwork, and as she gazed around she saw all the surrounding streets were the same. Then she spied a sign for a hostel.

Stepping inside, she enquired after a bed for the night.

'Tuppence a night,' the clerk said, 'or you can have a place on the "Penny Hang".' Seeing Orpha's puzzled expression, the clerk explained, 'We have a washing line strung across the hallway, pay a penny and you throw your arms over. Hang there for the night, hence . . . the "Penny Hang".'

'I'll take a bed thank you.' Orpha said with a shudder.

'Don't blame you,' the clerk said, 'we gets the drunks and tramps on the "Penny Hang", not a good idea for a lady such as yerself.' The woman grinned, showing blackened teeth, before taking Orpha to her room.

The place was filthy and Orpha seriously considered moving on and forfeiting the two pennies she'd given over, but she was at a loss as to where to find another place to stay. Pulling back the bedclothes, she saw the sheets were none too clean. She decided to remain dressed and sleep on top of the bed.

Leaving her carpet bag in the corner, she walked back to the clerk. 'Is there anywhere close by where I can purchase a meal?'

'Ar, you can try the café on the corner, good grub and nice and cheap,' the clerk answered before lighting the clay pipe stuck between her teeth.

Orpha found the place she'd been directed to and ate a good hearty meal of faggots and grey peas, with fresh bread and a pot of tea. Bread and butter pudding followed and Orpha's stomach groaned as she slowly walked back to the hostel.

As soon as she entered her room, the hairs on the back of her neck stood on end. Someone had been inside. Looking to the corner where she had left her carpet bag, she gasped. The bag was gone.

Rushing back to the clerk, Orpha was beside herself. 'Someone has been in my room and stolen my bag!'

'Oh deary me,' the clerk said, shaking her head. 'Left it there did you, while you went out for your dinner?'

'Yes, and now it's gone! All my clothes, my money . . . everything has gone!' Orpha wrung her hands together.

'Ah well, that's what happens when you leave things lying around. Some thieving buggers around here. You've seen the last of that, I'm afraid, my dear.' The clerk shook her head.

'I'm going to inform the police . . .' Orpha began.

'And just what do you think they can do? The thief is long gone by now. The bobbies will tell you the same. A hard lesson, but one well learned, I think,' the clerk said.

Orpha returned to her room knowing the clerk was right in what she'd said. All she had left were the clothes she stood up in and a few pennies in her drawstring bag. All her hard-earned cash had gone, along with her few good clothes.

Sitting in the one chair in the room, she berated herself for her stupidity. Then thinking again about her loss, she burst into tears. She was in a strange room, in a town she didn't know and had been robbed of her belongings. As she cried, she thought about her father. She should have gone home and then this wouldn't have happened to her. Thinking how cruel and nasty some people could be brought her thoughts inevitably to her mother. Her fear of the woman had brought her here, and now she had virtually nothing left.

Orpha's misery weighed heavy as she sat through the dark hours of the night, and her mind whirled with questions. Now what would she do? She had no money for a train ticket to Wednesbury. She would have to find a job here but had precious little to live on whilst looking for work. Was she destined to end up in the workhouse after all?

Feeling miserable to her core, Orpha stared out of the window watching people coming and going in the moonlight. She heard the drunken laughter as revellers passed by, but none of it registered in her mind. All she could think about was that in a day or so she would be penniless again. She would have no bed to sleep in and no food to eat. It would eventually come down to making the decision . . . go to the workhouse or starve on the streets.

Orpha walked the streets for the next few days looking for work but to no avail. She kept her few pennies and went without a proper meal, only buying an apple or a carrot to see her through the day. By the fourth day, her resolve began to crumble. If she bought a meal she would be without funds, then she would have nothing. Making a decision, she made her way to the market, maybe she could scavenge something to eat there.

As she trudged along, she considered again about going home but she could not face her mother's wrath, besides which she couldn't afford the train fare now. She also wondered about returning to the Toyes in Birmingham; she knew they would take her in, but her stubborn pride wouldn't allow her to go cap-in-hand to them. It would seem like she'd failed them and then she would have to explain how, on impulse, she had come to be in Wolverhampton. No, she would have to find work of some sort to at least pay for some food. Stiffening her resolve she marched on.

CHAPTER 12

Peg Meriwether stood by her cart in the last of the sunshine. She had very little to sell; the winter, she knew, would continue to be harsh and nothing would grow in her garden. She hated the cold months when she had to resort to having to sell her bottled produce to earn a living. All the pickling and bottling had been hard work, but Peg was glad now that she had pursued the task. She silently thanked Rufina for giving her the knowledge of how to get by. Chutneys, jams, pickled onions would sell and contribute to her meagre savings.

The weak sunshine was cut through by a chilly wind that whistled around the market stalls, and Peg rubbed her hands together for warmth.

'You cold wench?' asked Lottie Spence.

Peg nodded, saying, 'I am. It's a lazy wind today.' Tying her shawl across her chest, Peg pulled the corners around her back and tied them together before shoving her hands into the sides like pockets. Slowly her fingers warmed and she stamped her feet to get the feeling back into her frozen toes.

Peg's eyes roamed the women walking around the market and a sudden intake of breath caused Lottie to look her way.

'You all right there Peg?' Lottie asked.

Peg didn't answer as she stared at the girl walking towards her cart. Following Peg's line of sight, Lottie also gasped before saying, 'Bloody hell! I'm seeing double!'

Peg nodded as the girl approached her cart, looking at the jars of pickles laid out before her.

Picking up a jar of pickled onions, the girl said, 'Oooh, how much are . . .?' Words failed her when she looked up at the girl behind the cart.

Two heads of black hair shook in disbelief as green eyes met green eyes.

'Bloody hell is right!' Peg whispered as the girls eyed each other. 'I don't believe it!'

Lottie moved closer to listen in as the girls began to speak to each other.

'Neither do I! Hello, my name is Orpha,' the younger girl said.

Shaking hands, the older of the two spoke, 'Peg, nice to meet you . . . Bloody hell!' Both girls burst out laughing.

'It's like looking into a mirror!' Orpha said, staring at the other girl.

'Ain't it just!' Peg answered.

Both were unaware of the stares of the other stallholders; the girls' shock holding them fast.

'How is it you look so like me?' Orpha asked.

'Or how you look like me?' Peg countered.

Again they laughed together, their green eyes sparkling like the best cut emeralds.

'I have no idea,' Orpha said.

'Me neither. Look . . .' said Peg, 'I'm packing up to go home now . . . where are you going?'

'I had planned to go to Wednesbury, but I'm unable to now as I've had all my money and clothes stolen!' Orpha answered woefully.

'Well in that case, why don't you come home with me and have some supper? You could stay over and think about what to do tomorrow.' The likeness between them had startled Peg and she wanted to know more about the girl who had happened on her cart in the market.

'If you're sure, that would be wonderful, thank you,' Orpha replied, the same thoughts running through her own head, as well as gratitude to the girl who had offered her a bed for the night just when she was beginning to despair.

Shouting their goodbyes to the other stallholders, Peg led Orpha out of the market and across the heath to her small cottage. As they walked, they talked excitedly and Orpha told her new friend about being thrown out by her mother and then being taken in by Hetty and Henry Toye. She explained how she had learned to make chocolate and her idea of trying the fudge process and its subsequent success.

Peg told Orpha of her vegetable garden and of her bottling onions and the like in readiness for the lean winter months.

Arriving at the cottage, Peg poked the coals in the grate as soon as they entered the kitchen and flames burst into life, giving out much-needed heat. Warming themselves first, Peg then set about making a cup of tea and pushed the broth bracket over the fire. Their supper would not take long to heat through and as they sat at the table they again marvelled at the similarity between them.

As the girls devoured the lamb stew with home-made bread, they each related their stories again. Orpha said, 'Hetty mistook me for a prostitute when I leaned against the shop wall. I was exhausted from walking around the town.'

Peg laughed, saying, 'Hetty's eyesight must be poor; anyone in their right mind could see you're a lady.'

Orpha explained, 'I was grubby at the time from sleeping beneath a tree at the canal side and must have looked an awful sight.'

Peg shared her own tale, 'Rufina Meriwether found me abandoned on the doorstep all those years ago and she raised me as her own, giving me the name of Peg Meriwether.' Sadness crept over her face as she told of how she had nursed Rufina through pneumonia but the illness had finally won over and her foster mother had died.

The girls talked long into the evening until Peg said, 'Orpha, it's uncanny how alike we are; I mean to say, there can't be many who have the same features as us. Black hair, green eyes . . .'

'There is another that I know of,' she said.

'Who? Tell me . . . who?' Peg's excitement began to bubble up.

'My father,' Orpha said.

The girls sat together in silence, each trying to piece together the puzzle that surrounded them.

The girls had shared the big feather bed out of necessity to keep warm and the following morning Peg decided to stay home from the market. There were questions that needed answers and over breakfast the girls talked in depth about their lives up to the point where they had met in the market.

'So what we have is . . .' Orpha said finally, 'that my mother threw me out when I was fourteen. Your mother abandoned you as a baby. My father, I know, has no siblings, so is my father your father also? Is my mother, your mother? Or, is your mother someone else?'

'Whoa . . . no more! My brain is addled at the thought of it all!' Peg said as she shook her head. 'I ain't got a clue, Orpha, but something tells me we should find out. Something here . . .' Peg laid a hand over her heart as she went on, 'tells me you and I are related somewhere along the line.' She felt the excitement grow in her at the prospect.

Orpha nodded, saying, 'I believe you're right. Look at us, how can we not be related? I think we could be sisters, or half-sisters at the very least!'

Peg continued with, 'Thing is, how do we find out?'

Orpha nodded her agreement. 'I did think to go

home, Peg, to find my father, but I can't. I just cannot face my mother. She threatened to kill me if she ever saw me again! Besides, I have no money now.'

It was Peg's turn to nod before she said, 'Well, why don't you stay here with me? You would be very welcome, and it would be company for me.'

'That would be wonderful!' Orpha gasped. She was excited to have found Peg who may just be her sister, and also grateful for the girl being so hospitable and generous when it was clear she led a modest life.

'Well, I get ever so lonely here on my own. Sometimes I talk to myself just to hear the sound of somebody yacking!' Peg confessed.

'I know how it feels to be lonely, Peg,' Orpha said sadly.

'You know, we could go together to see your dad, and when everything is sorted out I could come back here,' Peg ventured.

'No! I wouldn't dream of dragging you into our family mess. I can't imagine what my mother would do if we turned up on the doorstep. I mean, look at us – we're almost like twins! She'd go stark staring mad! I can't risk the possibility of her hurting you as well as me, Peg.'

'Right then, that's settled. You'll stay here with me.' Peg smiled at having made the decision.

'If you're sure it's no imposition . . . and I could make some chocolate and you could try and sell it on your cart!'

The girls then chatted excitedly about how they could start the making of chocolate to be sold alongside Peg's fruit and vegetables.

Peg added her savings to Orpha's few pennies and they set off for the market to buy the ingredients for the first batch of chocolate. On their return to the cottage, Orpha took over the kitchen and Peg worked in the garden, settling the soil for the oncoming winter. By evening, the first of the chocolate was cooling and setting on the cold slab in the tiny scullery. Orpha had already cleaned her utensils and had started to ready their supper when Peg came into the room. The rich aroma of chocolate filled her nose as she sat at the table.

'If that tastes anything like it smells,' Peg said, 'we could have a nice little business going in no time!'

'You can try a bit and let me know what you think,' Orpha said with a smile. Her words evoked thoughts of the Toyes and her face warmed with guilt at not returning to them, but then she knew Hetty would have encouraged her to go her own way and lead her own life. Certainly she felt at home here with Peg slipping into the relationship like a hand into a glove.

Peg popped a tiny square of chocolate into her mouth and closed her eyes. It seemed forever before she spoke. 'That was the best thing I've ever tasted in my life! I've never had chocolate before!'

Satisfied, Orpha cut the chocolate slab into tiny squares and making a paper cone she dropped a few pieces inside before folding the cone over at the top. With all the chocolate now in small paper cones, Orpha set them on the cold slab to keep cool overnight.

'If,' she said, 'this goes well and we sell it all, we will have to get more supplies. The money from the sales should cover that, and if we buy our sugar and flour in bulk, we should get it at a reduced rate.'

Peg was all for the idea and was excited at the prospect of selling the confection from her handcart the following day.

They were amazed at just how quickly the cones of chocolate sold at the market. The queue of women wanting to buy were disappointed when it was all gone. With the jars of pickles gone too, Orpha said they should get their supplies on the way home, saving them another journey later in the day. Dragging the cart behind them, Orpha and Peg chatted happily about how well their sweets had sold.

'Whoever would have thought it,' Peg said, 'us meeting in the market in the first place, then before you know it, we're working together!'

'I know, of all the places in the country I could have gone and I came to Wolverhampton. Then, out of the hundreds of people here, I meet you,' Orpha said, still hardly believing it herself.

'Divine intervention,' Peg said.

'Do you believe in the Fates, Peg?' Orpha asked. Seeing her new friend screw up her mouth, she went on, 'This was meant to be, it was our destiny.'

'You reckon?' Peg asked.

'I do indeed,' Orpha answered.

Over supper, Orpha said, 'I'm going to make some fudge later, then we can see how well that will sell too.'

Peg drooled as she helped Orpha make a slab of chocolate then begin making the fudge. Before long the cold slab was piled high with cooling confectionary. As they sat at the table with a cup of tea and making the small paper cones which would hold the chocolate and fudge the following day, their conversation once again turned to their lineage.

With the cones made, their tea drunk and still no answers to their questions, the two girls climbed the stairs to bed, tired but happy.

Orpha lay next to her friend in the big bed, snuggled under the eiderdown all warm and cosy. Listening to Peg's gentle breathing, her thoughts turned to her good fortune. How was it each time she found herself at her lowest with nowhere to turn, Lady Luck stepped in to save the day? She certainly felt she had a guardian angel watching over her.

CHAPTER 13

'You wouldn't believe me if I told you,' Ezzie Lucas said to his mother, Edna, as they sat eating their evening meal in the belly of the narrowboat they called home.

'So tell me, then I'll tell you if I believe you,' Edna replied.

'Well,' Ezzie began, 'you remember that young girl, Orpha, the one we gave a lift to in the summer?' Edna nodded. 'Right, well, I saw a lad in the Golden Cross Inn in the marketplace who looked just like her!'

Edna lifted her tin cup to her lips, sipped her tea then said, 'And your point is?'

'Mother, he had the same black hair and green eyes! He looked like he was searching for someone!'

Edna studied her son for a moment before saying, 'You still got that wench on your mind then?'

Ezzie flushed to the roots of his hair as he nodded. 'It's hard not to,' he replied.

'Ar, she was a beauty,' Edna cast her mind back to the girl who had been through so much in her young life. 'I wonder where she is now.'

'Maybe the lad was looking for *her*,' Ezzie put in. 'Maybe they are related.'

Edna smiled gently at the memory of the refined young lady they had taken to Birmingham aboard 'The Sunshine'. 'It's most unlikely, son; she said she was an only child. Besides, he wouldn't be looking for her in a place like the Golden Cross, now would he?'

Ezzie conceded Orpha would not have been in a public house – it was a men-only environment. 'Well I was stunned at the likeness, mother, I can tell you. So what do you make of it?'

'I don't make nothing of it, lad. It was just a coincidence, I'm sure.' Edna tried to quieten her son's agitation and changed the subject abruptly. 'So did you find us a backload?'

'No, not as yet, but I'll try again tomorrow. There's bound to be someone who wants something transporting.'

'Fair enough,' Edna said as she began to clear the supper things away. Out of the corner of her eye, she watched Ezzie brooding; he was clearly taken with the young girl named Orpha. One brief meeting had ensured her son would not forget the pretty girl with the sparkling green eyes. Her boy was infatuated if she wasn't mistaken. With a heavy sigh Edna moved along the boat to her bed, leaving Ezzie to his thoughts. As she climbed into her bunk, Edna thought about what Ezzie had told her about the boy who looked so much like young Orpha. Although she had tried to take Ezzie's mind off the subject, she began to think there must be a connection there somewhere. Mulling it over as she lay in the darkness, Edna could not fathom what that connection might be.

As he sat by the light of the oil lamp, Ezzie saw Orpha again in his mind's eye. He remembered how her tears had welled up as she told them of her journey and his heart ached. He recalled how she had fiercely fought off her attacker on the heath the day he had rescued her, and he smiled into the coming darkness. There was nothing about her he had forgotten, and as he ran his hands through his hair, he wished with all his might that he would see her again someday soon.

Taking the oil lamp, Ezzie moved to the other end of the boat and his own bed. As every night since he'd met her on the heath, Ezzie fell asleep with Orpha on his mind.

The bitter wind bit sharply at his nose as Ezzie trudged up Portway Lane from the Monway Branch of the Birmingham Canal. Looking up at the sky, he shivered; there would be snow before the day was out. Ezzie knew he had to find a backload soon, no work meant no pay – no pay, no food.

Striding out in an effort to keep warm, Ezzie made his way into Wednesbury town, his mind no longer on the weather. He wondered again about the boy he had seen in the Golden Cross Inn. His mother had said the boy's likeness to Orpha was purely coincidental, but Ezzie was not so sure.

What were the odds of such a thing? No, he felt there was far more to it than that, but for the moment his priority was finding work. Ezzie stepped up his pace as snowflakes began to fall.

As he walked down Trouse Lane, he heard his name being called, and turning in the direction of the shout, Ezzie saw the pawnbroker. 'Ezzie lad, you looking for a load?'

Ezzie nodded as he entered the pawnbroker's shop. 'Come in out of the cold. I have a load of stuff . . .' the man spread his arms around the shop, '. . . I need taking to Birmingham, if you've a mind to transport it for me.'

Ezzie nodded and they shook hands, sealing the deal. Being paid the agreed sum to transport the cargo, Ezzie thanked the man.

'I ain't going to sell this lot here and folk can't afford to retrieve the things they've pawned, so I'm sending it to my shop in Birmingham. It might sell better there.'

The pawnbroker assured the boatman a wagon load would be at 'The Sunshine' by the afternoon. It would not be a heavy load; boxes of costume jewellery, pots and pans, junk furniture . . . all had been pawned by those desperately in need of money to survive.

Giving his thanks again, Ezzie moved on in the hope of another cargo that needed to reach Birmingham; his boat needed filling to make it worth his while and he needed the money the journey would bring.

Ezzie marched across the town, cursing the snow which had begun to fall earlier than usual whilst he was in the pawn shop and now fell thick and fast, coating everything in a cold, white layer. Reaching Walsall Street, he ducked into Etchell's factory, where a small load was known to be had on occasion. Ezzie was lucky, a cargo of nuts and bolts needed to be sent to Birmingham and striking another deal Ezzie pocketed the money and set off back to the boat moored up off Portway Lane.

With his head down against the snow, his hands in his pockets, Ezzie trudged down Portway Road heading into Portway Lane. He was frozen to the bone and was thinking about the warm stove on the boat as he passed the Portway Inn.

His head shoved down into the muffler around his neck, Ezzie didn't notice the young man who stepped out of the inn door just as he passed by. Had Ezzie looked up at that moment he would have seen the boy with the green eyes.

CHAPTER 14

Seeing the snow begin to fall, Orpha had insisted on going to the market with Peg. The weather was in for the day and she intended to help pull the cart trying to be as useful as she could. Besides, she wanted to spend as much time with Peg as possible; they got on like a house on fire. Both wrapped up warm against the biting wind they set out. Orpha had borrowed some of Peg's old clothing and although slightly too large, it was clean and warm. With a woollen shawl wrapped around her shoulders, crossed over at the chest, it was tied at the back. Another shawl lay over her head, wound beneath her chin and was secured at the back of her neck. A thick long skirt covered her side button boots beneath which men's woollen socks covered her already cold toes. She wore hand-knitted woollen mittens, yet again courtesy of Peg.

The girls dragged the cart laden with bottles and jars of pickles and jams; the cones of chocolate covered by a blanket so the snow would not ruin the paper.

Peg muttered as they trudged on, 'I hate the bloody snow!'

Orpha giggled, saying, 'But, Peg, look at the beauty of it, Mother Nature is a wonderful thing!'

Peg muttered again, 'Well, Mother Nature can take her white beauty and stick it up her arse!'

Orpha fell about laughing at Peg's words as they dragged the cart next to Lottie Spence's stall.

'Hiya girls,' Lottie said as they stood by the cart. 'Christ it's so bloody cold today. I ain't standing here long, I can tell you!'

'Bloody snow!' Peg mumbled again as Orpha stepped out from behind the cart. 'Where you off to?'

Bending down, Orpha grabbed a handful of snow and threw it at Peg. A loud screech echoed across the market and all eyes turned in the direction of the shout. Smiles crossed the faces of the women in the market as the two girls were now firmly in the grip of a snowball fight.

A crowd began to gather as they watched the fun the girls were having and they began to cheer and side with one or the other. Finally out of breath, the cold air stinging their lungs, the girls retreated to the cart where Orpha grabbed Peg's hand and, holding it in the air, declared her the winner. Orpha shouted across the cheers that there was chocolate to be had at Peg's cart and they were suddenly mobbed by women wanting some of the sweet confection for their children.

Money was hard-earned everywhere so Orpha kept her prices low; mothers would always find an extra half penny for some 'suck' for their children. Orpha smiled as she thought about the Black

Country term for sweets. Normally the mothers would buy half an ounce of boiled sweets and would tell their children to suck them to make them last longer. Hence the term 'suck' came into being.

Orpha was delighted at the rate the chocolate and fudge sold, as well as the jams and pickles, and before the morning had ended, the girls were on their way back to the cottage. Day after day, the sweets sold quickly, always leaving a disappointed line of women wanting chocolate for their families. Night after night, the girls worked hard, making as much confectionery as their ingredient supplies would allow.

That evening, sitting by the fire with hot tea in hand and outdoor clothes steaming on the backs of chairs, they toasted their toes in the hearth. Orpha began to think over the time she had lived with Peg and how she'd settled into a new chapter in her life. She smiled inwardly at how close they had become in such a short time. The subject of their parents was still mentioned every now and then, but Peg would bring it to a swift close when Orpha's tears welled.

Peg, sitting next to her, was thinking much the same thing. She was glad of the company and she liked Orpha immensely. They never had a cross word and they laughed a lot together. However, Orpha had a sadness about her sometimes and Peg put it down to her lousy mother. She also knew, one day, Orpha would return home to confront the woman, but for now the girls were happy.

Glancing over, Peg asked, 'What's on your mind?'

Orpha glanced over at her friend, saying, 'How much money do we have?'

'I dunno,' Peg answered. 'Why?'

'Well I was just thinking about the chocolate and how well it is selling. I was wondering how we could make more.'

Peg shook her head as she stared into the dancing flames in the fireplace.

'I have some ideas about the confection itself, Peg, but it would mean putting the prices up and then the women at the market probably couldn't afford to buy it.'

'What ideas have you got? Tell me about them,' Peg asked, all ears now.

'In the summer . . .' Orpha began excitedly, '. . . when you grow your soft fruits, we could cover them in chocolate; strawberries, raspberries, cherries . . . then we could experiment with flavours like orange, lemon . . . anything we can get our hands on!'

'Orpha, I don't want to rain on your parade, but that's gonna be mighty expensive!'

Orpha laughed loudly at Peg's expression before saying, 'I know some fruit is hard to come by and expensive to buy, but we'll never know if we don't try!'

'Ar, you're right there, but it ain't summer for a long time yet.' Peg watched the light in Orpha's eyes dim but it didn't go out.

'True enough,' Orpha agreed, 'but in the meantime

how about we see about getting hold of some almonds and coat them in chocolate? I know it would cost, but if we up the price, we should be able to see a small profit.'

'Who would buy them?' Peg asked, watching Orpha as she grew more and more excited by the prospect.

'Everyone!' Orpha exclaimed, 'We could wrap them individually in paper and set them in a cardboard box . . .!'

'Whoa! Hang on a minute, yes we could do all that, but . . . what about the money?' Peg hated that she was knocking the wind out of Orpha's sails but she needed the girl to take one step at a time with her exciting new venture.

'I need a pencil and some paper,' Orpha said as Peg got out of her seat to set the kettle to boil. Going to a drawer, Peg provided the requested articles. 'Right,' Orpha went on, 'we need to list what we need, where to get it from, how much we would need and how much we could pay. Then we need to check our capital. We would need to work out how much it would take to make a particular sweet as well as a profit margin; that would give us the price to sell it at!'

Peg grinned, saying, 'Easy as that, eh?'

The two girls burst out laughing as they collected their hard-earned savings and spread the money out on the table.

'Bloody hell!' Peg said. 'Fifty pounds! I had no idea we had that much! Hell's teeth!'

Orpha grinned at Peg's colourful expression, saying she'd put every spare penny away and between them the fifty pounds was the result.

Settling once more with hot tea, the girls began compiling a list of ingredients and packaging they would need. By the side of each, Orpha wrote the name of where they could purchase the items and how much of each they would need.

Agreeing to go into the town soon in an endeavour to strike bargains with the ingredient sellers, they continued to talk excitedly about their new 'business', as they began once more to make the chocolate for the market the following day.

As Peg lifted down the bottles and jars full of chutneys and jams, Orpha asked, 'Peg, do you have any spare jars?'

'Ar, good and clean an' all, why?'

'I thought we might put the chocolates in them and sell them from the jars. We could use the cones as wrappers, and the customer could see what they're getting.'

'Good idea! I'll give them another scalding before we do though, just to be sure they're properly clean.'

The jars were thoroughly washed in hot water and left to cool and dry.

Once cold, the next morning, the jars were filled with chocolate squares and fudge chunks and with the cork stopper in the top, they were ready for loading onto the cart. The paper cones were flattened and slipped between two jars for safekeeping.

After loading the cart, Peg threw a blanket over the top in case of more snow or rain, and they set off in the direction of the market.

Placing the sweets in the jars for all to see was a resounding success and Orpha and Peg dragged the cart with its empty jars homeward.

One day more at the market would see their stocks depleted and Orpha knew she would have a job on persuading merchants to deal with them for large orders. She also knew from experience that men dealt with men; women having no place in their business world.

Well, she decided, she was about to right that wrong. Businessmen *would* deal with her. She would be relentless and eventually they would see the error of their ways if they dared to refuse her! Orpha Buchanan was on a mission!

CHAPTER 15

Abel was glad he'd stayed over once more at the Gentlemen's Club in Squires Walk, watching through the window as the snow fell. Sitting by the roaring fire in the Club Room, Abel knew he had to return to Buchanan House before the snow became too deep to traverse. In his own little world now, Abel was deep in thought about the last couple of months and his life with Hortense. He had been staying over more at the club rather than at home with his wife. Life with Hortense was becoming unbearable; they barely spoke to each other and when they did, it was with spite and hate. He had not yet reconciled with Mahula and Zachariah either and this played on his mind. He missed them but couldn't return until he'd left his wife. Then he could explain the whole thing and pray they would forgive him. He knew he had to decide once and for all to leave Hortense and move in with his mistress and son. Still spending time searching for his daughters, Abel realised he was putting the whole thing off. He had opted for the quiet life and chosen to distance himself from the woman he had married.

He *had* to be a man and face Hortense; he must tell her he was leaving her.

Walking to the stables housed behind the Club, Abel tipped the lad who tacked up his horse. Climbing into the saddle, he walked the horse into Brunswick Terrace, cursing the weather as he made his way home along the slippery cobbled streets.

Arriving at the house, Abel went straight into his study. It was time to sell the emeralds he had taken from the bank. His intention was to sell them on and then with some of the money make sure Hortense was taken care of financially. The time had come for him to move on. Looking around he cursed again, 'Bloody new furniture!' Flipping the rug aside, he retrieved the box holding the emeralds. Tipping them onto the new desk, he scanned them quickly then gasped. Nudging them one at a time, Abel counted, eleven . . . but there had been twelve! Counting again confirmed there were indeed only eleven. Replacing them in their hiding place, he marched out of the study and into the parlour.

'Assemble your staff!' Abel bellowed at Hortense who sat by the fire with her knitting.

'Why, dear? Is there something wrong?' Hortense replied.

'Hortense! Do as I say, woman, and do it *now*!'

Hortense stood and tugged on the bell pull beside the fireplace. Within minutes Simmons appeared in the parlour.

'Ask Beulah, Jago and Alice to join us please, Simmons,' Hortense said.

Giving a slight bow, Simmons left the room, closing the door quietly behind him.

Hortense waited in silence as she watched Abel pace back and forth not saying a word until a knock came to the parlour door which then opened and the household staff trooped in.

'The master would like a word with you all,' Hortense said, looking as mystified as her servants.

Clearing his throat, Abel kept his temper even as he spoke. 'There is something missing from my study and I want to know where it is!'

The butler looked at Hortense, who looked at the maid, who turned her eyes to the stable boy, who glanced at the cook, who stared open-mouthed at Abel.

Gathering herself together, it was Beulah who spoke. 'Begging your pardon, Mr Buchanan, but none of us have ever been in your study. It ain't our place for starters, and besides, the mistress informed us when we came that your study was even out of bounds for the maid! The mistress cleans that room herself.'

Alice, the maid, nodded emphatically and was joined by Simmons who added, 'Mrs Jukes is correct in what she says, sir. If you've a mind to elaborate on the missing article, we would all be very happy to help search in order to discover its whereabouts . . . sir.'

Abel faced his wife and asked, 'Is what they

say the truth? Are you the only one to go into my study?'

Hortense nodded, a feeling of cold dread consuming her, but she pushed it away. Had Abel discovered one of his jewels was missing? If so, and he accused her, she would deny it vehemently.

Turning to the staff, he said, 'Please understand I am not accusing any one of you of theft. I thank you for your honesty and offer of assistance. Mrs Jukes, a cup of tea would be nice right now and a slice of your excellent Madeira cake, if you wouldn't mind.' Abel gave the cook a beaming smile, which she returned before the staff all filed out of the room.

Turning back to face his wife, Abel said menacingly, 'So, Hortense, you are the only one to go into my study, eh? In that case, I suggest you return the item you stole from there.'

Feigning shock, Hortense asked timorously, 'Abel, what is it you think I have taken from your study?'

'Don't!' Abel snapped as he walked to stand by the fire. 'Don't you dare play games with me, madam!'

Hortense rounded on her husband. Attack was the best form of defence, and Hortense attacked with venom. 'Games! I play no games with you! Firstly you humiliate me in front of the servants, then you accuse me of theft! How dare you, Abel? How bloody dare you!'

'A certain item was stolen from my study, Hortense, and since you are the only one, other than myself, to go in there, well . . . you see how it looks. So, let's get this over with. What have you done with it?'

'With what?' Hortense asked, stalling for time.

Abel let out an exasperated sigh before saying, 'If that's how you want to play it . . . I have no option but to send for the police.'

'For God's sake, Abel, what's so important that you would call out the constable in this awful weather?' Hortense began to lose her composure. 'Talk to me, Abel, tell me what all this is about!'

Dropping into a chair, Abel ran his hands through his hair. 'I had some emeralds in there. I took them out of the bank with the intention of selling them, but there is one missing.'

Hortense thought quickly and then said, 'How many do you have?'

'Eleven, but there should be twelve,' Abel said as he looked up, 'and before you ask, I counted them twice.'

Taking a deep breath, Hortense asked, 'Have you considered you may only have taken eleven out of the bank . . . in error?'

Abel stared at her and Hortense knew her planted seed of doubt had already begun to grow. Quickly she went on, 'It may be that in your haste, you miscounted at the bank.' The doubt in Abel's eyes showed clear and Hortense knew she had beaten him.

'I suppose it's possible . . .' Abel started just as a knock came to the door and Alice brought in their tea. Laying the tray on the table, she dropped a quick curtsy and beat a hasty retreat back to the kitchen.

'Bloody hell!' Beulah said as Alice finished telling them what she'd 'overheard' as she'd stood with her ear pinned to the parlour door. 'No wonder the master was riled!'

'The question is . . .' Simmons said with a straight face, '. . . did the master "miscount at the bank", or . . . did the mistress take the emerald?'

Alice and Beulah looked at the butler as he sipped his tea, his eyebrows raised; his eyes on them.

'Why would her do that?' Alice asked.

'*She*,' corrected Simmons, 'Why would *she* do that?'

Alice rolled her eyes as she went on, 'Well it ain't as if her . . . *she* . . . needs it. *She* has enough money of her own.'

'Indeed,' Simmons answered, 'but *she* may not have sold it, *she* may have it hidden away for a rainy day perhaps.'

'Well I don't care either way,' the cook said, 'I'm just glad the master knows it ain't down to us. And . . .' she went on, 'I'm also glad we're looking out for each other down here!'

Alice added, 'I know the master didn't rightly accuse any of us, but that ain't to say he wouldn't have though.'

Simmons nodded saying, 'We should be extra vigilant, ladies. I hate to say this, but I don't entirely trust our mistress.' The women nodded their silent agreement. 'Another thing I find very odd . . .' Simmons paused to ensure he had the women's attention once more, '. . . is the tale of the missing children of this household.'

'What you mean?' Alice asked.

Simmons sighed at the maid's lack of good grammar and corrected her again, 'What *do* you mean?' He watched Alice sigh before he said, 'The baby, many years ago, was purported to have been stolen by gypsies, correct?' He looked at the cook who nodded. 'Although no gypsies had been sighted in the area for a long time.' Another nod from Mrs Jukes encouraged him to go on. 'So where did the child go? At a few months old, it wasn't as if she ran away by herself!' The women exchanged a glance as Simmons resumed, 'Which brings us to the second daughter who apparently did just that. I ask myself why? Why did the teenage Miss Buchanan run away from all this?' Rolling his eyes around the room, he swept a hand to emphasise his point.

'Could be lots of reasons,' Alice put in, 'but if I had a mother like the mistress I'd run off an' all!'

Simmons nodded slowly as he looked at each woman in turn and then Jago, the stable boy.

'Do you think . . .?' Beulah began.

'I do indeed, Mrs Jukes. I think the mistress ran the second daughter off. The daughter who would inherit from her father. As to the first child . . . who knows?'

Mrs Jukes' hand flew to her chest and Alice, who had sat enthralled, almost jumped out of her skin as the parlour bell tinkled in the now quiet kitchen.

CHAPTER 16

The winter months finally began to move aside, allowing the weak sunshine of spring to encourage new growth everywhere.

Peg's bottled chutneys and jams, along with Orpha's chocolate and fudge, had sold well and kept the girls going throughout the long winter months. They had lived together for some months without them having a disagreement. They had worked side by side throughout that time and when Orpha's ideas soared, Peg gently brought her back down to earth. Often they discussed the likeness they shared but still they had no proof of their being related. Orpha felt her father would be able to answer the many questions that plagued her. But, over time, their work became more important than finding answers, and so they continued to further their little business.

Dressed in their Sunday best, the girls set out to attempt to accomplish what they knew could be the turning point in their lives. They intended to visit all the grocers in the area in an effort to strike a deal for a regular bulk order of sugar and cocoa powder. They would then move on to the dairy regarding a supply of fresh milk and the mill for an order of flour.

Arriving at Cooper's Grocers shop in Melbourne Street, they marched boldly through the door. Asking to see Mr Cooper himself, they waited amid the stares of the few customers waiting to be served.

Mr Cooper, a tall thin man, came from the room at the back of the shop. Squinting over the top of his glasses perched on the end of his nose, he asked, 'You ladies asked to see me?'

'Yes,' the girls said in unison. Peg flushed and stepped back, allowing Orpha to take the lead.

'Yes, Mr Cooper, we have come to ask about placing a regular bulk order for cocoa powder and sugar.'

Mr Cooper eyed them over his spectacles once more before saying, 'Is that so? Well now, *girls* . . .' he emphasised the word, before continuing, 'I don't rightly know what to say.'

Orpha stepped closer to the man as all ears in the shop turned to listen. 'You can say yes,' Orpha said commandingly.

Raising his eyebrows, Mr Cooper stood with his hands on his hips before saying, 'As I'm sure you know, other than my customers in the shop . . .' he paused as he spread an arm towards the gaping women who stood hanging on his every word, 'I only usually deal with businessmen.'

Orpha nodded knowingly. She had expected this and Mr Cooper had not disappointed her with his words. He had all but rebuffed them because they were women. Orpha felt Peg stiffen beside her; the anger building in the other girl was palpable.

'I see.' Orpha nodded again. 'That's a shame, Mr Cooper, because you see, we hope to be opening our own chocolate shop before long and . . .' she paused for effect, 'who knows, we could be making confectionery for Queen Victoria one day!'

The women in the shop gasped as they only registered half the sentence. *'Making confectionary . . . Queen Victoria!'*

Orpha went on before the shop owner could speak, 'I'm sure Her Majesty would be interested to know where we purchased our ingredients and . . . who had refused our custom.'

Mutters sounded quietly in the shop as Orpha looked directly into the eye of the man standing before her. He didn't for one moment think this girl would ever be supplying the Queen with her chocolate, but he had to admire her gumption. Rubbing his whiskers, he squinted again, asking, 'Of course it would depend on how much of each of the products you would be ordering and how often . . .'

Orpha knew she had him. Now she pushed her luck as she said, 'I would also expect delivery of said items.'

Mr Cooper's eyebrows launched themselves towards his scalp as he said, 'Well now, I'm not so sure about . . .'

'Fine!' Orpha snapped. 'Then we will take our

business elsewhere. Good day, Mr Cooper.' As she turned to leave, Orpha gave Peg a quick wink.

'Wait!' the shopkeeper called. 'Perhaps we can work something out between us.'

Orpha turned back to face him, then glancing at the gawking customers, said, 'In private, Mr Cooper, if you don't mind.'

As the two girls followed Mr Cooper into his back parlour, Orpha heard the disgruntled murmurs of the customers who had been robbed of any more of the conversation.

Their requests – the bulk order plus delivery – were met and their first order would be arriving in a few days' time. Orpha said that, as in all business, she expected to be invoiced and would pay at the end of the month.

As the girls walked towards the dairy, Peg gasped, 'Bloody hell, Orpha! You don't half tell a good lie!'

Turning to her friend, Orpha said, 'Peg, I told no lie. I *do* intend to open a chocolate shop and *maybe* Queen Victoria will order our confectionery.'

At both the dairy and the flour mill the same scenario played out and on their way back to the cottage, Orpha said, 'Peg, we will have to make room in the cottage . . . we are now in the chocolate-making business!'

Orpha and Peg began to clear the cottage of any unused furniture and clutter, piling it outside at the back of the building on a patch of waste ground. It was vital they made as much space as possible to store ingredients as well as the ready-made chocolate while it cooled. Junk was moved out of the scullery and kitchen when Orpha said suddenly, 'Peg, we don't have nearly enough trays for the chocolate to cool in!'

'Right!' Peg said. 'Why don't you go to the market and get some more while I shift the stuff out of the spare bedroom to give us more space.'

Counting out some money, Orpha ran out of the door in order to catch the market before the stallholders closed down for the day.

Peg began the task of emptying her jars and bottles from the bedroom and as she stepped out of the back door a while later, she was faced with a handsome young man. His blonde hair fell over his twinkling blue eyes.

'Oh . . .' he said, 'Orpha?'

Shaking her head, Peg said, 'No, she's gone out. I'm Peg.'

'Ezzie Lucas,' the man said, extending his hand. 'Sorry I thought . . .' His voice trailed off, leaving his mouth open.

'Ar, everybody thinks the same. Blimey you gave me a start when I saw you standing there.'

Ezzie apologised and said he was looking for Orpha Buchanan as he was led into the kitchen and given tea.

A couple of hours later, Orpha ambled into the kitchen loaded down with tin trays of all shapes and sizes, wooden spoons and tin mixing bowls.

Seeing the man chatting happily away to Peg, Orpha gasped, 'Ezzie!'

'Hello again, Orpha,' he smiled.

'How did . . .?'

'Lottie Spence at the market told me where to find you,' he said, 'after I explained about our previous meeting.'

Sitting at the table, Orpha asked after his mother, Edna, and they caught up on what had been happening since they last met. As they talked, Orpha saw the looks that passed between Ezzie and Peg and felt the sting to her heart. Jealousy turned her eyes a brighter shade of green, but the others didn't notice, they only had eyes for each other.

Orpha sat quietly listening to them chat and laugh together and her thoughts spiralled. Although she was still very young, she had thought Ezzie was as taken with her as she was with him. She couldn't deny she had thought of him often despite leading such a busy life. Peg had proved that to be wrong. She and Peg had set out on a venture to see their chocolate-making become a business. Now Ezzie had come along and could spoil it! What if Ezzie and Peg got married? Surely they would want to live in the cottage together; then where would that leave her? Orpha knew she would have to move out if that happened. Where would she go? What would she do? All her money would be gone and she'd once again be penniless. Well, if Peg and Ezzie became a couple, she would go into business by herself!

Snapping her mind back, Orpha berated herself for her foolish thinking, she'd blown a simple visit out of all proportion. After all, Ezzie and Peg had only just met!

'What a lovely chap,' Peg said after Ezzie had left to return to his mother aboard their boat, 'The Sunshine'.

Orpha said nothing as she took the last of the jars from the bedroom down into the kitchen. As she did so, she wondered when they would see the 'lovely chap' again. Orpha knew it wouldn't be too long. The happiness she'd had when she'd first seen Ezzie in their kitchen now turned to sadness.

Later in the week, Ezzie's visit pushed to the back of their minds, the girls saw their supplies neatly packed in the spare bedroom and the scullery empty in readiness to house the trays of chocolate to cool and set, the girls began their preparations.

'Oh Peg! I need to go to the cardboard factory, we have to have some boxes made for our confectionery!'

'Christ Orpha! We can't afford to spend any more money. What if we can't sell them, we'll be up to our eyeballs in debt!'

'Don't worry, Peg, we'll sell them, be sure of it. It's my intention to take them to every shop in the town and get them to sell the chocolates on our behalf. I'm also going into Birmingham to do the same. Firstly though I have to get some labels printed for the boxes.'

'Labels? What labels?' Peg asked, her mind's eye seeing their hard-earned money disappearing like smoke in the wind. She knew Orpha only had their best interest at heart and she was the person to make this business succeed, but she also knew she had to rein her in somewhat. Peg was the one to be wary of the risks and after all it would be her cottage on the line if things backfired.

'Business labels,' Orpha said as she spooned smooth chocolate into a large oblong tin tray. 'We need labels to say what we're selling, who we are and where we can be found.'

'Oh right, yes of course.' Peg muttered. 'So who are we?'

'We are . . . "The Choc's Box"!' Orpha said proudly.

'I like that!' Peg said, suddenly enthusiastic again.

Orpha spoke as if to herself, 'I wonder if the printer could put a picture of the cottage on the boxes? If I spoke to the photographer in the town, maybe he could sort that out with the printer and cardboard manufacturer.'

Peg drew in a breath and shook her head as she looked around her small kitchen. Things were moving fast, but were they moving too fast?

CHAPTER 17

Mahula, after much thought, decided to go in search of Abel at the Club. She hadn't seen him since she gave him his ultimatum several months ago, and this was the only place she knew of that she might find him. She didn't know where he'd gone or where he was spending his days, or more importantly his nights, but the club was a good bet to find him. Zach had told her exactly where it was. The weather was bracing as she set out, but the walk would do her good after being cooped up for most of the time, and it would give her time to think.

As she strode out onto the heath, she knew she would not be allowed into the Gentlemen's Club when she arrived, but she could request Abel be notified she was waiting outside to speak to him.

She had worried about how they had parted on bad terms and she wanted to apologise. She also needed to know precisely what he was keeping from her. It was time for some plain speaking. Not knowing when he would be visiting her at the house again, she had made the choice to go to him.

Mahula quickened her pace as the wind took up and she wrapped her shawl over her head. Keeping her eyes to the ground, she trudged on, wishing she'd taken a cab.

Hortense climbed into the trap, dismissing the stable boy with a wave of her hand and a look that could sour milk.

Jago walked back to the stable, wondering why he bothered to stay working for Mrs Buchanan, but then he considered his position. Most stable lads were housed in or near the stables themselves; he, however, was fortunate enough to have his own room in the big house. Jago Morton could endure his mistress's harsh tongue and dismissive ways in exchange for a warm bed every night. He could put up with her surly comments whilst he ate in a cosy kitchen with the rest of the staff. As he began to muck out, Jago smiled; once finished he could go indoors for breakfast. Maybe he didn't have it so bad after all.

A bitter wind blew as Hortense steered the trap down St James' Street and out along the Holyhead Road. She needed to think, she needed to find a way of relieving Abel of more emeralds without him finding out or at least implicating herself in the theft. She just had to hope he hadn't moved them to another hiding place. As the trap reached the heath that separated the smoke-blackened town of Wednesbury from the not much cleaner city of Birmingham, Hortense flicked the reins, setting the horse to a faster gait. Pushing her head down into the muffler around her neck, Hortense urged the horse on, she wanted to be out of the icy wind that raged all around her. Hortense squinted as she flicked the reins again; the cold wind making her eyes water.

Unable to move any faster, the poor horse endured the sting of the whip. Hortense shoved her head further down on her neck and as she did so she did not see the woman walking towards her.

The woman also had her head down against the biting wind which howled its warning across the empty open heathland. She didn't hear the trap trundling towards her as the wind blew full force around her shawl-wrapped ears. She only heard the screaming wind; it was the last thing she would ever hear.

The horse's hooves slipped on one of the patches of ice still remaining on the heath and its back legs skidded sideways. Hortense yanked on the reins in an effort to halt the beast, but the trap's wheels were now on the ice patch. The wheels could find no purchase on the frozen earth and the trap slid around in an arc. The trap hit the walking woman full on and she sailed through the air before landing with a sickening thud some way from the trap.

Hortense managed to halt the horse and sat on the driving seat breathing heavily. She was scared out of her wits as she saw the woman who lay unmoving on the heath a short distance from her.

Looking around her, Hortense could see no one; the heath was empty. Climbing down from the trap, she walked against the wind to where the woman lay. Looking down, Hortense gasped. Mahula Buchanan lay dead at her feet. What on earth was she doing on the heath in the first place?

Rushing back to the trap, Hortense turned the horse and urged it back the way she had come. She had to get home before anyone saw what she'd done. It had been an accident, but who would believe that? It would come out, under investigation, that Abel and the woman were known to each other and that Hortense had visited the woman in Birmingham. Worse than that, she would be made to look a fool and probably carted off to jail for murder. No, she had to get away from the scene as fast as she could.

Jago came running from the stables as he heard the trap crunching on the gravel of the driveway. He thought it strange the missis had not been gone long. He thought it stranger still when Hortense nodded to him as she climbed down from the driving seat. She was as white as a ghost as she hurried into the house.

Pulling the bell cord in the parlour, Hortense dropped into the chair by the fire. She was shaking but not from the cold.

Alice brought the tea tray and left the parlour quietly. Hortense tried to steady her nerves as she poured the tea. Adding extra sugar, she sipped the hot liquid. She had to calm herself, she had to think rationally. Her horse and trap had knocked the woman off her feet and now she was dead. Hortense had left her on the heath. She had looked around, but the heath had been empty. Could anyone have seen what had happened? If so, could they recognise her or the trap? Hortense was convinced no one had seen her and slowly she brought her nerves under control. An evil smile formed on her lips as she realised she was, at least, free of Mahula Buchanan.

Jago unhitched the horse from the trap, noting the horse's wild eyes as he did so. What had this horse so frightened? Slowly the horse settled as Jago brushed him down, talking softly as he did so. Eventually the horse was calm and Jago moved to clean the trap. The missis would have his hide if her trap was still dirty the next time she needed it.

With a bucket of water, the lad began to wash down the trap and as he worked his way round, he saw blood splashed all over the side and the wheel. Catching his breath, Jago knelt down to take a closer look. Yes, it was blood and it was fresh. What the hell had happened? As he stood again, the boy considered his options. Obviously, from the blood on the trap, the missis had had a collision with something . . . or someone. Had the person or animal been killed or were they just hurt? Had the missis informed the police? What should he do? Should he just clean the trap and forget what he'd seen or should he inform the police? Thinking now of his fortunate position in the household, Jago dipped his rag in the water bucket and washed away the blood.

CHAPTER 18

Zachariah heard the commotion and saw two men carrying his mother in through the door. Laying the woman down gently on the couch, one said, 'Sorry, lad, we found her on the heath as we was coming home from the pit; she was dead before we got to her. I'll send the doctor to give a death certificate. She was a nice lady, your mother, we're real sorry, Mr Buchanan.'

Zachariah merely nodded, shock written all over him. The men left after giving their condolences once more and Zachariah stood looking down at his mother lying lifeless on the couch. Sitting down in the chair beside her, he took her cold hand in his and quietly asked, 'What were you doing out on the heath, Mother?' Staring at the face of the woman he loved beyond all measure, Zachariah Buchanan's tears streamed silently down his face.

The doctor came and went, having recorded death by misadventure so she could be buried, saying he would inform the undertaker of Zachariah's sad loss. Thanking him for his kindness, the boy again sat by his dead mother unable to take his eyes from her face. Although the doctor had said she had been knocked over, probably by a cart, Mahula looked like she was sleeping. Zach could see no signs of injury or a wound.

Seth, the stable boy, was sent to fetch a constable. It was the constable's opinion it would be unlikely that, as the woman was out on the heath alone, the person responsible for this would ever be found. The constable left the boy to his grief.

'Mother,' Zachariah whispered when he was alone with her once more, 'what shall I do without you? Please don't leave me like this, I need you!' Again his silent tears fell as he kept vigil over his mother's dead body.

The undertakers arrived next and Seth let them in.

Zachariah saw the two men dressed in black approach his mother and lift her very gently, to take her to the wooden box. Jumping up, he yelled, 'No! Don't put her in there . . . please . . .!'

The man in charge held the boy back, patting his shoulder. 'Come away, lad, let the men do their work. She'll be all right with us.'

Zachariah watched as the lid was placed on the box and it was carried out to the cart that waited at the front of the house. He watched the horse pull the cart down the drive and out onto the street taking his mother away for good.

Closing the door, Zachariah sat in his chair in the parlour and looked at the now empty couch where his mother had lain. Grief swept over him and it held him fast as he howled his unhappiness into the quiet of the room. Great shudders racked his body as he dragged in breath after breath only to let them go with howl after howl like a wolf in the moonlight.

Zachariah sat in the chair all night. He didn't move even to light the oil lamp. He neither ate nor drank, so deep was his despair. Without a wink of sleep, Zachariah was unaware of the morning light that crept quietly into the room as if afraid it would disturb him.

'Mr Buchanan sir,' a small voice filtered through his haze of grief. 'Mr Buchanan sir,' it came again.

Looking up, Zachariah saw the stable boy standing in the doorway.

Seth Walker looked at the young man who sat in the chair with hunched shoulders. 'Sir, I'm sorry for your loss,' Seth said.

Nodding, Zachariah's green eyes returned to the couch.

'Sir, if you don't mind me saying . . .' Seth watched as the other man looked at him again, '. . . maybe you should go and look for your father.'

Zachariah nodded once more but made no attempt to move, he simply stared into space.

Unable to hold his own emotions in check, Seth turned and walked back to the stables. With a horse saddled and tears coursing down his face, Seth led the horse to the front door of the house. Although it was not his place, Seth would not see his master alone at this awful time. He set his mind to helping, and climbing into the saddle Seth took off down the gravel driveway intent on reaching the Gentlemen's Club in Wednesbury as fast as possible. The stable lad, on his days off, spent his time with others in the same profession and gossip of their masters and mistresses was rife. Seth knew exactly where he would find Abel Buchanan.

Abel sat in the Club Room of the Gentlemen's Club in Squires Walk talking quietly with the man who owned a string of shops all over the district. Abel was a business consultant and advised businessmen about how to improve working conditions for workers and thus increase output of the business they owned. He was very successful and was often sought out for his expertise. He commanded a huge fee for his consultations and was paid without quibble. The owner of the shops, obviously delighted with the advice he'd been given, shook Abel's hand and left the Club Room.

Looking towards the door, Abel heard the commotion going on in the hall. A steward rushed in, looking around hastily. His eyes alighted on Abel and he strode purposefully over.

'Sir,' he began all of a fluster, 'there is a stable boy by the name of Seth Walker insisting he sees you right this minute!'

Abel nodded and followed the steward into the hall in order to avoid further gossip.

Spotting Seth, he crooked a finger and the boy walked over to him. 'Now then Seth lad, what's this all about?' Abel asked, not at all pleased that the boy had come to the Club to find him.

'Sir,' Seth drew in a breath, 'I'm real sorry to come here, but I didn't know what else to do!'

'All right lad, calm down and tell me what's happened.' Abel rested a hand on Seth's shoulder.

'It's Mr Zachariah sir . . .' Seth said the pain in his eyes showing clear.

'What about him?' Abel urged the boy to continue.

'Sir, it's his mother . . .' Seth's tears began to fall as the older man watched him.

'Mahula? What about her?' Abel felt the panic begin to rise in him.

'Her's dead sir!' Seth gasped at last.

Abel stared at the boy who stood before him now crying openly. Seth grabbed his employer as Abel's legs gave way beneath him. The steward rushed over to help and they sat Abel in the nearest chair.

'How?' Abel asked on a sob.

'Doctor said her was run over. Two men carried her back from the heath. Undertaker came and . . .'

'The heath?' Abel asked. 'What was she doing on the heath?'

'I don't know, sir, but Mr Zachariah . . . he's just sitting there. I can't get no sense out of him!' Seth shook his head as he looked at the steward.

'Get my horse now!' Abel yelled as he grabbed Seth's arm and stood.

Zachariah didn't hear his father and the stable boy enter the parlour; he didn't see them walk towards him. All he saw as he stared at the empty couch was the image of his dead mother lying there.

'Zachariah,' Abel said softly. 'Zach . . .'

Nothing. His son never moved a muscle.

Abel spoke to the stable boy, 'Seth, I need you to fetch the doctor.'

Seth shot from the room and Abel slowly walked over to his son.

'Zach,' he called again. 'Son, can you hear me?' Still nothing, Zachariah never moved. Abel touched the boy's hair, saying again, 'Son . . . Zach, look at me.'

Zachariah finally looked up at his father, silent tears welling in his eyes. 'Fa . . . Father . . .' he stammered, 'It's Mother . . .'

'I know, lad, Seth fetched me. I'm here now.' Abel sat in the chair he pulled up next to the boy. 'I'm here, lad, everything will be all right.'

Zachariah looked at his father again before saying, 'How will everything be all right, Father? How? Tell me!' The boy's anger rose and he began to yell. 'How Father? Mother's gone, she's dead! How can anything be all right ever again?' Zachariah was on his feet now and his fists bunched and relaxed, before bunching again. Bringing them to his forehead, the boy let out a bone-chilling scream which rocked Abel to his core. He'd never seen such grief before even from women who had lost their children.

Abel rushed to his son and threw his arms around him, holding him tightly as they both wept their anguish into the quiet room. He was riddled with guilt at not seeing his son for months and vowed to try to make it up to the boy somehow.

The funeral of Mahula Buchanan took place a few days later at St Bartholomew's Church on Jennens Road, with Abel holding up his son at the graveside. Zachariah had spoken barely a word in that time and watched with dry sobs as his mother's coffin was lowered into the ground. Abel held his son back as a handful of dirt was dropped into the grave by the mourners.

Seth had been tasked with looking after Zachariah in the interim while Abel rode over to the police station, which sat between Duke Street and Woodcock Street, right next to the Corporation Baths. He learned nothing more than he already knew concerning Mahula's death, and although the police were still making enquiries, it was unlikely anything more would come to light regarding the accident. Over the last few days, Abel's emotions had fused together leaving him exhausted. He was distraught at losing Mahula and guilt weighed heavily at the way things had been left with her. He wished he had done things differently. He was sad that his son had been left without a mother and angry at whoever had taken her life.

Abel rode home wondering what he would do now. Zachariah could not be expected to live alone, the boy was in no fit state to care for himself let alone the property he lived in.

Sitting in the parlour, brandy in hand, Abel considered his options. He had a wife, Hortense, and a house in Wednesbury. He had a son, Zachariah, and a house in Birmingham. Where did that leave him? Which house would he live in? He could not forsake his son to live with Hortense. On the other hand, he could not trust Hortense to live quietly without him; she would cause an uproar in the town blackening his name to all who would listen.

Swigging his drink, Abel mulled over his dilemma. He could not sell his house in Birmingham for it would see Zachariah out of a home and Seth out of a job. He could not take the boy home with him to live at Buchanan House – Hortense would never allow it and . . . he would have some explaining to do.

Abel sighed wearily as he drew no nearer to resolving his predicament. Sitting in the parlour alone, Abel's thoughts drifted back to his daughters, Eugenie and Orpha. Where were they now? Were they still alive? How could he find them? These same questions he'd asked himself many times rolled through his mind and, yet again, he had no answers.

CHAPTER 19

The cardboard factory was situated in Brunswick Street near where Cleveland Road and Bilston Street merged. As Orpha and Peg walked up Vicarage Road, they took in the warehouses which lined both sides of the road. Each crammed firmly against the next, they let no sunshine through unless the sun was at its zenith. On the corner of Vicarage Road and Cleveland Road stood the Wolverhampton and Staffordshire General Hospital, an impressive building.

The girls walked into the factory and Orpha asked to speak with the owner. The foreman said she could talk to him, but Orpha insisted on seeing the owner. With a loud sniff, the man walked off. A moment later, a short, rather overweight man waddled towards them.

'Foreman said you wanted to see me. The name's Bertram . . . Bertie Bertram.' The little fat man stuck out his hand and Orpha shook it, introducing herself and a grinning Peg.

'I wish to broker a deal with you, Mr Bertram,' Orpha said haughtily.

Seating the girls in his office, his tiny brown eyes

moved from Orpha to Peg and back again, amazed at their likeness, then he said, 'Now, Miss Buchanan, what is it I can do for you?'

Orpha reached into her bag and drew out a jar of her chocolates. Placing the jar on his desk, she saw his eyes light up at the sight of the confectionery. 'This is our product, and as you can see we need packaging for our chocolate,' she said as she took the stopper from the jar. The sweet aroma travelled on the air to Bertie's nose as she pushed the jar over to him. 'Please, help yourself, Mr Bertram.'

Bertie's fingers dived into the jar and he shoved a square of chocolate into his mouth quick as a wink in case the girl changed her mind. Savouring the flavour with his eyes closed, Orpha and Peg exchanged a smile.

Smacking his lips, the little man gave his compliments, 'Ah, delicious . . . in fact, the best I've ever tasted! Now as you said, you will need some boxes.'

Orpha nodded and said, 'Yes, providing of course that the price is right.' She watched as Bertie eyed the jar and added, 'We would welcome your advice regarding the best design to house our sweets.'

Bertie raised his eyebrows as Orpha offered him the jar again.

With his mouth full once more, Bertie listened as Orpha explained. 'At present, we make chocolate, fudge and dipped almonds. However, we are looking to move into flavoured chocolates.' Orpha watched the man's eyes grow wide at the thought of such delicious confectionery.

'We will need to discuss your order requisite and the price to be paid, naturally,' Bertie said, although it was clear the girls could get whatever deal they asked for.

By the time the girls left the factory, having left the rest of the jar of sweets with Bertie Bertram, they were assured their first order of boxes would be delivered within the week, and . . . at a decent price.

Walking down Brunswick Road into Commercial Road, Peg said, 'I think that man's parents had a sense of humour.'

Orpha looked at her friend, asking, 'Why?'

Peg giggled, 'Bertie Bertram . . .!'

Orpha laughed too as they walked into the printer's shop. Ordering the labels in the best copperplate script, Orpha explained what was to be printed on them.

The Choc's Box
Buchanan & Meriwether,
Purveyors of the finest chocolates.
The Cottage, Derry Street, Wolverhampton.

She was assured they too would be delivered within the week.

Over tea in the kitchen of the cottage, Orpha worked out the figures on a piece of paper. Sitting back in her chair, she said, 'If my calculations are correct, and providing we sell everything, we can pay our invoices, order more ingredients *and* make a profit!'

Clinking cups, they saluted their good fortune

before they began in earnest the task of chocolate production.

The end of the week saw Orpha and Peg with boxes of chocolate, fudge and dipped almonds all piled up in the spare bedroom. The labels stuck on the box lid added a touch of class to the product and the girls were trying to decide whether to travel to Birmingham or tout their wares in Wolverhampton first, when a knock came to the back door. Peg answered and in walked Ezzie Lucas, a big grin on his face. Peg followed behind him sporting a grin of her own.

Offering tea, Orpha watched the two chatting happily and she tried to suppress the jealous ache in her heart. She heard their conversation but didn't join in. Ezzie was telling Peg about delivering fresh fish to Bilston and how long it had taken him to wash the boat clean of its odour.

Orpha saw the sparkle in Peg's eyes as she listened intently to Ezzie talking, hanging on his every word.

Ezzie ate lunch with the girls before leaving to return to 'The Sunshine', moored in the basin in Old Limekiln Wharf. Orpha gave him a box of chocolates to take back to his mother. By the end of the visit, Orpha had managed to rein in her jealousy somewhat.

Although it was afternoon, the girls were too excited to wait until the following day, and they loaded the handcart with their boxes. Throwing a blanket over the top, they set out for the town. The intention was to sell their boxes to the grocers, who would then sell them on, making themselves a small profit in the process. They walked in silence: Peg's mind was on Ezzie and Orpha's mind was on selling their products.

Orpha began to worry. Would they be able to sell the boxes of confectionery? If not, how would they pay their bills? Her face flushed with worry as she thought it was her, after all, who had pushed for them to develop the business and spend their savings, so if it didn't work she would feel terribly guilty.

Arriving in Melbourne Street at Cooper's Grocers where they had ordered their cocoa powder and sugar, Orpha grabbed a box from the cart and marched inside. She also had a jar for the grocer to taste from. Mr Cooper was pleased to see her and after tasting the creamy sweet he said he would take one dozen boxes, eventually agreeing to her asking price. The girls moved on through the town repeating the process, and by the time their cart was empty, their purses were full.

They chatted happily on the way back to the cottage and Orpha's worries had abated. The following day, and each day after, their sweets sold 'like hotcakes'.

Orpha kept a careful tally in a ledger book of what was bought, what was sold, who it was sold to and for what price.

'Balancing the figures shows that after two weeks

trading we are already in a position to pay what is owed and have a healthy profit to boot. I think it's high time to put the money in the bank for safekeeping,' Orpha said delighted with the success.

She later walked into the town, taking the money with her, and after paying her invoices and being presented with receipts, she marched into Lloyd's Banking Company to open an account. Orpha returned happily to the cottage.

As Orpha walked in she could hear laughter coming from the kitchen and she saw Ezzie at the table with his mother sitting next to him.

'Edna!' Orpha laughed as she hugged the older woman.

'How are you, wench?' Edna asked.

'Fine, I'm so pleased to see you! You've met Peg then.'

Edna nodded, her mind working overtime trying to make the connection between the two girls. Then her thoughts roamed to the green-eyed boy her son had seen in the pub. Were they all related? Would the pieces of the puzzle ever slide together and provide an answer? Edna hoped so.

The chatter went on as they shared their evening meal. Orpha's mood had been uplifted by the arrival of Edna.

Before they left the cottage, Ezzie turned to Peg and asked, 'Would you be kind enough to allow me to court you?' Peg readily agreed; she had known he would ask. The only one not smiling was Orpha. She knew it would not be long before they became sweethearts, and her fears for the future and the business began to weigh heavily on her once more. She had slowly come to realise that her feelings for Ezzie had been only a childish infatuation based on his rescuing her, and that her jealousy was very much misplaced. Her saving grace at present was that Ezzie worked his boat with his mother. He would be unable to give that up, and besides, he had his mother to think about. The woman could not work the boat by herself. If Ezzie did quit the canals, what other work could he do? Jobs were scarce enough as it was. Orpha began to relax as these thoughts dissipated her concerns somewhat.

Alone again in the kitchen, talk of the business they had started resumed when Orpha said, 'Now the question is . . . how do we get the boxes to Birmingham?'

CHAPTER 20

Hortense Buchanan sat in the parlour with the accident still on her mind albeit having taken place several days ago. By rights she should have informed the police, but the repercussions of that didn't bear thinking about. They might charge her with murder. Abel would find out it was his wife who had killed his mistress, or whoever she was to him. God knows what would happen to her then. No, Hortense convinced herself she had done the right thing in fleeing the scene, leaving the dead woman on the heath and returning home. Self-preservation was her uppermost concern.

Meanwhile, in the kitchen, Jago Morton, the stable boy, pondered his cleaning the blood off the side of the trap and having told no one. Lost in his own thoughts, he pushed his brown hair out of his eyes and sighed.

The butler cast a glance at Mrs Jukes who nodded her head towards the boy. Simmons nodded back then said, 'Jago, is there something on your mind? Something you might want to discuss?'

The boy looked at Simmons, then Mrs Jukes who nodded to him, and lastly at Alice. 'I'm not sure it's something I can discuss,' he said.

'Well,' Simmons went on, 'whatever it is, maybe we can help.'

Jago wavered then said in a whisper, 'You must promise, all of you, not to tell anyone else . . .'

'It's all right, lad, what goes on in this kitchen *stays* in this kitchen. Agreed?' The butler eyed the cook and maid, both of whom nodded their agreement as they sat forward in their seats.

'When the missis brought the trap back the other day . . .' Jago started, 'there was blood on the side and on the wheel.'

'Christ!' Mrs Jukes gasped.

'What did you do about it?' Simmons asked gently.

'I . . . I washed it off!' Jago's words rushed from his lips. 'Should I have gone to the police?'

'What would you have told them? It could be that the mistress hit an animal with the trap and then you would have had to face her wrath for involving the constabulary.' Alice shivered at the butler's words. 'However, I feel you think there's more to this than meets the eye. Am I right in my observations?'

Jago shifted uncomfortably on his chair, saying, 'The missis was white as a ghost. She all but ran indoors and she was shaking, I . . . I did wonder if . . .'

'If she had injured someone?' Simmons asked

185

and watched Jago lower his eyes. 'I have to say, that was my first thought too.'

Jago's head shot up, relief showing clearly on his young face that someone else thought as he did.

Simmons continued, 'If, and I say *if,* the mistress was involved in some sort of accident, did she report it to the police herself? My guess would be no.' Seeing the puzzled faces around the kitchen table, the butler continued. 'The police have not been to the house to speak with the mistress. Now, if she had knocked down an animal, it would have been more of an annoyance to her than a shock.'

Murmurs of agreement sounded as Jago spoke up once more. 'The missis was going to Birmingham but she wasn't out long enough to have got there, do what she went for *and* come back again. Then when she came in, she had a face like a slapped arse!'

Alice giggled at his expression as Jago apologised for his language.

'Hmmm,' Simmons scratched his cheek, 'then that lends support to our thinking.'

'So you think her . . .' Alice saw Simmons' frown and corrected herself. 'So you think *she* knocked a person over with the trap?'

Simmons smiled at the maid; praise for her self-correction. 'The question is, I think, did she injure them or . . . were they killed?' The women gasped at the thought. 'Either way,' Simmons continued, 'we need to make no mention of this to a soul.'

Seeing puzzled looks yet again, the butler sighed. 'Let me lay this out for you. Firstly, an emerald goes missing – and I'm convinced the master did not miscount them at the bank. Now we come to the trap covered in blood. *If* the mistress struck a person and left them either injured or dead, and didn't report it . . . that gives us leverage over her.'

'What?' Alice asked, feeling even more confused.

Mrs Jukes explained, 'It means we have one over on her upstairs.'

'Oh yeah,' Alice said as the penny dropped.

'This could prove useful in the future,' Simmons added with a wry grin.

It was later that night when Simmons noted down all he'd been told by Jago about the trap. This information needed to be passed to his superiors at some point, but first he needed to find out exactly what had occurred.

He sighed as he replaced his notebook in the pocket of his uniform hanging in the wardrobe. Being a policeman under cover could be frustrating at times.

Sitting on his bed, he recalled why he'd been asked to take on this role.

The police in Birmingham had been contacted by a pawnbroker regarding expensive jewellery he had bought from a young man. The broker had considered this suspicious, firstly because it was a woman's earrings and necklace, and secondly the young man came in again some days later with more. The police requested the broker continue to deal with the young man whilst they conducted their enquiries.

Snippets of information had come in from informants that this young man was believed to be stealing this jewellery from older women. What he was doing in their homes in the first place remained a mystery.

The police were keeping tabs on the man's activities and whereabouts. Unable to arrest him without absolute proof, they continued to watch him closely. It appeared he lived in Wolverhampton. It was considered this man would possibly try to rob the Buchanans, who were the wealthiest family in Wednesbury.

Then there had been the incident with the missing emerald. Simmons thought it unlikely that the young man had been responsible, which led him to suspect that Mrs Buchanan wasn't as innocent as she made out.

The two missing daughters raised more questions and was a cause for concern and now he was embroiled in a mystery of a trap covered in blood and a mistress who was keeping quiet about it.

With a sigh, he climbed wearily into bed. He needed sleep.

The springtime came in all its glory and Jago Morton met up with the other stable boys on their afternoon off. Being a quiet boy, Jago listened to the gossip as they sat in the bar room of the

Elephant & Castle on the High Bullen. Talk turned to their employers and Jago was envied as he said he had a room in the main house, the others having their quarters in the stables with the horses. The boys complained about how mean their employers were when one asked if they'd heard about the accident on the heath some weeks before. Jago's ears pricked up as he listened to the tale of a woman knocked over and killed during the high winds. There was no mention of who the woman was, only that she had lived in Birmingham. No one knew why she was walking on the heath in such bad weather. Jago stored the information; he would pass this on to Simmons. The accident may not have been the one they had discussed, but then again . . . it may well have been.

Returning to the kitchen of Buchanan House for his evening meal, Jago related what he'd learned about the accident on the heath.

'I think it might be time to make some discreet enquiries,' Simmons said.

'Oooh,' Alice muttered, 'it's like one of them Sherlock Holmes stories. You know, that series of short tales published in *The Strand* magazine about ten years ago!'

'And how would you know about them?' the cook asked indignantly.

'I read the copies the Master keeps in the parlour!' Alice said simply.

'Alice Danby!' the cook gasped.

At the girl's grin, she rolled her eyes as she served

Jago an extra portion of rice pudding. The boy was looking peaked even in this good spring weather, and Beulah Jukes was making it her mission to feed the boy up.

'Alice,' Simmons said as the maid prepared the tea tray for her mistress, 'are you able to keep a keen eye on her upstairs . . . without her knowledge of course?'

'Oh ar,' the girl said excitedly.

'Discretion, Alice,' Simmons reminded her as he tapped the side of his nose.

Hortense watched Alice place the tray on the table then snapped, 'What are you staring at, girl? Get out!'

Alice bobbed a quick curtsy and fled the room.

'The missis is in a foul mood again,' Alice said as she entered the kitchen. 'I'll be glad when the master gets home, she's a bit more civil when he's here. Mind you, he don't seem to be around much of late and when he is he takes himself straight off to his study and doesn't come out.'

'I suggest we keep our heads down, all of us, until we discover exactly what's going on in this house,' the butler said quietly. 'My gut tells me something is definitely amiss with her upstairs!' Lifting his head, Simmons rolled his eyes before seeing the others nod in agreement.

Upstairs, Hortense was considering removing another jewel from its hiding place in the study, but no, it was far too risky at the moment. Of course she could always steal one and blame the staff, but the gossip in the town would be horrendous. She would be shame-faced, it would be known far and wide that Hortense Buchanan was incompetent in hiring household staff. No, she would bide her time, a better opportunity would present itself, she felt sure.

Hortense shivered as she thought again of the dead woman on the heath. There had been no visit from the police, and no talk in the town that she could discern. Although it had been an accident that had taken Mahula's life, Hortense thought how simple it had been. Getting rid of the woman's son however would not be so easy . . . not so easy at all.

CHAPTER 21

Abel and Zachariah walked into the grave-yard at St Bartholomew's Church on Jennens Row and placed their flowers on the grave of Mahula Buchanan. Looking at the headstone, they both said their silent words to the woman who meant so much to them.

Turning away, Abel said, 'I have an appointment, son, and I'd like you to come with me.' Seeing Zachariah look up at him, he went on, 'I want you to learn the art of business consultancy.' Abel saw the boy smile for the first time in weeks as they strode out of the churchyard.

Riding down Albert Street, they passed factories and warehouses on their right; the hide and skin market was situated on their left, the awful smell of the tanning riding on the air. Coming to a crossroads, they turned left into Moor Street, passing the Roman Catholic Chapel and many more workshops and factories. The brick buildings lined one side of the street and on the other side stood the Great Western Railway Moor Street Station, and a small police station. At the end of the street was the hotel where the business meeting was to be held. Not far from the busy Bull Ring, the hotel owner needed advice as to how to attract more custom. Abel been thinking for a while of bringing Zach on board regarding the business. Since his mother's death, the boy had appeared to lose interest in everything, so Abel was hoping this would spark and hold his son's attention on something other than bereavement.

As they tethered their horses behind the hotel building, Abel said, 'Now Zach, I want you to keep quiet and listen good. Understand?'

Had Abel known at that moment just how successful the boy would become, he would have been delighted with his decision to bring the boy into the business.

In a town many miles from where Abel and Zachariah sat in their meeting, Edna Lucas sat at the table in the small cottage that belonged to Peg Meriwether. Her son and Peg were out strolling in the balmy spring evening as they did so often since they began courting.

'He does love you, you know . . .' Edna began, 'but he loves you like a sister.'

Orpha nodded, her eyes misted as she continued to stir and pour the creamy chocolate mixture into the tiny patty tins she had had specially made. These were placed on the cold slab to cool. Inside each dent of another tin she'd placed a small round of wax paper which she pushed down with a sawn-off piece of broom handle, making the wax paper crinkle up at the sides like a tiny cup. The cooling chocolate would be poured into each paper.

With all the trays now on the cold slab, Orpha sat and began to fill boxes with the small cups of confectionery that had set perfectly. Once the base board of the box was filled with sweets, Orpha pushed the lid on and ran her hand over the label on the top.

Orpha began to fill another box with fudge and said, 'Edna . . . what if they marry? What will become of us . . . you and I?'

'Ah, you think they'll want to live here . . .' the woman rolled her eyes round the room, 'and you'll be sent packing.'

'It would be only right that I move out if they were married, Edna, I understand that, but where would I go? Also, would Ezzie continue to work the boat with you?'

'I think he would; there's no work anywhere else for him, that's for sure.' Edna shook her head. 'Anyway, let's cross that bridge when we come to it. Ain't no use meeting trouble round the corner. Now, give me a box and I'll help with the packing of these here chocolates.' As the last words left her mouth, a sweet filled the space and Orpha laughed watching the woman devour the fudge.

As time rolled by, 'The Choc's Box' business grew rapidly and the girls were working flat out. They were exhausted, only having a few hours' sleep each night to keep the orders for their product fulfilled, as well as working the garden.

Doing the accounts at the kitchen table one day, Orpha said, 'Peg! We have enough in the bank to open a tiny shop!'

'What?!' Peg dropped into a chair.

'It would make sense if we could find a building that was suitable and cheap,' Orpha replied.

'Wait,' Peg held up her hands, 'we were going to take our business to Birmingham, which we ain't done yet.'

'True enough,' Orpha agreed, 'but we haven't needed to as yet. I can't believe how well we've done here in Wolverhampton. If we carry on like this we will have to take on more help.'

'Pay someone you mean?' Peg queried.

'Yes,' came Orpha's reply as she looked at the figures again, 'it would be the only way to fill the orders in time.'

'No!' Peg snapped. 'I ain't paying someone my hard-earned money!'

'Peg, they would be working for us . . . they would earn their wage,' Orpha explained.

'I don't give a bugger!' Peg slammed her hand on the table. 'Orpha, we've worked so hard to get to this point . . .'

'Yes we have, Peg,' Orpha agreed, 'and if we take on more help we can make more chocolates, sell more and see a higher profit!'

Peg considered Orpha's words, seeing the sense

of them, then conceded with, 'Who we gonna get to help?'

Orpha smiled as she said, 'We could ask Lottie Spence; it would get her out of that freezing market.'

'Now that's a bloody good idea!' Peg beamed.

'First though, I think we need to speak to a financial consultant. That way we will have all of our incomings and outgoings at our fingertips. The consultant will advise us of the best thing to do.'

'Where are we going to find a consultant?' Peg asked.

'I suppose Birmingham would be the best bet. We could go next week . . . on the train!' Orpha watched Peg's grin widen.

'Orpha,' Peg said suddenly, 'ain't your father a consultant of sorts?'

Orpha's face showed surprise then a frown appeared. 'Yes . . . he is. But to go to him would enrage my mother and, even after all this time, I couldn't face her, Peg . . . I just couldn't!' Orpha became distressed at thinking about how much she missed her father and how he would be feeling about her disappearance. She had so desperately wanted to go back to him, but fear of her mother, ingrained from an early age, had forced her to keep her distance.

'All right girl, don't get yer knickers in a twist, we'll find someone else.'

Orpha giggled at Peg's expression as she gathered her papers together from the table. In spite of her giggles, thoughts of her father left her feeling a little sad.

The last few months had seen the young Zachariah Buchanan become an extremely competent business adviser who was in as much demand as his father. The partnership had worked well, so much so that they had located an office in Burlington Passage next to the Midland Hotel and the bank in Birmingham. Running parallel with Stephenson Street, Burlington Passage was situated behind New Street Station. It was an ideal position for catching trade not only from the station but also from the bank. An advertisement in the local newspapers informed anyone interested of their whereabouts, and the office proved extremely busy.

Peg and Orpha alighted the steam train at New Street hardly able to contain their excitement of being in the big city. Buying a newspaper from the boy standing outside the station, Peg suggested finding a tea shop. Walking down Station Street into John Bright Street, they spotted a small coffee house near the Alexandra Palace. Never having tasted coffee before, they decided to try it. As they waited for their order, Peg glanced through the newspaper and came upon an advertisement that caught her eye.

Messrs Buchanan are proud to announce the opening of their new office for financial consultancy. The office can be found behind New Street Railway Station in Burlington Passage, next to the Midland Hotel.

Peg folded the newspaper and tucked it into her bag as the waitress delivered the tray of coffee to their table.

Looking at the tray, the bewildered girls then looked at the waitress. The girl leaned over to unload the tray, whispering, 'Pour the coffee then add milk and sugar.' Winking conspiratorially, she left them to their drink.

It was as they drank their second delicious cup that Orpha said, 'You know, Peg, this would be perfect with our chocolate, I'm sure.'

'Hmmm,' Peg said, smacking her lips, 'let's get some!'

Enquiring of the waitress where the coffee could be purchased, Orpha noted down the address the waitress whispered to her. She had definitely earned herself a big tip today.

Orpha had decided, since she was in Birmingham, she would go and visit Mr and Mrs Toye who had been so kind to her. Peg said she wanted to explore some of the town and they agreed to meet back at the coffee shop for more of the delicious drink at midday.

Paying their bill and giving the waitress a large tip, the girls parted company outside the shop. Orpha strode out for Upper Priory to visit the Toyes and Peg watched until she was out of sight. Walking along Stephenson Street, Peg turned into Burlington Passage where she immediately spotted the Midland Hotel. Striding purposefully towards it, she stopped outside a building next door which held the nameplate 'Buchanan Financial Consultants'.

A little bell tinkled as she walked in and a secretary sat at a desk in front of her asked with an astonished look, 'Can I help you?'

'Yes,' Peg said as the woman stared at her, 'I'd like to make an appointment with Messrs Buchanan for two o'clock this afternoon.'

Dragging her eyes away from Peg, the woman checked in her appointment book. 'Mr Buchanan Junior could see you at two . . .'

'No,' Peg interrupted her firmly. 'I need to see *Messrs* Buchanan at two this afternoon.'

'I'm afraid Mr Buchanan Senior has a client at . . .' the woman began.

Peg leaned forward, saying quietly, 'Mr Buchanan Senior will not be at all happy with you should he miss this appointment with me. In fact, you could well find yourself out of a job by the close of business today, so . . .'

The woman readied her pencil and asked, 'Your name please?'

'Peg Meriwether. I will return precisely at two and I expect to be seen by both gentlemen. Good day to you.' Turning on her heel, Peg left the office.

Remembering the address the waitress had given them, she hailed a hansom cab telling the driver where she needed to go. Arriving at her destination, Peg asked the driver to wait. The smell of coffee was almost overwhelming as Peg strode into the building.

Half an hour later, Peg thanked the cab driver for waiting and climbed inside, instructing him to take her back to New Street Station. As she rode along, Peg took a paper from her bag and read it. It was an invoice for four bins of roast and ground coffee. Orpha would be delighted.

Paying the driver and adding a generous tip for his patience, Peg walked back to the coffee shop and saw Orpha waiting for her. Sitting at the same table as previously, awaiting their order, Peg passed the invoice from her bag to Orpha.

Reading it, Orpha gasped, 'Oh Peg! How lovely, thank you so much!'

'I know we ain't tried the coffee with the chocolate yet, but I also know you'll make it work somehow.'

Enjoying their drink, the girls chatted happily about how they could combine the new ingredient with the chocolate.

Orpha had made up her mind she would visit the Toyes often, if only briefly, and this had proved the ideal opportunity. Hetty and Henry were delighted to see her as she stepped into the small shop. Orpha told them of how their little business was working out, and they in turn explained they were ready to sell up and move away to live by the seaside before they were too old to enjoy it. When Orpha left them, the goodbyes had been tearful.

'Mr and Mrs Toye want to retire, so they're looking to sell their shop, Peg! If we could strike a deal, we could buy the shop ourselves, it's an ideal opportunity!'

'Orpha, it's in Birmingham . . . we live in Wolverhampton!' Peg said. 'I have the cottage and our suppliers are there, whatever are you thinking? It just ain't practical!'

'Well, you could carry on the business at the cottage and I could work from the shop,' Orpha suggested. 'Besides, when you and Ezzie are married, you'll be wanting to live in the cottage, I imagine.'

'Married? Whoa Orpha, there's been no mention of a wedding as yet. Anyway, what about Edna? Orpha this is all becoming too complicated!' Peg pushed her black hair back in exasperation. 'We're running before we've learned to walk!'

'But, Peg, we simply *can't* pass up this chance! If we do, we'll regret it. Please Peg . . . Please!' Orpha's eyes were begging her friend to agree.

Looking at the clock on the fireplace, Peg said, 'Come on, we have to go.'

'Where?' Orpha asked as she paid the bill.

'We have an appointment to keep.' Telling Orpha she would say no more, Peg threaded her arm through her friend's as they headed for the Midland Hotel. She was feeling anxious now the time had come and prayed all would turn out well.

'An hotel?' Orpha asked as they neared it.

Peg opened the door to the building next door to the hotel, standing in front of the nameplate attached to the wall in order to hide it.

'Miss Meriwether,' the secretary said without looking up. When she did finally raise her eyes, her mouth fell open and she stared blatantly from

Peg to Orpha and back again. Pointing to some seats, the secretary rose and disappeared through a door without knocking.

A moment later the secretary reappeared holding the office door open and crooking a finger for the girls to enter.

Walking through the door, they saw an easy chair area and on a large couch sat the Messrs Buchanan.

CHAPTER 22

Hortense had not seen Abel for many weeks, but that did not unduly worry her. She knew where he would be. He came home on occasion where he sat in his study alone, he had even taken to having his meals in there.

It had been a while since Mahula's death and Hortense had not as yet found a way to dispose of her husband or his son, but she would, given enough time. There was no way that boy would get his hands on the money that should come to her.

Hortense Buchanan reflected how she had spent her time entertaining her high-society friends who gossiped cruelly behind the backs of those not in attendance during the afternoon tea parties. She never contributed to these wicked conversations but listened instead in a state of pure boredom. The gatherings were essential to her maintaining her social standing in the town. Besides which, her only pleasure during these afternoons was to show off some new piece of furniture she had bought, or her new china tea service. Hortense revelled in the fact she had a butler, cook, maid and stable boy. Her 'friends' were not so fortunate.

She ensured they had no call to discuss her behind her back by attending every meeting.

After the ladies left, Hortense settled herself in the parlour, feeling exhausted by all the backbiting and cruel gossip she had been forced to endure. If she had her way, she would see them all in hell alongside her husband and his children.

Alice brought the last of the crockery into the kitchen saying, 'That's the lot. Her "Ladyshit" is exhausted.'

Simmons and Mrs Jukes exchanged a tight grin at Alice's description of their employer. Neither chose to challenge or correct her.

'Right then. Alice, go fetch Jago from the stables and we'll have our tea now,' Beulah instructed. Alice sauntered out of the back door and the cook shook her head. 'She's a card, is that one.'

Simmons, understanding the meaning, agreed, 'She can certainly have a bob on when it suits her, but she means no harm.'

Sitting at the table, Beulah cut into a farmhouse cake fresh from the range as the maid and stable boy fell in through the back door laughing fit to burst over some joke they shared.

'You know,' Simmons mused, 'we never did find out much about the accident with the trap.'

'Indeed,' Alice said, borrowing the butler's stock word. As Simmons raised his eyebrows, she grinned back at him.

'I find it very strange that there was no other

information forthcoming. However, whatever it was the mistress hit with that trap, she appears to have got away with it.'

Leaving it at that, Simmons watched the others mull over his words and he knew they were all thinking the same thing. Their employer may well have got away with murder.

Hortense sat in the garden of Buchanan House and looked over the plants and shrubs that were withering in the late spring heat. With no rain for weeks, everything had become tinderbox dry. No doubt there would be fires breaking out on the heath, which only usually occurred on the driest of summers. With a sudden thought, she allowed her considerations to roam through her mind. She had not seen Abel for some considerable time, so it stood to reason he was staying at the house in Birmingham. The upkeep of that house would be down to him; he would be paying all bills connected to the property and the boy who lived there.

Now, if the house was no longer standing, the money paid for its upkeep would stay in the bank at her disposal.

An evil grin formed on her lips as Hortense connected the thoughts. Taking them one step further, she considered how she could get away with burning down the house which would become Zachariah Buchanan's inheritance.

Trying to remember the house itself, she knew the brick structure would remain but everything inside it would burn to ashes. The wooden furniture, the paintings, the beautiful drapes, all would be consumed by the fire as it swept from room to room. In a matter of minutes, the house would become a ranging inferno. Everything that constituted the boy's life would be lost and if he were in it at the time . . . all the better!

The fire station was situated behind Upper Priory which led onto Corporation Street. The fire truck pulled by two great shire horses would have to travel the length of the road and along the tramway to get to the house. Ideal; by the time they arrived the house would be razed to the ground.

Hortense knew daytime arson was out of the question, she might easily be spotted by nosy people passing by. But setting the fire at night would mean traversing the heath in the dark; not a very sensible option. No, she would need to stay overnight in the city in a hotel.

She had to be mindful also that the police station was not far from Aston Street where the boy lived. She would need to set the fire, ensure it had taken hold and be away before the authorities were alerted. Casting her mind back to the layout of the streets, the only hotel fairly nearby was the one which stood on the corner where Corporation Street joined Lower Priory. That would have to do.

Over the next couple of days, Hortense worked out a plan. She decided a shopping excursion in Birmingham would be the perfect cover. A day round the shops would see her far too exhausted to return home in the evening, so she would book into the hotel. The Grand Theatre was right opposite the hotel she had in mind, which would afford her an alibi if she needed one. Moving her mind to the house itself, she wondered where would be the best place to start a fire to ensure it would gut the whole building. It would have to be at the back to shield her from prying eyes. Hortense had not seen around the house or grounds, she had only been in the parlour when she visited. It was a minor complication, one she felt sure she could overcome.

Happy she had thought of everything, she walked to the fireplace and pulled the bell rope summoning the maid. A few moments later Alice walked into the parlour.

'Ah Alice,' Hortense said pleasantly, instantly making the maid feel uneasy, 'tea please.' Seeing the maid bob a slight curtsy, she went on, 'Oh and Alice, please inform the staff I intend to spend tomorrow shopping in Birmingham and I will stay the night there as I intend to visit the Theatre. I will return the following day.'

'Yes ma'am,' Alice muttered then left the room.

In her mind Hortense had set her plan. The following night she would burn down Zachariah Buchanan's house and it was her fervent hope he would be inside it at the time. If Abel were there too . . . so be it. That, in fact, would be an added bonus.

Alice set the tea tray with milk jug and teapot, cup and saucer, saying, 'Lady Muck is off to

Birmingham tomorrow. Her's . . . *she's* . . . going shopping then to the theatre and, she ain't coming back 'til the following day.'

Simmons and Mrs Jukes exchanged a glance.

'Is that so?' Simmons asked.

'Ar,' Alice added over her shoulder as she left the kitchen with the tea tray.

Beulah said quietly, 'What's the mistress up to now I wonder?'

The butler shook his head. 'Nothing good I'll be bound.'

'I'd love to know though,' the cook added.

'If the mistress plans to be away from home for two days . . .' Simmons said, 'she would not be aware that one of us was away too.'

'What's on that devious mind of yours Simmons?' Beulah asked as she poured his tea.

'The mistress never stays away from home, Beulah, so it's my contention she's up to something. Now, if we want to discover her plans, it stands to reason one of us must be there too. One of us should follow her, but we would have to be back here before she returns. She must not be aware of what *we* are up to.'

'Bloody hell! Sherlock Holmes strikes again!' Alice said as she stood in the doorway.

'Alice,' Simmons said, 'this must be of the utmost secrecy, do you understand?' Seeing her nod, he went on, 'Right, pop out and fetch Jago, we need to formulate a plan.'

CHAPTER 23

Zachariah stared at the two girls stood before him in the office he shared with his father.

'Orpha! Oh my God!' Abel gasped, not really knowing which of the girls to look at, they were so alike.

'Eugenie? Oh my dear girl!' Abel stared at the older of the two young women. Looking from one to the other even he was amazed, they looked like identical twins.

'Father!'

'Father?' Orpha and Zachariah spoke in unison.

Abel's eyes moved between his three children in utter disbelief. Then holding his arms out he rushed to Orpha. 'Dear God thank you! Oh my dear girl, I thought you were lost to me forever!' Orpha wrapped her arms around her father and held him.

Father and daughter cried as they hugged tightly.

Finally breaking his hold on his youngest child, he turned towards his other daughter and saw she had stepped back a pace. He desperately wanted to hold her in his arms again as he had when she was a baby. He wanted to rush to her and never let her go again. However her moving back told him she was allowing him time with Orpha before introducing herself. Abel then saw Zach standing staring at them with an open mouth. Abel laughed out loud as he watched his children looking at each other hardly able to believe their eyes. Then their father burst into tears again.

'Thank you God for bringing my daughters back to me!' he sobbed. 'I can't tell you how worried I've been; I had the police out searching for you both. Where were you?'

'I've been staying with Peg,' Orpha sniffed.

'Peg?' Abel asked.

Orpha pointed to the girl standing staring. Peg couldn't understand why Orpha's father had called her Eugenie?

Abel was confused. Why was his other daughter calling herself Peg?

Zachariah and Peg exchanged a quizzical look as Orpha sat Abel in a nearby chair.

'I don't understand, your name is Eugenie,' Abel said, then with open arms he stood and moved towards her; she stepped back out of his reach.

'Erm . . . I think you're mistaken, my name is Peg Meriwether.'

Dropping onto the couch, Abel motioned for Peg to take the seat next to Orpha. 'Oh dear Lord! I don't believe this! All together in one place. Heaven surely shines her light on me today.' He was elated as he looked at each in turn.

The girls looked at each other and then to Zachariah and finally Abel.

It was Zachariah who spoke first, 'Father, I don't understand . . .'

'All in good time son, all in good time.' Abel's eyes moved back to the two green-eyed girls sat before him.

Orpha gasped, her father had called the boy 'son'. She had a brother or half-brother, it seemed!

Peg snapped her attention back as she said, 'Sorry, Mr Buchanan, but we don't have good time. We, or at least I, have to get back to Wolverhampton.'

'So that's where you've been all these years!' Abel said as his hands came to rest on his cheeks.

'Yes,' Peg continued, feeling confused, 'I've lived there all my life.'

'Not quite,' Abel said, 'the first few months of your life you lived at Buchanan House with me and your mother.'

Shock took Abel's three children, who stared at him open-mouthed.

'Let's have some tea and then we can discuss this whole thing. But first, let me introduce you all to each other.' Pointing to Peg, Abel said, 'Eugenie Buchanan my firstborn daughter.' Sweeping his hand to the boy, Abel went on, 'Zachariah Buchanan my son, second child to me, born of a different mother.' Looking at the youngest, Abel added, 'Orpha Buchanan, my third child, sister to Eugenie.'

'Bloody hellfire and damnation!' Peg said. 'I knew

I wasn't Peg Meriwether because Rufina gave me that name, but I never knew my real name.'

'No my dear, you are Eugenie Buchanan,' Abel said with a laugh.

Orpha grasped Peg's hand saying, 'I knew we must have been sisters. Look at us, is there any mistaking we are family?'

Shaking heads verified his words and as Abel stood to call the secretary to bring tea, the silence of astonishment hung heavy in the air.

An hour later and back at the house in Aston Street, Abel and his children exchanged the history of past years, beginning with Eugenie going missing as a baby of a few months old.

'Hortense swore you had been taken off by gypsies, Eugenie, although I never believed her, nor did the police, I suspect. They and I searched for you and when they eventually closed the case, my despair dragged me down into a terrible depression. Oh my dear girl, I looked for you everywhere!'

Seeing tears well up in his eyes once more, Peg grinned, 'Well, you searched everywhere but where I was.'

Abel laughed loudly then went on. 'It was by happenstance that I met your mother Zach. Not looking where I was going, I bumped into her in the street! I was still searching for Eugenie . . . Peg . . . and I didn't see her coming.'

Zach cut in, 'My goodness, I bet she chewed your ears off for that!'

Laughter sounded at the quip as Abel said, 'You have no idea, lad!' Again they all laughed. 'I was taken with Mahula immediately and in time we began a relationship . . . in secret of course. I swear I never intended to hurt Hortense but things between us were difficult, especially after Eugenie disappeared, and when Mahula came into my life it felt as if I was given a second chance. Then you were born Zach and life for me improved. It has always been my one true regret that I could not marry your mother as I was already married to Hortense, but the only recompense I could make was to give you both my name. I carried on my search over the years for you Eugenie and then Orpha came along. I was overjoyed at having a son and daughter that I could spend time with, but my heart ached to find my firstborn.'

Zachariah now understood why he had seen so little of his father whilst growing up. He also remembered visiting his father at the Gentlemen's Club and how he had been sent away. The pieces of the puzzle were finally coming together. Any anger he was feeling was tempered by the fact he had discovered he had two sisters. He did feel a little sad for his mother being deceived by his father, but then again he was grateful they had found each other and had spent many happy years together.

'I met a lady called Hortense Eldon in the town and then she came to the house . . .' Zach said suddenly. He wondered at what a coincidence it was then saw shock register on his father's face.

'Yes, Eldon was her maiden name, she's mother to the girls,' Abel confirmed. He could hardly believe that had all met – what were the chances of that happening?

Abel asked, 'Eugenie, tell us of your years in Wolverhampton.'

'Rufina Meriwether found me on the doorstep. No one ever claimed me so she raised me as her own. She named me Peg. She died of pneumonia some years ago. I still live in her cottage and I made a living growing and selling fruit and vegetables. Then I met Orpha in the market and . . . well now we make and sell chocolate.'

'Orpha,' Abel said to his youngest. 'Why did you run away? Your mother said your temper tantrums were getting out of hand and . . .'

'No, Father! I didn't run away – she threw me out! She threatened to kill me if she ever saw me again, that's why I couldn't come home!' Orpha watched the shock on the faces of her family. 'She beat me often, for no reason. I was constantly covered in bruises . . .'

'Oh my God! Why didn't you tell me?' Abel's voice was a mere whisper.

'How could I? She would have made my life hell as opposed to just miserable. Then, that day after you left for work, she threw me out. I walked for hours before I was accosted by a carter.' She heard the sharp intake of breath from those around her. 'I was saved by Ezzie Lucas who took me to his mother Edna on their boat. They were so kind and gave me a ride to Birmingham. I walked the town in the hope of seeing you, Father, then in exhaustion I leaned on a shop wall. Mrs Toye, the owner, thought me a lady of the night plying my trade. When I fainted from lack of food, she took me in and she and her husband took care of me and taught me a trade . . . how to make chocolate.'

'Thank God for kind people!' Abel said.

Orpha continued, 'I had saved some money, so decided to travel home and face mother's wrath. However, in the end, I was too scared. So I bought a train ticket to Wolverhampton. I stayed overnight in a hostel where my belongings and money was stolen. I visited the market to scavenge food, which was when I met Peg. It was like an invisible thread drawing us together.'

They explained their reason for being in Birmingham and how Peg, seeing the advertisement in the newspaper, had made an appointment while Orpha visited the Toyes.

The family talked long into the night until Abel suggested they retire to bed. Zach helped his half-sisters make up the beds in the spare rooms and bidding them goodnight he went to his own room.

Each lay in their beds going over the conversations. Abel felt a deep relief at having his daughters back and they had met their half-brother. He had shared with his children his guilty secret and they had not stood in judgement of him for which he had been grateful. He was convinced now that he would leave Hortense after the way she had treated his daughters. He had his children and that was all he needed.

Peg was hardly able to believe she had a family after having so long thought she'd been abandoned because they didn't want her. In fact, she had a father who had loved her, and it was clear he still did. She had found a sister and half-brother and her smile in the darkness stretched wide.

Zach was astonished at having two half-sisters who looked exactly like him. He knew, without question, his mother would have loved the girls. He was able now to understand his father's extended absences as he was growing up.

Orpha was delighted beyond belief to have her father back and meeting her half-brother for the first time. It seemed all was well in her world and she hoped long would it continue.

Finally exhaustion took them all into dream-filled sleep.

The following day saw the Buchanan family board the train for Wolverhampton. Abel wanted to see where his daughters had been living and Zach was eager to visit the town, never having been there before. Sitting in the comfortable first-class carriage, the family chatted together as though they'd never been apart. No one else was in the carriage and Abel thought this a good time to explain about his adventure mining emeralds and the inheritance that would come their way one day.

Abel's children gaped at him as he explained about his journey to Colombia and mining for the green stones

When they arrived in Wolverhampton, Peg led them down Raby Street and out across the small heath to the cottage, her home. Ushering everyone into the small kitchen, she set and lit the fire while Orpha pumped water from the standpipe outside. Before long, they were all seated with hot tea and a meal of bread and cheese. The girls began to explain about their business of chocolate making and how they wished to expand. They wanted their own shop, and eventually a string of shops.

Zachariah enquired about supply and demand and Orpha pulled her account ledger book from a drawer and passed it to him. Going over the figures, he passed the book to his father. Rolling his eyes down the columns, Abel said, 'I think you could do better if you ordered your cocoa and sugar from Birmingham. It's cheaper there and you could have it brought by barge.' Zachariah nodded his agreement.

'Ezzie!' the girls suddenly said in unison. Orpha explained, 'Ezzie runs a boat; maybe he would bring it in for us. We would have to find a supplier first though. I'm sure Ezzie wouldn't mind if it meant seeing Peg . . . sorry Eugenie!'

'I can't get used to that name,' the girl said with a blush. 'I'd rather be known as Peg by you all, if you don't mind. I'm a little more used to it.' With smiles all round it was agreed.

'Oh my goodness!' Orpha said suddenly. 'We'll have to get new labels printed! That's more expense.' Rushing to get a box of chocolates, she placed it on the table.

The men looked at the box and nodded. 'You will indeed, you'll have to change Meriwether to Buchanan,' Abel said as he watched Zachariah take the lid off.

'Oh Father, look at these!' Taking a chocolate from the box, he eyed Orpha, 'May I?'

'Please do,' she replied as she glanced at her sister.

Abel snatched up a sweet too and both men chewed, the pleasure on their faces saying all.

'Bloody hell, girls!' Abel said at last. 'These would rival Cadbury and no mistake.'

Zachariah agreed, helping himself to another.

'Brother,' Orpha said to the boy, his eyes opening at the endearment, 'we're going to need your help to find suppliers in Birmingham. Peg, you're going to sweet-talk Ezzie, if you'll pardon the pun.'

They all laughed as a knock sounded on the back door and Edna Lucas yelled out, 'It's only us.'

Ezzie and his mother strode into the kitchen to be faced with four black-haired, green-eyed people. Ezzie gaped.

'Found yer father then I see, oh gel I ain't half pleased for you!' Edna said as she sat in the chair Zachariah vacated for her. 'Thank you, young man.'

Introductions were made and Abel noticed Ezzie only had eyes for Peg. A sudden thought popped into his head; and he wondered if it would not be long before he was paying for his daughter's wedding. Smiling at the thought, he watched as his family excitedly related their plans to the friends who had joined them.

Ezzie readily agreed to the transporting of the goods needed from Birmingham and suggested Zachariah and Abel travel back with them on the boat as they were going straight through with no stops. Once there they could sort out suppliers for the products the girls needed.

It was agreed that they would rendezvous at the wharf the following morning as Abel and his son wanted to spend more time with the girls. 'I only have one available bedroom,' Peg said, but as their discussions flowed freely no one felt the need for sleep. All were too busy reaffirming their bonds. Abel reiterated it was never his intention to hurt Hortense or Mahula, and that he was only trying to do his best by both women. Now it was his plan to do right by all three children. He determined that his family would never be parted again.

Abel now knew where his daughters were and that he could visit any time he chose to. As for Hortense, she would see a side of him she wouldn't like one bit.

The next morning, hugging both girls tightly, he and Zachariah set off for the wharf. Ezzie and his mother welcomed them on board 'The Sunshine' for their boat ride to Birmingham.

CHAPTER 24

Hortense bought newspapers from the boy standing outside New Street Station in Birmingham as she made her way onto Hill Street. Hotfooting it along Corporation Street, she saw the hotel she was looking for. Once inside she booked a room for the night, saying she was shopping for the day then visiting the Grand Theatre that evening. The bored receptionist gave her a key to her room and yawned. *Insolent girl!* Hortense thought as she shoved the key into her bag and walked out of the hotel.

Roaming the town, she knew for her story to hold water she would have to buy something. After purchasing a vase and a carriage clock and a few other items, she settled herself and her packages in a tea shop to read the newspapers. She hadn't bought them to read but thought she might as well before she used them as kindling at the house in Aston Street.

After more shopping Hortense returned to her room at the hotel, instructing the receptionist she would be eating in the dining room at seven o'clock sharp. Relaxing on her bed, Hortense went over her plans for the evening. She would have her meal then spend a few hours in the theatre before using the darkness as cover whilst she walked to Aston Street. With the newspapers and the small tin of lamp oil tucked safely in her bag, she would round the house and set fire to the back door. The oil would be an excellent accelerant.

Happy with her plans, she closed her eyes for a brief nap.

On strict instructions from Simmons, Jago Morton, the stable boy from Buchanan House, had been very careful not to be seen by Hortense as he followed her everywhere she went. He had waited in a nearby doorway while she had been in the tea shop. Then he had followed her to the lamp oil shop before she went back to the hotel. Leaning in a nearby doorway once more, Jago pulled out the food the cook had given him for his journey. Simmons had provided the money for the train and extra for any eventualities that may arise. Finishing his bread and cheese, Jago lit a hand-rolled cigarette and continued his watch on the hotel door. If Mrs Buchanan didn't come out again, it would be a long night for Jago standing in wait.

The weather had threatened storms and it brought the darkness earlier than usual. Jago prayed it wouldn't rain as he walked a few paces to stretch his tired legs. Just then he saw her come out of the hotel. *Thank the Lord for that!* the boy thought as he watched her cross the road. His glee evaporated as he saw her enter the Grand Theatre. *Bloody hell! More hanging around!* Jago moved to the theatre and stood to the side. Finding a patch of grass, he was relieved he could sit down and still keep watch.

Leaning back on his elbows, Jago surveyed his surroundings, his eyes flicking back to the theatre every few minutes. Lying back fully on the grass, he propped his hands behind his head. The walking and standing around had made him tired and he fought to keep his eyes open.

A sudden shout had Jago sitting bolt upright and at that moment he saw Hortense leave the theatre and walk further up Corporation Street. Jumping up, the boy followed as he realised the shout of nearby revellers had woken him. He had been asleep! He could have missed her exit from the theatre! Thank goodness he hadn't, how would he have explained that to Simmons and Mrs Jukes who had entrusted him with this task! Walking on the opposite side of the street some way back, Jago watched the woman as she turned right into James Watt Street. Hanging back at the intersection, he waited to see where she would go next. The shops were all closed now and he felt it was a bit late for a woman alone to be going for a stroll. Reaching the end of the street, she turned left into Stafford Street. Sprinting forward, Jago endeavoured to make as little noise as possible. His boots on the cobbles would give him away as surely as eggs were eggs. He smiled in the gathering darkness as he watched from the end of the street. Taking off his boots, he tied the laces together and flung them over his shoulder. Hortense continued up Stafford Street and straight on into Aston Street. From his position, Jago waited. He could see where the woman went from where he was and he could run silently forward in just his socks if he lost sight of her.

Hortense stopped and looked around her before ducking into a house driveway. Jago shot forward. Out of breath, he reached the house standing in its own grounds. What was she doing here at such a late hour? He knew she didn't have family in these parts so what had brought her to this house? Looking around him, he could not see the woman he had followed all day. He cursed under his breath. He had lost her! What should he do now? He could wait a while to see if she came out again, or he could sidle up the driveway and chance being seen. If he *were* seen, he might be taken for a burglar, then he would have to explain to the police that he had followed the woman as he believed she was up to no good. It sounded ridiculous even to him and it was hardly a defence against jail time. Jago considered what to do next.

Suddenly a flash of light from the back of the house caught his attention. Pushing himself into the huge hedge that surrounded the house, Jago watched. A faint glow showed at the back of the house and the boy wondered what it could be. As he peered around the hedge, he caught sight of Hortense walking hurriedly towards him. Dashing a short way up the street, Jago hid in the hedge of another house as Hortense emerged from the driveway. Looking both right and left, she hurried back down Aston Street, the way she had come.

Jago walked back to the house driveway and looked at the building. Gasping, he was horrified to see large flames shooting upwards. As he watched, the windows exploded and he prayed there was no one inside. Shoving his feet into his boots, he quickly laced them and took off at a run. Out of Aston Street, Jago shot across the tramway and ran down Steelhouse Lane. Barging through the door of the police station, he shouted, 'House on fire in Aston Street!'

The sergeant of police immediately sent a constable to the fire station off Upper Priory. 'Wait!' he shouted to Jago as he made to leave the station. 'What can you tell me about the fire?' the sergeant asked.

Jago caught his breath and said he'd seen a woman in the vicinity of the house at the time of the fire.

'I see, and where did this woman go?'

'I think she's gone back to the hotel on Corporation Street opposite the Grand Theatre.' Jago had misgivings about relating his story to the police. Would they believe him? Would they think he had set the fire for some reason? Knowing they would keep him there until he told all he knew, he told the sergeant everything. Jago saw the other man's scepticism as he finished speaking.

'So,' the sergeant said sarcastically, 'if we were to visit the hotel, we would find this arsonist?'

'Yes!' Jago insisted. 'We have to go now.'

'All right lad, hold your horses, but I tell you now if this is a wild goose chase, I'll lock you up myself!' The sergeant sniffed as he told another constable where he was going and to watch the desk whilst he was away.

The sergeant and Jago walked quietly down Corporation Street to the hotel. On entering, the sergeant asked which room Hortense Buchanan was in. The receptionist pointed the way and the man and boy walked to the room. Knocking on the door, the sergeant held up a warning finger. Jago cowered.

The door opened and Hortense gasped, 'Jago?'

'Madam,' the sergeant began, 'I wish to ask you a few questions in connection with an incident which occurred earlier tonight.'

Seeing the policeman had made Hortense gasp with surprise. She invited them in, wondering what mess the stable boy had got himself into.

'Now then,' the sergeant began, 'our boy here tells me he saw you in Aston Street tonight.'

Hortense shook her head, saying she had been to the theatre.

The sergeant cast a frown at the boy stood beside him. 'She was in the theatre,' Jago said, 'then she went to Aston Street!'

'Why would I go there?' Hortense asked. 'I have no business in that street.'

'Except to burn down a house!' Jago snapped before the sergeant could stop him.

The colour drained from her face as Hortense realised she had been seen doing the dirty deed.

'How dare you accuse me of such a thing?' she rasped. Trying to get herself back on track she added, 'Do not bother to return to Buchanan House, Jago Morton . . . you now find yourself without a job!'

'Now, madam, let's not be hasty here . . .' the sergeant said with a sigh, but Hortense cut across his sentence.

'Hasty! This boy has accused me of arson!' She was clearly rattled and the sergeant wasn't sure of who to believe.

Jago saw the dilemma the policeman was in and said, 'If I had set that fire, would I have come to you to report it?'

Looking at Hortense, the sergeant said, 'The lad has a point there.'

Hortense whirled away from them and plonked herself on the only chair in the room, gathering her long skirt about her knees.

'Would you mind answering me one more question, madam?' the sergeant asked, casting a glance at Jago.

Hortense nodded indignantly.

'Can you tell me what that is on your skirt?'

Looking down, Hortense made to brush the

mark from the material and her hand came away covered in oil. As her eyes met those of the policeman, she saw him draw his lips together. 'I think you need to come along with me to the station. You . . .' he said to Jago, 'get yourself off home, I know where to find you if I need you.'

'There's no train until tomorrow,' the boy said.

'In that case, stay here. Mrs Buchanan won't be needing the room now and I'll explain to the girl on the desk on the way out.'

The sergeant grabbed Hortense by the arm and dragged her unceremoniously out of the room. All the way back to the station she protested her innocence which the Sergeant duly ignored.

Jago sat on the bed and sighed with relief it was all over, but then he wondered why his mistress had set light to the house in Aston Street.

While Jago Morton watched from the street, Seth Walker, the stable boy at the house in Aston Street, had heard someone approach the house from his bed in the stables. Usually staying in the house, Seth had made up his sleeping quarters to tend an unwell horse. Creeping to the stable door, he peered through the top which had been left open for fresh air for the horses. Watching intently, he saw a woman bending down by the back door. What was she doing? He watched as he saw her stand and take a step backwards. Suddenly a flash of light impaired his vision for a few seconds before he saw the woman turn and walk away. She had set fire to the house! Seth's shock had him pinned to the spot and as the fire took hold the woman looked around her before rushing away from the house. Recognition registered as he saw her face in the firelight. He'd seen her before . . . at this very house!

Seth could see by the way the fire licked the building he would be unable to put it out himself. He could ride to the fire station for help, but he also knew he would be too late. Smoke billowed then he heard the windows shatter with the heat. He knew there was no one in the house as he'd seen the masters leave that morning with the two green-eyed girls and they had not returned.

The three horses in the stable began to whinny and paw the ground as the smoke from the burning building reached their nostrils. He had to get them safely away. Working quickly, he grabbed the tackle and shoving the bit into each of the horse's mouths he connected a rein to each, talking quietly to the agitated animals. Holding the reins to the first, he opened the stall door and tried to coax the frightened beast forward. It refused to move. Walking to the side, he slapped its rump sharply and the horse walked forward. Holding fast to the rein in case the horse bolted, Seth encouraged the others out of their stalls. Walking them slowly forward, the boy talked gently to his charges. Jumping up onto the bare back of the lead horse, he nudged it with his knees. The horse walked on, and holding the leads of the others, Seth managed to lead the horses down the driveway and onto the street and safety.

Eventually coming to Cardigan Street, Seth jumped down and banged on the blacksmith's door. He quickly explained what had happened and the blacksmith agreed to his request of housing the horses until he could come back to claim them. Remounting the horse, Seth rode back the way he came and was dismayed and very shocked to see the house a raging inferno. He was right; it was too late to fetch the fire service now. If he had gone for the firemen first the horses would have been killed. Slowly making his way back towards the smithy's house, Seth would spend the remainder of the night with the horses and decide what to do the following day.

Not knowing where Mr Abel or Master Zach were, Seth decided to visit the office in Burlington Passage. Walking through the streets, he wondered how he would break the news of the house having burned down to his master. He was grateful, at least, that the smithy had allowed him to sleep in the stables until such time as he would find his master and rectify his housing problem.

The secretary had opened the office and greeted Seth with a disdainful stare. The boy stood in front of her desk still blackened by the smoke from the night before. Bits of hay clung to his torn and dirty clothes from sleeping in the stable.

'What do you want?' the secretary asked sharply.

'I'm looking for Mr Abel or Mr Zachariah,' Seth replied, feeling tired to the bone.

'Really?' the woman said with her nose in the air.

'Yes really!' Seth snapped. His patience with the snotty-nosed woman instantly gone. He was tired, dirty and homeless and he certainly didn't need her attitude right now.

Leaning his dirty hands on her desk caused the woman to sit back in her chair. Pushing his head towards her, he said through clenched teeth, 'I need to see one of them and I need to see them now!'

'They're . . . not in,' the secretary babbled.

'Right. Now why couldn't you have said that in the first place?' Seth sneered right back at her. 'When will they be back?'

'I don't know,' the woman said quietly.

Without another word, Seth strode from the office, leaving the secretary with her mouth hanging open. Out in the street, Seth was at a loss as to what to do. Walking back to the smithy, he reasoned one or the other of the Buchanans would have to come back to the office at some time. All he could do was wait and visit the office again the following day in the hope that one of them had returned.

The smithy's wife took Seth in and giving him some of her son's old clothes sent him to the stand-pipe in the yard to wash. Another mouth to feed was no hardship to her and she knew she would be well compensated by Abel for the kindness she showed to his stable boy.

Seth cleaned himself up and dressed in the clothes

he had been given, he washed his dirty ones in a bucket of water in the yard. Throwing the wet clothes over a nearby fence to dry he went into the kitchen to the smithy's wife.

Placing a large bowl of porridge before him, she cut thick wedges of home-made bread and butter and passed them to Seth.

'Thank you, missis,' he said as he tucked in.

Ruffling his hair, she gave him a smile. 'It ain't no bother, lad, you can stay here as long as you like,' she said warmly.

'I'll go look for Mr Abel again tomorrow,' Seth said with a forlorn look. Nodding, the woman went back to her chores leaving Seth to eat his breakfast in peace.

CHAPTER 25

Ezzie steered 'The Sunshine' out of the basin at the Old Limekiln Wharf and out onto the Birmingham Canal, showing a fascinated Zachariah how it was done.

Edna and Abel sat in the belly of the boat with hot tea and discussed what had happened over the last few days, and how astounded Abel was to have found his family again. He asked, 'Edna, what will you do if Ezzie and Peg decide to marry? Will you continue to live on the boat?'

Edna said, 'I couldn't work the boat alone, but I'll decide if and when talk of marriage is mentioned.' Both were delighted that their children marrying would bring the two families together. Abel also told Edna, 'If ever you or your son need anything, you should come to me; after your kindness to my younger daughter, I would be more than happy to help you in any way I can.'

'Thank you. It's nice to see you ain't snobby about cut-rats.' Edna smiled.

'People who work the canals are just hard-working folk, Edna, and for that reason alone they should be shown respect, in my opinion.' Abel smiled back.

'Tell me to mind my own business, Abel, but why the hell ain't you divorced that Hortense?' Edna asked in her forthright manner.

'I suppose it was cowardice to a point. I thought the scandal of a divorce would see her in her grave and I couldn't have that on my conscience. I have considered it many times, and if I'd known she'd abandoned Eugenie and abused Orpha, I would have done so immediately.' Abel sighed loudly. Then he went on to tell Edna all about his wife and what she was like; her love of money and prestige, and keeping up appearances.

'Ah well, it ain't no use crying over spilt milk, what you have to do now is decide what you'll do next,' Edna said on a sigh.

'I agree, and I know exactly what the next step is,' Abel said.

Edna nodded, suspecting she knew what he would do, and Hortense Buchanan would most definitely be in for a shock.

The day passed peacefully on the canal network and Ezzie eventually moored up in the basin at the Old Wharf in Birmingham. It was decided that the two young men would search out suppliers for the girls' products the following day, then Abel and Zachariah, giving their thanks for their first journey on a boat, waved goodbye as they left Edna standing on the deck of 'The Sunshine'.

Needing to get their 'land legs' back, the men decided to walk back to Aston Street. Zachariah was excited about the boat, saying, 'I would enjoy having one of my own – for leisure purposes only of course.'

Turning into the driveway of their home, both men stopped dead in their tracks. Their house was a smoking ruin. Rushing up the drive, they surveyed what was left of their once beautiful home.

'Oh my God!' Zachariah said, looking at his father. 'Whatever could have happened?'

Shaking his head, Abel ran his hands through his black hair. Both walked around the remains of the house, wisps of smoke still escaping from the brickwork. There was nothing left to say anyone had ever lived there. All of their possessions were burnt to ashes. However the fire occurred, it had left them homeless and in total shock.

'Seth!' Zach said, dashing to the stables. 'He's not here, Father!'

'He must have got out, God willing he's all right.' Abel panted then added, 'Let's see if the police can shed any light on this.' Running down to the small police station on Steelhouse Lane, Abel said, 'We were lucky we weren't inside when it went up, lad.'

Stepping into the station, Abel introduced himself and his son to the duty constable and asked what was known about the fire in Aston Street. The constable said he would fetch the sergeant. Once seated in the Sergeant's office, the story unfolded before them.

'Young Jago Morton reported he had seen Mrs Buchanan set the fire before rushing back to her hotel room. I brought the lady back to the station for questioning and Jago was instructed to go home and stay there in case we needed to speak with him again.'

'What?' Abel asked incredulously. 'Why on earth would Hortense do such a thing?'

The sergeant answered by saying, 'Mrs Buchanan denied having set the fire, sir, and it came down to her word against the stable lad's. Although Mrs Buchanan had lamp oil on her skirt, it didn't prove that she had burned the house down. She said she had brought a bottle of lamp oil but had dropped it; she had not seen said oil on her skirt until I noticed it during questioning her at the hotel.'

'Then why would Jago accuse her? In fact, why was the boy following her in the first place?' Abel queried.

Shrugging his shoulders, the sergeant said, 'The lad said he thought the woman to be up to no good. He would tell us no more, sir. Maybe you should be having words with him, maybe he will explain it all to you, that's supposing he went home after I left him at the hotel.'

Zachariah asked, 'You don't think . . .'

The Sergeant assured them, 'No, I don't think the lad set the fire; after all, he was the one who alerted us to it in the first place.'

'What will happen to my wife, sergeant?' Abel asked, dreading the man's answer. He didn't know if his wife was to blame in this debacle but he had his suspicions.

'Well, sir, we let her go this morning. We couldn't rightly charge her with arson without proof. She could have been telling the truth about spilling the oil, and the lad could have been mistaken in his identification of her. It was dark and stormy after all. I'm sorry, but you must see the predicament I was in.'

The two men thanked the sergeant for his efforts on their behalf and left the police station.

'We need to get to Wednesbury, son, but first I need a drink!' Abel said as they crossed the tramway and walked down Ryder Street. Turning right at the end into Gem Street, they passed the Gaiety Palace and walked into the Three Swans Inn. Sitting at a quiet table in the corner with their beers, father and son looked at each other.

'I can't believe it has all gone, Father. You have Buchanan House in Wednesbury, but I have nothing left!'

'Don't you worry your head about that, son, we can get you another house. I'm just thankful you and I are still alive and breathing!'

Discussing their options, Zachariah wondered if he could stay over in the office in Burlington Passage until they could find another suitable house while Abel returned to Buchanan House in an effort to ascertain what had gone on during his absence. Abel suggested they book into a hotel.

Jago Morton had arrived back at Buchanan House still shaking with fear and shock, and it was a while before Simmons could get a word out of him. Mrs Jukes fussed with hot sweet tea for the boy and slowly the story of the previous day and night came out. At the end of relating his tale, Jago burst into tears, whereupon Mrs Jukes grasped him to her ample bosom.

'Beulah . . . you are suffocating the boy!' Simmons said, raising a smile on the boy's face as he gasped for breath.

'I'll have to go,' Jago said as he controlled his breathing. 'The missis gave me the sack.'

'Well, Mrs High and Mighty bloody Buchanan ain't here!' Alice said sharply.

'Let us all calm down and evaluate the situation,' Simmons said quietly as he held up his hands. 'Now, Jago, do you think the police will charge the mistress with arson?' Simmons asked.

'I don't know! I mean, there was lamp oil on her skirt, but that don't prove she did it, does it? But, Mr Simmons sir, I saw her! I saw her set light to that house, I swear!'

'I believe you, lad,' Simmons comforted the stable boy who was again beginning to shake. 'The question is, do the police?'

'They must do, otherwise they would still have him in the station!' Mrs Jukes interjected.

'Good point, well noted, Beulah, but consider this . . . it is Jago's word against the mistress's.' Simmons kept his voice low.

'Well, they ain't gonna believe him over her are they?' Alice asked.

Jago's tears flowed again and Alice caught a disdainful look from Simmons and a clip across the back of her head from Mrs Jukes.

'Bloody hell Jago! See what you've done now?' Alice complained, but she didn't miss the small smile on the boy's face.

The slam of the front door and a screech filled the house. 'Simmons, where the hell are you?' Shocked faces looked at each other across the table as Hortense's voice reached them.

'We know nothing,' Simmons said, instantly assuming a commanding role. 'You,' he pointed to Jago, 'get in there, and for God's sake keep quiet!' Simmons pointed to the butler's Pantry. 'Mrs Jukes . . . the kettle, Alice . . . find something to do!'

Hortense's footsteps could be heard descending the steps into the kitchen.

'Ah, welcome back, ma'am,' Simmons affected his speech, 'I trust you enjoyed your trip?'

'Where is he?' Hortense yelled across the kitchen. Alice dropped a cup, which shattered on the tiled floor. All eyes went to her as she scampered off for the broom. 'Stupid girl!' Hortense shouted after her. Turning back to the butler, she said menacingly, 'Where is Jago Morton?'

'I presume, ma'am, that he is in the stable where he usually is at this time of day.' Simmons kept his calm.

His sarcasm was not lost on Hortense as she yelled again, 'Fetch him to me . . . NOW!'

Simmons sniffed his disgust at being sent on such an errand and walked out of the back door. Waiting just outside for a few minutes, he then returned saying, 'I'm afraid he's not there, ma'am.'

'Well where is he?' Hortense's voice rose an octave.

Wincing at the screech Simmons replied, 'I'm afraid I have no idea . . . ma'am.'

Hortense spun on her heel and as she left the kitchen she shouted over her shoulder, 'Tea . . . immediately!'

Alice sidled into the kitchen saying, 'Has her gone?'

Simmons did not correct the maid's grammar, in fact he replied in the same vein, 'Her has!'

Booking into the Midland Hotel next door to their office that evening, Abel and Zachariah sat in the bar, neither tired enough to sleep. Drink after drink was consumed but drunkenness was staved off by shock. They quietly discussed the events that had brought them here.

Abel cast a glance around the room. It was late and there was no one around save for the bar keeper who was busy washing glasses and tankards.

Looking back at his son, he saw the tears roll down the young man's cheeks. 'Cry it out, lad,' He whispered.

Zach's shoulders heaved as he covered his face with his hands but he made no sound other than his breathing. After a moment he dried his face on his handkerchief and said, 'All of mother's things . . .'

'Aye lad, I know and I'm sorry in my heart for that.' Abel cut across, 'But Zach, we have our memories and no one can take those away.'

The boy nodded and they clinked glasses before finishing their drinks.

Eventually they retired to bed to rest, both knowing that sleep would evade them.

CHAPTER 26

Orpha and Peg had chatted all the time they worked in the kitchen at the cottage in Wolverhampton. The boxes of chocolates began to pile up as taking time off had seen them a little behind with their work. Now they were working hard to catch up.

A knock came to the door and Orpha was delighted their bins of coffee had finally arrived. Thanking the man who carried them into the scullery for her, Orpha gave him a box of chocolates and his eyes lit up. 'Thank you, miss,' he said, 'the wife will enjoy these!'

'Peg,' she said after the man had left, 'let's take a break and make some coffee!' As they sat with their drinks, Orpha spoke again, 'I wonder if the men have managed to find us new suppliers yet.'

Peg shook her head, saying, 'I wonder what we'll do with all that coffee.'

Laughing, Orpha set her mind to experimenting with their new ingredient. As she was thinking she absent-mindedly brought a chocolate square to her mouth. Slipping from her fingers, it landed in her cup and began to melt as it floated on the hot coffee. Peg watched as Orpha shrugged her shoulders and took a sip. With a look of surprise she said, 'This is delicious . . . try it!' Passing her cup to her sister, she watched as Peg sipped.

'Bloody hell! Well at least we know now how to combine the two!' With that she dropped a piece of chocolate into her own cup.

The girls rose early the next day so that they could deliver their orders to the grocery shops around the town. Dragging the handcart behind them Orpha said, 'There has to be a better way than this!' Peg nodded in agreement wondering what Orpha was planning next.

Delivering to Cooper's Grocery, they trudged up Raby Street, the cartwheels rattling on the cobblestones. 'Peg,' Orpha said emphatically, 'we *have* to have our own shop! This is ridiculous. Look at us . . .' She stopped and pointed at the cart. 'How can we be taken seriously in the business world?'

Looking back at the cart, Peg nodded and answered with, 'I tell you what, let's get this lot delivered then we'll have a look round for a suitable property.' She didn't mention the Toyes' shop again, as it was in Birmingham and much too far to travel every day.

Orpha gave her sister a hug and they set off once more invigorated by the prospect of becoming shop owners.

On their return they walked down St George's Parade and they passed the vicarage on the corner of Old Hall Street. On the opposite corner stood Belcher & Son, Estate Agents. Leaving the cart outside, they walked in through the door and a little bell tinkled their arrival. Mr Belcher senior sat behind a desk and, over a small pair of spectacles, he looked up at the girls. He had a full head of silver-white hair with beard and moustache to match. Orpha smiled, thinking he looked like Santa Claus. Standing to greet them, she smiled again; the man was no more than five feet tall.

'Ladies, come in . . . come in. Please take a seat.' He motioned to a couple of straight-backed chairs near his desk. 'Now, how may I help you?'

'We are looking to open a shop,' Orpha said, 'and living in Derry Street we would be looking for a property not too far from there . . . at the right price of course.'

'Ah, a shop. May I ask what kind of shop?' Mr Belcher sat with fingers brushing his beard.

Orpha took out a jar of chocolates from her bag; pulling out the stopper, she offered the jar to Mr Belcher. Slipping a chocolate piece into his mouth, he savoured the creamy taste. 'Delicious!' he managed eventually. Riffling through papers on his desk he located what he was searching for. 'Here we are,' he said, wafting the papers up and down. 'Now then, may I ask if you are looking for a shop only or a property that will include manufacturing facilities also?'

The sisters looked at each other; this was something they had not considered. Then Orpha spoke up, 'Well, not having millions of pounds to spare . . .' Mr Belcher smiled kindly. 'Maybe you could find us something with a shop area and an upstairs or back rooms we could use as kitchens and cold storage.'

Riffling through his papers yet again, Mr Belcher waved a paper under Orpha's nose. 'I think I may have just the thing! This property is in Oxford Street.'

'We know where that is and it's not too far from the cottage!' Peg said excitedly.

'Would you care to take a look at it?' the whiskered man asked.

'Yes please!' Orpha was beside herself.

Noting down the address, Mr Belcher gave the details to Orpha. Giving their thanks, the girls rushed from the office and dragging the cart they set off for Oxford Street.

They finally found the address Mr Belcher had given them and standing outside the building they looked up and down the street. Both sides were lined with houses interspersed with shops. It was in the middle of the town not too far from the market and quite near the dairy. Looking at the building, Peg said, 'I like the little bullion windows, although it looks dark inside.'

Orpha nodded and opened the door with the key Mr Belcher had entrusted to her. Walking inside, they saw it had obviously been a shop at one time. Having a good look around, Orpha felt it would be ideal for their purpose. Peg agreed and locking the door behind them they wandered back to Belcher & Son to return the key, but more importantly, to discover the asking price.

Mr Belcher welcomed the girls in his office once more, seeing their excitement. After some discussion about the building and location, Orpha drew in a deep breath and asked the sale price.

An astonished look passed between the girls as Orpha repeated what Mr Belcher told her. She gasped, 'Two thousand pounds!'

Zachariah was up bright and early and met with Edna and Ezzie on 'The Sunshine' moored at the Old Wharf. Over tea, he explained how he and his father had found their house a smoking ruin on their return the previous day.

'We turned into the driveway and then we saw it . . . our house had been razed to the ground!'

'Bloody hell!' Edna gasped, her hand flying to her chest.

Zachariah choked back the tears once again threatening to erupt. 'The police said Mrs Buchanan had been seen setting the fire, but with no proof they couldn't arrest her, so they released her.'

Shock evident on Edna's face, she wisely kept her thoughts to herself. That woman had meant to hurt the boy and his father . . . maybe even kill them!

As Zachariah and Ezzie set off for the town, Edna's mind went over what she'd been told. Although there was no proof that Hortense

Buchanan had burned down the house, Edna knew in her heart it was the case. The question was, why? More questions unfolded in her mind. What would Hortense do now? Would she make another attempt on Abel's life? Did she know Zachariah was Abel's son? Did she know about the girls living in the cottage in Wolverhampton? If not, and if she *had* dumped Peg there as a baby, then she might decide to return and then discover the sisters living happily together; she might even try to harm them in the same way . . . by burning down the cottage! She would have to warn her son and Zachariah when they returned.

Meanwhile, having found and struck a deal with suppliers for his half-sisters, Zachariah suggested to Ezzie they have a pie and a pint in an inn before returning to Edna on the boat. Sitting at a small table in the bar, the two men discussed the arson attack and what Zachariah would do regarding living accommodation now. The green-eyed boy said, 'I will have to stay at the hotel for the fore-seeable future, but my first priority is work. Keeping the consultancy business open is imperative; no work means no money.'

Climbing aboard 'The Sunshine', the young men were happily telling Edna of the deals they had made with the new suppliers when Ezzie noticed his mother's sombre mood. When pushed, Edna related her fears regarding Zachariah, his father and his half-sisters.

'If she did set fire to your house, lad, she may

well try the same thing at the cottage if she gets wind of the girls living there. Also, if she finds out about the office you and your father have together . . .' Edna let the sentence hang.

'Christ, Edna!' Zachariah put in. 'I never thought of that!' Then another thought struck him and turning to Ezzie he said, 'You have to be extra vigilant too. If Hortense discovers your part in the girls' business and that you and Peg are courting, God knows what she's likely to do.' Seeing Edna pall, he continued, 'Edna I don't wish to frighten you, but we must take extra precautions just in case. Ezzie, you must not, under any circumstances, leave your mother on this boat alone!'

Ezzie nodded his agreement, all three now aware of the peril they could be in if Hortense Buchanan made it her business to investigate them further.

Mother and son had no load to return to Wolverhampton as they set the boat in the direction of the town, but that was the least of their worries at that moment. Zachariah had assured them they would be financially compensated by Abel for the loss of load. For now, they had to get back and warn the girls that they could all be in great danger. As their journey continued, Ezzie's mind whirled with thoughts on how to keep them all safe from Hortense's wrath.

CHAPTER 27

Abel had boarded the first train to Wednesbury out of New Street Station and mulled over his situation as the train rumbled along the tracks.

The more he thought about what the sergeant had told him, the more he began to believe Jago's explanation over Hortense's. The question he kept coming back to was, why? Zachariah had told him his wife had visited the house in Aston Street. She had met Mahula. She had met Zachariah, so obviously she knew who he was and the connection to Abel. Could it be she wanted rid of them as she had her daughters? Had she hoped her husband and his son were inside as she lit the fire at their house? Why go to such lengths? Why not just divorce him? Scandal and money. That was the answer, Hortense could not bear the thought of scandal.

Alighting the train at the end of his journey, Abel hailed a carriage and gave the cabbie the address of Buchanan House. Another thought formed in Abel's mind as the carriage trundled through the cobbled streets. Could it have been Hortense who had knocked down and killed his beloved Mahula? The shock of losing his home to the fire had worn off somewhat and anger had replaced it.

If it was ever proved that Hortense had caused Mahula to lose her life . . . then God help her!

Abel strode through the front door of Buchanan House yelling for Hortense. His voice echoed through the hall and the staff in the kitchen tensed.

Jago ran to hide in the butler's pantry.

Striding into the parlour, Abel marched across to the fireplace where Hortense sat.

'What the bloody hell has been going on?' he shouted.

'It's all the fault of your stable boy!' his wife spat back.

'Hortense! You were arrested by the police for God's sake!' Abel began to pace back and forth in front of the fire.

The butler, cook and maid had tiptoed from the kitchen and now stood outside the parlour door listening intently as the argument raged on.

'You were arrested for arson!' Abel yelled.

'I was released as there was no proof of my guilt! I was exonerated!' Hortense was on her feet. 'If you spent more time at home instead of . . .'

'Instead of what?' Abel asked, trying to draw her out.

'Working so much,' his wife's temper calmed a little.

'I have to bloody work so hard because you keep

spending the money on all this damned rubbish!' Abel swung his arms around, encompassing yet more new furniture.

Hortense's temper flared again, 'I will not be blamed, Abel!'

'No, you won't,' he was quick to answer, 'you won't take responsibility for anything, will you?'

'Just what are you referring to now, Abel?' Hortense sneered.

'What about the disappearance of Eugenie and Orpha . . . I suppose you had no hand in that either . . .!' Abel's voice was laced with sarcasm.

'So you are still singing that old song,' Hortense rasped nastily. 'How many times do I have to tell you? It had nothing to do with me!'

'Is that so?' Abel screwed up his mouth and arched his eyebrows. Watching his wife carefully, he saw the flicker of doubt on her features as her colour drained.

Hortense harrumphed as she retook her seat. Rapid thoughts flicked through her mind as she produced a handkerchief from her dress sleeve. Did he know she'd abandoned Eugenie? Was he aware she'd driven Orpha from the house? If so, how had he found out?

'Yes, that is so,' she sniffed as she dabbed her eyes with her handkerchief pretending to be upset.

'Hortense, you are a liar, a bigot and a very evil woman! I thought I loved you once, but be sure now that any love – if that was what it was – has died, never to be resurrected!' Abel watched his wife's head snap up, her eyes wide with shock.

Outside the door, Simmons looked at Beulah who had her hand across her mouth. Pulling his mouth down at the sides, he pinned his ear back to the door.

Abel's voice rose again as he continued his tirade, 'I want you out of this house by tomorrow!'

'Abel!' Hortense gasped. 'How will I live? What will I live on?'

'Live on the money you got for the emerald you stole from me!' Abel yelled.

'But there wouldn't be enough . . .' Hortense blanched as she realised her mistake.

'I knew it!' Abel shouted, triumphant again.

'No Abel, you don't understand . . .' Hortense managed before her husband cut off her sentence.

'What is it that I don't understand, Hortense? Please enlighten me,' he said almost soothingly.

Hortense rounded on him her voice full of fire. 'You, with your daughters – always doting on them! You never showed me love like that!'

'Hortense, you never warranted it. You are a thief and I won't have you in this house any longer, now I suggest you call for Alice, I think you need a cup of sweet tea!'

Hearing the last, the staff scuttled swiftly back to the kitchen in time to hear the tinkle of the parlour bell.

Simmons sat with his tea and thought. So it *was* the mistress who had stolen the gem after all!

A little while later, Abel stomped into the kitchen at Buchanan House. 'Alice go upstairs and pack the mistress's things.' He then instructed Simmons to find Jago Morton and bring him to the kitchen table. Alice fled up the stairs as Simmons called Jago's name loudly.

Stepping from the butler's pantry, the stable boy walked towards Abel, his head down.

'Sit down, lad. Mrs Jukes, tea if you'd be so kind,' Abel said. 'Now, I want you to tell me everything you know.' Raising a hand slowly, he went on, 'You are not in trouble, Jago, so don't worry about that; just tell me the all of it.'

Jago related his experience of the day he followed Hortense to Birmingham, interspersed with Simmons' confirmation here and there. Then they went over it all again; Mrs Jukes providing sustenance with tea and cake.

Hortense had quietly crept to the kitchen door behind Abel and listened in to the beginning of the conversation. The little weasel was telling Abel everything – something he would come to regret if she had her way. Silently making her way back to the parlour, Hortense eyed the study door. Slipping into the room, it was a matter of minutes before she came out again – eleven emeralds in their velvet bag tucked safely in her bodice.

Hearing a noise upstairs, Hortense ran to her

252

bedroom where she saw Alice folding clothes and packing them in a large trunk.

'What the hell do you think you are doing?' Hortense yelled at the girl.

Alice quivered as she replied, 'The master told me to pack your things, ma'am.'

'Well you can just bloody well unpack them!' Hortense shouted as she left the room.

With a heavy sigh, Alice began to unpack the trunk and hang the clothes back in the wardrobe.

Hortense stamped into the kitchen and, spotting Jago sitting at the table, she yelled, 'What are you doing there? I thought I said you were sacked!'

Abel stood to face his wife. 'Jago is in my employ, not yours!'

'Are you keeping him on? Even after the lies he told about me?' Hortense was astonished.

'They were not lies!' Jago also stood which gave him confidence to continue, 'I saw you! I saw what you did!'

'You lying little . . .!' Hortense took a step forward with her hand raised to strike the boy.

Abel caught her arm, saying, 'I thought *I* told *you* to get out of my house! Alice is packing your things!'

'Well I told her to put them back!' his wife spat.

Dragging her upstairs by the arm he still held, they entered her bedroom. 'Alice, pack her things, she's leaving today! And you . . .' he poked a finger at his wife, '. . . leave Alice to do my bidding or else you will leave in what you stand up in!'

Nodding to a muttering Alice, Abel let go of Hortense's arm which flew to her bodice, giving the impression of shock. Feeling the little bag of emeralds, she watched Abel stalk from the room and an evil grin curled the corners of her mouth.

'I will send for these things when I'm settled elsewhere, so hurry up, you lazy girl!' Hortense marched from the room, down the stairs and, grabbing her coat from the coat stand in the hall, she walked out of the front door, slamming it behind her.

Finally settled in a hotel room, Hortense fumed her anger. How dare Abel believe a stable boy over her? Even if she was guilty, it was still his word against hers. She had been foolish in her anger by letting Abel know she had taken the emerald, but he was unaware she had stolen the other eleven. Abel did not know where she was now so he would be unable to recover the gems. Abel was angry with her, but he was not distraught which told her his blasted son was still alive. This thought then led her to remember the girls; were they still alive, she wondered. Having no idea where Orpha might be, she knew where she'd left the snivelling baby so many years before. Maybe it was time to revisit the cottage where she'd abandoned Eugenie. Touching again the emeralds in her bodice, Hortense smiled. To ensure everything Abel owned reverted to her on his death, she had to be rid of his children . . . all of them.

CHAPTER 28

Zachariah had gone back to the office in Burlington Passage where his secretary informed him of a visit made by a young boy who was filthy dirty asking for either Mr Buchanan. Being told the boy had not left his name but would call back, Zachariah prayed it was Seth Walker and that his stable boy had not perished in the fire. Certainly, the police made no mention of having found a body in the ashes and Zachariah, noting the horses were missing, was confident now the boy had got them and himself safely away before the house had been claimed by the flames.

Sure enough, an hour later saw the boy standing in Zachariah's office wearing old clothes supplied by the blacksmith's wife.

Speaking to his secretary, Zachariah said, 'I will be out for the rest of the day, and I have decided to find a couple of men to watch over the premises at night. Be assured you are quite safe.' Explaining he would be back before she left for the day, he and Seth strode out and headed for the 'Golden Peacock'. With beer in hand, the boy related what he'd seen on the night of the fire.

'You are certain it was the same woman who visited my mother?' Zachariah asked.

The boy nodded. 'Beggin' your pardon, sir, but your mother didn't get many visitors so I was very curious. I got a good look at that one and I'm sure it was the same one who fired the house!'

Zachariah and Seth left shortly after to attend the police station in Steelhouse Lane where the stable boy gave a sworn statement to the sergeant about what he saw on the night the house in Aston Street had burned to the ground.

Seth Walker sat before the sergeant in the police station in the torn and tattered clothes he had been given. The policeman nodded every now and then as he listened to Seth's story unfold. A young constable sat in and took notes then he waited as Seth finished speaking. Zachariah sat in silence throughout.

'You have any more to add, lad?' the Sergeant asked.

'No sir,' Seth said respectfully.

Turning to the constable, the Sergeant asked, 'Where was it this woman lives?'

Riffling through a stack of papers on the table, the constable replied, 'Buchanan House in Wednesbury, sir.'

'Hmmm,' the Sergeant mused, 'I think it's time to be having another word with the lady. Where can I find you gents if I need you?'

Zachariah said he had a room at the Midland

Hotel next door to his office and would be booking a room for Seth there too, after they had bought the lad some new clothes.

Thanking Seth for coming forward with the information, the sergeant scratched his head as he watched them leave the station. This case was turning out to be a right mess, and he had an unsettling feeling there would be a lot more to it before he could close it and file it away.

Once the room was booked in the hotel for Seth, he and Zachariah went back to the blacksmith's where the smithy and his wife were compensated for their kindness in taking Seth and the horses in. The smithy agreed to keep the horses until such time that Zachariah could retrieve them.

The men then walked into the town to buy some new clothes for them both. As they walked, Seth said, 'I thank you, Mr Zachariah, for taking care of me.' Zachariah waved a hand, dismissing the boy's words kindly and Seth spoke again. 'Do you think they will arrest that woman?'

'I would imagine so now.' Zachariah explained about Jago Morton, the other stable lad, following Hortense and seeing her commit arson and he had alerted the police. 'So,' Zachariah went on, 'if two independent witnesses saw her, I would think the police would have no alternative but to arrest her.'

'Mr Zachariah sir . . .' Seth began tentatively, 'if this woman was Mr Abel's wife, then . . .'

Zachariah picked up the boy's sentence, 'Then what was my mother to Abel?' He saw the boy nod as they walked along the street. 'I always understood them to be married, Seth, but apparently it was my father's one regret that they never were. He couldn't marry my mother because he was already married to Hortense Buchanan.'

'I see,' Seth muttered quietly.

Returning at the end of the day loaded up with boxes of new clothes, the two ate a hearty meal in the hotel before retiring to the bar for the rest of the evening to speculate what would happen next to the woman, who thought she'd got away with the arson attack on their home.

CHAPTER 29

Orpha and Peg looked over the figures in their accounts ledger; they did not have nearly enough to purchase the empty building on Oxford Street. Peg was disappointed but Orpha was sobbing.

'It don't matter,' Peg said, trying to comfort her sister as they sat by the fire in the cottage kitchen, 'we can keep looking. There's bound to be somewhere we can afford, we may just have to wait a while longer.'

'No Peg, I want that one!' Sounding like a petulant child, Orpha apologised to her sister for snapping.

'How long would it take us to get the money together for that building?' Peg asked.

Orpha took up her pencil and worked the figures. Looking up, she said, 'We could afford it by the time we were Methuselah's age!' Both girls collapsed in a fit of giggles.

'Best get to it then,' Peg said after they stopped laughing.

'Yes,' Orpha agreed, 'and, we have to put our prices up.' Suddenly a thought struck her and she

259

added, 'We could find buyers in Birmingham and maybe Ezzie would help out with transportation!'

Peg gave a coy smile saying, 'Oh I'm sure he would.' Laughing together again, the girls settled to their work.

'Speak of the devil,' Peg said with a smile as a 'Yoohoo' sounded at the back door and Edna and Ezzie walked in. Looking at Edna, Peg said, 'Kettle has just boiled.'

Edna clicked her teeth as she muttered good-naturedly, 'I don't know what the world's coming to. I come for a visit and I have to make my own bloody tea!' She moved to set four cups ready for the brew.

Once settled, Edna and Ezzie related their fears about Hortense possibly finding the girls at the cottage, and maybe discovering their father's office in Birmingham. They watched the girls' shocked faces as they told them about Zach's house being razed to the ground.

'What are we to do?' Orpha said in a panic.

'Well, worrying about it won't help,' Edna put in, 'after all, this is just "ifs and buts", we don't exactly know yer mother even knows about you being here.'

Orpha relaxed a little as they discussed ways to keep themselves safe.

Ezzie and Peg went for a stroll and she told him about the building they had looked at and their idea of finding buyers in Birmingham. 'I can transport your products any time I am near, but I can't guarantee dates and times, not knowing where we'll be at any given time.' That was something the girls had overlooked.

Meanwhile, Orpha brought Edna up to date regarding the building and her sadness at being unable to afford it was evident. The woman's heart went out to the girl who worked so hard; life could be very harsh and sometimes it was harder on the good folk. Trying to hide the tears that threatened, Orpha continued to work as they chatted.

Sitting on a bench by the allotment gardens which were bordered by Major Street, Ezzie took Peg's hand. Pulling her to her feet, he led her into the gardens proper. Like a park, it had walkways and plant beds with trees dotted about on the grassy areas, although now the branches were bare. As they ambled along, Ezzie gently steered Peg to a large oak tree where he kissed her tenderly on her cheek. Then dropping to one knee his words came in a rush, 'Peg, will you marry me?'

Looking around and feeling a little embarrassed, the girl nodded as she dragged him back to his feet.

'Thank God for that!' Ezzie breathed through his grin which spread from ear to ear. 'I love you Peg, with all my heart and soul.'

Peg laughed, 'I love you too Ezzie. We'd better go and tell your mother she needs a new hat!' Hand in hand they walked back to the cottage, already making wedding plans. They agreed to a spring wedding which would be a small affair in St George's Church which stood between the market and St George's Parade. Close enough to the cottage, everyone would walk to the church on the allotted day.

Edna and Orpha were delighted with the news that there would be a wedding and their families would be joined. Edna cried buckets at the idea of her 'little boy' getting married. They celebrated with cups of tea and massive slices of cake before Edna and Ezzie said it was time for the off. Hugs given all round, they parted company.

A few days later, Ezzie delivered the first of the ingredients from the girls' new suppliers in Birmingham. Having borrowed a sack truck at the wharf, he stacked the goods in the scullery, then warmed his hands by the fire.

Orpha was due to meet her brother Zachariah at the office and was readying herself for the train journey to Birmingham. They were to go in search of buyers for the chocolates.

Ezzie had a backload to go to Bilston so finishing his tea, he kissed his bride-to-be and set out for 'The Sunshine' at the wharf.

Being assured her sister would be fine, Orpha also left the cottage, heading for the railway station.

Zachariah was waiting for Orpha as she alighted the train. Leaving the platform, they walked into the town together and he passed her a paper. 'This is a list of the grocery shops I thought might be interested in your products.' Walking up Corporation

Street, Orpha checked the paper and stopped at the first shop on the list. Confidently striding indoors, she asked to see the person in charge. Zachariah followed behind and smiled as the shop girl asked if she could help.

'Are you the person in charge?' Orpha asked.

'No,' the girl replied.

'Then you cannot help me. I wish to see the owner or the manager please.' Orpha stood her ground, confident but polite.

Disappearing into the back room, the girl returned with a disgruntled man who barked, 'What do you want? I'm busy!'

'Too busy to make money?' Orpha asked, not put off by his gruff manner. Seeing the spark in his eyes, she went on to explain about her chocolate business and produced a box from her bag. Then offering a sweet from her ever-present jar, she waited. Examining the box, the man chewed the confection with raised eyebrows. Inviting them into the back room, they sat down to discuss business.

Walking to the next place on the list, Zachariah said, 'Congratulations, Orpha, on your business acumen and how you dealt with the man whom you softened to the consistency of your chocolate!'

By the time they stopped for tea, Orpha had acquired ten new clients. Over tea and cake she began to realise how much extra work this would entail, and she had only visited a few streets so far!

'Birmingham City is spread over a vast area and I will need to visit many more times to expand the business. I also know we will need help in the cottage.' She recanted all this to Zachariah who agreed with her every word. Orpha then told him about the building they had looked at in Wolverhampton; his eyes growing wide when she said, 'The asking price is £2,000!'

Over more tea, Zachariah gave Orpha the benefit of his experience in the financial world, and as they left the tea shop, Orpha now had a better understanding of how to deal with Mr Belcher at the estate agents.

Zach returned to the office and Orpha decided to visit with the Toyes before going home.

As usual, Orpha was greeted with hugs and tears of joy. Hetty was ecstatic at seeing her young friend and it was Henry who made the tea in an effort to hide the tear in his own eye.

Orpha updated her friends on the goings on of the last few weeks and said she felt sure it was her mother to blame for all of it.

When it was time for her to return home, Hetty clasped the girl to her bosom saying she should keep herself safe and have nothing more to do with Hortense.

CHAPTER 30

Hortense had taken the train to Wolver-hampton and found the place where she had abandoned her firstborn child. She had watched the girl leave the cottage. So, Eugenie was still alive and living in the same place. That would make things easy when it came to disposing of her.

Trudging back to the railway station, Hortense boarded the train back to Wednesbury. Now she just had to find Zachariah and Orpha. Once she knew their whereabouts, she would get rid of them too. That would just leave Abel.

On her train ride back to the hotel in which she'd been staying since Abel had so harshly thrown her out, she silently fumed at the way her husband had treated her. When his time came to cast off his mortal coil, it had to be something very special indeed. She was going to make sure he suffered before meeting his maker.

Abel was assuring the staff at Buchanan House. 'Despite Hortense leaving, your jobs are safe.' Just then a knock came to the front door. Simmons excused himself from the meeting in the parlour. Opening the door, he nodded to the sergeant and constable from the Birmingham constabulary. Given tea, the sergeant explained his visit. 'Zachariah Buchanan and his stable boy, Seth Walker, have been into the station and given a statement.' Usually staff would be sent out of the room during such discussions, but Abel felt as they had been involved from the start, they should remain. After all, without Jago Morton they may never have found out about Hortense and the house fire. 'Not wishing to step on the toes of the Wednesbury constabulary,' the Sergeant said, 'I suggest you and I . . .' he nodded at Abel, 'plus the constable here, should pay a visit to the local station.' Abel asked Jago to ready the carriage and join them on their journey to the Holyhead Road police station.

Walking into the hotel, Hortense was stopped by the receptionist who said the police sergeant had visited. Hortense nodded and without so much as a thank you, she hurried to her room. How did the police find her here? How did they know where she was? The lad who had brought her luggage from Buchanan House! The little rat had sold her out. He must have told the house staff where he was taking her things, who in turn had told the police. It had been a mistake hiring that boy to transport her belongings, she should have left them behind.

Gathering a few things together, she shoved them

into her carpet bag; she had to move to another hotel now, so she would have to leave most of her things behind. It was no matter; she would buy more after she sold the emeralds that were hidden snugly in her bodice. Hortense decided it might even be better to travel light and keep on the move.

Leaving the hotel once more, Hortense informed the receptionist she was going to the theatre in Birmingham and it would be late when she returned. Seeing the girl nod without looking up from the desk, she stepped out onto the street and made straight for the railway station. She needed to get out of Wednesbury. Trying to decide where to go, she considered her options. It would be a million to one chance she would see Zachariah in Birmingham and she had no idea where Orpha was. The police in Wednesbury would be searching for her. She now knew Eugenie lived in Wolverhampton . . . if she went there she could dispose of the green-eyed girl before moving on.

Increasing her stride, feeling happy with her decision, Hortense bought a railway ticket for Wolverhampton.

Peg had worked hard in the kitchen at the cottage and the boxes of chocolates were piled up when Orpha walked in feeling chilled to the bone. Settling by the fire, she told her sister of her day. 'We have ten new orders,' she said. She also explained what Zachariah had said about the building on Oxford Street. After agreeing the decision to visit Mr Belcher again the following day, they settled into filling the cold slab with trays of chocolate to cool.

Weak winter sunshine greeted the girls as they dressed warmly for their visit to the estate agent the next day. Mr Belcher was pleased to see them as they took a seat in his office. 'Zachariah Buchanan, our financial advisor, has given us instruction on the property we are interested in.' They saw Mr Belcher's eyes widen as he stroked his white beard and listened.

'*The* Mr Zachariah Buchanan?' he finally asked.

Orpha nodded. 'Yes, *the* Mr Zachariah Buchanan, he's our brother.' Clearly Zachariah's reputation had spread far and wide.

'So what are you proposing?' Mr Belcher asked.

'My proposal is this,' Orpha began, 'we have given the bank the money we have in our account as a down payment to enable us to take over the building straight away . . . initially to give it a damn good clean!' Orpha watched the older man nod and she continued, 'We have borrowed the rest from the bank, who will then pay you. Then, as we begin our business, we will pay off the balance owing monthly. I believe it is known as a mortgage facility; all of this was arranged yesterday with the bank in Birmingham.'

Surprised at her sensible suggestion, he asked, 'That's all well and good, but what if your business fails? Where would you find the balance owing then?'

'Mr Belcher,' Orpha said confidently, 'our business will *not* fail. Only yesterday we had ten new orders from Birmingham which covered only a small part of the city. It is my intention to cover the whole of the city eventually before moving on to other towns. I assure you, Mr Belcher, the bank will have their money for the Oxford Street building in no time at all and not long after . . . *you* will have a search on *your* hands . . .' Watching silver-white eyebrows raise Orpha clarified by saying, '. . . because *you* will be finding us our second shop!'

Having signed the papers with the bank beforehand and now with Mr Belcher, Orpha left the office in a daze. With the keys clutched tightly in her hand, she had just bought their first shop!

Orpha and Peg hurried round to the market to buy cleaning materials. They also had a question to ask Lottie Spence, the woman who had a stall next to where Peg had once parked her cart.

Lottie was standing at her stall in the cold.

'Hey up wenches, how's tricks?'

'Lottie,' Orpha said excitedly, 'we've just bought our first shop and we wondered if you fancied working there? It would get you out of this freezing market!'

'I most certainly would! I was thinking this would be the last time to stand the market in the winter anyway. I thank you both.' Lottie blew on her cold hands.

Looking at the sky, the threatened snowfall added conviction to her excitement. Peg explained where the shop was, and Lottie said she would be there the following morning to help with cleaning and painting. When Orpha asked about Lottie's stall, the woman replied, 'Damn the bloody stall!'

Bidding Lottie farewell, the girls rushed round to the shop which now belonged to them; they wanted to get started straight away. Peg immediately began the cleaning when they unlocked the building; they had agreed the shop needed to be ready first then they could start scrubbing down the kitchen. Orpha left Peg to her cleaning and went to the sign writer's office. She knew exactly what she wanted on the sign to hang above their shop door. Agreeing to her request, the signwriter handed her an invoice, which she promised to pay at the end of the month.

Walking back to the shop in the cold winter wind, Orpha realised that Christmas was just around the corner; it was already November and she wanted the shop up and running before Yuletide arrived.

Taking off her outdoor clothes, Orpha knuckled down to cleaning the shop with Peg and said, 'We need to be open in time for Christmas.'

Peg looked around her, shaking her head. 'Don't make me laugh, girl!' she said, 'We'll never be ready in time . . . look at this place! It will take a month to get it clean, never mind painted!'

Orpha looked around too and sighed heavily.

'Well we can try! Come on, between us, and with Lottie's help, we can do it!'

Peg shook her head again and continued her scrubbing. As the light began to fade, the girls locked the shop and wearily walked home. They had an evening of chocolate-making to face before they could retire for the night.

Lottie was waiting for them bright and early the next morning outside the shop with her two daughters, Joan and Hilda. 'Thought a little help might be needed,' she said as they entered the shop, 'looks like I was right!'

They all scanned the room – it was a formidable task to clean, paint and open the shop in just under two months. Besides which, they had to transport everything from the cottage, notify their suppliers of the new address and have new labels printed.

Joan and Hilda Spence set to in the kitchen area, both glad of the work. Jobs were scarce everywhere and they worked in the hope they might be taken on as cleaners by Orpha. However, the girl had other ideas, and when they stopped for tea – Hilda having managed to get the range working – she explained her idea to them all. 'If you ladies help with the chocolate making, we can pay a small wage; Lottie has agreed to be the saleswoman in the shop.' Delighted at this turn of events, cups clinked in the now sparkling clean kitchen of 'The Choc's Box'.

The sisters were totally unaware that Hortense had booked herself into a hotel in the same town they now had their shop, and was busy hatching a plan to rid herself of her first born daughter.

CHAPTER 31

Abel excused himself while Jago ran out to the stables. Walking quickly to his study, Abel went directly to the floorboards knowing instantly something was amiss, for the rug was not properly aligned. Checking the hiding place, he gasped as he realised all of the emeralds were missing. Rushing back to the parlour, he yelled at the sergeant, 'My treasure has been stolen!' It stood to reason Hortense had taken them before she left. As he explained about the emeralds, he watched as the constable added this latest information to the file he carried with him.

Jago drove the others in the carriage and after a lengthy meeting with the Wednesbury police about the thieving arsonist, the case was given priority in this jurisdiction also. Everyone was now on the lookout for the woman known as Hortense Buchanan.

Being driven to the railway station, the sergeant, the constable and Abel Buchanan caught the train to Birmingham while Jago returned to Buchanan House. Abel hadn't seen his son for a couple of days and he was still living in the hotel.

'I will keep you updated,' the policeman said as he left Abel at New Street Station.

Going to the office in Burlington Passage, Abel met with Zachariah and they exchanged news. He agreed hiring a couple of nightwatchmen was an excellent idea. Suddenly he said, 'Zach son, why don't you come and live with me at Buchanan House? We could commute to the office by train!'

'That would make perfect sense, Father,' Zachariah answered, excited about the idea.

Collecting Zachariah's things from the hotel next door and telling Seth Walker to join them, they all set off to fetch their horses from the smithy.

Arriving at Buchanan House, Zachariah was introduced to Mrs Jukes the cook, Simmons the butler and Alice Danby the maid. The staff were shocked at the revelation that Abel had a son . . . by another woman, but they all warmed to the man immediately and anyone was better than their previous mistress. A dewy-eyed Alice was sent to make up a room for the handsome young man with the sparkling green eyes.

Overnight, the threatened snowfall had descended and Orpha wrapped up warmly against the cold the following morning. Trudging through the thick snow, her skirt hem was wet almost in an instant and she felt the cold wetness seep through to her woollen stockings. She noticed how grimy windows held a latticework of frost and the snow had piled up on dirty doorsteps. Passing people in the street, she saw many had no outdoor clothes to speak of. Too poor to buy coats, she guessed their money, what little they had, would be spent on food.

Orpha felt sorry in her heart for the men standing the 'bread line', their shoulders hunched and chins shoved deep into mufflers. She heard their feet stamping and saw them blow on their cold hands. She shivered as she wondered how many of the stick-thin figures would manage to survive until the spring came round again.

Walking on, she brought her mind back to the reason for being out in the cold herself. She had decided to visit the bank manager to seek his advice on pertinent matters such as informing their clients of the new address.

The meeting went well with the manager, who said, 'The bank would be happy to pass on this information on your behalf; a courtesy afforded to our valued customers.' His eyes sparkled at the thought that Orpha might bring new business to his bank by way of her own customers; the box of chocolates given over sweetening the deal.

Having left the bank, Orpha trudged round to Oxford Street to open the shop, having no idea she was being followed. There was more cleaning to be done yet and Lottie would be arriving soon with her daughters to begin whitewashing the walls.

Orpha immediately lit the range and, as it burned, the heat began to warm the kitchen. Lighting the fire in the living area made the whole place look and feel homely. Readying the cups for hot tea she knew the women would need when they arrived, she moved back into the shop area and looked around her, envisaging its look once the boxes of confectionery were in place. Stepping towards the mullioned windows, she turned and stared at the space that would hold her chocolates, the place where customers would stand with their mouths watering. Orpha was lost in her vision of the shop when it was finished, so much so in fact, she was unaware her shop was under surveillance from further along the street.

Peg had loaded the cart with pots, pans and utensils to be taken to the shop, cursing the snow as she did so. Dragging the cart through the snow-covered streets, she smiled to herself; today was the day Ezzie and Edna would be visiting them. Brightening, she thought about her wedding in the spring, it wouldn't be too long before she became Mrs Peg Lucas. Dragging the cart to Oxford Street, her head down against the driving wind, she didn't notice the woman hovering in a doorway on the other side of the street.

Parking the cart outside the shop, Peg opened the door and Orpha came out to help relieve the cart of its cargo. The two girls laughed and chatted as they worked until the cart was empty and they disappeared inside closing the door behind them.

★　★　★

Hortense left early in order to make her way to the cottage but as she walked through the town she caught sight of a raven haired girl. It was Orpha! Hardly able to believe her eyes she followed the girl. Hiding in a doorway she had gasped her disbelief as she saw the two sisters. So, they were both alive, and what's more they had found each other! What were the odds of that happening? How had it come about? Hortense Buchanan stared at the building that now held both of her daughters. The look of shock left her features, being replaced by one of pure evil. The old saying of two birds with one stone popped into her mind as she walked stiffly away.

Sitting in the warm teashop, Hortense wondered again how the girls had come to find each other. Some might say it was inevitable, others might say was it was impossible – either way, they had managed it. The likeness between the two was striking; surely they must be aware by now that they were related in some way. Jealousy reared its ugly head again as Hortense pictured the girls in her mind. They were beauties, there was no denying it, and she snorted her hatred of them into her teacup. She could see nothing of herself in those girls. Mousy hair and brown eyes she'd always known she was plain, but next to her daughters she would be seen as positively ugly! Hortense felt the sting of jealousy bite again which then began to turn to anger. *Bloody girls!* She thought. *Bloody family!*

It looked like they were intending to open a shop, that much was evident, and she wondered what they would be selling. Pots and pans had been unloaded from the cart – could it be cheap household items? Well, whatever it was, if Hortense had anything to do with it that shop would never see its opening day!

Feeling warmer, she made her way back to skulk in the doorway where she had previously hidden from view. She needed to be sure the girls were still there. As she sheltered in the doorway, she saw an older woman emerge and begin to clean the windows. They had help it would seem. Hearing voices, she pushed herself further into the doorway watching as a young man and an older woman passed by across the road. As they walked into the shop, Hortense thought the whole scenario was becoming ridiculously complicated. Turning on her heel, she marched indignantly across the town back to her hotel. This needed thinking about in more detail. She had to make her plans carefully.

In her room, she considered how to be rid of the girls. She also had to find and dispose of her husband and his son. Once she had achieved all this she would go after Jago Morton, the stable lad who had brought her to living in a hotel room.

Joan and Hilda Spence had carried the tins of whitewash into the shop and began scrubbing out the scullery. Edna set to cooking the food she had brought with her from the boat as Ezzie slapped the whitewash on the walls in the shop. Orpha and Peg went back to the cottage with the cart to transport the last of the things they would need. The shop was coming together in remarkably quick time and Orpha was ecstatic on her return to see the signwriter hanging the sign over the shop with a picture, exactly like their boxes, at the side of the name 'The Choc's Box'. Beneath, in beautiful lettering, read, *'Proprietors, Orpha Buchanan & Peg Lucas'*. Orpha had pre-empted the wedding when ordering the sign, she did not want the added expense of having it changed in the spring. Everyone stood outside watching the signwriter do his work; all oblivious to the cold in their excitement.

Congratulated by one and all, the signwriter left and they all trooped inside to toast the business with hot cups of tea. After lunch of boiled potatoes, cabbage and lamb stew, Ezzie fixed the tinkling bell above the door as the girls arranged their utensils in the kitchen.

A little while later the bell tinkled and Edna yelled from the kitchen, 'Ezzie, we know that bell works, so leave the bloody thing alone!' Amid raucous laughter they heard an unfamiliar voice call out. Rushing into the shop area, Orpha apologised to the man who was delivering their till. Smiling widely, he set it on the countertop before doffing his cap and leaving the building, a box of chocolates tucked under his arm. Everyone was surprised, not knowing Orpha had ordered it, and scuttled in to have a go at working the new till. Pressing down the appropriate keys, the price tags popped up in the window at the top of the big black contraption. Turning the large handle on the side, the money drawer flew open. With a shove, it shot back into place.

Whilst ingredients were being stored; boxes stacked; pots, pans and utensils put in their places, Orpha left to visit the newspaper office. Front page news was centred on the first suffrage bill which had been defeated in Parliament. Orpha hoped that paying for an advertisement for their shop for three months would bring its own rewards. They were all set to begin work on the confectionery as she returned. As the daylight began to fade, Orpha suggested they start bright and early the next morning. Locking the shop, Orpha said as they all trudged homeward, 'I will have extra keys made for you, Peg, as well as you, Lottie.' They all tramped home happy with the work they had achieved. They might just be open for Christmas after all.

Hortense waited near the cottage for the girls to return. Standing behind a building on the corner where Raby Street and All Saints Road converged, she rubbed her gloved hands together to warm them. The temperature was dropping with the coming of night and she stamped her feet to beat off the cold. Not having a plan as such, she watched for the girls coming down the street. She could burst into the cottage and . . . No, there were two of them and they were younger than her. She could burn down the cottage with them both inside. That seemed a better idea. She still had the daily newspaper in her bag, but this time she had no lamp oil. Shaking her head at her own lack of forethought, Hortense peeped around the edge of the building. There was still no sign of the girls. Could they have gone somewhere else before deciding to come home? Maybe they were off with their friends. Hortense snorted into the darkness just as she heard voices. Risking another peek round the building, she saw them. Her daughters were walking towards her arm in arm. The jealousy in her was combatted in part by her excitement at knowing she was finally going to be rid of them once and for all.

Watching from her hiding place, Hortense saw the girls disappear round the back of the cottage and after a moment a light shone out through the window. Checking the coast was clear, she hitched up her skirt and ran across to stand in the lea side of the small house. Voices carried on the still air and then laughter sounded.

Enjoy, Hortense thought, *you won't be laughing much longer!*

Taking the newspaper out of her bag, she folded a sheet and slipped it into the gap beneath the back door. Another joined it and another, then she waited. Once they were in bed, she would light the newspaper and would ensure it was burning well before she made her escape.

Standing in the cold for over an hour, she cursed silently. She wished they would go to bed so she could get out of the cold night air. Her fingers could barely move and she couldn't feel her toes, but it would be worth the discomfort when she saw the cottage begin to burn. Deciding she could wait no longer, she fumbled with the box of matches, dropping a few onto the snow. Finally managing to strike a match, she shielded the flame with her other hand and touched it to the edge of the newspaper beneath the door. A slight breeze blew the match out and with a sigh she struck another. This time the paper caught and began to burn slowly. Watching the flame consume the paper, she could only pray it would continue its journey into the cottage. With a bit of luck there would be a curtain hanging by the door to help keep out the cold, a practice used in many old houses. Striding away from the building, Hortense smiled into the darkness. Tomorrow she would know whether the fire had taken the cottage and the girls with it, or whether the paper had gone out before doing its work. She hoped it would be the former.

Orpha woke with a dry throat and an acrid smell filling her nose. Instantly she rose and shook Peg awake.

'Fire! Peg, I smell fire!' she screamed at her sister. Grabbing their clothes and boots, they bolted down the stairs.

'It's coming from the kitchen!' Orpha coughed at the smoke burning her lungs.

'How will we get out?' Peg yelled.

'Come on, out the front door . . . NOW!'

The front door, not having been used in a long time was stuck. The girls coughed as they heaved together.

'It won't open!' Peg gasped.

'It has to, we have to get out! Come on, pull again!' Orpha shouted.

Peg let out a strangled cry as the fire licked the walls and crawled along the old wooden floorboards, an errant flame catching at her nightdress. The cotton began to burn slowly.

With a sudden crack the door sprang open. Grabbing Peg's arm, Orpha dragged the girl behind her and both shot out of the front door and into the freezing night. Orpha threw her sister to the ground and rolled her in the snow to snuff out the flaming nightgown. They shoved their cold feet into their boots and dragged their clothes on over the top of their nightdresses. Having moved well away from the burning building, they held tight to each other as they watched their home engulfed by flame.

'Oh my God!' Peg gasped as the windows blew out with the heat. 'Orpha . . . how? We're always so careful with the fire! How did this happen?'

Orpha shook her head but in her heart she knew exactly how it had happened.

They stood in the snow, clinging to each other, and Peg sobbed her heart out as she watched her home burn. Everything she owned had gone up in flames.

Orpha shivered more from fear than cold; the heat of the cottage being razed to the ground was fierce and she dragged Peg further away from the intense glare. *We could have died in there!* She shuddered in horror as she realised what a terrible death that would have been.

Dragging a sobbing Peg behind her, Orpha felt in her coat pocket. It was still there, thank goodness, the key to the shop still lay snugly where she had placed it. 'Come on,' she said, 'we'll go to the shop, at least we can have a fire there.'

Peg burst into fresh tears as Orpha realised her faux pas. Giving the girl a hug, they stepped double time towards Oxford Street.

Entering the shop, after a cold, quiet walk, Orpha locked the door behind her. Peg lit the fire in the living room as Orpha lit the range. A hot cup of tea was called for and then in the morning they would visit the police station.

Discussing the incident by firelight, Orpha said, 'I am almost certain our mother had a hand in this somewhere, although proving it is an entirely different matter. After we report it to the police we can return to what is left of the cottage to see if anything is salvageable.'

'Oh Orpha . . . it's gone! My home, all my things . . . gone!'

Hugging her sobbing sister, Orpha replied, 'I know, but at least we have each other and we're still alive!'

CHAPTER 32

Simmons watched the cook set out the cups for their mid-morning tea. 'It's odd, don't you think . . .' Beulah Jukes said as she fetched the cake from the pantry, 'that the master had a son in Birmingham?'

'No,' Simmons replied, watching her movements, 'I think it's no wonder, knowing what we do about the mistress.'

Beulah nodded as Alice came through the back door followed by the two stable lads. Sitting around the scrubbed wooden table, Beulah took up again, 'We was just sayin' about Mr Zachariah, and us having no knowledge of him until the both of you come here with the master.' She looked at Seth as she spoke.

'We never knew anything about you lot either,' the boy answered.

'Seth,' Simmons interjected, 'where is Mr Zachariah's mother?'

'She's dead,' the boy lowered his eyes, 'she was killed some months ago.'

'Killed!' Beulah gasped. 'Did they find the bugger who did it?'

Seth shook his head, his tear filled eyes lifting to meet the cook's. 'No. She was a lovely lady . . . she was killed out on the heath . . . police reckoned she was run over by a cart. She died of her terrible injuries.'

Jago's eyes immediately shot to Simmons whose slight frown and imperceptible head shake told him to keep his tongue between his teeth.

'Our sympathies,' Simmons said, 'so they never found the person responsible?' He watched the boy shake his head. Simmons' head rocked slowly up and down.

'Police said Mrs Buchanan was dead when the two men got her home, she never stood a chance,' Seth continued.

'Mrs Buchanan?' Simmons probed gently.

'Yes, Mr Zachariah told me the other day that she weren't married to his father, but Mr Abel gave them his name anyway.'

The discussion continued and before long they pieced together the puzzle of Mahula Buchanan walking the heath in the bad weather; of Hortense Buchanan taking the trap out and bringing it back covered in blood; of both stable boys seeing Hortense set fire to the house in Aston Street; and of her stealing Abel's emeralds.

'What are you saying, Mr Simmons?' Seth asked. 'Are you saying the master's wife killed his mistress?'

'That would be my contention,' Simmons said. 'However, whether by accident or design, it would be impossible to prove.' Now nodding to Jago, he gave the boy leave to impart the information regarding the blood-spattered trap.

'Bloody hell!' Seth muttered. 'I think Mr Abel is well shot of that one!' Then he added, 'Do *they* know?' He raised his eyes to the ceiling as he spoke.

'They are not aware of the incident with the trap, but I think it's time to enlighten them, do you all agree?' Simmons' eyes passed to each person sat around the table. All were in agreement and Simmons said he would inform the master.

Abel and Zachariah sat in the parlour and listened carefully as Simmons related the discussion below stairs. Zachariah cried openly as the butler finished speaking. Abel was fuming and yelled, 'Get two horses saddled. Zach and I will ride over to the Holyhead Road Station and pass this information to the police!' There appeared no end to what Hortense would do in her quest for her husband's money.

Ezzie and Edna Lucas had moored up in their usual spot at Old Limekiln wharf and trudged through the snow towards Oxford Street. Both were surprised to see the girls looking so distressed when they arrived and almost immediately the reason was explicated. Sitting by the fire in the warm living room, Orpha told them of the cottage being razed to the ground. Ezzie held Peg tight as she cried; the only home she had ever known had gone forever.

Orpha said on a sob, 'We have no option but to stay at the shop as we are not in a financial position to find another home; all our money is tied up in "The Choc's Box". There are two armchairs we can sleep in, and fortunately everything we needed for the shop had been moved before the fire had started. But Peg has lost everything; all her mementos of Rufina have been destroyed.' Orpha's tears escaped her dark lashes.

Edna wrapped her arms around Orpha and held her while she let loose her emotions.

'We think Hortense started the fire,' Peg said with a sniff.

'I think you'll be safe enough here at the shop. There are lots of prying eyes in this street; if it *was* your mother, she won't try anything here. I'm going to see Abel and Zachariah when we get back to Birmingham, and they can inform the police,' Ezzie said, comforting the frightened women. 'You just go on about your business in the shop, but keep an eye out just in case.'

Ezzie and Edna spent the day with the girls helping out with the chocolate making in the kitchen. Lottie Spence and her two daughters were informed of the previous night's incident when they arrived to begin their work. They were instructed to be vigilant on their comings and goings from the shop.

Orpha decided she would not wait for the police to be informed at a later time, she was going to tell them today. Ezzie said he would accompany her to the police station and they set off, very much more aware of the people they passed in the streets. They didn't, however, see the woman skulking to the side of a building further down the street.

Hortense had returned to Oxford Street to see who arrived, and whether the girls were amongst them. Anger burned in her when she saw the young man and her daughter leave the shop. Her plan had gone awry . . .

Guessing they would return before long, Hortense decided to stay put and watch the shop. Who else could be in there? She needed to know. All the time she waited there she saw no one come or go until Orpha and the young man returned a couple of hours later. By now Hortense's legs ached from standing but she maintained her silent vigil. Still she waited, trying to decide what to do and where to go from here.

Seeing the young man and the older woman leave the shop after lunch she followed discreetly behind. She needed to know who they were and what the connection was to her two daughters. As she walked, she thought about the cottage fire. With her frustration mounting, Hortense stamped through the snow-covered streets until she reached the wharf. So, the lad was a 'cut-rat'! Watching, she saw the young man help the woman aboard a boat –'The Sunshine' – and that must be his mother.

Walking back to the town, Hortense made a mental list of what she would need to carry out the next part of her plan. The added complication of the two people on the boat vexed her, but she would deal with that first, then she could return her attention to being rid of the Buchanan family.

Later that day, Hortense bought what she needed and set out once again for the wharf.

'There ain't no one aboard, mate,' a voice called out, seeing a figure standing in front of 'The Sunshine'.

'Ar, I know,' the figure called back, climbing aboard, 'I been asked to do a job on her.'

'Fair enough,' the man shouted and went back to his task on his own boat.

The figure moved to the belly of the boat and began to move possessions around. Taking out a hammer and chisel from a tool bag, work began. Finding a suitable spot, the chisel was rammed into the side of the boat and the sound of the hammer sounded as it hit the chisel square on. Pounding away, the figure eventually smiled as a trickle of water was sighted. Moving further down the boat, the hammer sounded again. On and on until each of the four holes in the side of the boat were letting in the dirty canal water. Moving to the other side of the boat, the task was repeated. Satisfied, the figure repacked the tools and climbed back out onto the towpath. Waving to the man who had called out earlier, the figure strode away.

Once more in her hotel room, Hortense stripped

off the men's trousers, shirt, jacket and cap and kicked them beneath the bed along with the tool bag. Dressed again in her long skirts, she went down to the dining room for an early dinner.

Relaxing in her bedroom later, she thought about the boy and his mother finding their boat sinking on their return and her luck at finding the craft empty. She really thought she might be hanging around waiting for the pair to leave. After reporting it to the wharf master they would return to the shop. After all, they would have nowhere else to go! Being 'cut-rats' they would not have the means to stay in a hotel that was for sure. The serving girls would leave at the day's end which would leave the two girls, the boy and his mother alone in the shop. Hortense smiled as she thought *four birds with one stone!* Everything worked out for a reason. This time she had to plan very carefully; she needed to ensure the building burned quickly and fiercely, taking the occupants with it.

Ezzie and Edna walked along the wharf on their way from the 'Choc's Box' in the early evening and saw the melee by their boat. Running on, Ezzie then saw what all the commotion was about. 'The Sunshine' was sinking fast.

Seeing Ezzie approach, the man who had spoken to the stranger earlier in the day explained what he'd been told. 'The bloke said he was on her to do some jobs,' the man nodded to the badly listing boat.

Edna joined them, crying, 'We always do our own jobs! This was sabotage!' Tears rolled down her face and her shoulders heaved as she watched everything she had ever owned disappear into the cold water of the canal. Ezzie paced up and down on the towpath, dragging his hands through his hair.

Stomping along to the wharf master, Ezzie asked that he inform the police, which the man agreed to do. He needed to get his mother out of the cold and told the master where they could be found. Leading a sobbing Edna away, Ezzie said, 'Come on, Mum, we'll go back to the shop. Peg and Orpha will take us in for sure.'

A frightened Orpha heard the banging on the shop door and was relieved to see it was Ezzie and Edna. Letting them inside, she relocked the door and ushered them into the living room. Seeing Edna's tears, she asked, 'What's happened? Edna, whatever is the matter?'

'Our boat's been sunk!' Edna wailed as Orpha gasped.

Looking at Ezzie who nodded, Orpha asked, 'How . . .? Who . . .?'

Ezzie shook his head as Peg gave him and Edna a cup of hot tea.

'You don't think . . .?' Orpha began.

'Yes! I bloody well do think!' Edna snapped. 'I'd lay money on it, it were your mother burned the cottage down, then went over and sunk our boat!'

'But why?' Orpha asked. 'Why would she do that to you? You are no threat to her . . .' Then Orpha dropped onto a chair and said, '. . . But we will inherit everything from Father!'

Peg spoke as she banked up the fire, 'Bloody hell, Orpha! Your mother ain't half a spiteful bugger!'

Orpha glanced at her sister, saying, 'I know, but she's your mother as well, don't forget!'

Peg grimaced at the thought.

Sitting around the fire, the four discussed the events of the last few days.

Peg questioned, 'Do you really think it is Hortense who is disrupting our lives so drastically?'

Edna snorted, 'Yes, I for one, believe it is! That cow has taken everything from us!'

Ezzie said quietly, 'I'm out of work now too.' All eyes turned to him, seeing the sadness on his face. 'There's no work to be had on the land, so where we go from here I have no idea.'

Misery hung heavy in the room until Orpha said, 'Tomorrow I'm going to see Father and Zachariah in Birmingham! I want you all to stay here, and for God's sake be extra vigilant!'

'I'll come with you,' Ezzie said.

'No!' Orpha said sternly, then more gently went on, 'I need you here to protect everyone and the shop.'

Ezzie nodded and silence descended as they watched the flames dance in the hearth. Fire held a different fascination for them all now.

★　　★　　★

Early the following morning Orpha alighted the train at New Street Station and ran through the snow to her father's office in Burlington Passage. Rushing through the door, she saw the nod of the secretary telling her to go straight through to her father's office.

'Father! Oh Father!' Abel dashed to hold his distressed daughter. Eventually stemming her tears, she explained to Abel and her brother what had happened in Wolverhampton. 'I know it doesn't prove it was Mother but . . .'

'But it's a fairly safe bet!' Zachariah concluded.

'Right!' Abel said, 'Looks like we're all going to Wolverhampton!'

Boarding the train once more, Orpha related the tale in more detail for her father and brother.

Abel assured her, 'I will inform the police, who will then contact the other police stations in Wednesbury and Birmingham. They will catch Hortense before she can wreak any more havoc.' He knew he should have returned sooner and the guilt of not having done so weighed him down.

Orpha was not convinced but was pleased to have her father and brother on side.

Going first to the shop to ensure all was well there, Abel and Zachariah went next to the bank in the town.

Orpha said, 'I'm going to the cottage . . . I need to see if there is anything I can salvage from the fire.' Although she was scared, she walked down

Oxford Street, keeping a keen eye out as she passed the doorways of the other buildings.

Eventually coming to the cottage, she stared at the burnt-out ruin, and despair covered her like a shroud. There was nothing left of the little house she had once shared with her sister. Turning away, she made her way back across the heath and into the town. It was then she saw a woman walk briskly up Raby Street. It was her mother, she was sure of it! Following some distance behind, Orpha kept her eye on the woman in front of her, hoping she wouldn't be seen. Keeping close to the buildings, Orpha moved from doorway to doorway where she could hide herself if the woman turned around. The woman turned the corner into Powlett Street and Orpha ran to catch up. Peeping around the corner of a building, Orpha watched the woman walk towards and enter an hotel.

Orpha was unsure as to what to do next. She could go to the police station in Lower Walsall Street and risk the woman leaving the hotel, or she could walk in and confront her. Not certain the woman *was* her mother, Orpha would look a fool if it wasn't. On the other hand if it *was* her mother, then this confrontation was way overdue.

Taking a deep breath, Orpha strode towards the hotel.

'Can you tell me the room number of the lady who has just come in please?' Orpha asked politely. Orpha received a bored shake of the head from the receptionist. 'The lady is my mother and I was late for our arranged meeting.' Orpha crossed her fingers behind her back in the hope the superstition would cancel out the little white lie. The receptionist relented and told her the number. Orpha strode towards the room and stopped outside. Remembering her mother's words of years before, Orpha wondered if she really would kill her if they met again. There was only one way to find out. Taking her courage in both hands, Orpha rapped smartly on the hotel door.

CHAPTER 33

The manager at the bank having been told of Abel's plans, said he would have to confirm these with their Birmingham branch in the first instance. Desperately wanting to use the newly installed telephone system, the manager was delighted when Abel nodded his consent. Explaining to the manager at Birmingham he had Mr Buchanan in his office at that moment who was intending to spend extremely large amounts of money, he was taken aback at the reply. *'Mr Buchanan has wealth to a degree you would never believe. If Abel wishes you to lick his boots you had better ensure you make a good job of it!'*

'Well now,' the manager gave a little cough, 'that seems to be all in order. Please accept my apologies, sir, but it is bank policy we check to protect our clients.'

'I appreciate that you do, sir, and I thank you for your help,' Abel said as he stood to leave. Bending down, he brushed off a little snow still left on his boot. The bank manager gulped loudly as he recalled the words spoken on the telephone.

Hailing a hansom cab, Abel and Zachariah

returned to the shop, asking the cabbie to wait. Zachariah remained at the shop and Abel and Ezzie climbed into the cab and set off for the wharf.

'The Sunshine' had been dragged out of its mooring place by a tugboat and was now resting in the boatyard nearby. It had been placed in the 'graveyard' there. Ezzie sighed loudly as he saw his home on her side, never to grace the canals again. Abel had spoken with the wharf master who now led them to the other side of the boatyard. There on supports sat a brand new seventy-foot-long narrow boat, and . . . it was for sale!

Abel urged Ezzie to look around her whilst he spoke with the master. Ezzie toured the boat with its beautiful deck and fixtures in her belly. An engine would power her and she was ready for the water. The new owner was to name her and she could be launched as soon as money exchanged hands.

'My God but she's a beauty!' Ezzie said as he climbed down the wooden ladder.

'Then it's settled!' Abel said, and going to the master's office, Abel wrote out a banker's order saying the bank had already authorised the money transfer.

Abel felt he wanted to return Edna and Ezzie's kindness as they had helped his daughter in her hour of need. Orpha had been saved by Ezzie out on the heath, he had been told, and they had taken her aboard to care for her as best they could. Despite having lost some of his emeralds, he was happy in the knowledge that the rest were in the bank, therefore he could easily cover this expense which was nothing compared to his daughter's safety. Besides, he felt certain it was his wife who had caused this further suffering, so the onus was on him to rectify the situation. His hate for Hortense intensified as he thought of the heartbreak she was causing.

Giving the paperwork to Ezzie, he clapped the young man's shoulder.

'What?' Ezzie looked at the older man.

'She's yours, son,' Abel said with a laugh. 'Compensation for my wife's actions . . . and yes, I do believe it was she who sank 'The Sunshine'.'

'Abel, I don't know what to say!' Ezzie gasped.

'Don't say anything, lad, just enjoy her.' Abel then led them back to the waiting cab.

Inside the cab, Abel asked, 'What name will you give her, son?'

Ezzie thought for a moment then said, 'The Emerald . . . in honour of your family's eyes!' Both men laughed as the cab took them back to Oxford Street.

Edna cried her thanks into the corner of her shawl as Ezzie told her of their new boat and the name which would be painted on the side as soon as possible.

'Where's Orpha?' Abel asked after the excitement died down.

'Didn't she say she wanted to go to the cottage . . .' Edna muttered.

'Oh Christ!' Abel said as all eyes looked to him.

Rushing out of the door with Zachariah, Abel ran down the slushy street, the snow at last beginning to melt. Hailing another cab, Abel told the driver to hurry to Derry Street. Standing in front of the ruined cottage, they looked around; Orpha was nowhere to be seen.

'We may have passed her on the way here, Father,' Zachariah said, staring at the burnt-out building.

Abel nodded, 'You're right, let's get back to the shop.'

The hotel door opened and Hortense gasped, 'what the . . .?'

Orpha barged past her mother into the room and turned to face the other woman who closed the door.

'Hello Mother,' Orpha said confidently trying her best to keep her anger under control, which had flared instantly even after all of this time and the way they had parted.

'What the bloody hell are you doing here?' Hortense snapped nastily.

'I've come to tell you to leave us alone,' Orpha replied, as she watched the familiar evil grin shape her mother's mouth.

'I don't know . . .' Hortense began.

Orpha held up her hand as she took the only seat in the room. 'Don't even try to deny what you've done, there is proof. You burned down

Father's house in Birmingham; you burned down Peg's cottage and you stole Father's jewels.'

'He was living there with his mistress!' Hortense's face contorted with anger.

'Yes, Zachariah's mother was father's mistress. I'm aware of that fact,' Orpha said, maintaining her composure.

'Yes she *was!* But she is no longer; I made sure of that!' Hortense's anger boiled over.

'You killed Mahula!' Orpha gasped in disbelief.

'It was an accident with the trap, but who would believe that? Besides, it did me a favour . . . one less to have to be rid of!' Hortense was screeching now.

Composing herself again, Orpha spoke quietly. 'And what of the cottage, Mother? Did you know Eugenie and I were inside at the time?'

'Oh yes!' Hortense rasped through her clenched teeth. 'I knew all right!' Pacing the room, she went on, 'I warned you! I told you if I ever saw you again . . .'

Orpha cut off her sentence. 'You would kill me, yes Mother, I remember. However, you came looking for me, I did not seek you out. You see, if I never saw you again it would be too soon!' Keeping her mounting anger under control, Orpha felt her confidence soar to new heights.

Hortense snapped her head up, 'You've grown cocky!'

'I'm a businesswoman now and I have no reason to associate with you further other than to give you this warning. If you persist in trying to harm me, my family or my friends, I *will* seek you out. I *will* find you and I *will* kill you!' Orpha watched her mother's eyes widen and continued, 'Should any hurt come to any of us by your hand, I will hunt you down and make you wish the police had found you first!'

Orpha walked from the room, leaving the door and her mother's mouth wide open.

As she walked swiftly down the street, once round the corner Orpha broke into a run. Her confidence had exhilarated her and the cold air added to it. Flying along the streets, she reached the shop out of breath but proud of herself. She was no longer afraid of the woman who had terrorised her for so long.

Everyone was in the living room, debating on where next to look for Orpha when she charged into the room, a broad grin on her face.

Telling them where she'd been, Abel berated her. 'You were silly to tackle Hortense alone!'

'I know and I'm sorry,' she acknowledged, 'but I think that's the last we will hear of Hortense Buchanan.'

'Somehow I doubt that!' Abel snapped. 'I'm going to keep the police informed.' Turning on his heel, he left the shop.

Hortense sat on the chair that her daughter had not long since vacated. So they were on to her. Orpha now knew it was she who had killed

Zachariah's mother too, albeit by accident. They also knew that she had stolen Abel's emeralds. Her nerves jangled as she wondered what to do next. She needed to sell the gems and quickly, which then provoked another thought. Had Abel replaced the missing emeralds with more? How could she find out? If he had, how could she get into Buchanan House and steal those too?

It would be dangerous, but if she chose her moment wisely it could work. She had no idea how many gems Abel had, but another handful would see her settled and happy – and away from the 'Black Country'.

The very next day, Abel had a telephone system installed at the shop. 'You can speak with me immediately by ringing rather than travel to see me. I will brook no argument,' he told his daughter as the engineer left the premises.

Orpha realised it was the way of the future. She could telephone her orders through to her suppliers now too.

The girls had taken rooms at a hotel near the shop until they were in a position to look for a house. It appeared Orpha's prediction had come true . . . they had heard nothing more from or of Hortense Buchanan.

Abel and Zach returned to Birmingham that same day; work awaited them at their offices, and Edna and Ezzie settled themselves on their new boat which had now sat nicely on the canal manoeuvred into place by crane, overseen by the wharf master.

The shop had opened and business was brisk much to the delight of its proprietors.

Realising springtime was creeping ever nearer, Orpha and Peg took a day off from the business and went in search of a wedding gown. The first day of spring, 21st March, was to be Peg's wedding day and the girls were excited as she tried on gown after gown in the wedding shop in the town.

Orpha looked at her sister as she stood before her. Shaking her head, she said, 'No. Little Bo Peep is not your style at all!'

Peg laughed and tried another gown.

Again Orpha shook her head. The pale pink chiffon lay over layers of net swelling out from the waist. 'It makes you look like a blancmange!'

The one she chose at last was a white silk slip dress with long sleeves and it was covered all over with Nottingham lace which trailed behind into a short train. A fine lace veil covered her black hair and a small tiara held it in place. Simple in its design it was the epitome of elegance.

'Oh yes!' Orpha gasped. 'Peg, you look divine! This is definitely you!'

Orpha realised how silly she had been to be jealous of Peg and Ezzie, and how now she only felt joy for them both.

Orpha chose a long emerald green tulle skirt and jacket which nipped in at the waist; it was the exact colour of her eyes and she chose shoes in matching green.

With their boxed packages tied with string and looped into a handle for easy carriage, they hailed a cab back to the hotel where they were still staying.

'St George's Church is booked for the service and the flowers are on order. Now all we have to do is wait for the day to arrive.' Peg beamed her happiness.

After lunch the girls returned to the shop where the others were busy. They saw Lottie had a room full of customers and Joan and Hilda Spence were working flat out in the kitchen.

The chocolate making business had taken off in a big way and the new telephone was constantly ringing bringing in new orders every day.

Orpha spoke as they worked. 'We need more help in the kitchen.'

Joan answered, 'I have friends who are unable to find work.'

Orpha asked, 'Could they come to see me as soon as they can?'

Joan smiled broadly, 'You bet your life they will!'

Before the week was out Orpha had two more employees in her kitchen being trained up by Peg. The girls learned quickly and their output increased in no time at all.

For all that was going on in the business and with the wedding, her mother was never far from Orpha's thoughts.

★   ★   ★

Hortense watched Simmons, Mrs Jukes, Alice and another stable boy as they stepped into the carriage. She snarled as she saw Jago Morton climb into the driving seat and flick the horse's reins. The carriage moved off down the drive of Buchanan House and out onto the street. Where were they all going? They were dolled up to the nines in their Sunday best clothes and the cook even sported a feather in her hat. It looked like they were off to a wedding.

Waiting a moment in her hiding place at the other side of the garden, Hortense debated. Should she risk trying to break in? Was the danger of being caught too great for emeralds she wasn't even sure were there? In her mind she saw again the sparkle of the gems in her hand, and she made up her mind; this would be her only chance. She had been to-ing and fro-ing to Wednesbury to keep her eye on the house for a while now and this was the first time the property had been completely empty whilst she was there.

Walking up to the front door, Hortense slipped her key into the lock. Nothing happened – they had changed the locks! She wasn't going to give up that easily so slipping round to the back of the property, she picked up and hurled a rock through the kitchen window. Pushing out the rest of the glass with her arm wrapped in her shawl, she clambered inside. Going straight to the study, she flung back the rug and lifted the floorboard. Yes! The box was still there! Highly excited she took out the box and lifted the lid. The excitement of a moment ago turned swiftly to anger as she threw it across the room. It was empty! Swiping the oil lamp off the desk in temper, it crashed to the floor. Looking at the mess, she debated whether to set the oil alight but decided against it. This was her beloved house, one she intended to return to once the Buchanan family were disposed of. Riffling the desk drawers drew a blank, there was nothing there.

Leaving the study, she ran up the stairs and into Abel's bedroom. Checking all around, there was nothing to be found. Walking down the stairs she unlocked the front door and walked out, leaving it wide open behind her.

Fuming all the way back to the railway station, Hortense boarded the train back to Wolverhampton and yet another hotel she had recently moved to. At least if she stayed put she would know where that damned family were! During the journey she thought about the emeralds; they must still be in the bank and therefore they were out of her reach . . . for now. The only way to get her hands on them was to see Abel and his descendants dead. Once they were out of the way, the bank would *have* to give her access to the gems. Then she could sell them and go abroad, somewhere warm and clean; away from the filth and grime of the 'Black Country'. Away from the poverty and disease and choking black smoke. She would find her own little paradise by the sea, and a wealthy man who would shower her with expensive gifts. Someone who would show her the love and affection she had lacked for so many years.

Leaving the station, she trudged back to her new hotel room to plan how to exact her revenge on her husband and all those he called family. She would not be leaving this town until she saw them all under the sod!

CHAPTER 34

Everyone was at St George's Church for the wedding. The staff from Buchanan House in Wednesbury; Lottie Spence and her daughters, plus the girls working in the shop kitchen. Orpha and Edna sat in the front pew and watched a nervous Ezzie as he was calmed by his best man Zachariah. The organ struck up and Abel led his eldest daughter down the aisle towards her soon-to-be husband. As the service began, Orpha scanned the church for any signs of her mother. When she saw none, she relaxed and handed a freshly laundered handkerchief to a quietly bawling Edna.

She had noticed again, however, the tall dark-haired man who had been introduced to her as Simmons, the butler, and he had his eye firmly on her. She blushed and turned back to face the front of the church.

Dressed in their finery, people sat in the pews which had fresh flowers attached to the end of each one. The vicar and Ezzie stood waiting as Abel, in his morning suit, began to lead Peg down the aisle.

Everyone turned to see the smiling girl as she walked sedately with her arm looped through her father's. The light glinted on her tiara, sending out tiny sparkles which looked like diamonds. In the silence of the church, the whisper of silk against her legs sounded like a breath of air.

Then the first sob broke the spell. Edna sniffed loudly as she watched her son waiting for his bride, silent happy tears slipping from his eyes. She hadn't seen him cry since he was a little boy and she was undone. Others in the congregation shed their tears of happiness for the couple as the service was conducted. Then applause sounded as Ezzie kissed his beautiful bride.

The bells rang out as Mr and Mrs Lucas stepped from the church and were pelted with rice. The wedding had gone off without a hitch and Orpha revelled in her sister's happiness. Orpha had booked them a night in the honeymoon suite in the best hotel in town as a wedding gift. As the happy couple set off in a carriage decorated with white ribbon, everyone waved them off before making their way to the hotel. Drinks flowed and supper was provided in the dining room and before long Mrs Jukes and Edna were kicking up their heels to a tune being played on an old piano. Simmons had cast surreptitious glances at the bride's sister – she was a beauty and no mistake! Abel had booked rooms in the hotel for everyone knowing the party atmosphere would go on until dawn. Proved right, Abel and the guests dragged themselves wearily to their beds in the early hours.

People with headaches and hangovers greeted each other in the dining room the following morning. Breakfasts were forced down before the guests drifted away and back to their everyday lives.

Orpha, Zachariah, Edna and Abel lingered over tea as they discussed the situation now Peg and Ezzie were married.

Edna asked, 'Do you think Peg will want to work the boat with her new husband?'

Orpha said, 'I think things will go on much as they have before they were wed.' She explained, 'I am meeting with the accountant tomorrow to see how the business is faring and whether it could stand us buying a small house instead of renting the room at the hotel. Peg can move in with me, and when the boat is moored up, Ezzie can stay at the house and I can stay with Edna on the boat. I know it's not ideal, but at least they can have the odd night together when Ezzie is home. What do you think?' All agreed it was an excellent plan.

The next morning and after her meeting with Jonathon Peasbody the accountant, Orpha went over to see Mr Belcher. The estate agent said, 'I will be sure to inform you of any property I deem suitable that comes onto the market.'

Thanking him, Orpha wandered back up

St George's Parade. She looked at the small church where Peg and Ezzie had been married. The church dominated a massive plot of land which was dotted about with gravestones. Trees and bushes added a serenity to the scene. She walked back to the shop wishing one day she could be married in that church.

Having moved yet again to another hotel, Hortense scanned the article in the local newspaper. She was surprised to see Eugenie had married that 'cut-rat'. Moreover, the bugger had a new boat! Hortense deliberated whether she should take her money and run; leave the damn family to each other. As she folded the newspaper, placing it beside her breakfast plate, she thought of the green-eyed family and their emeralds. She knew, however, she would not leave them to inherit what she saw as rightfully hers.

Twice now she had burned down their houses and twice they had escaped the flames. She had sunk their friend's boat and he had acquired another – no doubt with Abel's help. There *had* to be a way to get her hands on those jewels at the bank. Previously concerned with getting rid of the family, Hortense now concentrated her mind on ways to snatch the emeralds from under Abel's nose. Formulating a plan, she retired to her room to work out the details.

Hortense spoke sharply to the hotel receptionist, 'I wish to make a private telephone call.' The bored girl left her to it. Speaking quietly, she arranged a meeting with the owner of 'The Choc's Box'. Using a false name, on the pretext of being a customer, Hortense requested a face-to-face meeting with Orpha at a bogus address.

'My shop is the last building on the left at the bottom of Major Street. Thank you my dear, I will see you at six o'clock this evening.' Pleased the first step of her plan was in place, Hortense dropped a coin on the counter for the telephone call. Walking into the town she made a mental list of the things she needed to buy.

Hortense waited in the building for her rendez-vous with Orpha. Checking her bag and that she had everything she needed, she watched the girl approach and look at the paper in her hand and then at the building before her. Hortense guessed what she was thinking. Yes, she had the right place but the whole area was dotted with derelict structures. Was someone playing games with her? Orpha moved towards the old building, calling out, 'Hello is anyone there?'

Then Orpha's knees buckled and she crumpled to the ground unconscious.

Abel answered the telephone as he sat in his office in Birmingham. 'Abel Buchanan . . . I have your daughter Orpha.' A gruff voice filtered into his ear. 'I want you to bring your emeralds to the old disused coal shaft off Pond Lane, Wolverhampton at midnight tonight . . . NO POLICE! Then you will get your daughter back!' The line went dead and Abel stared at the receiver in his hand. Replacing it on the cradle at the side of its stand, Abel's brain processed what he'd heard. In a blind panic he snatched up the telephone again and immediately rang the police.

'Someone has kidnapped my daughter!' Abel was beside himself with fear for her safety. 'I was told not to inform you . . . I have to be at Pond Lane in Wolverhampton at midnight tonight!'

Abel was advised to do as he was bid by the mysterious caller; the police would be there to apprehend the person responsible. Abel then rang Orpha's shop and was told she'd gone to meet a new client and hadn't yet returned.

He realised he couldn't get the emeralds from the bank now as it had closed for the day. He had to get to Wolverhampton and find Pond Lane before darkness fell.

Zachariah was with a client and Abel instructed his secretary to pass on the information regarding Orpha's disappearance. Without waiting for a reply, Abel was out of the office on his way to New Street Station.

Once in Wolverhampton, Abel bought a small leather case and as he walked around he collected a few small pebbles, dropping them into the bag. Asking directions, he was pointed in the direction of Pond Lane. Although very early, Abel found the disused mine shaft and sat down on the grass to await midnight. Looking around him, he saw old ruined buildings a little way off and more in the opposite direction. Other than that there was nothing but heathland. Sitting with his head in his hands, Abel sobbed. Could it be he would lose his daughter yet again? All for those bloody emeralds! Quite suddenly realisation struck. Who knew about the jewels other than his children and the bank? Hortense! Was her greed for the green gems such that she would go this far? Was it she who was holding his daughter? If so, where was Orpha being held? Was she in one of those buildings? Springing to his feet, Abel ran from one ruin to the next. All were empty save one which held two police constables. They nodded and, without a word, Abel returned to the coal shaft and waited for darkness to descend.

Once more dressed in trousers, jacket and cap, Hortense picked her way to the meeting place. The moon shone brightly and she could see a man pacing back and forth. Hiding herself behind a crumbling wall, she watched for signs of any other movement. Just then, a small light came from the shell of the building on the opposite expanse of ground. Someone was there! Abel had brought someone with him, and they had been stupid enough to alert her to their presence by lighting a cigarette!

Hortense shrank back into the shadows and left Abel waiting for a meeting that would never take place.

★   ★   ★

The morning after the botched rendezvous, having had no sleep and with a headache from hell, Abel sipped hot tea as he sat in the shop. He telephoned Zachariah and said, 'I will be staying in the shop until Orpha is found.' Replacing the receiver, the telephone immediately began to ring.

Peg answered it and heard someone say they wanted to speak to Abel Buchanan.

'I thought I told you no police!' the voice rasped. 'Now I suggest we try this again, same place, same time, drop the bag and leave. When the emeralds are in my possession, you will get your daughter back! Get it right this time or I will kill the girl!'

'Hortense! Is that you? I swear I will . . .' Abel yelled into the telephone but the caller had already rung off.

Immediately ringing Zachariah again, Abel said, 'I need you as fast as you can get here . . . and bring the two stable lads from Buchanan House with you.' He had no intention of informing the police this time. Somehow the person who had his daughter knew the police were there. Running his fingers over the leather case holding the pebbles, Abel rocked his head back and forth. This time he was taking charge.

A few hours later, Zachariah dashed into the shop, followed closely by the two stable boys. 'Father!' he gasped. 'Are you all right?'

Abel, seeing the concern on his son's face, shook his head. Suddenly he bent double and Zachariah ran to him.

'Father! Are you ill?'

Abel shook his head and grasped the front of his son's clothes with one hand, the other leaning on his own bent knee. Abel Buchanan gasped short breaths before letting loose his despair. His shoulders shook as he wept openly. Dragging in a deep breath, it escaped his lips like a howl from a wounded animal. Peg's hands shot to her mouth as she saw her father's distress.

Zachariah held Abel until his father was spent. Then, slowly, Abel raised himself up. Wiping his eyes on the handkerchief his son produced, he nodded. With a sniff, he said, 'Now then . . .' His words broke the spell the others appeared to be under. 'This is my plan. Seth, I want you to hide on one side of the coal shaft and Jago on the other. I will take the case along with two oil lanterns already lit. I will place the case on the ground and leave one lamp beside it to show its position; the other lamp will lead me away from the area. When you see the bag being retrieved, I want you to silently follow the person. Do not be seen! Hopefully you will be led to Orpha. Should the kidnapper not lead you to my daughter, you are to bring that person back to the shop unharmed. *Then* I will discover where Orpha is being held!'

CHAPTER 35

Orpha's senses slowly returned and she realised she had a rag round her mouth and another round her eyes. Her hands and feet were tied and she was lying on a cold stone floor. Her head ached and the smell of damp around her said she was in an old building. Then she remembered; she had gone to meet someone but the area she went to had seen no trading life for many years. Is that where she was now? Was she still in Major Street or had she been moved elsewhere?

Listening keenly, she heard nothing, not even a bird was singing. Who had taken her? *Why* had they taken her? The fear she felt at first waking was slowly being replaced by anger. Wriggling her feet, she tried to break her bonds, but to no avail. She tried feeling around with her fingers, endeavouring to untie the ropes that bound her hands behind her back. Persevering made her fingers ache and she had to rest them; all the time, she listened for any sounds of her kidnapper.

Thinking about her predicament, she realised if she straightened her body she could bring her hands down past her backside and then, bending double, she could bring her feet through her arms. It would be awkward, but she had nothing to lose in trying. Dragging a breath through her nose, she let it out slowly before she leaned her upper body backwards. Pushing her arms down, her shoulders strained until her muscles screamed their protest. She tried pushing her bottom out through her arms, but the pain caused her to drag in a breath and she lessened the pressure on her arms. Resting a moment she thought the process through again. She had to keep trying! She had to escape before her abductor returned. Making another attempt she pushed her arms down ignoring the agonising strain on her muscles then she leaned her upper body forward and slid her arms down the back of her legs. Bending her knees, she pulled her hands over her feet and skirts and, with her hands now in front of her, Orpha fought to control her erratic breathing. Dragging the rag first from her mouth, she drew in large breaths. Then snatching the blindfold from her eyes, she squinted around her. She was alone and she breathed a sigh of relief. Taking a moment to take a few deep breaths and steady her beating heart, she then freed her feet. Dragging the ropes from her hands with her teeth, and keeping a keen eye out for anyone approaching, she moved quietly to the edge of the building and peered out into the fading light. There was no-one to be seen and gathering the last vestiges of strength left to her she took a step forward.

Slipping silently out of the ruin, she had been held captive in; Orpha's eyes swept the area for any signs of her assailant. Seeing no one, she picked up her skirts and ran. Direction didn't feature in her thoughts; she just needed to get away from that awful place. Suddenly seeing the allotment gardens on her left, she knew where she was and ran like the wind for the shop in Oxford Street.

Dashing in through the door, she fled into the living room where Abel and the stable boys were finalising their plans.

Rushing to throw his arms around her, Orpha explained to her father amid sobs and snatched breath what had happened to her in Major Street.

'I didn't see who it was, Father! I was looking for the woman who had telephoned me and then I was hit on the head. When I came to I found myself tied and gagged!'

Peg provided hot sweet tea as Abel related what he knew of the incident then said, 'We will go ahead with our plan as if Orpha was still missing. We have to catch the perpetrator red-handed.'

They all agreed to inform the police *after* the event this time; after all if it had been Hortense, wouldn't she have been apprehended already had it not been for their bungling of the situation in the first place?

Darkness fell and the three men set off for the old coal shaft. A lit oil lantern in each hand and the leather case tucked beneath his arm, Abel strode out with determination. With Jago and Seth safely in their hiding places amongst the ruins, Abel set the bag and one lantern down as a marker. Looking around, he could see nothing but the silhouette of the old abandoned buildings. All was silent; he could not see the stable boys, but he knew they were watching him. Abel began to walk away from the lone lantern on the patch of waste ground.

Hortense arrived just as Abel had placed the lantern on the ground. She watched him look around before leaving. Waiting until she could see him no longer, she waited just a few more moments. Seeing nothing move, she stole from her hiding place and retrieved the leather case and lantern. Almost at a run, she fled the scene. Abel, the fool, had complied with her orders. Walking quickly, she smiled into the darkness; he had even been kind enough to leave the lantern to light her way home. Being so occupied with her thoughts, Hortense didn't see the two young men who followed some distance behind as they crept from one shadow to the next. With rags tied around their boots their footsteps were silent as they watched Hortense disappear into a hotel.

Hortense placed the lantern on the small table in her room and, opening the leather case, she tipped out its contents. Seeing the gravel stones, she let out a hiss of utter frustration.

'Bastard!' she growled through clenched teeth, then threw the bag across the room before dropping into the solitary chair. Tears of complete misery formed in her eyes as she looked at the gravel on the table again. How was it that girl and her family seemed to beat her at every turn? She should have killed Orpha when she had a chance, she knew that now. Scraping the gravel from the table, she threw it into the fireplace. The girl was going nowhere and no one knew where she was. That settled it, tomorrow would see Orpha Buchanan take her last breath!

Jago Morton took shelter in a doorway opposite the hotel in Hospital Street while Seth Walker, taking the rags from his boots, hotfooted it to the shop to report back to Abel.

Undecided whether to pass this onto the police immediately or wait until the following day, Abel watched Peg bathe the cut on the back of Orpha's head with saltwater and deliberated. Voicing his thoughts, he began, 'We cannot prove the voice on the telephone was Hortense. The boys watched the person they assumed to be Hortense, but in the darkness it was difficult to tell, take the bag and lantern back to the hotel opposite the Wolverhampton & Staffordshire General Hospital, but that person could say they had found the items. With my daughter now safely back in the fold of our family, there is nothing to say it had been Hortense who had carried out the assault on Orpha. I am at a loss. There is no evidence for the police to arrest my wife therefore, Seth, if you would be kind enough to bring Jago back to the shop, there is nothing more we can do.'

'Beggin' your pardon, Mr Abel, but I think we should tell the police. They could go to the hotel and arrest her.' Seth said tentatively.

'I suppose it would make sense, lad. Right, off you go and I'll get down to the police station,' Abel agreed.

Hortense had spent the night in yet another hotel thinking of ways to dispose of her daughter without suspicion falling on her, then she had left the next morning leaving her things in her room. Stomping over the cobblestones, Hortense was belligerent – she was going to kill Orpha Buchanan! On her way back to Major Street, she had stopped and bought a 'gulley', a bread knife with a serrated edge. Anger at being duped by Abel was mounting in her and she stamped her ire into the cobblestones of the street to the last building. Casting a quick glance around and seeing no one, she stepped inside. The girl was nowhere to be seen but the rags and ropes lay on the floor where she had been left.

'God damn the bloody blinding girl!' she growled as she kicked the ropes across the floor. With a huge sigh, Hortense left the building and marched back up Major Street. Now what? With the girl gone, she had no leverage. Obviously concentrating solely on acquiring the emeralds had been a mistake on her part. With the money gained from the stolen gems which she'd sold to the same jeweller almost immediately after acquiring them, Hortense knew it would dwindle fast. Having to move from one hotel to another was costing her, but she daren't stay in one place too long lest the police catch up with her. She *had* to get her hands on either Abel's money or his jewels, otherwise she would end up in the workhouse!

The police telephoned Abel at the shop and said that after going to the hotel in search of Hortense they were told the woman in question had already left. However, should she be found, they would question, and possibly arrest her regarding both the arson and the kidnapping. They would keep him informed.

Orpha insisted, 'Father and Zachariah, you must go back to your work in Birmingham; we will be safe enough as Ezzie and Edna are due back with supplies for the shop.' Father and son acquiesced albeit begrudgingly.

It was a few days later when once more in the shop, Orpha sighed as the telephone rang.

'Is that "The Choc's Box"?' a snooty voice said and Orpha confirmed it was, saying she was the owner and giving her name. The voice went on, 'Miss Buchanan, my name is Travers and I am in Her Majesty's employ.'

'Oh,' muttered Orpha, not believing a word of it. The voice said, 'I am to inform you that Her

Majesty has heard of your little shop . . .' Travers paused and Orpha felt the heat of disdain creep into her cheeks . . . *little shop indeed!*

'Mr Travers, I'm having difficulty believing this. How would the Queen have heard of my shop, may I ask?' Orpha said.

'It would appear she has read of it in the news-papers,' the man said, his voice holding a sharp frustrated edge. 'Her Majesty likes to keep abreast of the news, as I'm sure you are aware.'

Still unsure whether someone was playing a joke on her, Orpha snapped. 'Mr Travers, what exactly can I help you with?'

'Ahem,' the man went on, 'Her Majesty Queen Victoria . . .' Orpha sighed audibly into the telephone – she knew who the Queen was '. . . would like you to make available some of your confectionery.' The sound of the man's sniff ended the sentence.

'Oh my goodness!' Orpha said with the utmost surprise.

'Indeed. In which case, her servant will be at your shop at four o'clock prompt tomorrow after-noon.' The line went dead as soon as he finished speaking.

Orpha wandered into the shop area in a daze. 'Lottie,' she said, 'it would appear the Queen has requested some of our chocolates. Her servant will be here at four tomorrow afternoon.'

Lottie squealed with delight as she scrambled around stacking boxes of everything they produced in readiness for collection.

Orpha sighed at the activity not at all sure the telephone call was genuine and not someone playing a hoax. However, she left Lottie to her task. After all, if it proved to be true, then they needed to have the confectionary ready for collection. Now she needed to await the outcome of the telephone call and pray it was authentic.

The following day at four on the dot a cabbie reined the horse to a halt and a young man stepped into the shop. Orpha was there to greet him. The young man nodded his greeting and placed a small card on the counter, the Queen's coat of arms emblazoned upon it. Orpha's eyes widened as the boy turned over the card to reveal the Queen's signature. So the call the previous day had been honest and sincere.

The boy picked up the boxes which had been strung together and walked from the shop, leaving the card on the counter. Lottie and Orpha exchanged a glance before bursting out laughing when Lottie said, 'He never even paid for them!'

Peg and Ezzie arrived back to the excitement of the tale of the Queen's envoy.

Orpha rang Abel. 'Father, you'll never guess! The Queen sent an envoy for some of our chocolates!'

Her father's voice filtered into her ear. 'Oh sweetheart, I'm so pleased for you! Well done, I'm so very proud of you!'

Some days later, Orpha was busy in the kitchen, dipping small home-made biscuits into creamy chocolate and setting them to cool. This was a new line she was trying out and so far it was proving very popular. She was also in the process of testing new flavours with the chocolate; some she was pleased with, others she disregarded.

Lottie yelled through from the shop that the postman had a letter for her. Looking at the envelope, Orpha took it through to the living room to open it. Reading the letter, her excitement began to mount.

'*By Appointment to Her Majesty Queen Victoria . . .*'

She had received a Royal Warrant from the Queen for her chocolates! Letting out a whoop, she rushed to tell Peg in the kitchen. 'We have received the highest accolade; a mark of recognition from Her Majesty!' Orpha gushed.

'Bloody hell!' Peg said as she dropped onto a kitchen chair.

'Peg, I have to go to the signwriter straight away and to the box factory . . .' Orpha said in a panic.

'Telephone, Orpha . . . you can telephone them now,' Peg said with kind sarcasm. Both girls laughed as Orpha went to order their new sign for the shop and new boxes from the cardboard factory. The Royal Warrant needed to be displayed for all to see.

The following week the new sign was hung above the shop and a reporter from the local newspaper came to see Orpha wanting to write an article on her shop and the Royal Warrant awarded to her. He said, 'You will be able to read the article in the next edition which is out tomorrow.'

Orpha guessed she would have to hire more staff very soon as she tucked the letter and card into a box in the drawer until she could get them framed and mounted on the wall. It seemed at last that things were getting back to normal. Abel and Zach were keeping in touch regularly via the telephone and there'd been no more sign of Hortense. Orpha prayed they had seen the last of her mother.

In her room at the hotel, Hortense thought long and hard about what to do next. Anger, disappointment and frustration fused together, leaving her feeling wretched. She felt weary to the bone and lying on the bed she closed her eyes. The last picture she saw in her mind before falling asleep was the face of Orpha Buchanan – smiling defiantly. Hortense was determined she would wipe that smile off the girl's face eventually.

Orpha and Peg decided to see if Mr Belcher had found a suitable house for them. It turned out he had indeed discovered a massive house for sale which stood in acres of its own ground between the towing path at Shrubbery Basins and the Stour Valley Railway Line. The house had only recently been vacated and the girls were eager to take a look.

Having had a good look around and standing in the hall once more, Peg said, 'Orpha, this will cost an arm and leg!'

'I know . . . but I want it!' Orpha replied, her green eyes sparkling.

'We can't possibly afford it!' Peg retorted.

Looking at her sister now, Orpha related her plan excitedly. 'If we persuade Father to sell Buchanan House we can borrow the money from that sale to buy this!' Orpha twirled on the spot with her arms out.

'What!' Peg was aghast. 'All right, say if Father agrees to your idea, what if there's still not enough to buy this house? What about the staff over there, what will happen to them?'

'We bring them here! Everyone . . . family and staff! There's more than enough room. We could also give Edna a room too if she felt in need of a break from the waterways. We could pay Father back in instalments. It would make far more sense for us all to be under one roof as a . . . proper family!'

It was that last sentence that clinched it for Peg and the girls made their way back to Belcher & Son to look at the paperwork and to brace themselves for the shock of being told the asking price.

The butler, Simmons, sat in the kitchen of Buchanan House and reflected. On their return from the wedding they had found the front door ajar. They had also spotted the broken window. Having had the glazier replace the pane, Simmons paid him from the household accounts. The study was cleaned and tidied by Alice and sitting in the kitchen over their evening meal they had all felt they knew the identity of the culprit who had broken in.

'This woman is becoming a menace,' Simmons had muttered over his teacup.

'Trouble is . . .' Beulah added, 'nobody knows where she is!'

'We ain't safe here!' Alice had wailed much to the amusement of the stable boys Jago and Seth.

He smiled inwardly as he recalled Beulah shooting the boys a desultory look before reprimanding the girl. 'Don't be so silly Alice! Of course we're safe. We have the boys here and Mr Simmons.'

He had tipped her a haughty nod of thanks, and heard the lads giggle again.

'Besides,' Beulah had gone on, 'Mr Abel and Mr Zachariah are here at night too.'

On his return to the house, Mr Abel had gone immediately to the police station to report the break-in.

Just then Simmons' attention was snapped back to the present as he heard footsteps on the stairs into the kitchen and father and son joined the gathering around the table.

'I need to talk to you all,' Abel said, accepting tea from Beulah. 'I believe none of you have family here in Wednesbury?' He watched each shake their head before continuing. 'So there is nothing tying you to this town?' More head shakes. 'Good. Now I have spoken with Orpha and she has suggested I sell Buchanan House.' Holding up his hands at the gasps from the staff, Abel continued. 'Hear me out, then I will ask for your opinions. It seems Orpha has found a bloody great house in Wolverhampton but can't afford to buy it . . .' Smiles turned to frowns as they listened to Abel's next words. 'So, she suggested I sell this place and loan her the money to buy the house. I'm telling you all this as it directly affects every one of us. Orpha also suggested we all move, and that includes all of you, to this new house, which she intends to name Buchanan Mansion. Now, how do you feel about the proposal to move?'

Everyone spoke at once and excited chatter filled the kitchen. Then a few bottles of sherry were brought out in celebration of the impending move. There would be a lot of sore heads the following day.

Mr Belcher was instructed to oversee the sale of Buchanan House and Orpha and Abel, having reached an agreement, signed as the new co-owners of Buchanan Mansion. This would help protect Abel from Hortense.

Each servant packed their own personal effects and Beulah and Alice, with help from the stable boys, packed up the kitchen utensils the cook refused to leave behind. Zachariah and Abel collected their business papers together and, along with their personal things, everything was loaded onto carts. Abel had hired six carters for a couple of days to transport it all to Wolverhampton, along with their horses. Everything else was to be sold along with the house. Nothing would be kept that reminded them of Hortense.

Abel had paid Mr Belcher for the new house and the money from the sale of Buchanan House would be sent to his bank as and when it sold.

Boarding the train to Wolverhampton, Abel and Zachariah watched the excited staff chatter amongst themselves. Beulah and Alice had never been on the train and marvelled at the railway station with its high glass roof. The platform stretched out and before long they heard the engine puff its way into the station. Beulah gasped as the iron giant pulled up with a screech of its brakes. Not at all sure it was safe, she reluctantly climbed aboard. Abel had secured first-class tickets; the ladies' first train ride was to be in style!

CHAPTER 36

Ezzie and Edna Lucas were on hand at the new property along with Peg and Orpha to help unload everyone's belongings and carry them to their allotted bedrooms.

The overawed staff wandered around the mansion familiarising themselves with it while they awaited the carts carrying their belongings. Beulah cried buckets when she saw her new kitchen and instructed Alice to fire up the range straight away. Orpha had bought in a few food supplies which she'd left on the huge wooden table. A nod from the cook to Orpha showed her pleasure at the girl's forethought and deference to the woman who now stood in her holy of holies.

The carts arrived mid-afternoon and the unloading began.

The carters were paid, given a big tip and a box of chocolates each for their wives before they happily left on their homeward journey. They had only been needed for one day but had been paid for two, as per the agreement.

The next few days would see a hive of activity as everyone settled into their new home. New furniture was in situ before they had arrived and Beulah was in her element giving out orders like an army general. Amid the flurry of excitement and the bustle at the new house, no one noticed the furious woman watching from the canal towpath which lay to the west of the property.

With the staff downstairs in the kitchen, the others sat in the parlour and listened as Orpha voiced her concerns about lack of space and staff at the shop.

Peg argued, 'What with still paying the mortgage on the shop and now being in debt to Father for the loan to buy the mansion, we can't possibly afford to expand the business further!'

Abel watched the spark die in Orpha's eye and his heart ached to see her so unhappy when just hours before she had revelled in everyone's delight at their new home. The girl only ever thought of others, never herself.

'I may have the answer if my three children are in agreement,' Abel said. 'As you know, I have a fortune in emeralds in the bank. I am not boasting my wealth . . . I've told you already how I got those stones. They are your inheritance when I die. However, when I'm gone I won't see the pleasure on your faces, so what I propose is this. I will give each of you one emerald to do with whatever you wish.'

'Father!' Orpha gasped. 'We can't . . .! They belong to you!'

'No child, they belong to you, all of you. I'm just holding them in safekeeping for you.' He smiled at his youngest daughter. 'I can either give you the gem itself or I can sell it on your behalf and give you the money. They are worth a great deal and how you spend that money is up to you.'

'Well, I'll have the money please, Daddy!' Peg said in a little girl voice. Everyone fell about laughing and the tension was broken. It was agreed Abel would sell three of his emeralds; the money given to each of his children.

Zachariah and Peg planned to bank their money while Orpha decided to see if she could open another shop.

Peg spoke up and stunned everyone. 'Orpha, I want you to take my name off the sign at the shop. It belongs to you. I still intend to work alongside you, but I want you to put me on a wage.'

'No!' Orpha cried, rushing to her sister. 'I can't! Peg you've worked so hard for this . . . it isn't right!'

'It is right,' Peg said softly, 'this was your dream and I'm so happy to be living it with you but . . . there will come a time when you will have to do without me.'

'Why?' Orpha asked, tears streaming down her face.

'Because I'm going to have a baby!' Peg said quietly as she shared a beaming smile with Ezzie.

Excitement abounded in the parlour as everyone congratulated Ezzie and Peg on their happy announcement. Edna cried into her shawl and even Orpha, who would be the most affected, was jubilant. Abel clapped his hands for silence.

'I will be putting some money into a trust fund at the bank for my grandchild! Now, let's all have a drink to celebrate!'

Orpha ran down to the kitchen rather than pull the bell rope. 'Everyone! Come upstairs . . . oh and glasses for yourselves as well as us please, Mrs Jukes! Simmons, we need wine please and lots of it!'

'Certainly, ma'am,' the butler replied, giving her a beaming smile.

Orpha realised as she made her way back to the parlour that her heart was beating fast, and it wasn't from running to the kitchen – it was from the smile Simmons had sent her way.

Looks of puzzlement passed between the staff members as Beulah and Alice busily loaded trays with glasses which they found in a cupboard, and Simmons unpacked the wine bottles.

Upstairs, Abel poured wine for everyone then made a toast. 'Raise your glasses please to Orpha getting her new shop.' All toasted as Abel spoke again, 'Raise again please to Peg and Ezzie and the next addition to our family . . . Baby Lucas!' Edna's tears ran free once more.

Mrs Jukes choked on her wine and Alice banged her on the shoulders. 'Enough!' Beulah shouted, getting her breath back. 'I want to be alive when the new baby arrives!'

The wine flowed and all but Peg retired to bed a little worse for wear. She was happy enough without the wine and settled for the night wondering if she would have a boy or girl. Either way, she determined she would certainly be a better mother than Hortense and would strive to be as good a mother as Rufina had been to her.

The light began to fade as Hortense Buchanan stared through her opera glasses. Even from the towpath, with this aid, she could see directly into the parlour. Wine . . . were they celebrating? Seeing the staff there too, glasses in hand, she deduced they were indeed celebrating something. What was it? The new house maybe?

Hortense snorted as she shoved the opera glasses into her bag, and with one last disdainful look at the mansion, she strode off.

As she made her way back to the hotel, her thoughts whirled. Bloody family! Here I am having to live in a fleapit of a hotel because my money is dwindling and they are kicking up their heels in a mansion! And . . . fraternising with the staff no less! The injustice of it all caused her to stamp her feet as she walked, taking out her temper on the cobbles.

Trying to settle in her uncomfortable single bed later that night, Hortense determined to discover the reason behind the family's celebrations. Turning on her side, she harrumphed into the darkness.

Up bright and early, Hortense watched again

from the towpath as Abel rode away from the mansion. *Now where was he off to? Couldn't the damn family stay in one place? I'm spending my life following the buggers around!* Hortense sighed as she debated what to do now. *What I need is a horse!* Striding away, she made for the smithy where Steelhouse Lane and Portland Place intersected with Bilston Street. Despite running out of money Hortense hired a horse and saddle. She had to know which way Abel had gone. Back to Buchanan House in Wednesbury or off to Birmingham? Walking the horse through the streets, she surmised he may have gone to the latter . . . which meant the bank!

After all, that was all that was left to him in the city. Quite suddenly she realised what she had seen in the house the previous night. The staff . . . the staff from Buchanan House! Why had Abel moved them here? Had he sold her lovely house? Temper flaring at the thought, she urged the horse on. If he *had* sold the house, this time there would be no mistakes . . . she *would* kill him!

Abel withdrew his three emeralds from the bank. He could either catch a train to London to sell them or he could check their worth with the Abyssinian Gold Jewellery Company in Corporation Street. He decided on the latter. Paying a young lad to hold his horse, with the promise of more money later, Abel stepped into the massive shop. The owner strode towards him hand extended in greeting. Abel explained the reason for his visit.

'Emeralds you say?' the man queried. Abel nodded. 'How very strange. I don't often see them in here, but a lady sold me one a while back, then she brought in some more some time later.'

Abel's ears pricked up. 'Can you remember what she looked like?'

'Yes sir, an older woman with brown hair and a scowl that could sour milk!'

'How much did you pay her for them?' Abel asked sure now that it must be Hortense who had sold the man the gems.

'I can indeed! Five hundred pounds each and very pleased to do so,' the man grinned.

'Well I have three emeralds, and don't even think to offer me the same price, my London dealer will pay a lot higher for them.'

'Sir!' The man looked at Abel aghast. 'We are businessmen . . . let me take a look at what you have and we can discuss the matter.'

Dropping the emeralds onto the counter, the man gasped as he picked up his magnifying glass. Studying each stone carefully, he weighed each one. Giving the usual patter about colour, clarity, cut and inclusions, which Abel had heard before, the man sighed. Looking at Abel, he said, 'Sir, I will not bandy words with you, I want these stones! I am prepared to offer you . . . four thousand pounds each.'

'Is that your best offer?' Abel said, picking up

the emeralds and dropping them back into their velvet bag.

'Erm . . .' Imagining the gems leaving with the man who stood before him, the owner of the shop quickly rethought his offer. 'I can stretch to five thousand each, but not a penny more!'

Abel looked at the small bag in his hand as if considering the offer before looking back to the man. It was a much better price than he'd expected. Holding out his hand, he said, 'Done deal.'

They shook and the owner quickly telephoned the bank for them to supply the money from the shop's account to Mr Buchanan, saying he would be bringing along a signed authorisation.

Abel gave the lad outside sixpence for holding his horse and trotted round to the bank, laughing as he went. Out of Hortense, the owner and himself, *he* had had the better deal!

Hortense watched as Abel came out of the shop she had visited to sell her emeralds. So that was what he was up to! He was selling off his gems! Was he spending too much and topping up with finances from the sales? Hortense grinned, his children were bleeding him dry! Her grin turned to a scowl as she realised it would be less for her to get her hands on. It was definitely time to free herself from the Buchanans, but how?

Sitting in the tea shop with its pretty tablecloths and china, Hortense recalled her past efforts. She had tried to poison Abel with the death cap mushrooms . . . and failed. She had burned down his house in Birmingham, but he and his son were not there at the time . . . another failure. She had razed the cottage to the ground hoping Abel's daughters were inside . . . a further failure. She had tried to kidnap Orpha in exchange for the emeralds . . . the final failure. Her one success was getting rid of her husband's mistress, albeit by accident. It had all seemed so easy in the beginning but Abel had turned her world upside down when he threw her out. Now greed had her by the throat and would not let go. She *had* to find a way of getting those other emeralds! With a loud sigh, she knew she was running out of options. Although fire was her preferred method, setting the mansion alight was too risky; there were far too many eyes watching.

She could try going to the bank – she could walk in bold as brass and tell them she wanted to take out the emeralds on Abel's behalf. It was worth a try, the least they could do would be to refuse her. Knowing Abel had visited the bank that very morning, she knew she would have to wait a while longer. In a few days she would see the bank manager . . . in a few days she hoped to be richer than she ever thought possible.

CHAPTER 37

Mr Belcher explained, 'The Toyes are selling their shop in Upper Priory in Birmingham. Unfortunately they have had no takers in the time it has been on the market. Maybe, if you visit, you could reach a reasonable agreement concerning the asking price.' He gave Orpha a mischievous wink.

Returning his smile, she said, 'I will indeed visit, it's unbelievable that shop has not been snapped up. I learned of its being on the market some considerable time ago but was unable to make an offer then.'

Thanking him, she left the office and headed for the railway station. On her train journey, her excitement mounted at the prospect of possibly owning another shop. Not least the very shop where this had all begun and helping her friends the Toyes out in the same instance.

Arriving at New Street Station, Orpha pushed her way through the throng of people and walked briskly to Upper Priory.

'Orpha! It's so nice to see you, wench!' Hetty Toye raced around the counter to wrap her arms around the girl. 'My, look at you! You are a sight for sore eyes and no mistake!'

Sitting with tea in the living room, Orpha put her suggestion forward. 'I need to buy another premises now. The Royal Warrant has seen the business prosper at an unbelievable rate!'

Henry Toye patted her hand and whispered, 'We are so proud of you, girl.'

Orpha smiled and continued with, 'Thank you. None of this would have been possible without you two. Now, I know you both wish to retire and move to live by the sea.' She watched them nod in unison. 'So, my proposal is to buy your shop. This will mean you can have your new home and I can expand my business into Birmingham . . . What do you think?'

Hetty's tears of joy soaked the corner of her apron, and with fresh tea to celebrate, the deal was completed between them. Orpha gave them a good price in an effort to repay their generosity and kindness. She spent the rest of the morning listening to the Toyes' excited plans of achieving their life-long dream of retiring to the seaside. Orpha left the excited couple with a promise to visit them for a holiday once they were settled in.

Visiting the Servants' Registry Office in Scotland Passage, Orpha hired a cook to make the chocolate, two serving girls and four more to work under the cook's instructions in the new shop.

Visiting the Northern Flour Supply Company

in Coleridge Chambers, she requested them to supply the shop in Upper Priory as they did in Wolverhampton. Birmingham Dairy Company in Haydon Chambers was given the same request, as were Cadbury Bro's for the cocoa powder. She ordered a new telephone system to be installed in the new shop, so the staff could contact her easily in the event of any difficulties.

Orpha went to order two new signs for the shops in Wolverhampton and Birmingham.

'By Appointment to Her Majesty Queen Victoria'
Orpha Buchanan, Confectioner
'The Choc's Box'

On the train home, she thought about how she had made the money given to her by her father stretch a long way, and now it was up to her to ensure her businesses thrived.

Orpha had found a factory which made up and delivered the petit fours cases, so she and the workers no longer had to make up the wax ones by hand. This now freed up her staff to concentrate on the chocolate making. Everything was running smoothly at the Wolverhampton operation and other than meetings with her accountant, Orpha had time to spare. Using this time wisely, she and her head cooks had experimented with new ideas for improving her product. Her shop window displays were changed often and at times such as Christmas and Easter she determined to try out new ideas. New tin moulds were designed and pretty wrappers and ribbons adorned her specialty boxes. Now she could do all this in her new shop in Birmingham.

Orpha's thoughts roamed again as she sat in the parlour of Buchanan Mansion. She was happy dividing her time between the shops, working with the chocolate makers, and keeping a check on her finances via the bank. She was becoming a very wealthy young woman, but as time passed Orpha felt she was lacking something in her life. Would she find herself a man to share her life? How would she ever meet such a man? Her life was taken up with her work and socialising was not something she did. Maybe it was time to make the effort.

Then she found herself thinking again about Simmons. Something she was doing more and more as time went on. He was handsome and his eyes held a constant mischievous twinkle. Tall and straight, he was always immaculate. His smile was infectious and again she felt her pulse rate quicken. With a huge sigh, she knew it could never be between them. She was the mistress and he was the butler and any romantic notions she had about him must be pushed firmly out of mind. Try as she might she was finding this virtually impossible now they were all living under one roof and she was seeing him every day. No, she realised she must concentrate fully on her work in an effort to beat off the palpitations she felt each time she saw Simmons.

★   ★   ★

Hortense stood on the railway platform in Wolverhampton watching the girl with the green eyes. Pushing her way through the crowd, she hid amongst the people standing behind Orpha. The platform was busy with folk pushing and shoving in order to be first on the train when it arrived. Hearing the train whistle sound, Hortense prepared herself. If she timed her actions properly, she would be free of at least one member of that family. Watching the train approach, a murmur of excitement ran through the throng of people as they jostled for a prime position. The train slowed and Hortense moved forward, pushing the people in front of her. The momentum spread and Orpha was now on the very edge of the platform with people at her back and on either side of her. *One more push!* Hortense watched the train moving towards her, belching out steam on its approach. She took two steps forward, making the woman in front of her do the same. She watched the scene as if in slow motion as Orpha teetered on the edge of the platform before tipping forward. A loud scream sounded and Hortense closed her eyes for the briefest moment. Opening them as gasps sounded, she saw Orpha in a young man's arms.

What . . .! How . . .? The interfering man had prevented Orpha from falling onto the tracks and being crushed by the big iron train now at a hissing standstill.

Hortense ran away feeling angry at herself and

disgust at the young man. For God's sake! Why would that girl just not die?!

Sitting in a tea shop, she annoyed other customers by tapping the teaspoon on the saucer. Complaints were made to the waitress who quietly asked Hortense to refrain from tapping. In no mood to bandy words with the girl, she threw the spoon across the room as all eyes turned to her. She walked out of the shop as everyone stared. The waitress apologised to her customers and then muttered, 'She never even paid for her tea!'

Hortense couldn't believe her bad luck. What was it about Abel's family that saw them escape her at every turn? Catching the next train to Birmingham, she fumed inwardly before dismissing the incident from her mind. With her money just about to run out, she had a bank to visit.

'My name is Ashley Rochester,' the young man said after ensuring Orpha was all right.

'Thank you, Mr Rochester, I am Orpha Buchanan,' she said quietly, desperately trying to control her shaking body.

'My God but that was a close thing! We almost lost you there, Miss Buchanan,' he said with a dazzling smile.

Only now did Orpha look up at the man who had saved her from certain death. Chocolate drop eyes, which sheltered beneath hair almost as black as her own, looked back at her. A lopsided grin showed even white teeth and Orpha felt the stirring within her. He was strong, for hadn't he just plucked her out of thin air with the swing of just one arm?

'Indeed,' Orpha gasped as she lowered her eyes, all at once realising she was blatantly staring at him.

'Miss Buchanan, if you would allow, may I buy you a cup of tea . . . to steady your nerves of course.' He gave a small theatrical bow, making her smile despite the shaking that had overtaken her.

'Mr Rochester . . . that would be very nice, thank you,' she replied. His dazzling smile and her terrifying experience of almost being crushed beneath the train wheels had her forget all propriety regarding first meetings with strangers, especially men.

Parting the crowd, Ashley led Orpha out of the station and into the nearest tea shop. She began to calm, and chatting over tea she explained she was on her way to her shop in Birmingham when the incident occurred. She shuddered at the memory. Telling him of her businesses, he informed her he often shopped at 'The Choc's Box'. Orpha was surprised and delighted and as the afternoon wore on they laughed and talked easily in each other's company.

Realising how time had fled, Orpha decided to return home rather than visit the shop. There was always another day. Ashley Rochester said, 'I insist on walking you home; you are still very pale, Miss Buchanan, and I fear for your safety.' On their arrival, Ashley whistled softly through his teeth as he gazed up at Buchanan Mansion.

'What a beautiful house you have,' he said as they neared the front door, which was opened by Simmons.

'Please come in, Mr Rochester, and meet my family,' Orpha smiled.

Over yet more tea in the parlour, the young man was introduced to everyone. Orpha related his heroic action at the railway station and he was inundated with thanks, and then with questions from Abel.

'Did you see what happened Mr Rochester?'

Ashley nodded, saying, 'For all the people on the platform waiting, I saw a woman gradually moving forward. The mutters of disgust from others as she pushed her way through was what drew my attention in the first place.'

Abel frowned and asked, 'Can you remember what she looked like . . . can you give us a description?'

Ashely nodded. 'She was a middle-aged woman with brown hair and a fierce scowl!'

Abel instantly knew who it was the young man had described. No one could scowl like Hortense Buchanan!

Ashley Rochester rose to leave and turning to Orpha, he asked, 'May I call on you again, Miss Buchanan? I would like to assure myself of your well-being.'

Fire burned her cheeks as the blush rose to her

hairline and Orpha nodded shyly. 'You may, Mr Rochester, although you should be aware I spend most of my time at my work. Running two shops keeps me very busy, as you can imagine.'

After Rochester left, Abel warned the family to be aware. 'It appears my wife is again showing her evil nature. It is my contention it was Hortense who tried to force Orpha off the platform. However, I will report the incident to the police, therefore diligent observation is imperative to ensure everyone's safety.' Glancing at his youngest daughter, Abel felt that, if Mr Rochester had any say, she would be spending less and less time alone.

Ashley sat once more in the tea shop congratulating himself. He had read in the newspaper of Orpha Buchanan's success with her business and after discreet enquiries had discovered she stood to inherit a very large sum of money.

Visiting 'The Choc's Box' in Birmingham, he had been surprised at just how well her business was doing. Having spotted her in the shop, he had followed her home without being seen. He had gagged at the size of the house as he stared from the canal towpath. Keeping watch, he had followed her to the railway station, hoping to find a way of introducing himself. Little did he imagine it would be by saving her from being pushed beneath a steam train.

Smiling inwardly Ashley was pleased he had

finally met the woman he had targeted to bring him a fortune. Now all he had to do was marry her and his money worries would be over. Once they were wed, all of Orpha Buchanan's wealth would come to him by law!

CHAPTER 38

At the Capital & Counties Bank in Corporation Street, Birmingham, Hortense sat in the office with the manager, Mr Cunningham.

'I'm very sorry, Mrs Buchanan, but without a letter of authorisation from your husband, we cannot possibly agree to your request,' the manager said, trying to avoid the woman's glare.

'This is ridiculous!' Hortense snapped, 'You know who I am! I don't see what the problem is!'

'The problem, madam, is that both the emeralds and the money are in your husband's account, which means . . . you do not have access to it!' Mr Cunningham's calm demeanour changed at the woman's attitude.

'My husband will hear of this, sir, you can be sure of it!' Hortense stood and the cadence in her tone rose.

'If Mr Buchanan determines I have made an error in judgement, I would be happy to apologise to you both, but for the moment I stand by my decision. If you return with a letter of authorisation signed by your husband I'd be glad to grant your request. I'm sorry I have been unable to help you today . . . now if you will excuse me . . . I have another meeting.' Mr Cunningham rose from his seat, signifying the meeting was at an end.

Hortense's anger was barely containable as she stamped back to New Street Station. The man had dismissed her! How dare he do that to her! He would give her neither the stones nor the money. After all this time she was no further towards achieving her goal of being a rich widow. Maybe it was time to give up her quest for the emeralds. But then most of her money had been spent on hotels as she continued to dodge the police, for she felt certain they would be on her trail. Maybe she should go cap in hand to Abel, he was her husband after all. The thought was bitter in her mind as she rode the train back to Wolverhampton where she would change her accommodation once more.

Over in Birmingham, Orpha was helping out at the shop when the doorbell tinkled. Looking around the line of women waiting to be served, her heart fluttered. Ashley Rochester stood patiently at the end of the line of customers smiling broadly.

The handsome Mr Rochester watched Orpha as she smiled at each person she served. Her green eyes flashed as she finally looked into his brown ones and they smiled a silent greeting.

'Mr Rochester, how nice to see you again,' she said quietly.

'How are you, Orpha, fully recovered I hope?'

The girl flushed at his bold use of her Christian name; it rolled off his tongue so well.

'I am indeed, thank you for asking,' she said, suddenly feeling shy in the presence of the serving staff and other customers now entering the shop.

Seeing her eyes swivel to the rapidly filling shop and her discomfort at keeping people waiting, he asked for two boxes of confectionery; one of chocolate and one of fudge. He watched as she deftly tied the boxes together with string, making a small loop at the top as a handle. Paying for his purchase, Ashley hovered before saying, 'Orpha would you consider having dinner with me this evening?'

'That would be very nice, thank you Ashley,' she said, her cheeks flaming red at her own forwardness.

'Good. I will collect you at eight . . . you will be home by then I take it?' His smile disarmed her as she smiled and nodded. 'Until eight then.' With a wave he was gone from the shop.

Orpha struggled to concentrate for the next hour and eventually decided to go home and spend a little time with her family before preparing herself for her evening out with the delicious Mr Rochester.

Why did the young man affect her so? She felt the blush rise to her cheeks as she wondered whether she might be married to the man at some point in the future. Orpha felt Peg's eyes on her as she looked up. Did her sister know what she was thinking? Another blush rising to her hairline, she saw Peg smile. Yes, her sister knew her thoughts.

They had been close since the day they first met and nothing had changed.

'One day,' Peg said with a knowing smile.

'Maybe,' Orpha replied, 'but not for a while yet. I have plans for my life, Peg, and right now they don't include a husband or family.'

'What plans?' her sister asked.

'I want to expand the business . . . I'd like my own factory to make the chocolate to supply the shops . . . maybe open another couple of shops too!' Her excitement at the prospect was clear.

'Whoa! Hold on there, you've only just opened in Birmingham, where else were you thinking of having shops?' However, Peg began to feel caught up in her sister's excitement.

'Oh, Wednesbury, Darlaston, Bilston . . . there are so many towns; it would need some research, but I'm sure I could make it work!' Orpha was now in full swing. 'If I opened a factory here or in Birmingham . . . or both!'

Peg held up her hands, 'All right . . . one step at a time!'

'I have a meeting with Jonathon Peasbody the accountant tomorrow. Peg, why don't you come with me? It would do you good to get out and you would benefit from the fresh air!'

The girls agreed to the outing the following day and Orpha skipped off to make herself beautiful for her evening out.

★   ★   ★

Ashley Rochester arrived promptly at eight and Orpha was waiting for him. She was dressed in a burgundy velvet suit, the jacket nipped into the waist and the skirt hem rested on the top of her burgundy shoes.

Simmons held the door as Ashley stepped into the house. 'Madam is in the parlour, sir, if you will follow me.'

Everyone greeted the young man as he walked into the room. Kissing the back of Orpha's hand, he unwrapped an orchid corsage and placed it on her wrist. 'I had thought to have dinner at Michelle's, the new restaurant on Corporation Street, then we could take in the ballet at the Grand Theatre,' Ashley said.

'That sounds wonderful!' Orpha gushed as he took her elbow to lead her from the room.

Looking at Abel, he said, 'Don't worry, sir, I will have your daughter home safe and sound by midnight.'

Abel smiled at the quip and watched the couple leave.

Turning to Peg, Abel said, 'I wonder if I'll be paying for another wedding before too long?'

'Quite possibly, Father, but not for a while. Orpha has set her sights on owning her own factory!' She laughed as her father gasped his surprise.

'You look beautiful,' Ashley said as he helped Orpha alight the carriage outside the restaurant.

Thanking him, she looked up at the building

they were to eat in. It had only recently been opened and she was excited to see inside.

Taking her elbow, he led her inside and they were shown to their table. Wine was ordered and they chatted over the menus before giving their orders.

Orpha looked into the twinkling brown eyes and felt her heart skip a beat. Ashley Rochester was as handsome as the day was long.

They chatted comfortably throughout the meal, Orpha answering his questions about her life and business. She liked that he wanted to know all about her.

Ashley paid the bill and they strolled along to the theatre. He produced the tickets and they were led to a box where they could look down and have a perfect view of the stage.

Orpha was impressed that Ashley had gone to so much trouble to ensure their evening out was a success.

After a few moments the gas lamps on the walls dimmed and the orchestra in the pit began to play. The lamps lighting the stage were turned up and the ballet began. Orpha watched in amazement as the dancers held their bodies rigid whilst standing on the tips of their ballet shoes.

As the music and dancing came to a dramatic close, she caught her breath and her tears welled. Ashley gazed into her eyes seeing the tears making them glitter and sparkle as the wall lamps grew brighter once more.

She laughed as she clapped the performers along with the rest of the audience.

Ashley led her from the theatre to a waiting cab and helped her aboard. All the way home they talked and laughed.

'Thank you for a wonderful evening,' Orpha said as the cab stopped outside her home.

'It was you who made it wonderful, Orpha, please say you will see me again,' Ashley asked, helping her out of the carriage.

'I'd like that very much,' Orpha nodded.

Ashley took her hands in his and turning them he kissed each of her palms. 'Goodnight, beautiful lady,' he said quietly.

'Goodnight Ashley,' Orpha said on a breath.

The next morning Orpha told her sister all about her evening with Ashley as they walked to see Jonathon Peasbody. The wily accountant gave the girls a projected forecast of the business. 'If the shops continue to do as well as they currently are, then the possibility of setting up a chocolate-making factory is a distinct possibility in the near future. I suggest you put together a business plan to include outgoings and incomings. I will need the details of everything you plan for, such as the cost of the building, refurbishment should it be needed, how many staff to work there and what they would be paid, as well as the amount of stock needed and your prediction of sales thereafter.'

Orpha and Peg walked back through the streets

and chatted excitedly about the new venture. So intent on their conversation were they, they didn't notice the woman walking towards them until she spoke.

'Well now, what do we have here?'

Looking at the woman standing in front of her, Orpha gasped. 'Mother!'

CHAPTER 39

Edna Lucas spoke quietly to her son. 'Ezzie, I feel too old to be working the boats and now I have my own room at Buchanan Mansion, I think it's time to quit.' Ezzie had expected this; he had been aware his mother wanted to spend more time on the land and less on the canals. Edna suggested maybe Ezzie should consider giving up the 'cut-rat' life. He had thought about her words but didn't know what work he could do on land, he was a 'cut-rat' at heart and it was all he knew. Edna said, 'Why don't you talk to Zachariah about it as you have become as close as brothers . . . he might be able to help.'

Ezzie agreed and as there was no time like the present he strode to the stables, asking Jago to saddle him a horse.

There were always a few ragged urchins hanging around in Birmingham and Ezzie asked one to hold his horse while he went into the office to meet with Zachariah Buchanan. The promise of a few pennies secured the young boy's employment for half an hour.

Ezzie explained about Edna wanting to give up the boat, but he could not work it alone.

'Have you thought what you will do with the money Peg received from Father from the selling of the emeralds?' Zachariah asked.

'Well no,' Ezzie answered, 'it's her money, so it's up to her what she does with it.'

'By law it belongs to you,' Zachariah said.

'No,' Ezzie contested, 'I don't believe in that law, Zach, it's Peg's money as I see it.'

'I can make a suggestion, but you would have to discuss it with Peg first.' Zachariah emphasised his words.

'Let me hear it,' Ezzie smiled as his interest piqued.

'Right. If you bought another boat with some of Peg's money from Father, you could hire two men to work each boat. You would be their boss and they would work for you. If you pay them a wage and you also hired a manager on a wage, he could arrange the loads and backloads. This manager could ensure the boats were always working, and all you would have to do is broker the deals and reap the profits.' Zachariah sat back in his chair eyeing the man who'd asked for his advice.

Ezzie asked, 'Do you think Peg would go for it?'

Nodding, Zachariah answered, 'I do if she knows you'll be home more. Edna could stay home also, so she'll be happy too.'

'Nothing ventured, nothing gained,' Ezzie said and shaking hands he left the office in much higher spirits than when he had arrived, so much so he paid the boy minding his horse sixpence for his trouble. Ezzie laughed as the boy took off whooping his delight at being able to afford to help feed his family for one more day.

Orpha stared into the eyes of the woman who had cast her out.

'You're doing well for yourself, I see,' Hortense Buchanan ran her eyes over Orpha's tailor-made clothes. 'And you . . . got yourself a husband to go with that child have you?' she said spitefully as she looked pointedly at Peg's swollen stomach.

'That's none of your business!' Peg snapped. 'But as it happens, yes I have!'

'Well horse before cart is always a good thing!' Hortense said sarcastically.

'What do you want with us, Mother?' Orpha asked quietly.

Hortense saw that the fear her daughter had once held had vanished being replaced by a confidence which held her head high as she spoke.

'*Want*? What do I want? I'll tell you what I want! I want what's owing to me!' Hortense rasped and felt her anger rising as she went on. 'Your father threw me out! Did you know that? Yes, of course you did . . . all of you living in that big house . . . and I'm reduced to living in a fleapit of a hotel!'

'It's known as comeuppance, Mother,' Orpha replied, her voice steady. 'You abandoned Peg then you threw me out, what you sow you will reap.'

'Insolent girl!' Hortense's eyes flashed black anger as she rasped again through clenched teeth. 'Don't you dare speak to me that way, I am your mother!'

'Yes you are,' Orpha said quietly, 'more's the pity. Neither of us considers you fit to hold that title, so if you will move aside, we have business to attend to.' Orpha pulled Peg's arm and they walked around and away from the woman standing gazing after them, her mouth clamped into a thin line, anger shaking her body.

The girls walked briskly down the street and Peg muttered, 'Bloody hell! Bloody hell!'

'Keep walking and don't look back,' Orpha said as she urged her sister to move faster. Seeing her sister look at her from the corner of her eye, Orpha went on, "I suggest we tell Father and Ezzie – they really should be advised,' Orpha said as they walked home, although she didn't know how she would find the words.

Orpha, after visiting Mr Belcher at the estate agents, then went to visit a property in Bath Street which ran across the bottom of Oxford Street. If it was suitable for a factory, it wouldn't be too far from the shop.

The massive brick building had arched windows along the front and all were shuttered from the inside. Standing on the corner at the intersection of both streets Orpha was able to walk around to the back. Here again shuttered windows lined the building. At the one end were huge wooden doors which would be ideal for loading up the carts on delivery days. The door opened with a creak and she stepped into the shaded building. She was surprised to see this was a fairly big room with a door connecting it to the rest of the building. Orpha shivered, it was cold – it would be an ideal cold room for the setting chocolate.

Stepping through the connecting door Orpha stood in an incredibly large rectangular space with high ceilings. Moving to each window in turn she threw back the shutters and light flooded in. Walking the length of the building a plan formulated in her mind. Watching dust motes dance in the light she saw her plan come together in her mind's eye. Closing the shutters once more and locking the door behind her, Orpha was delighted with it and set off happily to return the key and endeavour to strike a deal with Mr Belcher.

CHAPTER 40

Ashley Rochester joined them all for dinner that evening and Ezzie explained Zachariah's idea about the boats. As predicted, Edna and Peg were delighted with the proposal when Ashley asked if there was anything he could do to help.

'Not unless you can drive a boat!' Ezzie said with a friendly laugh.

'Well I can't drive a boat, Ezzie, but I have many contacts who might be useful to you,' he replied, smiling back.

'What will you call your new business?' Orpha asked. 'You have to have a name that people will remember.'

Ideas went back and forth across the table, 'Lucas Loads' . . . 'Lucas Cargo Boats' . . . on and on the ideas came until Ezzie said, 'If it's all the same to everyone I'd like to call it the Buchanan Boating Line . . . after all, I hope to expand too if I can.'

They all toasted the new venture and Orpha suggested he spoke with Jonathon Peasbody her accountant to help set it all up.

Peg had been quiet and Ezzie noticed, thinking she was not so happy with the idea. Asking her outright if she preferred he didn't set up the business, she stated adamantly she was all for it.

Watching her sister, Orpha spoke up, 'We met Mother in the town today.'

Shocked looks passed from face to face as Orpha went on to disclose what was said.

'We need to inform the staff downstairs to be extra careful too, especially Jago. I think Mother is still gunning for him after he denounced her to the police for arson.'

A quick explanation later for Ashley's benefit saw them discuss safety measures around the family and staff. Who knew what Hortense might do?

The conversation turned to Ashley. He explained his father had died many years before, leaving him a wealthy man. 'I never knew my mother, and was raised by a nanny who I still live with over by East Park. My father owned a string of warehouses in St Matthew's Street which he hired out to wealthy businessmen to house their stock. The rent from these warehouses more than covers my living expenses and my inheritance is kept safely in the bank. This will provide for and be passed down to any future Rochesters.' Orpha blushed scarlet as he aimed this last comment directly at her. It was not lost on the family around the dining table.

'It would make sense for me to have a warehouse when I eventually get the chocolate factory running,' Orpha said shyly, her glance going to Ashley.

'Well if you had your factory somewhere near St Matthew's Street, I could provide you with a large dry warehouse for storage, and being close . . . transporting your stock to the factory wouldn't be a problem. After all, you can only keep so much stock at the factory at any one time.'

Orpha beamed her delight at this unexpected turn of events.

As conversation continued, Orpha reflected. Her father and brother's consultancy business was going well in Birmingham; Ezzie was to set up the boating line, and she was drawing up plans to have her own factory . . . and now maybe a warehouse too! Peg was married and happy with Ezzie and a baby on the way, and Orpha had met the man of her dreams. Ashley Rochester was everything she wanted in a man, even if he was as poor as a church mouse she would still feel the same. Orpha Buchanan was in love . . . properly in love for the first time in her life. She realised her feelings towards Ezzie when she first met him had been an infatuation, but her feelings for Ashley were so much stronger. He stalked her dreams at night and her days were spent mooning over him.

Orpha looked up at the young man sat across the table from her, and her green eyes sparkled brighter than ever as he smiled at her. God, she loved this man to distraction!

Hortense Buchanan sat in the tea shop in Portland Place overlooking the General Hospital. That girl had been so rude to her! Glancing at the hospital, she wished she could put her daughter in there . . . never to come out!

The age-old question sounded in her mind. How? How could she get her hands on their fortune and see them all penniless? She determined to keep watch and hopefully a solution to her problem would present itself. Nothing she had tried so far had worked, but she felt sure something would happen to see her either a rich widow or at the very least exact her revenge on the loathsome family in Buchanan Mansion.

Time marched on as Hortense watched the comings and goings of the family. With her money dwindling fast, she had had to downgrade the hotels she stayed in, much to her chagrin. She had spent the autumn watching and learning. She saw Orpha open a factory in Bath Street which ran parallel to St Matthew's Street and close to Oxford Street. She eyed the supplies being delivered to the factory. She stalked Orpha carefully as new workers were set on in the factory. She learned of Peg's husband starting up his own business with the boats, and now she knew where Abel and Zachariah had their office in Birmingham. The office that now employed two burly watchmen at night.

The family had appeared to cover every eventuality, but Hortense would yet see her day. One or the other of them would slip up and then they would experience her wrath.

The onset of winter curtailed her following the family somewhat and as the first snow fell, Hortense felt it more than time to face Abel once more.

Walking into the office in Birmingham, she told the secretary she needed to see Mr Buchanan senior. Watching the girl consult her appointment book, Hortense tapped her foot in frustration at being kept waiting.

Looking up, the woman said, 'He can see you next week, Tuesday at 11.30 a.m.'

Hortense silently fumed and snapped, 'He will see me NOW!'

'I'm afraid that's impossible,' the woman returned as she glanced at Abel's office door.

Catching the look, Hortense strode past the woman into the inner office, the woman trailing behind her full of apologies to the man sat behind the desk.

Dismissing the secretary with assurance all was well, he looked at his wife standing by the door.

'Well now, this *is* a surprise,' Abel said, his voice laced with sarcasm. 'I wondered how long it would take for your money to run out and you'd be here begging cap in hand for more.'

Hortense snorted then said, 'I am not here to beg, Abel, I am here for what is rightfully mine!'

'Rightfully yours!' Abel laughed. 'Woman, you have *no* rights!'

'Abel Buchanan, you owe me! You threw me out onto the streets with nothing! Now you have to pay me for that wrongdoing!' Hortense plumped up her bosom in defiance.

'Hortense, sit down, there is something I have to explain to you.'

Watching his wife sit stiffly in the chair by his desk, Abel leaned back in his chair, placing his fountain pen on the desk carefully.

'Now firstly, and let me make this perfectly clear, I owe you nothing. Yes . . .' his hands went up to prevent her speaking, 'yes, I threw you out, but it was not without just cause, and it was not with "nothing" as you put it. You stole and sold my emeralds for five hundred pounds each.' Seeing her surprise, he went on, 'Oh yes I know how much you were paid for the little gems, and I tell you now . . . with very much pleasure . . . you were robbed.'

Hortense's puzzled expression made Abel smile.

'The emeralds were worth so much more than what you were paid, my dear.'

His wife gasped as her thoughts went to the man who had bought the emeralds and she felt like wringing his neck.

'Also you tried to murder my son and myself in a fire at my house, as well as my daughters in their cottage.' Abel kept his temper under control as he watched his wife squirm in her seat. 'Added to that, you kidnapped Orpha and held her for ransom . . . but the worst of it all is . . . you murdered the love of my life. You killed Mahula, Zachariah's mother, my mistress!' Although not certain of all these facts, Abel had pushed in the hope she would admit to some, if not all, of what he had accused her of.

Hortense's eyes dropped to her lap for the briefest moment. 'Abel, you must understand . . . Mahula . . . it was an accident!'

'A fortuitous one for you though, eh?' Abel's smile was malicious.

'I never meant . . .' Hortense began.

'Stow it, Hortense!' Abel snapped, his patience all but gone as he automatically slipped into the vernacular of his days on the ocean sailing to Colombia. 'I really don't care to know the details! What I will say though is you have balls bigger than any man I know!'

Hortense closed her eyes for a moment at his crude expression. 'Abel, I *have* come here for money, I admit. Surely you would not see me in the workhouse! Even you would not be so cruel!'

'My dear, what you have to come to terms with is this. I don't give a shit what happens to you!' Abel's grin split his face as he saw the horror on Hortense's face before he added, 'And if you come near me or mine again I will have you disappear from the face of the earth!'

'But Abel . . . I have nothing left, I am destitute!' Hortense railed. She kept her counsel at having to spend what money she'd gained from selling the stolen emeralds on constantly moving from one hotel to another to avoid capture by the police.

'But Hortense . . . I don't bloody care!' Abel mimicked.

Hortense forced the tears from her eyes as she looked at her husband. Would he soften at her crying?

'Don't play that game with me, woman, it won't wash!' Abel snapped, seeing the tears.

'If you don't give me what I want . . . I will expose you as a wife beater!' Hortense shot back venomously.

Abel pulled his mouth down at the sides as he shook his head. 'Do what you like, Hortense, but remember . . . beating your wife is not a crime, and if you think I'm concerned about scandal . . . believe me, I am not!'

Temper getting the better of her, Hortense stood and jabbed a finger in his direction. 'You won't get away with this! I'll see you all in hell for what you've done to me!'

'Not if I see you there first!' Abel said. Then picking up the telephone he said, 'Please put me through to the police station.' He grinned as he saw Hortense flee his office. He repeated his conversation with Hortense to the police sergeant.

CHAPTER 41

Orpha sat in the open carriage wrapped in fur against the winter chill, Ashley by her side. Gloved hands shoved in a fur muff hanging around her neck and a fur hat on, Orpha laughed as the snowflakes landed on her face. Ashley had organised the winter ride around East Park for her pleasure and laughed at her childish delight. The trees were laden with snow and the whole landscape was draped with Mother Nature's white cloak. The weak sunshine made everything sparkle like tiny diamonds and Orpha thought she was the happiest she'd ever been.

'Orpha,' Ashley said, 'there's something I wish to discuss with you.' At her nod, he continued, 'Now that you have your factory and your shops are doing so well, I wondered if you had considered settling down.'

Orpha looked him in the eye. What was he saying? Was he alluding to her being married and having children? Was he about to propose to her? The blush that rose in her warmed her cheeks. 'I . . . I hadn't thought . . .' she faltered, not quite knowing how to answer.

'Orpha, what I'm trying to say is . . . will you marry me?' Ashley said all in a rush.

The carriage driver smiled to himself as he heard the question, at least the lad had style.

'Oh Ashley! This is such a surprise! You see, I have so many plans for the business!'

The driver's smile turned down as he listened to the conversation taking place behind him.

'Darling,' Ashley said with a smile, 'you can still run your business when we are married.'

'Well then my answer is yes!' Orpha said breathlessly. Blinded by love, Orpha rushed headlong into her decision.

The driver flicked the horse's reins, urging the horse to move quicker as he called out, 'Come on Bess, these young people are getting married!'

Laughing as they were thrown back in their seats as the horse picked up speed, Ashley kissed his bride-to-be gently amid the tinkling of the bells on the horse's reins.

The news of the carriage ride and proposal was given to the family over dinner that night and everyone was delighted, all that is except one. Simmons' heart weighed heavy in his chest.

Once more, Simmons, Mrs Jukes, Alice, Seth and Jago were invited into the parlour to toast the happy young couple. Copious amounts of alcohol were consumed and singing and dancing ensued. Hangovers the following day were not even considered as laughter and joy carried the revellers into the early hours. The only one not drunk that night was Simmons. He spent the evening watching the man who had so recently settled himself so easily into Orpha's affections and her life.

Ashley Rochester was delighted when Orpha accepted his proposal of marriage. She was a beauty, there was no denying that, and from a very wealthy family too. Now she was a very rich young woman in her own right. Once they were married he would want for nothing, her money would come to him.

Sitting on his single bed in the old ramshackle building in Ettingshall Road at the other side of Wolverhampton, Ashley held his cold hands to the meagre fire. Another few months was all he had to wait, then his financial problems would be over. Rubbing his hands together for warmth, he smiled, yes all this misery and poverty would be behind him. Looking at the few clothes hanging from a picture rail near the fire, he thought he would soon be visiting the best tailors in the town. He would be living in Buchanan Mansion and have his own horse in the stable there. With good food in his stomach and coin in his pocket, Ashley Rochester would receive the respect he felt he deserved.

Climbing into a cold bed fully clothed in order to stay warm, he shivered as the fire slowly died. He had used the last of the coal and would need to pick from the pit banks again tomorrow. He hated having to pick the coal bits from the mounds of earth moved by the miners, it was hard and laborious work, and the pit bank wenches laughed at him. But come the summer, he would pick no more coal; he would burn as much as he pleased once he had his feet under the table at that big house! The thought warmed him as he succumbed to sleep.

The following day, Ashley ignored the jeers of the pit bank wenches as he dug his hands into the slag heap, looking for bits of coal for his fire. There were women crawling over the mounds of earth and chippings. Unable to afford to buy coal, they would spend their days searching for anything that would burn. The task was made all the more difficult by the recent fall of snow, but Ashley pressed on. His bucket almost full now, he decided he'd had enough and started for home, to the taunts of the women shouting he had no stamina. Ignoring them, he trudged on as the cold and wet seeped through the holes in his boots. By the time he got back he was thoroughly miserable. Lighting the fire, he searched for something to eat; bread and cheese was all he had, so bread and cheese it was.

Sitting directly in front of the fire, his boots in the hearth to dry out, he wriggled his toes through the holes in his socks. Biting into the stale bread and hard cheese, he decided he needed to be invited to dinner at Buchanan Mansion again.

What he'd told Orpha and her family was true . . . to a degree. His father had left him the string of warehouses, but what he hadn't told them was, they were all empty. He could find no takers and he could not sell them. There was not enough money being earned by people to warrant their buying a warehouse. He had never known his mother; that was true enough. His father would never speak of it, so Ashley had no idea who or where she was, or even if she were alive or dead. He had been raised by a nanny who had died when he was in his teenage years.

Looking around the small room, he shook his head at what was left of his father's house. He had never found work, he wasn't trained in anything and had lived by his wits from that time on. He had coerced a few older wealthy women out of money on occasions by having secret liaisons with them, which he continued to do in order to survive as well as to provide him with the money needed to court Orpha Buchanan.

Ashley finished his food and rubbed his cold hands together. Very soon he would be a man of means. Once he was married to Orpha, no one would question or doubt him, no one would taunt or ridicule him . . . ever again.

Peg's time was near and she had not worked in the shop for a few months. With Ezzie and Edna still away on the boat, she was glad of the company of the staff at Buchanan Mansion.

Sitting with Simmons and Beulah in the kitchen one morning, Peg caught her breath then said, 'Oh Beulah, I think I've wet myself!' Bursting into tears from sheer embarrassment, she looked at the cook.

'No, girl, it's your time. The baby's on the way!' Taking charge immediately, the cook issued her orders. 'Simmons, send Jago for the doctor; Alice, get the mistress to her bed and into her nightgown; Seth, get some water on to boil; Simmons, fresh towels and linen. I'll get Mr Abel and Miss Orpha then I'll go up to see to Miss Peg!'

Peg's cries could be heard echoing around the house as Abel and Zachariah sat downstairs in the kitchen with the male staff and Alice, the maid. She kept busy, making tea, and Abel paced the floor. Zachariah winced with every cry he heard coming from his sister. Ezzie and Edna would not return for a couple of days and there was no way to let them know what was happening . . . or was there?

Zachariah jumped up and yelled, 'I'm going to the wharf to ask the "cut-rats" to get a message to Ezzie that his wife had gone into labour!'

Orpha held her sister's hand and bathed her forehead as Peg struggled to bring her child into the world. She was exhausted and the doctor and Beulah encouraged the girl to rest between the contractions that racked her body, stealing her strength and energy.

'Orpha . . . I can't do this . . .!' Peg gasped.

'Sweetheart, you can. Besides, you can't leave the little mite where it is now can you?' Orpha watched the faint smile cross her sister's face before another agonising wave of pain rolled over her.

The doctor and Beulah exchanged a look as Peg let out a screech. The cook shook her head and the doctor turned his attention once more to the girl who lay whimpering on the bed.

'Peg,' he said, 'the baby is breech . . . its legs are coming first . . . so we have to try and turn it.' With a nod from the girl, the doctor muttered as he worked, but the child would not turn. 'Right,' he said, wiping an arm across his sweat-soaked brow, 'legs first it is then!'

Screams ensued and with pushing from Peg and pulling from the doctor, the child came into the world with a plop and then let out a healthy howl. Passing the baby quickly to Beulah to swaddle, the doctor finished his ministrations with its mother. 'There now, Peg, you have a beautiful baby boy!'

Ralph Lucas was placed in his mother's arms and settled immediately.

Orpha whispered, 'Zachariah has taken a message to the wharf, it should get to Ezzie and Edna pretty quickly.' Then stroking the baby's cheek gently, she went on, 'Oh Peg, he's so beautiful, you are so very lucky.'

Orpha tearfully watched her sister and nephew as Beulah took the news to the others waiting in the kitchen.

Abel paid the doctor's fee and once he'd left he rushed upstairs to see his daughter and her newborn son. Each of the staff popped their heads round the door for a quick squint at the new arrival and offered their congratulations before retiring to the kitchen again.

After a cup of tea, Peg settled down to sleep off her exhaustion, the baby in the crib beside her and Orpha watching over them both from a chair by the window. Everything in her world was wonderful right now, but with her mother still roaming free, how long would her happiness last?

Having received the message via the 'cut-rat' grapevine, Ezzie and Edna immediately set off for home. Arriving the following morning, everyone congratulated the new father. Holding his newborn son, his tears flowed as he whispered, 'Oh Peg . . . he's perfect! Thank you so much my darling, thank you!'

Orpha watched the happy couple for a moment before slipping quietly from the room.

She wondered what her mother would say if she knew she was now a grandmother.

Throughout the bitter cold months of winter, Orpha's business steadily grew and more workers were taken on in the factory. The two shops were selling out so quickly Orpha had to rethink her policy. The bottom line was she needed another factory! Her accountant had assured her the business could stand the expenditure and so one particularly cold day she travelled to Birmingham with Ashley in search of new premises.

Mr Belcher, the estate agent, had informed Orpha a building had just come onto his books that might be just what she was looking for. The structure was in Albert Street, a couple of streets away from the shop. As luck would have it, the building was very like that in Bath Street in Wolverhampton. Pacing back and forth, Orpha was telling Ashley where the ranges would be placed; the packing and preparation areas, the sinks and . . . massive cold room. She would, however, have to install a lavatory and hand-washing basin.

'Orpha,' Ashley said, 'it needs a thorough clean and a coat of whitewash . . . you can't put your curtains up before your floorboards are down!'

Laughing at his analogy, she said, 'I know that, silly!' Her laugh echoed through the empty building, but Ashley did not laugh at being admonished. That would soon change once they were married, he would see to it.

Looking over the building, Ashley and Orpha agreed it would be ideal.

'Now all I have to do is find and train workers, and install the equipment needed,' Orpha said.

Orpha had agreed a price with Mr Belcher and had immediately begun to have the building cleaned and painted. New equipment was fitted and staff were on site being trained by her best chocolate makers, a bonus in their wages an encouragement. Going to and from the new building over the next weeks, Orpha thought she caught a glimpse of her mother every now and then. Was her mother following her? Or was it just coincidence? Orpha kept a keen eye out on her travels, especially in the railway stations where she stood well back from the platform edge.

Orpha wasted no time in getting the new factory up and running and by Christmas it was working flat out. The Christmas specialties were in the process of being made and chocolate novelties were displayed in her shop windows.

Orpha's profits soared and she was constantly looking for new ideas for the chocolate process. Nuts, fruit, toffee, fudge . . . all were covered in creamy chocolate and all were selling incredibly well. Orpha had designed special chocolate moulds for the different occasions such as Christmas and Easter. Tiny chocolates were made and wrapped prettily to hang on Christmas trees, small chocolate bunnies were made for Easter, tiny cakes and biscuits covered in the creamy mixture were flying out of her shops. Even with two factories and two shops, Orpha could barely keep up with the orders coming in. Taking on more workers for the Christmas period, she was determined to meet the demand, she knew from experience, she would be faced with.

With her work keeping her so busy, she'd had little time to spend with Ashley and even less time to think about her wedding. They had agreed to be married in the summer, so she had plenty of time to organise things, she felt.

Walking across to the new factory in Albert Street one day in early December, Orpha was wondering how the new Santa moulds were working out. Suddenly a voice behind her said, 'Got yourself another business, I see.'

Orpha turned and was shocked at the sight of her mother. Dressed in clothes that had seen better days, the woman was a shadow of her former self. Thin features stared back at her; brown eyes sunk deep into their sockets and wispy brown hair tried desperately to escape the confines of a battered hat.

'Mother! Mother . . .?' Orpha gasped in shock which quickly turned to sadness as her mother answered.

'Yes, it's me, not looking my best I'm afraid,' the gaunt-looking woman said, all haughtiness gone from her now.

'My God!' Orpha whispered. 'What happened to you?'

'No money, your father wouldn't give me any,' Hortense muttered.

'Mother, when did you last eat?'

Hortense just shook her head – she couldn't remember.

'Come with me!' Orpha ordered and taking her mother's rail-thin arm they walked to the nearest tea shop. Ordering food and hot tea for them both, Orpha stared at the woman sat opposite her. She couldn't believe her mother had come to this!

Orpha watched in horror as her mother devoured the hot food like she'd never been fed.

Pushing her empty plate away, she whispered, 'Thank you Orpha, I know I don't deserve this.'

'Mother, everyone deserves to eat!'

'I mean, the way I treated you and Eugenie . . . I noticed you called her Peg.'

'Yes, her foster mother named her Peg and she wanted to keep to it,' Orpha replied not unkindly, although she felt the need to answer truthfully It felt strange speaking in a civil manner with the woman who had only shown her abuse in her former years.

Hortense dropped her eyes to her lap.

'Mother, tell me, where are you living?'

'There's an old house . . .' Hortense began but was too ashamed to tell her daughter she lived in a derelict hovel.

'Oh Mother!' Orpha gasped, her hands coming to her mouth.

The waitress arrived asking if they would like anything else. Orpha ordered more tea and a stodgy pudding for her mother. 'We have to get you sorted out,' she said as the waitress ambled away with her order. 'You can't continue to live like this!'

Hortense attempted a smile, which looked macabre on her thin face.

The waitress arrived with the order and while Hortense ate, Orpha took the time to think about a solution. Once a proud woman, would her mother accept money if Orpha offered it? Would her pride prevent her from taking money from her daughter? She had to find a way of helping the woman without flaunting her own wealth in her mother's face. When Hortense had finished eating, Orpha said gently, 'Mother, how can I help you?'

'Oh you can't, I'm lost. This is God's judgement for my being so evil to you girls.' Hortense looked resigned to her fate. 'I just couldn't go into the workhouse! I would rather starve than go in there!'

'Mother, by the looks of you, you very nearly did! There's no question of you going into the workhouse!' Orpha was finding it difficult to forgive her mother for all the hurt she had suffered growing up, but she felt a pang of guilt should she allow her mother to end up in that dreadful place.

'I must accept God's punishment for all the bad things I've done.' Hortense's eyes misted over.

'We have all done bad things, Mother, there were times I wished you dead, and that's a terrible thing!' Orpha watched her mother attempt to smile once more.

'I was so jealous of you both. You are so like your father and nothing like me. Abel doted on the pair of you, he ignored me until you were gone. Then, instead of loving me again, he hated me. He blamed me for you no longer being in his life . . . and rightly so.' Hortense was pouring her heart out to the daughter she had once hated with a vengeance. Now sitting here talking quietly together she could see what a beautiful young woman the girl had grown into, and she felt wretched, but her jealousy still lay just beneath the surface of her shame.

'Oh Mother, why did we never talk like this before? So much could have been avoided if we had.' Orpha saw the emotions play on her mother's haggard face.

'I must go, you have your work to go to,' Hortense said finally.

'Bugger the work!' Orpha snapped.

So like your father, Hortense thought as Orpha stood to leave.

'Come on, we'll get you booked into a hotel and then we will sort out something more permanent.' Orpha gave her mother a determined look.

Slowly walking the length of Moor Street, they walked into a hotel behind the Bull Ring. Orpha booked and paid for her mother to stay for one month, after deciding it may take a while to sort out permanent accommodation. Going to the allocated room, Orpha looked around; it was clean and the clerk said she could light the fire to take the chill off. The coal scuttle was full and Orpha knew it would be warm in no time. Leaving some money on the bedside table for some new warm clothes, Orpha said she would see her mother the following day then she left. Hortense's thin face stretched into a macabre smile in a self-congratulatory manner on ingratiating herself with her daughter so easily. This was the first step to acquiring what she thought should rightly be hers – the family fortune.

Sitting on the train home, Orpha thought about the events of the day. Her mother's appearance had shocked her. The woman was half starved and dressed in rags. Why had she let herself get into such a state? Why had she not tried to find work? Hortense believed God was punishing her, that's why!

Hailing a cabbie in Wolverhampton, Orpha was on her way home. Now all she had to do was tell the family about her mother and what she'd done.

CHAPTER 42

Orpha sat at the dining table and listened to the family's news. Ezzie's boat business seemed to be going very well and he and Peg were pleased it was making money. Edna clucked over how her grandson, Ralph, was growing. Zachariah and her father were busy with consultations and the staff were happy in their work. She pondered how to broach the subject of her mother and their afternoon spent together. Suddenly everyone was silent and looking at her. Casting a glance around the table, she searched the enquiring faces.

'So how was the factory?' Zachariah asked, ending the silence.

'Oh,' Orpha said her eyes downcast, 'Erm . . . I didn't go in the end.'

'Why not sweetheart?' Abel asked.

'Well, it's a strange story,' Orpha began, 'and I will tell you, but you have to hear me out before you comment.' All nodded their agreement and Orpha related the tale of meeting and talking with her mother. She knew when she finished they would fire questions and accusations at her, but she was never more surprised when everyone sat in silence.

Abel eventually said, 'After all she did to you all and now you take pity on the wretched woman! Oh Orpha . . .!'

It was then that the questions came and answers were given.

Abel snapped, 'Hortense knows I will never forgive her for what she's done to this family, especially with regard to Mahula . . .' He cast a look at his son who nodded. '. . . But you are all grown now, so you make up your own minds. I, for one, will have nothing more to do with the woman!'

Abel rarely raised his voice and although he was not now shouting, the cadence kept everyone tight lipped on the subject. After a short hiatus, it was baby Ralph who broke the spell with a loud yell – he was hungry.

Orpha's first visit the following day was to her mother.

'Mother, I have an idea. I thought to find you a small house somewhere.' Orpha saw the surprise on Hortense's face and she added, 'We could go back to Wolverhampton where the property is cheaper and see what the estate agent has on his books.'

Orpha then had the shock of her life.

Hortense walked across to her and put her arms lightly around the girl and patted her back before quickly stepping back saying, 'Thank you.'

Orpha's heart was beating like a drum. All she'd ever wanted growing up was that hug; that small show of affection. Her hatred of the woman in front of her now appeared to melt away as she stared.

Taking a deep breath, she whispered, 'Thank you Mother.' Then turning quickly to hide her tears, she said, 'Now, come on let's go.'

Catching the train back to Wolverhampton, a cabbie drove them to the estate agents. Mr Belcher said he had an end terraced house in Park Street that Hortense could move into straight away, but Orpha wanted something a little more upmarket. There was a house, he said, standing alone behind the allotment gardens and Orpha agreed they should look at it. Orpha winced as she realised it was in Derry Street where she and Peg had once had their cottage.

Looking around the property, Hortense thought it was nowhere near up to the same standard as Buchanan House had been, but then beggars couldn't be choosers, and she accepted Orpha's offer to buy it for her. Hortense stayed to light the fire while Orpha went to organise payment for the estate agent. He was delighted; Orpha put a lot of business his way.

Once that was done Orpha went shopping for food to fill the larder. She arrived back to a roaring fire and a kettle boiled ready for tea. The two women discussed ideas of how to arrange the rooms when Orpha suddenly said, 'Oh Mother, is there a bed here?'

Going upstairs, they found an old iron bedstead with no mattress. They donned their coats and walked into the town.

With a new bed, linen, towels and blankets ordered, they sat in the tea shop in the warmth of the fire. After tea, they returned to await the delivery of the bed, which Orpha insisted should be sent out that day.

Orpha said, 'I have told the family what I am doing and no one has voiced any objections.'

Hortense nodded. It made no difference to her either way.

The men arrived with the bed and Orpha left her mother to settle in, saying she would call the next day.

That evening, Ashley Rochester, dressed in his set of good clothes, tramped through the snow to Buchanan Mansion to see his fiancé. As usual he was made very welcome and the wonderful aroma reached his nose as he sat at the dining table. They were having lamb . . . and not the scrag end he was more used to either.

Busy eating as much as he could get down his throat, he listened to the conversations taking place around him.

'You're hungry this evening, Ashley,' Orpha said with a twinkle in her eye.

Wiping his mouth with a napkin, he replied, 'I

am, darling. I had no lunch today and Mrs Jukes' cooking is so delicious . . .' He gave Orpha a wink as everyone agreed with his statement.

'Ashley,' Orpha reprimanded, 'you must eat during the day especially in this cold weather!'

His mouth full, Ashley merely nodded. *Chance would be a fine thing!* he thought as he swallowed his food.

The evening wore on with coffee and brandy in the parlour until eventually Ashley stood to leave. Thanking everyone for their hospitality, he kissed Orpha's cheek gently before stepping out into the snow to make his way home to his hovel in Ettingshall Road.

Lying in his cold bed, he wondered how he could wangle an overnight stay at the large house . . . or even a bedroom of his own. With a full belly, Ashley slipped into sleep as easily as a baby.

While the rest of the family were enjoying their meal, Hortense lay in her new bed in her new house and contemplated her good fortune. She had eaten well before retiring and her larder was full. Orpha had left her enough money to buy more food, coal and clothing. This house was not up to her beloved Buchanan House standard, but then it was better than the derelict property she had hidden away in. She had come very close to either starving to death or putting herself in the workhouse. Shivering at the thought, she turned her mind back to her daughter.

Orpha had done very well for herself with two shops and two factories and a Royal Warrant to boot. Peg had married and now had a son. Hortense thought about Zachariah, the boy Abel had with Mahula, and her mood turned sour as she lay in the darkness of the bedroom. Try as she might, she couldn't forgive Abel his indiscretions. She was grateful for all Orpha had done for her these past few days, but there was still a deep-down jealousy that raised its ugly head on occasions. There was also a hatred for the son Abel had fathered. In her heart she knew she would always be resentful of her husband's affair and that he had put her in the situation in which she now found herself. She was a social pariah. The afternoon meetings with her 'friends' had ceased and she knew she had been their topic of conversation and the brunt of their spite after her downfall from society. The old feelings of resentment and hatred began to stir in her once more.

Her attempts to do Abel's children out of their inheritance had failed. Trying to kill them all off had failed. Now she had Orpha on side she wondered how that relationship would pan out. The girl was clever, but was Hortense cleverer? Could she find a way to wheedle some more money out of Orpha? Could she eventually climb the social ladder again? Firstly she needed to get herself healthy again so she would accept the handouts Orpha was willing to give and bite her tongue while she did so.

Once she was strong and healthy again, then she could construct a plan that would see her rich and the Buchanan family dirt poor. Smiling into the dark bedroom, Hortense drifted off to sleep feeling better than she had in a long time.

Over the following days, Orpha began to feel the strain of stretching her time visiting her shops and factories, her accountant and her mother. Peg wanted nothing to do with the woman who had abandoned her as a baby. Zachariah did not wish to get to know the woman either, after all it was she who had killed his own mother. Abel had made his position perfectly clear both to the family and to Hortense when she had arrived unannounced at his office. He still had no idea where the woman was or else he would have told the police immediately. Therefore it was left to Orpha to take care of the woman who had brought her into the world.

With her business booming, Orpha struggled with the decision as to whether to open yet another shop. Her finances could cope, she had been informed by Jonathon Peasbody, but on the other hand it would be a further drain on her time. She needed to put an overall manager in place, which would relieve her of the pressure she was under, and Orpha thought she knew just the person.

The snow had turned to dirty slush as Orpha walked to Oxford Street and she was glad that spring was just around the corner. Realising how quickly time had passed, she further realised she had her wedding to plan. The summer would be hot on her heels before she knew it.

Walking into 'The Choc's Box', Orpha stepped into the back room, having made her way through the crowd of customers waiting to be served. The shop staff coped incredibly well, sharing smiles and jokes with the waiting women.

Lottie Spence followed her employer into the sitting room to give her usual update. Basically, everything was running true to form.

'Lottie,' Orpha said at last, 'I have a proposal to make to you.' Lottie listened carefully. 'I have need of an overall manager and I wondered if you would be interested in the position?' Lottie nodded again, allowing Orpha to lay out the proposal in detail. 'It would mean travelling between the shops and factories, keeping a check on stock . . . reordering where necessary, ensuring the staff are happy or whether we need to employ more staff to keep up with orders. Naturally, you would have the title of Manager and a salary befitting your status. If you are inclined to take up this position, I will ensure you receive the respect of all workers and you would meet with me once a week to report back.'

'Well,' Lottie said, 'this is a surprise and I thank you for thinking of me. It sounds like hard work, but I'm not afraid of that so . . . I accept the offer!'

Clinking teacups in salute, the women smiled then Orpha said, 'I will inform the girls here first . . . oh and we'll have to find someone to take your place in the shop . . . then I will need you to accompany me to the factories and other shop. Everyone needs to get to know their new manager.'

The girls in the shop were informed and Joan said, 'My friend Ann is looking for work.' Orpha agreed to meet with the girl with a view to employing her.

The following day saw Orpha and Lottie visiting the other premises and explaining that Lottie was to be the new manager. On the journey home on the train, Orpha answered any questions Lottie had regarding her new position in the business.

Before she went home, Orpha called in on her mother in Derry Street and found Hortense sitting by the fire.

'You should look for work, Mother,' Orpha said as sad eyes met hers, 'it would get you out of the house at least.'

Shock registered on Hortense's face for a fleeting moment but Orpha had seen it. Maybe she shouldn't have said that. Hortense had always considered it beneath her to work, but then she'd never had to. Orpha let it lie and went on to tell her mother about Lottie taking up the manager's position. Hortense listened carefully; all information stored. One never knew when it would come in handy.

Orpha left the house thinking one day it might be nice for her mother to hug her again, but she could not, in all honesty, ever see it happening in the future, but she remained hopeful.

CHAPTER 43

Ashley Rochester congratulated himself on keeping his secret for so long as he walked to Buchanan Mansion in the early spring sunshine. Orpha had pestered him on occasion to see his house, and he'd had to think on his feet as to why she should not. It was taxing coming up with plausible excuses for not taking her to his home. He smiled inwardly as he recalled some of them; he was going away on business, he was visiting friends in another area – one after another the lies had slipped from his lips. However he had got away with it and in just a few months he would be installed into Buchanan Mansion and wouldn't have to lie any more.

The snow had now disappeared, making his journeys far easier, and he whistled a little tune as he strode along the streets. Soon now he would be a very wealthy man. Soon he would be living in the lap of luxury, albeit with a wife he didn't truly love. Oh he felt affection for Orpha, but could it be called love? He thought not, but then everyone had a cross to bear. Yes, he would marry Orpha, but there was no reason to think he could not continue to enjoy his fun on the side.

Orpha was making preparations for the wedding and at this thought he did a small jump, clicking his heels together. 'Thank goodness spring is here at last,' he called to a woman who laughed at his antics.

St George's Church needed to be booked and invitations were being printed. Orpha would be choosing her flowers shortly and then her wedding gown. Suddenly stopping in his tracks, Ashley realised he would be expected to buy a new suit and boots. Swearing under his breath as he walked on, he wondered how he could get round this particular problem. What would he say when Orpha asked him about it? What would that father of hers say? His bright mood of moments ago darkened as he searched his mind for answers.

Arriving at the house, Ashley was surprised to see Zachariah and Abel there, he thought they would be at their office. 'We're all going to Birmingham to be fitted for our wedding garb,' Abel said. Ashley's mood darkened further. 'You will, of course, come with us,' Abel added. Ashley scrambled his mind for an excuse to refuse. Abel would have none of it and before he knew what was happening the three piled into the carriage with Jago on the driving seat. He was to drive them to the tailor's and wait to drive them home again.

Ashley spent the whole journey in a state of pure

dread. How could he get out of buying a new tailor-made suit? He didn't want the others to think him cheap, but he didn't have two halfpennies to rub together. The feeling of dread swamped him as they stepped into Beaty Bro's in Union Street, the most expensive tailors in Birmingham.

The tailor's assistant measured Abel, Zachariah and Ashley and wrote down each measurement carefully while the tailor himself spread out different cloths for them to choose from. Abel and Zachariah were regular customers and the tailor, being certain of a good sale, sucked up to them accordingly.

Ashley sat after being measured and took no interest in the cloth on show. He endeavoured to maintain an air of gentlemanly behaviour on the outside while inside he was in a blind panic. The tailor advanced towards him, the others having chosen their desired material and Ashley sucked in a deep breath.

'Has sir decided yet?' the tailor asked.

Shaking his head, Ashley felt all eyes on him. 'Unfortunately I find myself in rather a tricky situation, you see all my funds are currently tied up in my warehouses . . .'

'Oh that's all right, sir,' the tailor cut in, 'we will invoice you at the end of the month.' He looked down his nose at the man sitting before him . . . a real gentleman would have known this.

'Ah excellent!' Ashley breathed a sigh of relief as he removed an imaginary speck from his trousers before moving to choose the cloth for his wedding suit.

Going next to Warwick Place, they entered the Irish Linen Company, the shirt and collar manufacturer, where again they were measured and again the invoice would follow.

On the journey home Ashley chatted brightly about the forthcoming wedding. In the town he had been treated as a gentleman; he had enjoyed the shopkeepers' deference and felt he could become accustomed to it very quickly.

Meanwhile Orpha was in the kitchen at the shop in Oxford Street, having decided to get back to basics now Lottie had taken over as manager. Thinking about a wedding gown, she absent-mindedly popped a chocolate-covered almond in her mouth. As the flavour hit her taste buds, an idea sprang to mind. Dropping a few almonds into a mortar, she ground them with the pestle until they lay in tiny chunks. Sprinkling these into a small amount of chocolate, she spooned it into the little moulds she'd had specially made. When they were set, they would try them; hopefully they would have a new line to introduce.

Heating coconut oil, Orpha added honey and cocoa powder. Excited about the new nut confection, she realised the chocolate she was making looked darker than usual. Dipping her finger, she was surprised the mixture was slightly bitter. A tray of set chocolates sat waiting to be packed and

Orpha took a teaspoon of the bitter mixture and drizzled a tiny amount over them in a swirly pattern. Leaving them to one side, she wondered how they would taste. With more mixture in the moulds, she sprinkled the remaining nuts over the top and took them to the cold slab to set. She would ask the shop girls to try these new chocolate ideas later and if they thought they would sell, if so she would introduce her new line in both factories.

She thought about Joan's friend, Ann, who had been taken on in the shop and was proving an asset to the business, the customers loved how she chattered incessantly to each one and served at the same time. Word had circulated that Orpha Buchanan was the lady to see if one needed work. With two shops and two factories working flat out, more women were being taken on each week and output soared. The implementation of the new line would be discussed with Lottie at their next meeting, and with her inspirational juices flowing, Orpha experimented with yet more ideas. Mint, orange and lemon flavours were added to creamy chocolate and left to set. At the rate she was going she would need another factory! The thought thrilled and excited her and as she worked she pondered where it could be situated.

Excited voices exchanged news over dinner that evening and Orpha was ecstatic her new lines proved a success with the shop girls. Her happiness was pulled up sharply when Ashley snapped, 'Don't you think you have enough on your plate?' The talking ceased as everyone looked at him. 'I . . . I mean . . . darling, you are run ragged as it is. It's just that I worry about you!'

Appeased, Orpha smiled, 'Be assured it's fine now that Lottie Spence is my manager.'

Simmons, who was standing at the side of the dining room waiting to give the maid instructions to clear the table, also heard the exchange. There was something about this young man he didn't like, other than the fact that he was marrying Orpha. One thing was certain, the butler intended to keep an eye on his mistress's intended.

Once the family were settled in the parlour with drinks, Simmons and Alice related the sharpness of Ashley's words to the other staff. They all agreed there was something definitely amiss regarding Mr Rochester and it was Alice who pointed out the obvious.

'Have you ever noticed . . . he always wears the same clothes?'

Simmons nodded, his mind ticking over in measured beats.

Alice went on, 'Anyone would think he had nothing else to wear!'

The cook and the butler exchanged a quick glance and the stable boys looked up from their dinner. 'I wonder . . .' Beulah Jukes said.

'It's possible,' Simmons interrupted as Jago, Alice and Seth looked from one to the other.

'What?' Alice asked.

'Maybe those clothes *are* all he has. Maybe he doesn't have the means to buy more,' Simmons said quietly.

'Ar, but he owns a string of warehouses though,' Alice added.

'That's as maybe,' Simmons put in, 'so why is he always in the same clothes and why does he walk everywhere? Why does he not have a carriage or least a horse?'

'I'd love to know more about him,' Beulah said as she dolloped more potatoes onto Jago's plate. Seeing Seth eye the food, she smiled doing the same for him and watched them tuck in hungrily.

'Well . . .' said Simmons.

'Oh Blimey!' Alice snorted. 'Sherlock Holmes again is it?' Laughter rang out in the kitchen as Simmons shook his head at the forthright young girl.

After their meal, Simmons instructed the two stable boys to be ready to follow Ashley when he left Buchanan Mansion. He wanted to know more about the man, and discovering exactly where he lived would be the first step.

Closing the door on the departing man, Simmons rushed down to the kitchen and shoved the boys out of the back door, whispering, 'Now remember – stay out of sight!' Before the night was out they would know just a little more about Ashley Rochester.

Two hours later, Jago and Seth rushed back into

the kitchen out of breath, having run all the way back from Ettingshall Road. Dragging in great lungsful of air, Jago spluttered, 'Mr Simmons, you won't believe it!'

Settling the boys with tea, Alice and Beulah joined them at the table, heads pushed forward to hear the news.

Now with even breath, Jago went on, 'Mr Rochester lives in Ettingshall Road . . .'

Seth finished his friend's sentence with, 'In a hovel!' The boys smiled at each other. Had the staff not known better, the boys might have been taken for twins.

'Bloody hell!' Alice gasped. 'Who would have thought it?'

'We did wonder, did we not?' Simmons nodded slowly. 'The question now is, what do we do with this knowledge? Do we stay quiet and keep our noses out of upstairs business? Or do we tell the mistress what we know and risk being in the dog house for interfering?' Simmons looked at the shaking heads as silence descended in the kitchen.

CHAPTER 44

Orpha decided it was time to engage a solicitor, so making her way into town she headed for Walsall Street. Albert Hayes was a kindly-looking man, short in stature with hair that was dark but peppered with grey. Orpha sat opposite Mr Hayes and explained why she was there. 'I am shortly to be married and I have no wish to give up the business I've worked so hard for and become just a housewife. I would be bored to death sitting at home with nothing to fill my time.'

Thinking on the matter a while, Albert said, 'You could ask your husband-to-be to sign a formal waver to your estate.'

Orpha shook her head, saying, 'It is most unlikely Ashley would sign such a document, what man would? He would be a fool to do so. However, after all my hard work, I would be a fool to just hand it all over once married.'

The solicitor agreed and suggested she leave it with him; he would draw up a document whereby after marriage, Orpha would retain the rights to her property as well as her money. 'You will need to revisit later in the week to read and sign the document, which will be witnessed by myself and my clerk. I will warn you, however that if it comes to the put-to, the document might not stand up in court, but it is the best I can do for you.'

Satisfied, Orpha left the office having made an appointment for later in the week. Walking back to Oxford Street, she determined she would tell no one of her meeting with Albert Hayes or of the document she aimed to sign to retain her wealth.

Walking towards 'The Choc's Box', Orpha was amazed to see a line of women waiting patiently to get into the shop. Thinking no one had opened up, she swept through to the door amidst grumbles of, *'Some people have no manners!' 'There is a queue you know!'* Orpha apologised as she pushed through into the shop itself, seeing it crowded with jostling women.

'Thank God you're here!' Joan said as Orpha threw off her coat and donned an apron. Standing behind the counter, Orpha helped out serving the next person in line.

All day they served and shelves were restacked with freshly made produce. By the end of the day, Orpha locked up and they all sat in the back room with tea.

'What a busy day!' Orpha remarked. Seeing Joan, Hilda and Ann exchange a look she asked, 'What?'

Joan explained, 'Every day is the same! We are hard-pushed to keep the counter and shelves stocked and be able to serve as well.'

'I see!' Orpha's eyebrows raised in surprise. 'I had no idea! Would it help if we had another shop . . .? I do know of a property going begging in Commercial Road.'

'Too bloody right it would help!' Joan said, rubbing her aching feet. The others agreed, explaining they were not afraid of the hard work, but every day they were run ragged. They said Lottie was aware of it and had promised to inform Orpha at the next meeting.

Orpha said, 'Right. I'll speak with Mr Belcher regarding the empty property.'

Ashley Rochester had joined them again later for dinner and Orpha related her experience at the shop. 'I couldn't believe how busy it was, we didn't rest until the shop closed! This can't go on, the women are exhausted! Therefore I am to view an empty property tomorrow. If suitable, I intend to purchase it and open it as soon as possible.'

Peg asked, 'Orpha, what about the wedding? You really should be concentrating on that rather than business right now.' Edna nodded her agreement.

'No!' Orpha snapped. She was tired and she resented what she saw as Peg's interference, but seeing the hurt on her sister's face she softened. 'Peg, I'm sorry I snapped at you, but this has to come first! The women are exhausted, I do not want them being ill from overwork! I *have* to lessen their workload, and this is the only way I can do it!' Orpha looked at Ashley for his support, but he merely scowled at her and shook his head. Why was he not supporting her in this?

Looking at Zachariah and her father, she saw them nod their heads. At least they understood what she was faced with. Ezzie gave her a reassuring smile that he was also on her side.

'Well,' she said at last, 'I've made my decision . . . and that's that!' This particular conversation was brought to a swift close.

Watching Ashley carefully, Orpha silently fumed as she listened to everyone's daily news and he joined in the conversations as though the contretemps had not even taken place. Baby Ralph was doing so well; Ezzie's boat business had really picked up, so much so in fact he was considering buying another boat to add to the line. Zachariah and Abel were kept busy in their business consulting work and Edna and Peg were loving spending their time together with the baby.

Ashley looked from one to the other as comments were made but he deliberately avoided Orpha's eyes which he knew burned into him with hurt and frustration.

Saying his goodnights to the family, Ashley walked to the front door with Orpha.

'Why, Ashley?' she asked suddenly. 'Why did you not back me in there?' She swung her head towards the dining room.

'Why?' Ashley rasped. 'I'll tell you why!' His voice rose as he shouted, 'would you see opening another shop take precedence over our marriage vows?'

Orpha stared at the man she was to marry before she shouted back, 'That will not be the case, Ashley, and well you know it!'

'Is that so?' Ashley yelled. 'First it was the factory, now it's the shop, what will it be next? Maybe more premises in another town? If you are having second thoughts about marrying me, Orpha, why don't you just tell me? Think on this, *Miss Buchanan* . . . I will not wait forever!' Ashley left, slamming the door behind him, leaving Orpha staring with open mouth.

'Miss Orpha . . . ma'am are you all right?' Simmons had heard every word from the doorway to the parlour where he was checking the fire was roaring. It was all he could do to contain the anger he felt at the man who had shouted at the young woman he had feelings for.

Facing the butler, Orpha nodded.

'Miss Orpha . . . if you could find a minute . . . I don't wish to add to your troubles, but the staff would like a word . . . and now might be a good time.' Simmons turned in the direction of the kitchen and Orpha quietly followed behind him, still feeling shocked at her fiancé's outburst.

Ashley had stormed from the house, not in anger but with a smile on his face. He would be master in his own home and was already laying the foundation stones. He had left Orpha shocked; now she would realise he would not be messed about. He decided he would not visit her for a few days, which would give her time to think about their relationship. She would come to her senses about trying to make him play second fiddle to a shop! Orpha had no idea where he lived, so he felt safe in the knowledge she would not come looking for him and turn up on his doorstep. Just as well, he thought, as he approached the hovel he resided in. However, it would not be for much longer.

Once inside, he changed out of his good clothes and, again having nothing to burn in the cold dark grate, he climbed into bed to think about his good fortune.

Lying in the dark, Ashley knew his cupboards were bare, he had used the last of the coal pickings and he had no money. Maybe it was time to earn himself a few guineas in Birmingham with the rich ladies he had once courted for their money. Having been a highly sought after escort to wealthy widows wanting an outing to the theatre, he had soon learned to extend his business into their bedrooms and had been well paid for his efforts. When he had needed new clothes he knew his 'ladies' would provide, after all having a handsome young man at one's side drew envious glances from all their friends. Yes, Ashley Rochester would soon be back in the business of parting wealthy older women from their money with choice words and promises of lovemaking like they had never before known.

*   *   *

Orpha sat in the kitchen with the staff and listened to what Simmons was telling her. He spoke quietly. 'The stable boys followed Mr Rochester to his home in Ettingshall Road. It was a ruin. We all know this is none of our business and, although we are only staff, we have been made to feel like family. We all adore you, ma'am, and we wish only to protect and support you. I must apologise for overhearing your conversation with Mr Rochester earlier but I was not deliberately eavesdropping.' He crossed his fingers behind his back in the hope the white lie would not be brought into question.

Alice piped up, 'We'm sorry, miss, really we am . . . is . . . are!'

Orpha smiled at Alice's search for the correct grammar before saying, 'I had also noticed that Ashley has worn the same clothes for months now and I had considered whether he was just down on his luck or, in fact, destitute!'

The staff watched the nuances of emotion play over the girl's face before she added, 'I will tell you this, and it must NOT leave this kitchen!' Seeing the nods of affirmation, she went on, 'I have today visited a solicitor. Mr Rochester will not be getting his hands on my estate after the wedding should that be his ploy.'

Beulah Jukes could hold her tongue no longer, 'If you think that's what he's up to . . . why marry him?'

Orpha sighed as she ignored the question 'Don't worry about me please, I'm glad you cared enough to tell me what you knew, and I'm not angry – far from it. Thank you all for your concern, and I would be most grateful if this stays between us.'

Orpha left the kitchen to retire to her bed. So, Ashley Rochester had no money, and he lived in a ruined house. Did he have a string of warehouses as he purported? Was he only after her money? Did he love her at all? Questions flooded her mind as Orpha climbed into bed. Well, there was only one way to find out . . . she would ask him!

CHAPTER 45

Orpha stamped down Commercial Road the next morning still feeling upset and hurt at Ashley's behaviour towards her the previous evening as well as the news given to her by the servants. At one end of the road was a smithy, at the other end was Union Wharf. With small wharfs all down one side of the road, buildings lined the other. There were two schools and a few public houses and the building she looked for was opposite one of the schools. It was a huge structure with large domed windows looking out towards Waterloo Wharf and its basin. Unlocking the side door, Orpha stepped inside and flung open the window shutters. Dust motes danced in the air and twinkled in the light that flooded the room.

Walking the length of the room, a connecting door took her into a smaller room. Opening the shutters, Orpha knew immediately it would make an excellent shop. It was very well suited to her business and looking around she discovered a lavatory and a room which would serve as a scullery. She couldn't have been more pleased, so closing the shutters and locking the door behind her, Orpha Buchanan walked back to Belcher & Son to close the deal on her new shop.

Lottie Spence reported for their weekly meeting and Orpha gave the good news about the shop in Commercial Road.

'Are you able to find some girls to give the place a thorough clean, whilst I organise equipment to be delivered?' Lottie nodded. 'I proposed to move Joan and Hilda to the new building to train staff in the first instance, so we'll need to hire new shop girls to stand in for them in the Oxford Street shop. Once the new shop is up and running I would like Joan to manage the Birmingham shop. Hilda will manage the Oxford Street shop and Ann will manage the new one in Commercial Road, if you are in agreement.' She also disclosed to her trusted friend she would be on the lookout for a new factory premises.

Orpha Buchanan knew she had risen fast in the world of men; she provided work, she paid her bills on time and found herself well-liked by the businessmen she dealt with. She had long ago learned not to back down where these men were concerned and she had gained a good reputation as a wily but fair businesswoman. There were those, of course, who still felt women should not be in business but should stay at home and raise a family. Orpha simply dismissed these archaic notions, and once set on an idea she became an immovable force.

On her way to Derry Street to visit her mother, Orpha considered herself to be extremely fortunate. She had good friends and a loyal staff and a dedicated workforce. She had ensured her mother had a roof over her head and food in her belly. Now she had to find a way to confront Ashley Rochester!

Hortense Buchanan sat staring into the fire. They were all up at the big house and she was left in this poky hole alone. Misery and loneliness folded around her as she considered her lot. She should have more than this. She should be mistress of a big house with servants of her own. Instead she was reduced to being beholden to her daughter. Hortense snorted as she had thought she would never see the day that happened!

Envy began to mount inside her once more as she thought about her daughter's success. Shaking her head, she realised that success would never have been achieved had she not thrown Orpha out of Buchanan House. What was it the girl had said, *'You reap what you sow!'*

Hortense had Orpha truly believing she had been brought down to her cake and milk and she intended it should remain that way. She had formulated a new plan. She would play the victim a while longer and slowly worm her way back into the family fold. Once firmly ensconced, she would take over the running of that household and its servants. She would be the matriarch of Buchanan

Mansion! Once she was in there then she could work at removing the others.

The town grapevine had revealed Orpha was planning to be married in the summer and Hortense wondered whether she would be invited. It was unlikely, she thought; Abel would not want her in the same vicinity let alone the same room as his family.

Bastard! she thought again as she relived his throwing her out onto the streets. Shovelling more coal onto the fire, she knew she would have her day, she just had to be patient a little while longer.

Hortense feigned pleasure at seeing her daughter and Orpha explained about the new shop as they sat drinking tea by the fire.

'You are a very lucky young woman, I hope you realise that,' Hortense said a little unkindly.

'I do, Mother,' Orpha ignored the jibe.

Hortense harrumphed in a way Orpha remembered well from her childhood. 'As long as you do.' Hortense always insisted on having the last word.

Orpha asked how Hortense was settling into the house and caught the sneer on Hortense's face before a forced smile replaced it. 'The house is fine,' her mother said, 'if a little quiet.'

'You should get out more now the better weather is coming,' Orpha added.

Hortense merely nodded, not taking her eyes from the fire. 'I hear you are to be married.'

'Yes,' Orpha said, wondering how her mother had discovered that snippet of news, because as far as she knew she never went out of the door. 'At St George's Church in the summer.'

'I hope *he's* worthy enough to be included in the family,' Hortense muttered.

The note of sarcasm was not lost on Orpha as she told her mother all about her intended.

'Rochester, you say?' Hortense asked.

'Yes, Mother, Ashley Rochester,' Orpha confirmed.

Hortense stiffened at the familiar name.

'Got money has he?' Hortense was now leading the conversation down the path she wanted it to go.

Orpha explained about the warehouses Ashley had told everyone he owned, and although she was sure he was lying, she kept that to herself.

'So what does your father make of him?' Hortense pursued.

'They get on well, they appear to like each other,' Orpha said. Now feeling distinctly uncomfortable, Orpha made her excuses and left. She had felt like a child again under her mother's questioning gaze and she didn't like it one bit.

On her way home, Orpha thought about their discussion; what her mother's questions were all about. Then it hit her. Hortense was angling for an invitation to the wedding!

When Orpha had gone, Hortense sat by the fire and her thoughts raced through her mind. Rochester. She knew that name only too well. It was an unusual surname in these parts; could this Ashley Rochester be related to the family she knew many years ago?

With a huge sigh, she thought about Orpha's relationship with the young Rochester.

It was true she wanted to see the girl fail, but the ramifications of this upcoming wedding could be too great even to think about.

If she was correct in her thinking, and she would need to know for definite, then somehow she had to put a stop to that wedding – and quickly.

It had been a week since Ashley had visited Buchanan Mansion and dressed in fine new clothes he wondered if he'd been missed by anyone. He had slipped back into his old life in Birmingham without a problem; the older ladies of the town having paid handsomely for his services. He was now back in Wolverhampton with money in his pocket.

Simmons said the family were in the parlour and led Ashley into said room, saying to Orpha, 'Will I tell Mrs Jukes there will be one more for dinner, ma'am?' At her nod, Simmons closed the parlour door behind him.

Orpha greeted her intended, offering him a seat next to her as she silently noted his new attire. Now where had he got the money for those?

'I was just about to tell everyone my plans for the new shop,' she said, catching the scowl on Ashley's face. Ignoring it, she launched into her description of her plans excitedly. 'Now I'm the outright owner of the two factories and two shops I'm in a financial position to buy the shop on a mortgage facility and have it equipped. I have decided to have a dividing wall built one third of the way into the larger room, which will be the shop. The other two thirds will then become a storage facility for boxes, bags etc., which will leave the other room to be turned into a coffee shop!'

Peg gushed, 'Oh Orpha, that sounds delightful! Coffee overlooking the wharf . . . it will be very popular, I'm sure!'

The others were in agreement and Orpha beamed at their praise of her idea.

Abel asked Ashley what he thought of the idea and the young man smiled, saying, 'Orpha certainly knows what she wants, that's for sure, and she doesn't rest until she gets it. Nothing stands in the way of business, does it, sweetheart?'

No one but Orpha picked up on the sarcasm that lay beneath the statement. Ignoring it, Orpha chatted with Peg and Edna about tablecloths and china for the new coffee shop.

As they sat down to dinner, Zachariah made mention of Ashley's new clothes and Orpha watched his response carefully.

'Ah yes,' he said, holding out his arms, 'I was able to free up some capital at last.' Ashley had lied through his back teeth, she was sure, and Orpha had seen him do it. She felt her heart sink at Ashley's bare-faced lie. Now, more than ever, she wanted to know where his money had come from.

With a heavy feeling in her stomach Orpha tried to ignore the blatant untruth. As she watched him talk and laugh with the family, Orpha wondered if she was doing him an injustice. Maybe he *had* freed up some money. Maybe he *was* telling the truth. Feeling a little ashamed of herself, Orpha joined in the discussions around the table.

At the front door, Ashley said, 'So I was gone for a week and you didn't even miss me.'

'Of course I did, silly,' Orpha replied with a smile.

Tightening his arms around her, Ashley leaned down as if to kiss her. Instead he rasped into her face, 'Don't you ever call me silly again, do you hear me?'

'Ashley . . .' Orpha struggled to free herself.

Simmons stepped from the morning room, saying, 'Everything all right, ma'am?'

Orpha nodded with a held breath as Ashley walked out of the front door, her eyes brimming with tears.

Simmons moved to the girl who was mistress of the house and folded his arms around her, producing a spotlessly laundered handkerchief. Neither of them registered the impropriety of the gesture.

Ashley knew if he wanted to lay his hands on her money he should be nice, but the way she constantly put him down was enervating. He was feeling exhausted at keeping up the charade and it showed in his temper.

Deciding to go back to apologise and make his excuses, he strode back up the driveway.

Knocking then flinging the door open, Ashley stared at his fiancé wrapped in the butler's arms.

'Oh-oh,' Simmons said as Ashley turned and stormed away, 'that's done it now!'

Orpha tried to hide a smirk as Simmons closed the front door on a rapidly retreating Mr Rochester.

It was later in the kitchen when Simmons explained the situation to the others. 'Miss Orpha was in tears and I wonder if that man would have slapped her had I not appeared in the nick of time. I'm afraid I overstepped the mark . . . I gave Miss Orpha a hug.'

'Simmons! You never . . .!' Alice exclaimed as Jago nudged Seth in the ribs and they tittered.

'Oh my Lord!' Beulah Jukes lifted her hand to her mouth.

'However, that's not all . . .' Simmons continued as the staff watched him, 'Ashley Rochester walked back into the house and saw us.'

'Bloody hell Simmons! What *were* you thinking?' Beulah asked incredulously.

'I couldn't bear to see her cry.' Simmons lowered his eyes to his teacup.

'Simmons . . .' Beulah began as the butler looked at her, 'Don't tell me . . . Oh Christ Simmons! You're sweet on the mistress!'

He nodded, making his dark hair bounce and his eyes glistened in the lamplight. Then he said, 'I am, Beulah. I know it could never be between us, but it doesn't stop me feeling the way I do about her. I love her, Beulah, and I'll see no harm come to her!'

The stable boys ceased their giggles as they looked at their mentor, the man who protected them and showed them the ways of the house. Alice and Beulah exchanged a look then Alice said, 'Mr Simmons, beggin' your pardon, but you must be in your thirties . . . you're a lot older than the mistress.'

Simmons nodded. Beulah let out a gasp, saying, 'Age has nothing to do with it, you soft girl! *She* is the mistress and *he* . . .' the cook jabbed a finger at Simmons, '. . . is the butler! It just ain't done!'

Lifting a hand to quieten the cook's fury, Simmons spoke quietly. 'The hug I gave the mistress was in no way improper, Beulah.' The boys giggled again and shooting them a desultory look, he went on, 'It was a hug of friendship; a hug to let her know we all care about her, and to let her know she is not alone.'

'That's what her family is for!' Beulah shook her head.

'I know and I will offer my resignation to the mistress when she returns.' Simmons sighed loudly.

'Don't be so daft!' Beulah snapped. 'She wouldn't accept it and, anyway, where would *we* be if you weren't here?'

'Well I wouldn't be answering the bloody door . . . I do enough around this place!' Alice huffed, sending them all into fits of laughter.

'So what do you think Mr Rochester will do about it?' Jago asked.

'I have no idea,' Simmons said, 'but I will cross that bridge when I come to it.'

Orpha was making her way to the kitchen when she heard the staff talking. They were discussing her and Ashley! Stopping in her tracks, she listened to the whole conversation before retreating to the parlour to mull over what she'd overheard. Simmons said he loved her! The butler was in love with his mistress! Thinking back to the hug he'd given when she was so upset, Orpha was certain it was the comfort given a friend. There was nothing more to it, but she felt sure Ashley would not see it that way. Orpha determined to clear the air with her fiancé regarding this, as well as his living in a hovel the very next time they met.

After storming home, Ashley sat by his fire wondering what the hell was going on. He'd gone back into the house to apologise to Orpha and found her in the arms of the butler! Were they having an affair? It sounded like a seedy novel . . . wealthy heiress sleeps with the hired help! He needed to find out, and quickly. He had no intention of marrying a woman who had given herself to another. Calming himself, he knew he couldn't be so choosy. He had to swallow his pride and get on with making her his wife.

Watching the flames in the hearth, he thought

about his life of the past week. Had he not done just that? Had he not given himself to another . . . a few others in fact? Had he not been paid for doing so? Justifying his behaviour, he reasoned it was different for a man. It could be seen as sowing his last free wild oats before being married. Besides, didn't men still take a mistress after marriage? It was perfectly acceptable for men in this day and age to do just that. However, it was not the done thing for a woman. She would most certainly be seen as a hussy!

With his temper flaring again, Ashley made up his mind to confront Orpha on the issue the next time he visited . . . and he would visit the next time he was hungry.

CHAPTER 46

Orpha did not expect to see Ashley for a little while and she was not disappointed in this, so she set her mind to organising the new structure.

Zachariah had found a reputable builder who was busy erecting the dividing wall. Orpha and Peg, leaving young Ralph in Edna's care, had gone to choose tables, chairs, table linen and china for the coffee shop. Once the wall was erected, then cleaning and painting could begin. A new sign was ordered for the shop and Orpha was delighted at how quickly everything was coming together.

On the way home, Orpha suggested, 'Let's stop off at Derry Street and see Mother.' Peg was horrified at the idea at first, but when Orpha explained how much Hortense had changed, she relented.

Walking to the house, Peg asked, 'Why did you buy the house for her?'

'Oh Peg, you should have seen her! She was half starved and dressed in rags, I couldn't walk away and forget about her!' Orpha's voice caught as she remembered the state Hortense had been in that day.

'I would have!' her sister spat.

'No you wouldn't, Peg, for all she's done to us, neither of us would have left her to go into the workhouse or die on the street.' Orpha cast a glance at her sister as they entered the house.

Hortense looked up at her daughters and said, 'Well now, Miss High and Mighty deigns to visit today then!'

Peg walked to her mother, slapped her soundly across the face, turned on her heel and walked out.

Hortense forced her tears to fall as Orpha said, 'Mother, you did rather ask for that.'

'I suppose I did,' Hortense said quietly, 'I was just so . . . so surprised to see her.'

'Well I don't think you'll be seeing her again for a very long time, if at all,' Orpha said as she sat next to her mother. 'Why do you do it? Why do you have to alienate everyone?'

Hortense shook her head then wiped her eyes. 'I just want to be part of the family again.'

So that was it! 'Well,' Orpha said, 'that's definitely not the way to go about it!'

That very evening, Ashley arrived dressed to the nines.

Simmons opened the front door and stood aside as Ashley stepped in. Dropping his gloves into his hat, he shoved them at the butler and with a scowl he hissed into his face, 'I don't know what's going on in this house, but I intend to find out. Now my advice to you is . . . stay away from Orpha. You touch her again and I'll kill you!' Ashley marched away to the parlour as Simmons quietly closed the front door. Opening the cloakroom door, he threw the hat on the floor before slamming the door and going back to the kitchen.

All smiles again, Ashley kissed Orpha's cheek in greeting and she whispered, 'We must talk later.' Nodding, he moved to greet the rest of the family.

Simmons stood at the side of the dining room while Alice served the food. Having told the others of the threat made to him, each had decided their own retribution. Alice served the soup and slipped, spilling the contents of the dish on Ashley's new trousers. Passing him the napkin, she muttered her apologies and moved away, giving Simmons a sly wink as she did so.

Simmons poured the wine, only half filling Ashley's glass before moving to fill Orpha's. He felt the glare on him as he smiled down at his mistress.

Alice cleared the soup dishes and brought in the main meal. Beulah had served straight onto the plates, which everyone thought strange, but a good idea to keep the food hot. No comments were made other than it was delicious as always.

Ashley almost gagged on his food . . . it was smothered in pepper. He emptied his wine glass in an effort to relieve the burning in his throat.

Orpha motioned for Simmons to refill everyone's glass and she watched Ashley drain his once more. Orpha gave an imperceptible shake of her head as Simmons stepped forward. 'Ashley, would you care for some water?' At his nod, Orpha flashed Simmons a glance and, in that instant, when their eyes met, Orpha knew what the staff were up to. A very slight smile lifted the corners of her mouth before she covered it with her napkin.

Individual bowls of trifle followed and Orpha wondered what would be wrong with Ashely's until she saw his eyes water. 'Too much sherry, darling?' she asked as Ashley dabbed his eyes.

'No . . . no, it's delicious, sweetheart, it's just . . . it went down the wrong way.' Ashley began to cough as Simmons refilled his water glass. Looking up at the butler, Ashley saw the satisfied smile and his temper began to rise.

The rest of the family moved to the parlour and Ashley steered Orpha in the direction of the gardens. Once outside, he snapped, 'Your bloody staff are trying to kill me!'

'Ashley! Whatever do you mean?' Orpha feigned ignorance.

'That food! Meat laced in pepper, soup on my trousers, trifle floating in sherry!' He gagged.

'No one else complained, Ashley, I suspect you are making too much of it.' Orpha strolled down the pathway that skirted the lawns.

Grabbing her arm, Ashley whirled her to face him. 'And another thing . . . what's going on with you and that butler?'

'Ashley Rochester!' Orpha fumed. 'How dare you accuse me of such a thing?!'

'I saw you, Orpha! I saw you in his arms, remember?' Ashley yanked her arm.

Pulling away from him, she said, 'He was comforting me . . . I was upset at your aberrant behaviour!'

'Oh Orpha, I'm sorry, I didn't mean to upset you,' he said cautiously as he realised his temper was getting the better of him again.

Her anger was fierce as she continued, 'You are no saint, Ashley . . . you lied to me!'

'What makes you think that?' he asked.

'You do not live in a fancy house . . . I know you are living in a hovel! I know you have no capital to draw on and my question now is . . . how did you afford those new clothes?' Orpha was beside herself with rage and her hands clenched at her sides.

'My father's house has fallen into some disrepair, I have to admit.' Ashley's brain worked furiously. 'Unfortunately my warehouses have not provided enough income to rectify this as yet. As for my clothes, I thought it time to replenish my wardrobe as I've neglected it of late; I drew the money from my inheritance stored in the bank.'

'Oh Ashley . . .' Orpha's anger evaporated as she heard his explanation. 'I'm so sorry.'

Wrapping her in his arms, he smiled in the darkness.

★   ★   ★

Throughout the whole exchange, Simmons had stood in the shadows, his eyes never leaving the flashes of Orpha's green ones lit by the moonlight.

Armed with pencils and notebooks Jago Morton and Seth Walker, the stable boys, entered St Matthew's Street from either end and walked towards the centre. This was where Ashley Rochester purported to have a string of warehouses. All the buildings were grimy with the coal dust from the coal pits. The windows were dirty from years of street traffic kicking up dust and mud. Hardly any of the premises looked to be in use.

Dressed in their best clothing, they had been instructed to ask anyone they met about hiring the warehouses on their mistress's behalf.

Seeing a small shop selling tobacco a little way down the street, Jago entered and asked the shop-keeper about the warehouses.

'No lad,' the woman said, 'those buildings ain't seen no use for many a year; not since old man Rochester died.' Jago thanked the woman and left the shop. Noting down what he'd been told, he walked further down the street. The road was long and straight with buildings on both sides and he could see Seth at the far end.

Seth Walker had also asked the same questions in a tiny grocery shop and had received the same answers. He too noted down the information he was given.

Comparing notes in the centre of the street, it

became obvious that Ashley Rochester had again lied through his teeth.

Jago walked to the filthy window of one of the buildings and took out his handkerchief. Spitting on the cloth, he rubbed a small section of the glass clean. Peering through, he could see it was dark but he could also see it was quite empty. This was the proof they were looking for. It was time to let Simmons know what they had discovered.

The boys imparted the knowledge to the butler in the kitchen after dinner.

'The lying swine!' Alice remarked on hearing their news. 'Ashley Rochester should rot in hell!'

'Why has Mr Rochester not tried to make the effort to rent out the buildings over the years? That's my question,' Beulah Jukes put in. 'After all, it would earn him some money.'

Jago consulted his notes, looking for all the world like a policeman. 'Says here, he couldn't be arsed!'

Laughter sounded in the kitchen at his remark.

'You going to tell the missis?' asked Seth as he looked at a worried Simmons.

'I suppose informing Miss Orpha what we know about the empty warehouses would be confirming what she already suspects.'

'But her . . . she . . . needs to be told!' Alice snorted.

'Leave it with me,' Simmons said, 'I will inform the mistress of the lies told regarding the empty buildings, and you two boys . . .' Jago and Seth looked up, 'well done!'

CHAPTER 47

Orpha threw herself into getting the new shop in Commercial Road up and running, and at last the opening day arrived. With shelves stacked with mouth-watering confectionery and the coffee shop ready for custom, Orpha opened the doors. The already growing queue of women trooped inside and Orpha greeted them all with a smile.

The coffee shop did a brisk trade as did the shop, and by the end of the day Orpha left exhausted but happy at the success the first day had seen.

Hortense was pleased to see her daughter and over tea Orpha related how well the new shop had done on its opening day. Hortense watched the girl as a sadness clouded her face and asked, 'So what's up?'

Orpha glanced at the woman sat opposite her and said, 'I had a row with Ashley.' Hortense nodded and Orpha went on to explain the details of the. heated argument that had taken place in the garden.

'So how was it left then?' Hortense asked.

'We've made up now.' Orpha shook her head, trying to stem the tears she felt begin to line her lashes at the memory.

Hortense went on, 'Do you think he loves you? Or do you think he's just after your money?'

'I do think he loves me, Mother, but I'm afraid he may have designs on my money and business even though that may not be his intention. Regardless of any wealth of his own, I am aware of the law and I know it will all belong to him once we are married. Naturally, having worked so hard to build up the business, I don't want to give it up to become a bored housewife.' Orpha's tears cascaded silently down her cheeks.

'So what are you going to do about it?' Hortense asked, ignoring the girl's sobs.

'I don't know! What can I do?' Orpha's voice cracked.

'Seems to me you have a choice to make. You either marry him and hand over your business and money . . . or you tell him to go to hell and hang on to your hard-earned wealth!' Hortense harrumphed.

Orpha knew her mother was right in what she said. She knew she had to make a decision soon; the day of the wedding was drawing ever nearer. If she chose *not* to marry Ashley then she should tell him sooner rather than later. If she chose to marry him then she would have to live with his temper and hope the signed document stored with her solicitor would stand up in court if Ashley pursued his rights to her money. Orpha walked home lost on the horns of the dilemma.

Hortense smiled into the flames in the grate after Orpha had gone. Her daughter, it seemed, had met her match with Ashley Rochester. Orpha would not be rich for long if she married that boy, everything would belong to him after the wedding. Orpha would find herself dependent upon her husband, much as she had been with Abel. The High and Mighty Miss Orpha Buchanan would become the low and weak Mrs Orpha Rochester! Hortense laughed out into the emptiness of the room. However she would not see the day how the mighty had fallen this way. There was no way Hortense could let her daughter marry the man she had set her sights on. She knew it was up to her to prevent this wedding one way or another.

Her mind once more returned to Abel and she wondered how he would feel about seeing his daughter lose her money to her new husband. She considered asking him, but he had made it very clear on her last visit he wanted nothing more to do with her. She could always write a letter to him pointing out his daughter would be penniless once married. He would know this of course, but she would enjoy rubbing his nose in it.

Moving to the small sideboard, she took out pen, ink and notepaper. Sitting at the table, she began her letter to her husband.

⋆   ⋆   ⋆

435

Simmons was finding it more and more difficult to hide his feelings from the mistress of the house. He watched in silent anger at how her husband-to-be treated her; he would disappear for days on end with no explanation. The wedding day was almost upon them and Simmons couldn't bear the thought of the love of his life marrying another. Perhaps it was time to move on. Maybe he should submit his notice and leave the house . . . leave the town.

He knew he would never love anyone the way he loved Orpha Buchanan and he also knew they could never be together while he was a butler. Sitting by the fire in the kitchen lost in his own thoughts, he was unaware of Beulah Jukes watching him as she worked.

Where did Ashley Rochester go when he was not here in this house? Were those warehouses being used or were they standing empty? Simmons made up his mind, he *had* to find out!

'You've come to a decision then?' Beulah asked as Simmons banged his cup onto the table. As his eyes found hers, she added, 'I've been watching you this past hour and that cup tells me you've made up your mind about something or other.'

'I have indeed, Beulah!' he responded with a smile. Going to the back door, he whistled out for the stable boys. As they ran into the kitchen he asked everyone to sit and hear him out.

'Oh gawd!' Alice said. 'Looks like Sherlock Holmes is planning something again . . . he's called in Watson and his friend!' Laughter filled the kitchen before the serious discussion got underway.

Simmons related his thoughts about Ashley's life whilst away from Orpha. He said, 'I want to know where Mr Rochester goes, what he does, how he gets his money, and what is going on regarding the warehouses. I think the man is only after Orpha's money . . . he is a gold digger. I don't think Ashley loves Orpha at all, in fact I think he holds no respect for her either. This is not sour grapes because he is engaged to the woman I love, but I feel it imperative we find out more about Mr Ashley Rochester.'

Jago nudged Seth, saying, 'It looks like we're going out on a mission again!' Simmons' nod attested to this statement. 'How are we going to explain not being here?' Jago asked.

'If you are missed I'll think of something. Now I want you to take pencil and notepaper and write everything down. Times, places . . . everything! We could save the mistress from making the biggest mistake of her life . . . if we're quick enough!'

So with money in their pockets, the two stable boys set off for Ettingshall Road and the hovel belonging to Ashley Rochester.

Ashley had left Orpha quietly standing in the gardens of Buchanan Mansion and would make her sweat before his next visit. Realising she had been too harsh with him, she would be in a better frame of mind when he eventually returned to

Buchanan Mansion. He could not afford to push her too hard in case she called off the wedding and that would never do.

Now as a new day dawned he boarded the train for Birmingham dressed in his new clothes and drawing admiring glances from women sitting in the first-class carriage. It was time to earn himself some more money. Settling himself, he did not notice the two boys scrambling into the third-class carriage further down the platform. In fact he was unconcerned with anyone, he had a headache and was feeling quite unwell. He passed it off as the onset of a head cold.

Alighting the train at New Street Station, Ashley made his way through the crowded streets to Ladywell Walk. Walking up the drive of a large house, he banged on the front door with his cane. The door was opened by an older woman. She was well into her fifties but had retained her beauty and maintained her figure. Allowing him entry, the door closed them off from the street and prying eyes.

Jago and Seth ran swiftly and quietly up the driveway and hid beneath a window which looked into the parlour. Noting down the time and address, they peeped through the window. They watched as Ashley pocketed the money the older woman had given him before wrapping his arms around her and kissing her fiercely.

The boys exchanged a shocked look then went back to watching the scene unfolding in the parlour.

Ashley Rochester was undressing the woman, then he laid her on the couch as he disrobed.

Seth muttered, 'He's going to . . .!'

'Shhh!' Jago urged, slapping a hand over the other boy's mouth before they continued to watch the goings-on.

The boys followed Ashley discreetly all day, noting down the details as they had been requested to do. They could hardly believe the man was going to certain houses, ones he was welcomed at – ones he had obviously visited before – and was selling himself for money!

Sitting on the board seat in third class on the train home, they joked in hushed voices about the day and whether there was a word for a male prostitute!

Ashley was immensely pleased with himself. He had asked for more money and they had paid it. It could be distasteful work, but it beat picking coal any day. He decided he would stop off for a meal and a beer in the Coach & Horses on the Wolverhampton Road before going home. He needed to relax, after all he'd had a busy day!

CHAPTER 48

Simmons listened patiently to the story the boys told in the kitchen along with the oohs and ahhhs from Alice and Beulah.

'We couldn't believe it!' Seth gushed. 'All these old ladies . . . beggin' your pardon, Mrs Jukes . . . he was . . .'

'All right,' Simmons said, holding up a hand to halt the boy's words, 'I think we all understand now where Mr Rochester is getting his money from.'

'Oh my God!' Beulah said in absolute horror. 'What about Miss Orpha! Simmons, we *have* to tell her!'

'How?' Simmons asked. 'We can't just say "Miss Orpha your husband-to-be is a gigolo"!'

The boys exchanged a quick glance – so that was the word for it!

'I know that!' snapped Beulah. 'But we can't just let her go ahead and marry the swine!'

'We have to go about this very carefully, Beulah. We have again interfered in "upstairs" business . . . for all the right reasons, I grant you . . . but it's interference nevertheless.' Simmons shook his head at the quandary. 'The only way I can see is for me to tell her, then hand in my notice. That way she's aware of what we've learned about Mr Rochester and I can move on and spare her embarrassment.'

'You don't have to give in your notice, Mr Simmons, it was us who followed him, and it should be us for the chop!' Jago intervened.

'No lad. It was my doing, and besides, I'm not sure I could stand by and watch her marry someone else, however good or bad may they be.'

The mood in the kitchen settled into a sombre quiet as each mulled over the situation in their own mind.

Abel sat in the study at Buchanan Mansion reading the post. A letter had arrived . . . from Hortense. In it she pointed out the folly of Orpha marrying Ashley Rochester.

Abel knew the law and he had worried about Orpha's estate being taken over by her husband. His daughter knew the law also and yet she'd planned the wedding. Obviously marrying Ashley was more important to her. He thought of the hard work and long hours Orpha had put into the business; of her contending with men who were of the opinion she should be at home tending her children; of the Royal Warrant awarded her by Queen Victoria – was Orpha really willing to give all this up for a man?

Abel also knew the letter from his wife was her

way of shooting another barb at him for the way he had treated her. Looking again at the letter, he read that Hortense had suggested he pay Ashley off with some of the emeralds he kept safe in the bank. If he thought for one minute it would work, he would do just that. However, Orpha had been lost to him once before and he could not risk being alienated from her by doing such a thing; she would never forgive him for driving away her man. No, the best he could do would be to talk to her and make sure she knew exactly what this wedding entailed.

It was the day to try on her wedding gown for final adjustment, she had told the family. In fact she had secretly gone to Ettingshall Street to see for herself where Ashley lived. It was as she approached the old houses that she saw him emerge from one of them and he was dressed in his Sunday-best clothes.

Following discreetly, she saw him approach the station. Where was he going? How could she find out? Circling the queue of people at the ticket office, she stood with her back to them pretending to look out of the window. Listening carefully, she heard people buying their tickets. Then Ashley's voice had asked for a third-class ticket to Birmingham. Orpha wondered if he was trying to conserve his funds by not travelling first class.

Moving to the end of the queue, she waited her turn. Buying her own ticket, she boarded the train quickly and found a seat in the first-class compartment.

Orpha alighted the train in Birmingham, and as she left New Street Station she followed Ashley in the crowd. Pushing her way through the throng of people, she kept him in her sights.

Hurrying to catch up to him, she was delayed at almost every step by people coming and going. Fear of losing sight of him, Orpha fought her way along the streets. Where had all these people come from? Then she realised it was market day and folk came from miles around looking for bargains. Birmingham, she remembered, had a market twice a week unlike that of Wolverhampton which held its market every day. As she stepped around children playing hopscotch, a game of hopping on numbered squares chalked on the street, Orpha saw Ashley walk up the driveway of a house. She rushed along but stopped dead in her tracks as she saw him waiting at the door of the house. Orpha shot back behind the hedge as he turned in her direction. Had he seen her? Chancing a peep round the hedge, she saw Ashley kissing an older woman on the doorstep. This was not a motherly kiss . . . this was a kiss full of passion!

Shock held her to the spot for a moment then she ran up the drive to look in the window. She saw, although unbeknown to her, exactly what her stable boys had witnessed the day before.

The horror of the scenario had her stumbling

back down the driveway. Her stomach rolled as she walked away from the house. Her colour had drained from her face and she felt sick. Leaning against a hedge, she began to retch and suddenly lost the contents of her stomach. Wiping her mouth with a handkerchief, she thought, how could he do this to her when he had so readily professed his love for her? If he needed money so badly he could have asked her for it. But no, not Ashley, he would never ask her for money . . . he preferred to take it, all of it, after their wedding!

Dragging herself into a coffee shop drained of energy, Orpha sat with her drink thinking over what she'd witnessed. She should refuse to marry him and tell him why. Orpha paid for her coffee and strode out for the wedding shop to fetch her dress. She would pay for it now she'd ordered it, but she would not be wearing it.

In the wedding shop in Birmingham, Orpha collected her finished wedding gown. Tailored in the empire line style, the bodice was white velvet and the long white silk skirt reached to sit nicely on top of her white side-button shoes. The top of the leg-of-mutton sleeves were silk that matched the skirt, and the lower sleeve of velvet fastened with tiny silk-covered buttons. The back of the skirt had a velvet spoon-shaped train inserted. The finest piece of Nottingham lace draped her black hair, held in place with a small tiara on which sat three white silk roses. Checking her look in the long cheval mirror, Orpha felt none of the excitement she knew she should be feeling. Assuring the worried dressmaker it was exactly as ordered, Orpha asked for it to be boxed for its journey home.

CHAPTER 49

Simmons opened the front door and greeted Orpha, 'Welcome home, ma'am, been shopping I see.' He eyed the box as he relieved her arms of its weight.

'Hmmm,' Orpha muttered, climbing the sweeping staircase to her bedroom with Simmons and the box in tow. 'Just put it on the bed please, Simmons,' Orpha said as she looked at the butler. He knew what the box contained, she could see it in his sad eyes.

'Should I send Alice up to hang it for you, Miss Orpha?' he asked as he walked to the door.

'No thank you, Simmons, I'll do it later.'

'Very good, ma'am,' he bowed slightly and turned to leave.

'Simmons,' Orpha called him back, 'may I ask you something?'

'Of course, ma'am, anything,' he answered. Feeling a little uncomfortable at being in her bedroom, he stayed by the door.

Walking to face him, she said, 'Simmons have you ever been in love?' Then suddenly added, 'I'm so sorry I should never have asked you such a question, please forgive me.' Orpha blushed crimson as she lowered her eyes.

'Ma'am,' Simmons whispered, 'I have indeed been in love and it hurts like the very devil!' Orpha looked up at him and he added, 'Pardon me, ma'am, but I take it you are not experiencing that feeling with Mr Rochester?'

Shaking her head, Orpha's tears threatened once more.

'Ma'am, may I speak freely?' Simmons asked, and at her nod he went on. 'It is my contention you are not in love with the man you intend to marry.'

Orpha's head rocked back and forth on her neck as she thought about his words.

'If that should prove to be the case,' he added, 'then marriage to him would most certainly be a mistake.'

Suddenly a weight lifted off her shoulders and reaching up she kissed Simmons on the cheek. Stepping back she said, 'Thank you Simmons.'

Mrs Jukes watched the butler drink his tea, his other hand occasionally brushing his cheek.

'You got a shaving rash?' she asked at last.

Simmons shook his head and said nothing as he lapsed back into thought of that kiss. It was only a fatherly peck, he told himself, but his heart fluttered at the memory. His love for the mistress of the house was growing day by day and he found himself seeking any excuse to see her. He had to be careful; she might think he was stalking her and take offence.

Simmons was finding it extremely difficult to keep his secret. Yes, the staff knew how he felt about Orpha and they all knew it could never be, but day after day he yearned to hold the girl in his arms. He spent his life wishing it could be possible; wishing she felt the same for him. He agonised over the decision to leave or stay. If he left he would not see her at all and that would be pure torture. On the other hand, it was torture to see her every day and be unable to reveal his feelings for her.

Sitting by the fire, his mood darkened and his tea went cold.

Simmons spent the afternoon packing his meagre possessions into a carpet bag. Now he could leave at a moment's notice. He considered ways of broaching the subject of Ashley's behaviour with Orpha. There would be no easy way to do this, he would just have to take a deep breath and plunge in. He dreaded the thought of her shedding tears over this man, knowing he would be unable to comfort her in the way he would want.

Pushing his hands through his hair, he sighed audibly into the quiet of his room. There was no way to avoid this imbroglio. Standing, he checked his look in the mirror and strode from the bedroom.

Ashley Rochester had not joined the family for dinner that evening, Simmons noted, and he was glad of it. He also noted Orpha was not eating and her face was pale. Was she ill? Had something or someone upset her? He watched with concern as she pushed her plate away the food untouched. Something had happened, nothing put Orpha off her food!

CHAPTER 50

Abel requested Orpha meet him in the study after breakfast, he had something he wanted to discuss with her. Unable to face her food, Orpha said she would take a walk in the gardens while waiting for her father to finish eating.

'Ma'am,' Orpha heard Simmons' voice as she strolled the gravel path, 'may I have a moment of your time?'

'Of course, Simmons, what is it?' Orpha smiled at the butler approaching her. He was tall and straight-backed . . . and handsome. She had noticed this before and flushed at the thoughts running wild in her mind.

'Ma'am, there is only one way to say this, so I will say it outright.' The butler saw her tense. 'It appears Mr Rochester has been lying to you regarding his warehouses. They have stood empty for many years, so the locals say. In fact they have not been used since Mr Rochester senior died.'

Simmons was building himself up to informing her of Ashley's activities in Birmingham also, but as he drew a breath to do so, she turned to go indoors and his courage failed him.

Orpha said, 'Thank you, Simmons, I suspected as much.' She didn't ask where he'd got the information, she really didn't care.

'I'm sorry, Miss Orpha, both for his lying to you and for my having to be the one to tell you.' Simmons watched Orpha's green eyes sparkle with tears in the sunshine.

'I'm sorry too, Simmons. Everything was going so well until Ashley came into my life and now . . .' Orpha let the sentence trail off. Taking a deep breath, she touched the butler's sleeve and walked into the house to meet with her father.

'Ah there you are,' Abel said as she entered the study. Sitting together, Abel showed his daughter the letter he'd received from his wife. Surprise showed on her face as she passed the letter back to her father.

'She's interfering again it seems,' Orpha said.

Abel nodded, 'Orpha, you do know when you marry everything you own will pass to Ashley?' Seeing her downcast eyes and her head nod, he resumed, 'Not only that, but when I'm gone my emeralds will be shared between Zachariah, Peg and yourself, which means yours will belong to Ashley.'

Abel's sad green eyes met Orpha's shocked green eyes. 'Yes,' he went on, 'you will be completely beholden to him. Are you really prepared to give up everything you've worked for just like that?' Abel snapped his fingers.

Threatened tears now ran freely down Orpha's

cheeks as Abel continued. 'If you are determined to marry this man then his money worries will be over. However, you will be working your shops and factories to line his pockets . . . and unless he dies before you, you will never see a penny of it!'

'Oh Father!' Orpha cried. 'Everything is going wrong!'

'You have to make a decision, darling, one way or the other,' Abel said as he hugged his sobbing daughter.

Sitting on the train travelling back to Wolverhampton, Ashley knew he was slipping back into his old life, but it was easy money. Staring out of the windows, he saw nothing of the buildings as they flashed past. He was careful about the women he visited, it wouldn't do for Orpha to find out how he earned his income. Besides, once they were married, he'd have no need to see the women again. His old life would be gone and forgotten.

It was exhausting work pleasing these old dowagers, but he dare not let his performance slip; that was a sure way to find himself replaced by another and his reputation in tatters. Besides which, the knowledge would be spread all over town before he could blink an eye. He needed the money at the moment and his 'older ladies' provided that. Telling each she was the only one for him, he was amazed how readily they believed him. If he were to boil it down, it was sordid work, but he chose not to think of it that way. When he looked into pale eyes in wrinkled faces, he saw only money. Their appetites were small, hence there being so many to visit and not one knew about the others. He was doing these ladies a service, making them feel wanted in their old age. They were happy with his visits and he was happy with their money.

Ashley whistled a cab, waiting by the station. He needed a drink and a good cheap dinner, and he knew exactly where to find both. Climbing into the carriage, he called for the cabbie to take him to the Foresters' Arms in Green Lane.

Very much later he stepped from the public house a little worse for wear. He wove his way down Derry Street which crossed Green Lane and by the light of the moon he was singing loudly.

As he neared the end of the street, a woman's voice called out. 'Shut that bloody row up! Folks here are trying to sleep!'

Stopping where the woman stood in her front garden, Ashley leaned his hand on the gate. 'I'll have you know, mad . . . madam . . .' he slurred, 'I am celeb . . . celebrating my himminent marriage!'

'Then celebrate it a bit quieter or bugger off home!'

'How dare you!' Ashley tittered. 'Do you know who I am?'

'I don't care who you are! I do care that you are disturbing my sleep!' the woman spat indignantly.

'I . . .' Ashley went on haughtily, 'I, madam, am

Ashley Rochester, soon to be the owner of "The Choc's Box"!'

The woman glared at him in the light from her window and laughed, 'Oh I doubt that, young man.'

'Whatever do you mean?' Ashley asked as he swayed in an effort to stay on his feet.

'I mean what I say!' the woman rasped. 'Now, if you don't get your carcass off my gate, I'll be calling for a constable!' She made to move his hand from her gate and shock took her breath away. The little finger of his left hand was webbed to the next one right down to the first knuckle – as her son's had been!

Ashley snorted as he balanced himself up and took off down the street humming quietly to himself. All he had to do now was find his way home.

Back inside her house, Hortense was shaking as she made herself some hot tea.

Sitting comfortably her mind was cast back to a time before she married Abel Buchanan.

After the death of her mother Hortense had been given the post of maid in the Rochester household. Mr Rochester had taken an instant liking to her.

She frowned now as she recalled how he had promised to divorce his wife and marry her. Being young and impressionable, she had believed him. She saw herself becoming mistress in his house, and so the affair had begun. Her world had been turned upside down when she discovered she was pregnant. Mrs Rochester had sent her packing, thinking she had given herself to some young man in the town. Mr Rochester had watched her go with no remorse for what he'd done.

Living in a home for unmarried mothers, she had given birth to a baby boy whose two fingers on his left hand were fused together.

Once the child was born she had registered him under the name of Ashley Rochester. She had taken him along with his birth certificate back to the Rochester house. Leaving him with the cook, she had run hell for leather away from the place.

Smiling to herself now, she wondered how Mr Rochester senior had explained the child to his wife. Whether the baby remained there and been raised by the family was anyone's guess, but it seemed he had retained his name.

Hortense sighed as she thought about the forthcoming marriage. It had to be stopped. It would mean losing yet another chance at getting her hands on the Buchanan fortune, but more importantly, there was no way her son could marry her daughter!

Edna was minding baby Ralph, and she smiled as she stroked his dark hair. His eyes had turned from baby blue to a vivid green. He had all the Buchanan family features.

Orpha took Peg to see the new shop in Commercial Road. She explained her dilemma regarding the financial obstacles to her sister as they walked.

Peg said, 'Oh, that's a dreadful decision to have to make.' She'd not had that problem when she married Ezzie as she'd already given full rein to Orpha regarding the shops and now Ezzie had his own boating business. Peg asked, 'What will you do about the situation?' Orpha merely shook her head.

The shop and coffee shop were full of customers and Peg was delighted for her sister it had proved such a success, but could see it only added to the girl's burden. As they enjoyed a coffee, Peg thought how simple life had been when she thought she was Peg Meriwether; when she ran a market stall and grew her own produce; when she first met Orpha and they worked together in the cottage. Peg's life was still simple, she had a wonderful husband, a good mother-in-law, a beautiful baby boy and a family that loved her. Orpha's life, however, had become an entanglement of situations. She had to choose between her business she'd worked for years to build up, and the man she loved. She had their mother to take care of, but why she bothered left Peg at a loss. She wanted to open yet another factory but couldn't, as yet, due to the prospect of losing it all to a future husband.

Peg looked at her sister as she exchanged words with the customers, and her heart went out to her. Orpha had only a couple weeks left to make her decision. The wedding was almost upon them.

Trudging back to Buchanan Mansion, Orpha told her sister about the warehouse debacle.

Peg stopped and stared, saying, 'For God's sake Orpha! When will you come to your senses?'

Orpha dissolved into tears once more overwhelmed by the strain of it all.

Peg hugged her tightly. 'Oh girl! I'm sorry. That was a bit of the old Peg coming out. But surely you can see what I'm saying?'

Orpha wiped her tears and nodded. 'Father said the same as you did . . . and I have seen a side to Ashley that I didn't much care for . . . but I thought I loved him.'

'Do you though? Do you love him so much that you can't live without him? Do you love him so much that you've never noticed another handsome man?' Peg prompted.

Orpha's mind immediately went to Simmons.

'I thought so!' Peg said, seeing the change on her sister's face. 'Orpha, you are not in love with his man! Yes, he saved you from being swept under a train but that is being grateful . . . not being in love! You can't base a marriage on gratitude! It's obvious he only wants you for your money!'

'I know you're right,' Orpha said miserably. As they walked on, Orpha considered her sister's words knowing in her heart they were true. She had already made up her mind about the sybarite, but as yet she had kept it all to herself.

However, the time had come to tell him what she had decided.

Hortense Buchanan sat by her fire contemplating the crapulous young man she'd met at her garden gate. Ashley Rochester . . . what a dolt! If Orpha held true to her word and married him, she was in for more than one surprise. Hortense grinned at the flames dancing in the hearth. She could of course tell her daughter what she knew about young Mr Rochester . . . or she could stay tight-lipped and let the girl find out for herself. *Decisions, decisions,* Hortense thought as she cackled like a witch. Then she realised she could not allow that to happen for all she had enjoyed the thought.

'What's tickled you, Mother?' Orpha said as she stepped into the room.

'Oh I just woke myself up snoring,' Hortense lied.

The two women passed the afternoon in idle chat, both guarding their words carefully. As Orpha stood to leave, Hortense could hold her tongue no longer.

'Oh I met your Mr Rochester the other night. He was drunk as a Lord and leaning on my gate singing his head off.'

'Really?' Orpha asked quite shocked.

'Yes really. He told me who he was and . . . that he was to be the owner of your businesses very soon!' Hortense smirked at her daughter.

'Did he indeed?' Orpha's anger rose swiftly.

'Well, I think Ashley Rochester is taking a little too much for granted!'

Hortense chuckled overtly as Orpha stomped out of the house.

On her way home, Orpha did not notice the buildings becoming silhouetted against the darkening sky making them look dirtier than ever. She was thinking Ashley had not visited for some time. How dare he tell a total stranger he was taking over her business!

Simmons saw her coming and held the front door open for her. He saw her anger bristling as she stamped into the hallway. 'Ma'am, Mr Rochester is here . . . he's in the parlour with the family.'

'Good!' Orpha snapped as she flung open the parlour door.

The conversation stopped as they all looked at her. Marching up to Ashley as he stood by the fire, she jabbed a finger at him. 'How dare you tell people you are to be the owner of my business!'

'I . . . I . . .' Ashley blanched as he searched for an explanation. He knew he'd overstepped the mark when he'd been drunk.

'You what?' Orpha challenged him. 'You thought I wouldn't find out? You are despicable, Ashley Rochester! You are an acquisitive bully and if you think to get your hands on my money . . . you best think again! Now get out of *my* house and don't ever come back!' Raising her hand, she slapped him hard across the face.

Simmons had heard every word as he stood in the hallway. He also had the front door standing open for Ashley to leave, the broad grin on his face a testament to his feelings on the whole matter. As he closed the door on the departing Ashley, Simmons brushed his hands together in an act of finality.

He enjoyed every word he passed to the staff downstairs as he related the incident. Rubbing his hands together, he settled to enjoy the meal Beulah set before him.

CHAPTER 51

Ashley fumed his way home in the darkness. How had Orpha discovered what he'd said? It must have been the woman he'd talked to on that gate. But how did they know each other? *Did* they know each other? Or had the woman gossiped and Orpha had overheard the tittle-tattle? Either way, she'd heard. Then she'd thrown him out. Now what would he do? He could leave it a few days for her to calm down and then try to talk her round. It would give him time to invent a good excuse.

He could say the woman was lying. No, he didn't think Orpha would believe that for a moment. He could say the woman misheard him, that he told her he was marrying the owner of the business . . . not that he was becoming the owner. Yes, that might work. He would say he was so excited the wedding was just a week away he had gotten drunk and wanted to tell everyone who he was marrying. He was so proud of her he wanted to shout it from the rooftops. Yes, he felt sure now that would work.

In the meantime he would still have to earn

himself some money, but that was no great hardship. He would continue to visit his ladies in Birmingham for a little while longer, which he'd planned to do until the wedding anyway.

Looking around his drab room now, Ashley felt sure he could rescue the situation and be on course for his marriage once again.

Alice Danby straightened her maid's apron and cap and took the tea tray upstairs to Orpha. The rest of the staff followed silently behind her. They were all eager to hear the conversations of the family surrounding Orpha's outburst. Once the tea tray was delivered they all stood outside the parlour door listening intently.

Abel asked his daughter who had told her such a thing and when she revealed it was Hortense, Abel snorted. 'She's being evil again, Orpha,' he said.

'Father,' Orpha snapped, 'Ashley did not deny he'd said it!'

Zachariah interrupted, 'You really didn't give him much of a chance, Orpha.'

'I know . . . and I realise it was hasty, but I had decided to call off the wedding in any case.' Orpha watched her family as they took in her words. None were surprised at her decision. 'Look,' Orpha said, 'you all told me he was only after my money. Peg, you and Simmons both said the same thing . . .'

Beulah's eyes slipped to the butler on hearing his name.

Orpha continued, 'You both said if I really loved him the money wouldn't matter; if I couldn't live without him . . . that was true love. Well, it turns out I *can* live without him, and my business is more important to me.'

Abel asked, 'Orpha, what on earth were you doing discussing this with Simmons?'

The butler raised his eyebrows and rolled his eyes as he continued to listen at the door.

'Father, Simmons cares for me, he didn't want to see me hurt or make a mistake as big as this!' Turning to her sister's husband, she said, 'Ezzie, answer me this. How did you feel about marrying Peg?'

Feeling a little embarrassed at being put on the spot, he answered quietly, 'I adored her, I still do. I would have died if she had refused my proposal. I cannot live without her in my life and if she'd been as poor as a church mouse, it wouldn't have mattered to me.'

'See!' Orpha yelled. 'It's supposed to be that way, but with Ashley and me . . . it wasn't!'

'Right then,' Abel said simply, 'tomorrow you'd better cancel the church.'

'I cancelled everything last week,' Orpha said.

'But you got your dress!' Peg was confused.

'I had ordered it, so I paid for it, I couldn't let the dressmaker down regarding the sale,' Orpha replied.

Suddenly she burst into floods of tears and was immediately wrapped in her father's arms.

The staff quietly retreated to the kitchen to discuss what they'd heard said amongst the family members. Simmons felt happy enough to do a little jig but restrained himself. Instead he retired to bed later, safe in the knowledge Orpha would not be tying herself to the gold digger who was Ashley Rochester.

Orpha, feeling immensely relieved, walked up St George's Parade to attend a meeting with Jonathon Peasbody, her accountant. The audit of her accounts had been completed and she wanted to know if her business could stand to open another factory. The discussions ended positively and she walked happily to see Mr Belcher once more.

The summer sun was warm on her shoulders as she thought it would have been nice to be married on such a day. Pushing the thought aside, she stepped into the estate agent's office. Explaining her requirement, Mr Belcher sought through his papers before showing her what he thought would be an ideal building. Looking at the diagram of the structural plan, Orpha agreed it looked promising. The premises stood on the corner of Navigation Street and Commercial Road – right opposite her shop! Orpha couldn't believe her luck.

Hailing a cabbie, Orpha gave him the address and settled back in the carriage to enjoy the sounds of the horse's hooves on the cobbled streets.

As it happened, Lottie Spence was in the shop

as Orpha walked in. She asked, 'Lottie, would you accompany me to see the new building and give your opinion?'

Lottie gushed, 'Ooh yes, I'd love to.'

As they walked around the dusty structure, the two women formulated a plan between them.

Agreed the building would be an asset to the business, the women parted company; Lottie going back to the shop and Orpha asking the cabbie to return her to Belcher's where she began negotiations for the purchase of the premises.

Once again the cleaning and painting took place while Orpha and Peg scoured the town for utensils, pots and pans, trays and any other accoutrements they might need.

It was on one of these jaunts into town, that Peg said, 'Orpha, did you realise you would have been married tomorrow?'

'Bloody hell!' Orpha said, causing Peg to spill her coffee. They had rested in their coffee shop before tackling yet another shopping trip.

'You know, I wouldn't have thought Ashley would have given you up so easily,' Peg went on.

'Well it just goes to prove what he was after all along!' Orpha said quietly. Her statement closed the conversation about Ashley Rochester.

'Well,' Beulah Jukes said as she stirred the broth, 'you going to tell Miss Orpha now?'

'Tell her what?' Simmons asked.

Beulah sat at the table and exhaled through

her nose. 'Tell her about that bugger's activities in Birmingham!'

'Oh, the delightful Mr Rochester you mean?' Simmons asked with a grin. 'No, I don't think there is any need now, do you?'

'I suppose not. There's no reason to rake over old coals,' the cook answered.

'Precisely, and she's busy with the new factory at the moment too.' Simmons smiled indulgently.

'True. It's fair amazing what that girl has achieved over the years, and no mistake!' The cook was back to stirring the broth, the old edict coming to mind: a broth boiled was a broth spoiled. Looking at Simmons, she asked, 'You still carrying a candle for her?'

The butler nodded, 'Like you wouldn't believe, Beulah!'

'Bloody shame that, you know, that it can't be between you two . . . you'd make a good pair.' Beulah shook her head in dismay.

Simmons felt the pang sting his heart as he heard her words. He had loved Orpha for what seemed like forever and each day that love grew stronger. He tried his best to love her from afar, but the memory of her lips on his cheek was always with him. She plagued his days and haunted his nights; his dreams were full of her. Again he thought of leaving the household and again he dismissed it. He knew he would stay near her always or die trying.

CHAPTER 52

Ashley Rochester walked along Derry Street in an effort to remember the house where he'd exchanged those fateful words with that woman. There, it was the house which stood alone. Walking up to the door, he banged hard. Receiving no answer, he banged again.

'All right, all right . . . I'm not deaf!' The shout echoed through the house. As the door opened, the voice said, 'Ah Mr Ashley Rochester, I wondered how long it would be before I saw you again!'

'Madam, we need words!' Ashley snapped.

'Best come in then,' Hortense said as she closed the door behind him. 'Sit down, lad, and tell me what's on your mind.'

'What's . . .? What's on my mind?!' Ashley said aghast. 'The words you and I exchanged at your garden gate have put paid to my wedding!'

'Yes, I heard something of the sort,' Hortense said nonchalantly.

'Do you not realise what you've done?' Ashley asked sharply.

'What *I've* done?' Hortense's voice mimicked the cadence. 'I've done nothing wrong.'

'I don't believe what I'm hearing!' Ashley rasped. 'You either gossiped and it got back to my fiancé or you told her yourself! Now, I ask myself, how would you know my fiancé?'

'Not that it's any of your business . . . but I will tell you nevertheless. I know that you *were* engaged to Orpha Buchanan . . . am I right?' Hortense watched his face intently; she was enjoying playing with this young man's emotions. Seeing his nod, she continued, 'Well you could never have married her despite me passing on your words to her.'

'What? I don't understand.' Ashley said, shaking his head.

Hortense sighed again as though she were speaking to a five-year-old.

'Why not?' Ashley's voice rose in anger.

'Because . . .' Hortense drew the word out, 'she's my daughter.'

Ashley's anger was now at boiling point. 'And that would matter precisely how?'

Hortense gave him an evil grin. 'That, young man, is something I do not intend to divulge. Now I'll thank you to leave my house. Oh . . . and please do not think to return.'

Ashley stormed away from the house decidedly rattled.

Dinner was pleasant at Buchanan Mansion with the business of the day being discussed. Ezzie was busy brokering deals for his boat line and Edna was in her element taking care of baby Ralph.

Abel and Zach's business was thriving and Peg was enjoying helping out where she could with Orpha's shops.

Then a banging on the front door interrupted conversation.

Orpha could hear raised voices and went to investigate. Ashley was yelling to be let in and Simmons was quietly refusing him entry.

'It's all right, Simmons, let him in,' Orpha said.

'Orpha . . . I'm sorry you misunderstood what had been said when I was drunk . . .' Ashley said in a rush as he stood in the hallway. Simmons was standing to the side still holding the door open.

'Oh I see!' Orpha snapped. 'Now it's that *I* misunderstood, is that what you're saying? That all this is now my fault?'

'No . . . no, I was telling that woman, your mother, that I was *marrying* the owner of "The Choc's Box" . . . not that I was going to *be* the owner!' Ashley held out his hands in supplication.

'How did you know she is my mother?' Orpha demanded.

'I went to see her,' Ashley was all innocence now, 'and she told me, but Orpha . . . she said I could never marry you despite this misunderstanding. What did she mean by that?'

'I have no idea, Ashley,' Orpha replied, 'but she was right in a sense.'

'What sense? What the hell do you mean?'

Ashley's temper rose and he saw Simmons take a step towards Orpha in a protective gesture.

'Ashley, I know too much about you . . . you lied to me and . . . I know about Birmingham,' Orpha said, her voice laced with disgust.

Simmons bit his lip as he heard the words Orpha was unaware he understood. How did Orpha find out? He certainly hadn't told her!

'No, Orpha . . . you don't understand . . .' Ashley tried again.

'Ah, *I* don't understand again eh? Well, Ashley Rochester, let me tell you something, I understand perfectly!' Orpha was in full swing as her tirade assaulted his ears. 'You have lied to me about the warehouses. You have told others that you intended to own my business. You have no money of your own, save that given you by the lady in Birmingham in exchange for your . . . your . . . amour!'

Simmons stifled a laugh at Orpha's search for a polite explanation before he said impudently in an effort to goad the man. 'And he lives in a hovel . . . ma'am.'

'Mind your business, *servant!*' Ashley snapped at the butler.

Orpha repeated, 'And you live in a hovel! How on earth do you suppose I would want to marry you knowing all this?'

'Orpha, please . . . hear me out, let me explain . . .' Ashley was begging.

'Ashley . . . just get out! It is finished. I never

want to see you again! Go back to your whore!'
Orpha spat venomously.

'Whores . . . ma'am,' Simmons put in politely.

Ashley had had enough and took a swing at the
butler who deftly sidestepped and Ashley tottered
forward a few steps. Grabbing the man's arm,
Simmons twisted it up Ashley's back and steered
him out of the front door. With a mighty push, he
watched Ashley fall on his face. Closing the door,
Simmons brushed his hands as though they were
dirty and said, 'Would ma'am like more tea?'

The whole family and staff who had gathered to
watch the debacle fell about laughing.

Ashley was angrier than he had ever been in his
life as he strode down the driveway and headed for
his ruin of a home. He had lost her – moreover
he had lost her money!

Finally sitting before the empty fireplace, his
mind tried to make sense of what had happened.
He felt a headache begin to bang in his head again.

Orpha knew about the empty warehouses . . .
how? She knew about his women in Birmingham
. . . and that butler knew too . . . how? Had the
butler found out and reported it to Orpha? Had
Simmons followed him? No, he would have seen
him, surely.

Ashley rubbed his hands over his face. How
could he have been so stupid? He'd got drunk and
boasted his good fortune. What were the odds the
person he bragged to would be Orpha's mother?

It was rotten luck and there was no way now he could retrieve the situation. His acquisitive nature told him he had to rethink his strategy if he wanted to become rich.

All his father had left him was a tumbledown house and a string of useless warehouses. He could at least sell those, they wouldn't bring him a fortune, but some money was better than none. He could still see the 'older ladies' in Birmingham; their money would keep him from starving.

He made his decision, he would have to try again to sell the warehouses, but first he would visit Orpha's mother again. This time she *would* tell him what he wanted to know!

CHAPTER 53

Answering the new telephone that Orpha had installed, Simmons informed her a Mr Belcher wished to speak with her. As she made her greeting, the voice she knew so well said, 'Ah, Orpha my dear, I have something here you may be interested in. I wonder if your busy schedule might be interrupted so that you could call in and see me?'

Orpha said, 'I will come straight after breakfast.' Looking out at the beautiful day, she decided she would walk to Belcher & Son.

'Hello . . . hello . . .' Mr Belcher said as the doorbell tinkled her arrival. 'Please, do sit down. Now then, I have just acquired on my books six warehouses in St Matthew's Street and I wondered if they might be of use to your good self?'

Orpha's attention was grabbed immediately as she asked, 'May I ask who is selling them?'

Riffling through his papers in a constant mess on his desk, Belcher said, 'Yes, here it is . . . a Mr Ashley Rochester.'

So Ashley was selling the only things left to him. Orpha's feelings oscillated between feeling sad at how low her once-intended had sunk, and her relief at being able to keep her business. She was not surprised at having heard nothing from Ashley since the wedding had been abandoned.

'Mr Belcher,' Orpha said, 'I am indeed interested. However, I would only buy them at the lowest possible price naturally . . .'

'But of course!' Mr Belcher agreed.

'I also have a proviso . . . Mr Rochester is *not* to know who the buyer is. Under no circumstances must he find out that I am interested in his properties until contracts and money are exchanged. After that it will not matter. Mr Belcher, I must have your word on this.'

The estate agent saw Orpha was adamant and he agreed, saying, 'You have my word, my dear. I will negotiate the lowest price I can for you and be assured you will remain anonymous until after the fact.'

Shaking hands on the deal, Orpha left the office. What on earth would she do with six warehouses? Why had she said she would buy them? Was it to help Ashley out in his hour of need? Or, had it been out of spite; revenge for hurting her so badly? Whatever the reason, she knew Mr Belcher would have those warehouses for her very soon; within the week if she knew anything about Ashley Rochester.

Enjoying the last of the good weather, Orpha walked over to visit her mother in Derry Street.

474

'So how are you bearing up considering you're not a bride?' Hortense sneered.

'I'm fine, Mother, and you don't have to be so nasty all the time!' Orpha was in a good mood and didn't want Hortense to spoil it for her. She debated whether to divulge the information about Ashley's properties but thought better of it. Thought of Ashley sparked a memory and she asked, 'Why did you tell Ashley he couldn't marry me?'

'Because he asked!' Hortense's answer was caustic.

'Why did he ask?' Orpha said in frustration.

'Because he wanted to know!' Hortense loved playing mind games with people and her daughter was no exception.

'Mother! For God's sake!' Orpha's frustration turned to anger.

Hortense smiled, she'd got the girl rattled now. 'It's not your business what I said to Mr Rochester, so keep your nose out!'

Orpha let it go, she would get no answers from her mother on this matter. Instead, her anger boiling over, she left.

Simmons joined Orpha in the gardens of Buchanan Mansion as he carried out a tea tray. 'Penny for your thoughts, ma'am?'

'Ah Simmons,' she said, 'I tried to find out what Mother had told Ashley about why we could not be married, but she wouldn't tell me.'

'I wouldn't dwell on it, ma'am, I'm sure she was

only thinking of your welfare.' Both knowing Hortense as they did, they burst out laughing. Simmons spoke again, 'I'm certain it will all come to light in time.'

'Perhaps you're right,' Orpha said, then in a conspiratorial whisper she explained about buying the warehouses, and how it should remain a secret for now.

Simmons touched his index finger to the side of his nose as he left her to her tea.

Hortense opened the door at the knock and a sonorous voice said, 'Excuse me, madam, but I'm looking for Hortense Buchanan.'

'Well you've found her,' she said taking in the police uniform.

'I am Sergeant Jack from the Birmingham Constabulary and I'm making enquiries about one Ashley Rochester. I believe you know the young man?'

'Best come in,' Hortense urged the man into the house.

Both seated before the fire, the man said, 'Now then, what can you tell me about Mr Rochester?' The sergeant pulled out a small notebook and pencil. Licking the pencil lead, he prepared to take notes.

Hortense told the policeman everything she knew about Ashley and then the man asked, 'And why is it you told him he could not marry your daughter, madam?'

Hortense had dreaded the question but knew it would be asked.

The sergeant waited then said, 'I'm sorry to have to ask, but it could be important to our investigations.'

'Exactly what are you investigating him for?' Hortense asked, trying to change the subject.

'I'm not at liberty to say, madam. Now about the reason for the couple not marrying?'

Hortense realised the sergeant was not going to give up. She really didn't want to say, but this was a policeman in her house. She couldn't withhold information from the police, could she? She looked carefully at the man, there was something vaguely familiar about him, but she couldn't put her finger on quite what it was.

'Madam . . .' the sergeant prompted, 'we can always do this interview down at the station . . .'

'No!' Hortense had been in a police station before and she didn't want to go back. 'They couldn't marry because . . .'

CHAPTER 54

O rpha's half-brother, Zachariah, accompanied her to look at her new warehouses. They were massive structures, each standing one wedged against the next with no light passing between them. Orpha wondered if they had, in fact, once been one building . . . or could be used as one building. Each one was dry and of sound construction and as they looked around Orpha's mind worked in pictures. She could use them as storage for her products, although her factories provided sufficient storage areas. She could turn them into more shops and coffee shops, but thinking sensibly she realised the expenditure would be too great at the present time.

Moving from one to the next, the warehouses were all of similar size and shape . . . just big, square, empty buildings, exactly what they were meant to be . . . storage areas.

'Why on earth did you buy these, Orpha?' Zachariah's question echoed around the empty space.

'I really have no idea!' she said. 'These are the ones that belonged to Ashley . . . obviously he needed money and decided to sell them.'

'So as a charitable act you bought them?' Zachariah asked.

'In a way I suppose, but the offer was too good to miss,' she said, brushing dust from her long burgundy skirt.

'Ah now I see . . . you bought bones from the butcher on the off-chance you might get a dog!' Zachariah smirked at his half-sister.

Orpha's laugh resounded in the room and she turned to leave, saying, 'Zachariah what am I to do with them?'

Zachariah said simply, 'Use them as they were intended . . . rent them out!'

Zachariah and Orpha discussed her plans with Mr Belcher who said he would be able to help. He had two young men he knew who needed dry storage for their painting and paperhanging business. They agreed a sum to be charged for rent, and Orpha left her warehouses in the capable hands of the trusted estate agent.

Mr Belcher was true to his word and before long each warehouse housed goods of one sort or another and the money poured in, in the form of rent.

Ashley Rochester walked through Birmingham on his way to relieve yet another older woman of her money and any small trinkets he could pocket and sell. As he walked, he again began to feel quite unwell. Could he be getting yet another head cold? If this continued, he really would have to see the doctor.

He had sold the old buildings in St Matthew's Street left to him by his father and wasn't surprised that they had been snapped up. What had surprised him, he'd learned after the signing of the contracts, was who had bought them. Orpha bloody Buchanan! It wasn't as if she needed them. Or was it she was feeling sorry for the down-and-out Ashley? Well, he would show her! He would have money one day, and lots of it, and when he did . . . he would rub her nose in his success.

Banging on a front door, he was let in by an older woman who was very pleased to see him. Within an hour he was on his way to his next rendezvous, his wallet a little heavier and a pair of diamond earrings clutched in his sweaty palm. The woman would know he'd taken them, but he didn't have to go back there. He had lots of other ladies to visit, and besides, he was sure they had insurance for loss, damage or theft.

Not revealing where he lived was *his* insurance policy against anything going awry, such as being reported to the police for theft. Then of course was the aspect of scandal. These women would have to admit to having a young, virile man in their bed who was not their husband. Yes, the women would keep their mouths shut and suffer their losses. Not one would risk having her name sullied by the scandal that would be rife, and the police would be looking for a man who they would never find! Ashley considered himself safe enough to continue with his business for now, and if he

480

thought himself in danger . . . there were lots of other towns!

Simmons had hung the sergeant's uniform in his closet after visiting Hortense. He had washed the flour from his hair and put the spectacles and false bushy moustache and eyebrows in his dresser drawer. Then he had gone down to the kitchen to brood. What he'd learned from Hortense could not be shared with the other staff – at least not yet. He had to find a way to inform Orpha of the reason she could not have married Ashley Rochester, but all ideas eluded him. He was faced with an impossible task. Orpha was busy with her shops and factories and didn't seem overly bothered about Rochester any more. She had cast him from her life without a backward glance. Yes, the man had hurt her, that much was obvious at the time, but she had picked up her life and moved on.

Simmons smiled to himself. The girl he adored was very resilient, nothing kept her down for long. His mind slipped back to Ashley. How had the man gotten away with all he had? He had been caught out visiting other women and satisfying their desires in exchange for money. He had openly boasted about becoming the owner of 'The Choc's Box' . . . unfortunately for him he had bragged to the wrong person, Orpha's mother! That had been his undoing and now saw him out of the running for Orpha's hand in marriage.

Simmons' smile became a low chuckle. He would be keeping a close eye on Mr Ashley Rochester in the future. The man's money would completely run out at some point, as would his luck, and he would have to move on. When he did, Simmons would not be far behind him.

For all Rochester had done, he had been clever and left no evidence behind for which he could be arrested. Simmons was now aware of where Hortense Buchanan was living but had omitted to pass this information to his superiors as yet. Orpha was taking care of the woman who appeared to be behaving herself, so Simmons was content to let sleeping dogs lie – for now.

In the parlour, everyone was gathered for dinner. Young Ralph was sleeping soundly upstairs and Peg stood to make an announcement.

'Everyone,' she called out, 'I am very happy to tell you I am pregnant!' Hugs and kisses were passed around and Orpha yanked the bell pull by the fireplace. Alice scuttled in a moment later and was asked to bring the staff to join them in the celebration of some good news.

Orpha watched her sister as she beamed at the congratulations given to her, and felt a pang of sadness. She had her businesses and money but Peg was far richer. A husband, a son and now a new baby on the way, Peg was rich in love and luck.

Simmons watched Orpha watching her sister. He longed to take her in his arms and comfort her. He saw the sadness that weighed her down for all her efforts to hide it. He saw that sadness flit to joy in her green eyes as she hugged Peg. She too could be a master of disguise.

Mrs Jukes and Edna had their heads together discussing names for the new baby and Abel and Zachariah were clapping Ezzie on the back for a 'job well done'.

Orpha had marvelled when Ralph was born with a fine down of black hair like his mother, and how as he grew his eyes took on the sparkling green brilliance; the Buchanan family trait. The Buchanan Emeralds. Would this new baby be the same or would it follow Ezzie's fair complexion? Orpha didn't really care as long as mother and child were safe and well.

As it was a special occasion, Alice was asked to reset the dinner table, the staff would be eating with the family this one time.

Simmons knew it was completely unheard of for staff to eat with family and he revelled in his good fortune to be butler to the Buchanans. This was a very special family . . . and the staff were made to feel part of it. He watched Orpha closely over the dinner table, her green eyes sparkling in the lamp light and she returned his glances with a smile. The wine flowed freely and before long they were kicking up their heels in the parlour to the latest tune banged out on the piano by Jago. There would be sore heads in the morning but no one cared as they partied long into the night.

CHAPTER 55

C hill winds began to blow and winter made herself known. The trees had shed their leaves and the sun struggled to make a weak appearance. The fires in the house were banked high to keep the rooms warm and aired and Mrs Jukes pulled out her winter recipes for hot, wholesome food. The sky threatened snow, although, as yet, none had fallen. Orpha had increased her order for coal for both Buchanan Mansion and her mother's house in Derry Street; she didn't want anyone falling ill from the bitter cold she knew was just around the corner.

Gazing out of the parlour window, Orpha reflected on her life; of all the things that had happened to her and how she had come through stronger for the experiences. Her one regret was that she had no man to share it with. She had her family and she loved them all, but it was not the same. She had no one to cuddle her on cold nights, no one to share her thoughts with, her anxieties and her pleasures. Amid a house full of people, Orpha Buchanan was lonely.

'Penny for your thoughts again, ma'am?'

'Oh Simmons, I didn't hear you come in. I was just . . . wondering what the weather held for us,' she lied.

Simmons placed the tea tray on the table, saying Alice was busy baking bread so he'd stepped in to bring up the tea.

'Simmons, do you remember I once asked if you'd ever been in love?' Orpha asked innocently. The butler clamped his teeth together and nodded. 'May I ask you a personal question?' At his further nod she went on, 'Never mind, it doesn't matter,' Orpha said, shaking her head.

'If you are wondering why I never married, it's because she was set to marry another ma'am,' Simmons said guardedly.

'I'm sorry, Simmons, I shouldn't have pushed. It was rude of me.'

'That's all right, ma'am,' Simmons cleared his throat, 'Is there anything else I can help you with, Miss Orpha?'

The girl lowered her green eyes to the tea tray and shook her head. Simmons began to leave the room when a sob had him stop in his tracks. Turning back, he said, 'Miss Orpha, are you all right?' Instantly chastising himself for asking a stupid question, he could see she was very defin-itely *not* all right. She was sobbing for God's sake!

Rushing up to her, Simmons pulled her up from her seat into his arms and placed his lips on hers. He felt her body lean into his as she succumbed to his kiss. He felt her arms gently wrap around his shoulders and her fingers touch the back of his neck. His blood was on fire as he kissed her passionately. It was everything he had dreamed of and more.

Releasing her, he stepped back and saw her eyes were closed a fraction longer than they should have been. She'd enjoyed that kiss every bit as much as he had.

Now the lady of the house and her butler stared into each other's eyes, neither knowing what to do next.

Hortense had worried about the visit from Sergeant Jack but as time passed and she heard no more, she had relaxed. Obviously Ashley Rochester was still giving the police the slip, otherwise she would have known from the newspapers. He appeared to be a rogue although somewhat lacking in the brains department. She was wondering how she could learn more about him when opportunity knocked on her door and Orpha walked in.

Orpha greeted her mother and walked straight to the fire to warm her hands while Hortense made hot tea.

'I was just thinking about you oddly enough, when you walked in,' Hortense said as she eyed the girl over her teacup.

'Oh yes?' Orpha asked.

'Yes, I was wondering what happened to that Ashley bloke?' Hortense pursued.

'I have no idea,' Orpha replied. Her mother was on the questioning warpath again.

'Where is he living?' Hortense was enjoying the girl's discomfort.

'Over on the East Side he told me . . .' Orpha began.

'But you don't believe that?'

'No.' Orpha cut her answer short.

'Why not?' Hortense couldn't contain herself.

'Because, Mother, he lied to me about other things!' Orpha snapped.

'Oh I see,' Hortense grinned.

'Mother, you do not see! You have no idea what Ashley Rochester is like!' Orpha's patience was already threadbare.

'So tell me!' Hortense had no intention of giving up, so Orpha relented and related what she'd discovered about the man she almost married.

Hortense let out a cackle. 'Bloody hell, girl, you almost got wed to a gigolo!'

'Mother, don't be smug!' Orpha's embarrassment sailed up her cheeks in a red hot flush. 'It was pure luck I found him out before the wedding took place!'

'Indeed! Imagine the gossip . . . the newspapers would have had a field day with that!' Hortense was openly laughing now at her daughter's distress. 'You know, I take it, the police are looking for him?'

'No! Why?' Orpha was shocked at the words.

'I've no idea. They wouldn't tell me.' Hortense

was revelling in knowing something her daughter didn't.

'They came here?' Orpha asked, her eyes wide now.

'Yes, they wanted to know all about him, of course I couldn't tell them much as I don't rightly know him. I'm surprised the police didn't come to you too though.' Hortense watched Orpha's face as the girl shook her head.

'No, they haven't been to see me,' Orpha said quietly.

Leaving it at that, Orpha explained the good news about Peg's pregnancy and saw her mother's face screw up in disgust.

'Girl should learn to keep her knees together!' Hortense spat.

Orpha felt now was an excellent time to leave.

In the carriage on the way home Orpha's mind whirled. The police were searching for Ashley . . . why? What had he done to warrant police involvement? It was bad enough the way he had treated her, but this, whatever it was, must be far worse.

Then there was Simmons and the kiss they had shared. Whatever had she been thinking? He was the butler! She had openly kissed her butler, but she had enjoyed it, far more in fact than any kiss from Ashley. She remembered overhearing him tell the staff he loved her, and in the privacy of the carriage she smiled. She lived again his lips on hers, the flush of passion she'd felt as she kissed him back. She recalled how she allowed herself to fold into his arms and suddenly she realised she knew what true love was.

On reaching home, she went straight to her bedroom where she could analyse her thoughts and rationalise her feelings. Her mind compared the two men: Ashley was a lying, cheating bully; Simmons was kind and gentle, always ready to defend her. Ashley was greedy for money; Simmons never mentioned it. Ashley wanted her business for himself; Simmons supported her in her every endeavour. Ashley had hardly ever said he loved her; Simmons had told the staff he did. But with all this said, Simmons was still in her employ.

It seemed Orpha was destined to bounce from one crisis to another her whole life, never to be settled, never to be truly happy, never to be married.

CHAPTER 56

Ashley's funds were running very low and the business with his ladies was making him tired and listless, he was feeling ill far more often. Maybe it was the onset of winter that had him so low; he should really see the doctor but his lack of money prevented it. Maybe he should rest more, but he needed to earn money to feed himself. He never would have been in this position had it not been for Orpha's mother. Perhaps it was time to visit her again.

Wrapping up warm against the bitter wind, he trudged across the town. Coming to the house, he banged on the front door. As the woman opened it he pushed his way in, slamming the door behind him.

'What do you want with me?' Hortense rasped. 'I told you not to come here again!'

'Well I'm here now!' Ashley yelled into her face. 'I want to know everything!'

'I'll tell you this,' Hortense sneered, 'the police are looking for you! Whatever it is you've done, they are on to you my lad.'

'I am *not* your lad!' Ashley's anger bubbled up.

If only you knew! Hortense thought as she glared at him.

'Now tell me what you know or else!' He raised a hand as if to slap her.

Hortense smiled, she was not afraid of him. 'Do your worst . . . *my lad* . . . because I'm not telling you anything other than if you hurt me, the police will lock you up and throw away the key!'

Ashley's anger spilled over and he bunched his fist and drove it into Hortense's face and blood poured from her nose. The woman fell backwards onto the floor and hit her head on the corner of the fireplace. She was not moving . . . was she dead? His anger dissipated as he looked at what he'd done to Orpha's mother. Lifting her head, his hand came away covered in blood. Dashing into the kitchen, he wiped his hand on a tea cloth, cleaning the woman's blood from his skin. He was now very afraid he may have killed her. Taking one more look at the woman on the floor, he turned and ran from the house.

That afternoon, Orpha requested Jago drive her to see her mother. Stopping the carriage outside the house, she said, 'I won't be too long.'

After a moment Jago heard the scream.

'Mother! Oh my God!' Orpha saw her mother lying on the floor. Running outside, she yelled, 'Jago, help me . . .!'

The boy jumped from the carriage and ran into the house.

'Oh Christ!' he said as he gently lifted the woman

into his arms and carried her to the carriage. Urging the horse forward up Vicarage Road, he turned into Cleveland Road and then into the grounds of the Wolverhampton & Staffordshire General Hospital. Orpha had ridden in the carriage with her mother.

Hortense was carried into the hospital and Orpha went in with her. Jago was sent to tell the family what had happened. Orpha watched the doctor examine her mother who she thought might be dead, but Hortense's moans told her otherwise.

The doctor was asking Hortense questions as he checked her thoroughly. Orpha said her name was Hortense and the doctor nodded.

'Hortense, do you know where you are?' the doctor asked. Hortense gave a tiny nod of her head and the doctor continued. 'Do you know who did this to you?' Another tiny nod. 'Can you tell us?'

Hortense gathered her strength and whispered through clenched teeth, 'Ashley Rochester . . . he hit me . . .'

'Ashley Rochester?' the doctor repeated.

Hortense nodded once more, then sliding her eyes to her daughter, she said, 'I'm so sorry Orpha.' Closing her eyes, Hortense Buchanan let out her final breath.

Zachariah and Abel were in their office in Birmingham when Jago took the news back to the house. Ezzie was out on boat business and Peg refused to go to see *that* woman in the hospital.

492

Edna elected to stay with Peg. Therefore it was Simmons who rode back to the hospital with Jago. By the time they arrived the police had been contacted by the hospital and Orpha and the doctor had been interviewed. There was now a manhunt on for Ashley Rochester.

Orpha sat in the carriage on their journey home with Simmons who held her tightly as she shivered with cold and shock. Whispering to her, he enjoyed the closeness albeit under such difficult circumstances.

The doctor had given her a tonic to take when she arrived home, saying she needed to rest; the hospital would lay Hortense in the mortuary until such time as she was collected by the undertaker. Edna tucked Orpha into her bed after the tonic was drunk, and left the girl to try to sleep.

Simmons said he would telephone Orpha's father.

'Mr Abel, it's Simmons sir, I'm sorry to have to tell you that your wife is dead. Please accept my condolences.'

After a moment, Simmons replaced the telephone receiver and moved back to the kitchen. 'Mr Abel and Mr Zachariah will be on the next train home,' he said to the others. 'Jago, please take the carriage to collect them from the station.'

The boy nodded and grabbing his cap he walked to the stables to hitch the horse to the carriage once more.

On his arrival home, Abel called everyone, including the staff, into the parlour.

Orpha, unable to rest, had joined them. She looked tired and wan as she related the dreadful demise of Hortense Buchanan. 'I found her on the floor and Jago and I managed to get her to the hospital. When the doctor asked if she'd seen who had attacked her, she said . . . she . . . it was Ashley Rochester!' Orpha burst into tears and Abel rushed to enfold her in his arms.

Simmons and Jago confirmed the truth of the girl's words.

'What I don't understand is, why?' Abel asked. 'Why Hortense?'

Orpha said quietly, 'I think he wanted to know the reason why mother said we couldn't marry . . . mother refused to tell him. I asked her too but she wouldn't tell me either.'

'So he attacked and killed her all because she wouldn't answer his question? Oh my God, Orpha! I'm so glad you didn't marry him!' Zachariah moved to hug his half-sister as Abel walked over to the fireplace. Ezzie looked at Edna's shocked face before putting his arms around Peg who was upset at her sister's distress.

'Well, I'm sure it won't be long before the police have hold of him,' Abel said as he turned to Jago. 'You told them where he lived?' The boy nodded. 'Good, although I doubt he'll go back there. We just have to trust to luck they happen upon him.'

Dinner was a sombre affair both upstairs and

downstairs as everyone wondered where Ashley Rochester would be spending the night.

Abel contacted the funeral director, who tactfully said he would collect Mrs Buchanan from the hospital and lay her in the Chapel of Rest until such time as she could be interred. Abel explained he wanted her laid to rest as soon as possible and was willing to pay handsomely for the swift burial. It was therefore arranged for two days hence.

Orpha wandered around in a daze, unable to concentrate on anything.

'Father, I need to contact Mr Belcher. I need to get mother's house sold,' Orpha said.

'When you are ready, sweetheart, there's no rush,' Abel replied.

'No, I need to do it now.' Orpha went straight to the telephone.

Ringing the estate agent, Orpha spoke quietly. 'Mr Belcher . . . I need for you to sell the house in Derry Street. I'm afraid my mother has passed away.' Accepting his condolences, she went on, 'However, I must ask you to wait a while . . . my mother was murdered, Mr Belcher, and the police are still treating it as a crime scene. Once their investigation is concluded then you will be free to put it on the market. Thank you for your kindness.'

The police visited the family and told them they had no evidence from the house other than a bloodied tea cloth in the kitchen. They surmised it was the victim's blood. There was no murder weapon and no one had seen or heard anything untoward in the street. This was hardly surprising as the house was separated from two more by a patch of wasteland on one side. There was another patch on the other side, then half a dozen more houses. All were empty during the daytime when the crime took place.

The funeral was a sombre affair and Peg reluctantly agreed to attend. The staff remained at Buchanan Mansion awaiting the family's return.

Once ensconced in the parlour, Simmons asked if he could have a word with Orpha. Stepping into the hall, he said, 'Ma'am, I am sorry for your loss.' At her nod, he went on, 'I'm afraid it's not a good time to ask for leave, but I have an urgent matter to see to that may take a week or so to resolve.'

'Of course, Simmons, take whatever leave you need, but promise you will come back?' Orpha tried to force a smile.

'I will be back as soon as I'm able, ma'am, thank you.' Simmons watched her re-enter the parlour and he muttered, 'Wild horses wouldn't keep me from you for long!'

CHAPTER 57

Orpha rallied herself in the next few days but she missed seeing Simmons around the place. She wondered where he had gone and what the urgent matter was that he had to attend to.

With the police finished with the house in Derry Street, Mr Belcher had sold it almost immediately. He delicately informed Orpha that the fact that a murder had been committed there clearly held a macabre fascination for some people. Orpha was just glad it no longer belonged to her.

The chocolate business was doing a roaring trade and with Lottie and the girls managing the shops, Orpha found herself at a loose end. The family often found her brooding in the parlour and knew she needed time to recover from the shock of her mother being murdered by the man she once agreed to marry.

Sitting now with tea, Orpha watched the snow fall silently onto the lawns and pathways. Despite the cold, she loved the winter and was suddenly transported back to the days of dragging the cart to market with Peg. She smiled as she allowed her thoughts to recollect her sister's hatred of the snow, of her constant complaints of being cold and of the snowball fight that had amused the stallholders that day in the market.

Simmons searched the ruin of the house in Ettingshall Road and found nothing. Ashley Rochester had not been back there. Taking the train to Birmingham, he studied the notes the stable boys had made when they had followed the energetic Mr Rochester. He certainly had stamina, Simmons had to give him that!

He had visited each of the houses on the list and spoken to all of the women. He had explained why he was looking for their young lover and all of the women were shocked. Each in turn had reported discovering valuable items missing after Ashley had left and none of them had seen him since.

Simmons left them with a warning – do not let the man into the house should he come calling again!

Walking through the streets back towards New Street Station, Simmons remembered something that was said by the first woman he visited. She was very ill and would not be entertaining the delightful Mr Rochester in the future.

Alighting the train in Wolverhampton, Simmons hailed a cabbie and giving an address in Cockshutts Lane, he settled back in the seat. He had an idea, it may be pie in the sky, but it was worth checking out. Arriving at the destination, he asked the reluctant cabbie to wait, he would be just a moment. The cabbie nodded at the promise of a large tip for his trouble but moved the horse further down the street. This was not a building he wished to be in the close proximity of.

Simmons quietly congratulated himself, he had found the elusive Ashley Rochester!

Ashley had seen Simmons enter the room and he'd sighed. Lying on his death bed, this was the last person he wished to see. Simmons had smiled as he approached the bed.

'So this is where you are hiding yourself!' It was not a question. 'I was wondering where you had disappeared to, and now I know.' Simmons grinned.

'What do you want?' Ashley croaked. 'Can't you see I'm dying?'

'I can indeed, Ashley, and I thought you might enjoy one last visitor.' Simmons kept his hands in his trouser pockets lest he lose his reasoning and choke the last of the life out of the man in the bed.

'Why? Why would you visit me?' Ashley lapsed into a coughing fit.

'Because,' Simmons said as he walked closer, 'I have something to tell you.'

'What would you have to tell me?' His breath coming in gasps now, Ashley was not long for this world.

Simmons' head leaned in close and he whispered

in Ashley's ear then stepped back to see the man's reaction.

After another bout of coughing Ashley Rochester uttered one word with his dying breath, 'Nooooo . . .!'

Orpha was delighted at Simmons' return to the house and although she was desperate to know where he'd been and what he'd been doing, she welcomed him back appropriately and with decorum.

Simmons requested a meeting with the family after dinner as he had some very important news to impart to everyone, including the staff.

All gathered in the parlour eager to hear what Simmons had to say. When everyone was seated Simmons spoke.

'Firstly I would like to thank you all for granting me this meeting as protocol would not normally allow for such a thing. Now I would like to apologise for deceiving everyone into thinking I am a butler.'

Waiting for the shocked muttering to abate, Simmons went on. 'I am in fact, Sergeant Jack Simmons of the Birmingham Constabulary and I was placed here on a covert operation.'

Again mutterings ran round the room. Holding up his hand for silence, he continued. 'I must make a special apology to you, Orpha, for having to keep up this charade.' Orpha dipped her head and he noted she knew what was meant by his words. Nodding back to her, he returned his attention back to the family. 'We have been on Mr Rochester's trail for some years now. We knew he was thieving from wealthy women but could find no proof against him. The women would not come forth with a complaint as they were afraid of the scandal. They had enjoyed him as a lover and simply claimed on insurance for their 'lost' belongings. Now, this past week I have discovered that Mr Rochester passed away in the Borough Hospital for Infectious Diseases.'

He did not have to explain further as he watched faces scowl and wince before him.

There was a melee of gasps as everyone came to terms with what Simmons had told them. Ashley had paid the ultimate price for his philandering.

Sergeant Jack Simmons knew the family were aware Ashley had killed Hortense Buchanan; whether by accident or design no one would ever know now. He didn't feel the need to relate the information he had gleaned from Mrs Buchanan . . . that the late Mr Ashley Rochester was her long-lost son and he had, in fact, murdered his own mother!

'I will have to return to my station in Birmingham now my covert mission is complete,' Simmons said to Orpha as they strolled in the garden later.

'I understand,' she replied, 'but I will miss you. Oh Simmons, I can't believe everything that has happened!'

'It will take some getting used to for you I'm sure,' he said.

Orpha nodded and he saw crystal tears sparkling in her emerald green eyes. Desperately wanting to hold her, it took all his strength not to do so.

'You will have to hire a new butler now too, I'm afraid.' Simmons tried to lighten the mood but it only served to upset Orpha more. He watched the tears finally escape her lashes and roll down her lovely face. 'Now you know the truth of it there is no reason we cannot . . .' Simmons let the sentence hang in mid-air.

'Do you mean . . .?' Orpha asked.

Seeing her dazzling smile, he was undone. Wrapping her in his arms, he said quietly, 'I have loved you from the first time I saw you, and will continue to do so until my dying day.'

'Oh Simmons . . .' Orpha's words were lost as his lips closed gently on hers.

Looking into her eyes once more, he whispered, 'Orpha, in time would you consent to changing your name to Mrs Orpha Simmons?'

'Yes! Oh yes!' she breathed.

As they kissed again, Peg's words sounded in her mind. *Do you love him so much that you can't live without him?*

This time she knew the answer was yes.